Wilson indeed!

Steve Walsh

**SIN EMBARGO
PUBLISHING**

Sin Embargo Publishing:England

First published in England in 2019 by Sin Embargo Publishing.
This edition published 2019.

ISBN 978-1-9164861-0-2 (Hardback)
ISBN 978-1-9164861-1-9 (Paperback)

Printed and bound in Great Britain.
Sin Embargo Publishing

For more information visit www.wilsonindeed.com

"A dream you dream alone is only a dream. A dream you dream together is reality."

John Lennon

"Dreaming permits each and every one of us to be quietly and safely insane every night of our lives."

William Dement

"Yes: I am a dreamer. For a dreamer is one who can only find his way by moonlight, and his punishment is that he sees the dawn before the rest of the world."

Oscar Wilde

"Dreaming is an act of pure imagination, attesting in all men a creative power, which if it were available in waking, would make every man a Dante or Shakespeare."

H.F. Hedge

Chapter 1

The Brimstone

Two miles south of Stockport lies the well-to-do village of Davenport; a comfortable notch on the commuter belt of Greater Manchester. Its focal point is a busy railway station and according to the community website, 'it has a range of facilities within a short distance, which make Davenport a good place to live for those who don't drive a car'. Which is somewhat ironic, given the events I'm about to describe.

Sally Bennett was a small-boned, twelve year old girl with a bright, full moon face, a clutch of newly hatched freckles over the bridge of her nose and fine, silky hair that could crackle with static. She also had a problem with eczema. Raw patches of inflamed skin flared across the backs of her knees, painfully visible above the cuff of her school socks. She was being tormented by classmates and the stress from trolling on social media was inevitably making the skin disorder worse. Sally's stepmother had made her an appointment with a dietician whose clinic was above the row of shops, directly opposite Davenport train station.

"Perhaps you're lactose intolerant or it's something to do with gluten. Half an hour talking to an expert can't make things worse, can it?"

Wendy Bellamy was married to a famous footballer and ticked all the boxes for the demographic of a 'yummy mummy'. In the minutes leading to Sally's appointment, she was driving her white Land Rover along Bramhall Lane, a busy road that strikes a tangent with the curved frontage of Davenport station. It was early afternoon and she was heading to Sainsbury's to pick-up the dry cleaning and something for tea. Emily, her one-year-old daughter, was an arm's length away, strapped into her car seat, sucking noisily on a bottle of milk.

1

Wendy glanced at her daughter.

"Goodness Emily, it's like you've never been fed. You'll make yourself sick gorging away like that."

Wendy tried to think if something was missing from her shopping list, but a favourite song came on the radio so she started singing instead.

The exit from Davenport station spills onto the pedestrian crossing where Sally was waiting for the 'walk' symbol to turn to green. In other words, listening for the sequence of tones that tell someone engrossed in their phone it's safe to cross without looking up. Sally was deleting yet another cruel insult as the beeps started and she registered a car on her right braking to a halt. She stepped into the road. Her heart sank on reading a tweet from a boy in her class saying something about eczema and leprosy.

As the Land Rover proceeded diligently towards the station, from out of thin air, a large, yellow butterfly danced through the half-open, passenger window and settled on Emily's hand. The baby spluttered in surprise and half-threw, half-dropped the plastic bottle − which bounced off the rim of the car seat and lodged itself in a tight gap between the handbrake and the side of the passenger seat. The Brimstone, an unusual sight for October, waltzed back out of the window.

"Emily, you're so greedy, you'll choke one of these days. Anyway, serves you right for dropping your bottle. You'll have to wait now, till the traffic's stopped."

Wendy heard an infantile grunt and turned to her daughter. The rubber teat was still protruding from Emily's mouth. Wendy looked down at the bottle. Some of the milk was running into the plastic cowl at the base of the handbrake but most of it was soaking into the carpet.

It's almost impossible to clean milk from a nylon carpet, particularly in the tight space beneath a car seat. And milk dries very quickly. Come the next sunny day, the pungent aroma of curdled milk was going to make it insufferable just to sit in this vehicle, let alone drive it. The vehicle was as good as written off.

Wendy panicked at the thought, took her eyes off the road and frantically reached down to retrieve the wedged bottle. Wet milk made it difficult to grasp. The bulky Land Rover continued onwards at thirty-two miles per hour, even though the lights on the pedestrian crossing had changed to red.

Sally was more than halfway across before she felt the need to look up and check the cars on her left had also stopped. The part of the eye that handles peripheral vision did its job and Sally instinctively leapt backwards.

Wendy finally hooked the almost empty bottle from its lodgement by inserting her finger into the open neck, her eyes returned to the road, she slammed on the brakes and screamed.

The car wasn't going fast enough to knock Sally into the air. Instead, the bumper knocked both knees from their joints causing her to bounce off the bonnet like a rag doll bouncing off a tin drum. As Sally fell backwards onto the tarmac, the sixteen-inch gap between the vehicle and the road, like a gaping mouth, swallowed her up. The right wheel drove over a forearm. The scabrous surface of the tarmac grated skin from her arms and legs. Sally's right shoulder dislocated the muffler on the exhaust system which caused the exhaust pipe to fall and wrap itself, like a double helix, around her left leg. The car came to a halt without expelling her from other end. Sally was unconscious and trapped in the coils of a metal snake.

Though gruesome, the sum total of the aforementioned injuries was not life-threatening. Sally's petite build and the ground clearance of the four-by-four were fortuitous. Her left shoulder however, was more of an issue. A flange on the engine's oil sump had a razor-sharp burr. As Sally was consumed by the car, the burr sliced through her school uniform severing the axillary artery near her armpit. The axillary is a major artery of the upper torso and carries a lot of oxygenated blood. Seconds after the car screeched to a halt, a rivulet of thick, scarlet fluid inched over black tarmac. As the red tide advanced, life ebbed from Sally's body. Without urgent medical attention, she had about eight minutes to live.

All traffic in the vicinity of Davenport station quickly came to a standstill. Wendy was in hysterics and refused to leave the car.

"She's stuck under there, she's stuck, please take her away."

A number of people were on their phones pleading with the emergency services to get there as soon as possible.

"No, the victim isn't conscious. Yes, she is bleeding. Of course we've not tried to move her!"

A woman with hair coiled in perm rods and still wearing a hairdressers overall proposed jacking-up the car. The owner of the convenience store said it would be dangerous, the taxi driver insisted it would be better to wait.

People stood on the kerb on both sides of the road looking helpless, faces drained of colour, hands cupped over mouths. An elderly lady buried her head in the lapel of her husband's raincoat.

After three minutes, a police car with a reassuring blue flashing light nosed through the congested traffic and pulled alongside Wendy's Land Rover. Someone explained to the nervy young copper the gist of what had happened and it took a while for the gravity of the situation to sink in. Eventually, he put his walkie-talkie to his bloodless lips. His mouth was dust dry, his eyes ablaze like those of a cornered animal.

"Constable Edwards here. I'm at Davenport station. There's been a serious road traffic accident. Urgent assistance needed. I think there's a girl under a car!"

"Yes, Roger that," came the reply. "One casualty, is that correct?"

PC Edwards gritted his teeth and turned away from the civilians surrounding the car. He didn't want to do it. But he was a policeman, a figure of authority, someone to depend on in an emergency. He dropped to the ground, peered under the car and gagged. As he climbed to his feet his knees gave way.

Meanwhile, a valorous young couple had managed to extract Wendy and her daughter from the car and were leading them from the scene. People were frantically looking up and down the road, listening and hoping for a sign of heavier duty help arriving.

Constable Edwards had only been on the force for four months.

Four months spent booking people for parking infringements. He was blatantly unprepared for this. The stream of thick red blood crept ever closer towards the soles of his shiny, new boots. His eyes followed the flow and he took a step back.

"But there's a hospital just down the road," he pleaded with the sergeant back at the station. "I think she's dying."

"Yes, but the ambulance crew are not based at Stockport Infirmary. They're about six minutes away, fighting through traffic. Is there someone there with medical knowledge?"

"Well I don't know. How do I tell?"

"Look son, pull yourself together and find out – yell for a nurse or a doctor."

The policeman hooked his walkie-talkie back on his belt and began frantically shouting: "Is there a doctor here, anywhere, a nurse, anyone with medical knowledge?"

The crowd of people standing around the car shrank back in response, as though making room for a hero to step forward.

PC Edwards yelled at a bus driver. "Ask your passengers. We need a doctor or a nurse. Someone with first aid knowledge."

Moments later, as if by divine intervention, his prayers were answered.

A seventeen-year-old student, wearing a retro, khaki-green parka with a fur-lined hood and carrying a rucksack stepped out of the station and stopped in his tracks. The clogged traffic, the clusters of grim faced pedestrians and a frantic policeman were all hallmarks of a fresh accident and with no sign of an ambulance, he had to help. Wilson Armitage stepped off the pavement and ran towards a nucleus of people surrounding a white car. Forcing his way into the halo of free space he saw blood and dropped to one knee. He could see a girl, maybe five years younger than himself; the estimate was based on her physical size and the school uniform.

The policeman came rushing over.

"Hey! What're you doing? No bloody selfies, you little sod!"

Wilson stood up and put his hands in the air.

"Look, it's okay. I'm not taking photos. You were shouting for help and I've had medical training. At school. Manchester Medical School. I'm an undergraduate. She's losing a lot of blood. I need to get under there and take a look."

The policeman didn't know what to say. Was this lad for real? He didn't look old enough to have experience of mayhem.

Wilson sensed the uncertainty.

"Look, I'm advanced for my age and older than I look and we don't have time for this! Right now, I'm the best chance she's got. Maybe I can put a tourniquet on her wounds to stem the bleeding until the ambulance arrives."

Like a wind-up toy with a spent spring, the policeman blinked and stood motionless. Wilson turned to the bystanders. They stared back like waxwork figures.

"Jesus," he said under his breath.

Wilson shed his rucksack and parka and crawled under the car until only his feet were visible. After twenty seconds, he slithered back out, ran to the other side of the car and wriggled under again. He finally re-emerged, fingers tipped with crimson and faced the policeman.

"She's unconscious. At least one leg is broken and she's badly cut up. Worst is the shoulder – an artery is severed and she's losing blood. I can see the end of the artery, but I can't get it with my fingers. I need something to clamp it with. If I can stop the bleeding, she might be okay."

Someone turned the policeman's winding key and he looked back towards his car.

"I've got, err, a thingy, I think."

He was about to turn and escape to his vehicle when Wilson pointed to the policeman's belt and said, "What's that in there, in that black pouch. Is it a multi-tool?"

"It's a Swiss Army knife, a big one, with all the..."

"Yeah, I know. Give it to me. Quick."

The policeman's fingers fumbled with the clasp on the pouch. Wilson grabbed the knife, pulled out the short, snub-nosed pliers, checked the spring was working and shot back under the car.

Thirty, painfully slow seconds later, he shouted, "Policeman! Get under here. I need your help. NOW."

After a moment for deliberation and with no way to escape public scrutiny, the policeman reluctantly did as requested. Wilson had found the pumping end of the artery near Sally's armpit and the nose of the pliers was clamped down on it, hard. There wasn't much room for three bodies and six elbows in the claustrophobic space beneath the car, but the policeman manoeuvred himself into position nevertheless. The crumpled state of the poor girl made him whince and Wilson sensed his self-doubt.

"Come on. She's only a kid and she's depending on you. You signed up for the police, the responsibility, so this is where you do your job. Just hold this, exactly like this, with a firm grip and don't let go. If you do what I say, I think you might save her life."

There was a staredown in the aura of half-light as they slowly completed the handover.

"Don't let go, even when they prop up the car."

"I won't man, I won't."

As the urge for fight or flight lifted from PC Edwards, he sensed something other worldly about Wilson. This pimply youth who'd been able to stride through chaos with all the surety of an experienced paramedic. There was a transmission in the steely intensity of his eyes that hinted at a secret under restraint. As though the black orb within each iris was a gateway to something incomprehensibly deep. An obtuse thought accompanied the policeman's perceptions.

"You're not really at Manchester Medical School are you?"

"No, not that particular one," said Wilson, "but I have been to a sort of medical school. Managed to pick up enough, to know quite a lot."

"So who are you?"

Wilson thought about the question for a moment. He returned the policeman's gaze with a kind-of half smile.

"To be honest, I've no idea. But I'm working on it!"

Then Wilson rolled himself out and away, leaving PC Edwards to do the job of a real, award-winning policeman and save a young girl's life.

"Hey. Hey! What's your name, fella?" The policeman shouted at a pair of white trainers branded with a bloody swoosh. The trainers turned and started walking away. Wilson Armitage scooped up his parka and his rucksack. The policeman followed the trainers from his worm's eye view until they turned right at a corner shop. Then he heard the song of the sirens approaching and nothing had ever sounded so sweet.

Chapter 2

Twelve years earlier

Wilson Armitage was five-years-old when he first spoke French. Unusual, because Wilson was English, his parents were English and he'd never heard anyone speak French either. It was teatime, 29th of October, 2005.

Wilson's seven-year-old twin sisters, Kate and Megan were sitting at the kitchen table playing with stringy, plastic Bratz dolls. The process of changing miniature outfits was tongue bitingly difficult. 'Two peas in a pod' was how Gloria, Wilson's mum, described the twins. Wilson's dad, Alex, was on the phone in the hallway correcting the script for some hapless cold caller.

"No, I've not had an accident. Why can't you..."

We'll come back to him shortly.

Clearly, there's nothing remarkable in a five-year-old learning a second language; children at international schools take that as read. However, Wilson was only just approaching the foothills of the ABCs, so an attempt at Mont Blanc should have been unthinkable. More significantly, Wilson's French was not just a string of words assembled from a 'Speak and Spell' game. Gloria Armitage was loading the dishwasher as Wilson placed his spoon beside an empty pudding bowl and declared:

"Mère, je voudrais que nous puissions avoir ce repas tous les soirs."

Which means, "Mum, I wish we could have that meal every night."

Gloria's lithe figure froze.

Megan's doll fell to the floor.

Kate's mouth and eyes popped fully open.

Alex Armitage, totally oblivious to the *éléphant dans la chambre*, returned to the kitchen table and took a seat facing Wilson.

9

Megan had been trying to clasp a press stud on a tiny jacket and was captured by the notion the stud would be the size of a satellite dish if scaled up to adult proportions. (Funnily enough, the concept would never leave her.) Reaching down to retrieve the doll, she decided to 'out' the elephant.

"Mum, I think Wilson just spoke French!"

Observation verified, Gloria returned to *unloading* the dishwasher. Mash encrusted knives and forks were placed *back* in the cutlery draw.

Alex was reading a fly fishing magazine, his thoughts somewhere on the banks of the River Tay.

"Speaking French are we Wilson? Excellent. That's your favourite subject, is it?"

"No, it's not my best Dad."

Wilson began pulling faces on the convex side of his spoon. His chin cleared the table top by five inches and his legs swung to and fro beneath his chair.

His father looked up.

"So what is your favourite lesson then?"

Wilson didn't have to contemplate the question.

"Fire practice."

Alex rocked back on his chair, howling with laughter. The twins sniggered and snorted respectively. Even Gloria smiled, neglecting all thoughts of the outburst moments earlier. But they demanded her full attention when Wilson declared:

"Mais je ne veux pas être un pompier."

And he clarified everything for his dumbfounded audience by announcing:

"I don't want to be a fireman, because I don't like climbing ladders."

Then Wilson ran his tongue around his mouth to remove any remnants of rice pudding, crossed his arms and sat back.

Alex Armitage placed his magazine on the table and leant forward. He was totally and utterly astonished.

Alex was six foot tall and lean, rather than thin. His dress code was tartan shirt over a white t-shirt with cargo pants and desert boots. A spiky mop of unkempt hair gave him the 'just got out of bed' look. Work colleagues referred to him as Shaggy, as in, Shaggy from *Scooby Doo*.

Wilson's dad worked for British Telecom and if asked his occupation would reply: "I'm the cable guy." Which left the enquirer with the notion that Alex spent his days climbing telegraph poles. What Alex actually did, was plan the national network of fibre-optic cable that would one day supply super-fast internet throughout the UK. So if a line went down, Alex would be sitting at his laptop rebooting the digital superhighway and not in a van on the M60. The PhD in Electrical Engineering was redundant in helping him comprehend the minor miracle that had just been performed by his son.

"I didn't know they taught you French at school Wilson? You know, to speak like a boy who lives in France?"

Wilson laughed as though Alex was tickling his feet.

"No Dad, all we do is sums and colouring in. We don't talk like we're France people."

"But how do you know those words Wilson? Where do they come from? Did you hear them on TV?" Alex's voice quivered and rose in pitch as he asked the questions.

Megan and Kate switched from parents to brother.

Alex turned to his wife.

Gloria wiped her hands on a tea towel and walked over to the table. She lovingly ran her fingers through Wilson's hair. He was small for his age, but that was the only evidence to suggest he was anything other than a typical five-year-old boy.

Alex turned to his daughters.

"Megan, do any of Wilson's toys speak French? Like that 'learn to read by pressing buttons' game. Can it play a different language?"

His dry mouth was asking questions he thought would bring reassuring answers, but Alex was simply talking without thinking; what he'd just heard was not from a toy.

"No Dad, the Picture Computer's broken. The screen's cracked."

"Wilson's weird," said Kate. She bit her lip to kill a tremble and escaped to the comforting world of her doll.

Alex continued tacking into the storm.

"Okay, so how do you know how to talk like a French boy Wilson, if they don't teach you that at school? Do you have a friend who's French?"

"No Dad, I just know it."

Wilson's answer took the wind from his sails so Alex sat back, frustrated with his navigational skills. Gloria shot a concerned glance at her husband, who returned it with gravitas, courtesy of raised eyebrows.

Gloria's thoughts had been racing through a candidate list of explanations, starting with the most rational before considering more disturbing territory. However, since nothing could be ascribed to the rational column, it was a one sided race and Gloria quickly moved to the dark side. An intruder had entered her kitchen.

Wilson's miraculous ability to formulate sentences in what sounded like perfect French, meant he was not normal. In any mother, the realisation that your child is *abnormal*, brings a surge of fear that runs through the body like an injection of ice. It took Gloria to an unknown place, far from the cosy world she'd inhabited a few, worry-free moments earlier and she blamed herself.

"Yes, maybe, I have been over-protective, living in my little bubble, never wanting to think about all the bad things that can visit a family - but isn't that what all good mums do?"

She cupped her face in her hands. Fledgling possibilities were becoming fully grown certainties and her fingertips carried a sheen of tears. The fact that Wilson could speak French meant things would never be the same. He was autistic or seriously ill. Gloria imagined the inter-parent conversation outside the school gates.

"Emily already knows her six times table."

"Philip can tie his laces all by himself."

"Wilson can speak fluent French!"

She half laughed, half sobbed at the seeming futility of all her protective, maternal intentions.

Wilson rested his chin on the table top and peered up at his mum. The message he deciphered from her features told him that speaking in a different language was not good. Her mouth looked tight, her eyes were red and she seemed sad. So Wilson decided to stop speaking French and return to being the little boy he'd been minutes earlier.

Later that evening, Gloria interrogated the internet for examples of 'spontaneous speaking in French' and given the dogged tentacles of Google, it didn't take long to find examples of Wilson-like behaviour all over the world. The article she read from *Time Magazine* was a soothing balm.

A True Story. Published 24th October, 2001.

Teen Wakes Up From Coma Speaking Fluent Spanish.

A Georgia, USA, teenager who suffered a head injury while playing soccer last month awoke from a light coma and spoke fluent Spanish for the first time in his life. Rueben Nsemoh, 16, shocked family members and doctors when he opened his eyes and began uttering sentences in Spanish, despite having known only a few words before his accident.

"It started flowing out," the teen told TIME on Monday. "I felt like it was second nature for me."

It's not unprecedented for patients to start speaking a different language or using different accents after a major trauma. In June, a Texas woman made headlines after she had surgery on her lower jaw and then suddenly started speaking with a British accent.

That case was diagnosed as foreign accent syndrome, a very rare condition in which people speak with a different accent, usually after head injury.

As the day drew to a close, Alex Armitage activated alarms, switched the house to night mode and entered the bedroom of his sleeping son. Despite the internet evidence, he knew he'd witnessed more than a strange anomaly. To a logical, educated man, the night's remarkable event was beyond plausible explanation. Which meant only one thing: Wilson was truly different. In a dark corner of his mind, Alex opened the top drawer of an imaginary filing cabinet and inserted a folder, labelled: 'Incident One – Speaking French'. He suspected more folders would be joining it in the coming years.

He pulled the duvet under his son's chin and kissed his forehead. A gentle sigh confirmed that Wilson was sleeping contentedly, dreaming of who knew what – firemen, faces in spoons? Alex closed the bedroom door, switched off the landing lights and joined his wife for an autopsy on the evening's strange event.

A conversation between Gloria and Mrs Franks, Wilson's primary school teacher followed the next morning, but in the cold light of day, claims of Wilson speaking French were met with looks of concern for the mental health of the mother rather than the precocious abilities of the son. Mrs Franks suggested that Wilson's recently acquired habit of falling asleep during lessons and the dark shadows under his eyes should be of greater concern.

Alex Armitage didn't know that Wilson had indeed been dreaming as he adjusted his duvet at the end of that memorable night. Dreaming not of firemen or faces in spoons, but about school and a French lesson.

Wilson was sitting at a desk in Classe 6a of L'École.

A boy by the name of Cecil Didier sat to his left and Daisy Meadowcroft, a pretty girl with a ponytail, sat to his right. They were focusing on a large blackboard, on which a strict looking teacher by the name of Miss Angeline was writing a list of French verbs.

A large glass vase, brimming with flame-red poppies stood blazing on her desk. Daisy was mesmerised by the flowers.

Chapter 3

The Market Square

Four weeks prior to speaking French, Wilson had followed his usual bedtime routine of a quick bath, two chapters of Doctor Seuss and a goodnight kiss from Mum and Dad. At 7.45 p.m., as the hands on his Mickey Mouse alarm clock waved goodnight, Wilson drifted away. To the outside world, a small boy cuddling a toy giraffe was fast asleep, safely cloaked beneath a Batman duvet.

Light sleep was followed by deep sleep and sometime around nine thirty, a faint smile stretched Wilson's lips as his eyelids began to flutter. He was making his first journey to The Market Square where 'Rocket Man'; a surreal visual experience in three parts, was about to begin.

To help you visualise the opening scene, imagine the centre of a traditional English market town such as Ludlow in Shropshire or Abingdon near Oxford. In the good old days, market towns were the hub of the local community where farmers came to trade. So they had a spacious open area at the centre — a market square — where townsfolk could buy fresh vegetables, chickens and jugged hare from a variety of stalls and handcarts.

The Market Square in Wilson's dream was flanked on all four sides by an assortment of period properties, including a terrace of chocolate box cottages, rows of shops with bay windows inset with bullseye glass, an inn with a tudoresque facade and an imposing looking bank building. The surface of the square consisted of smooth, rounded cobbles laid in a herringbone pattern. A wide, uneven pavement of foot-worn flagstones bordered the perimeter while four narrow alleyways marked the entry and exit points in each corner. Towards one end stood a majestic Clock Tower, constructed from blocks of local stone and about fifteen metres in height. A neighbouring structure to the immediate left, was a pompous-looking chap cast as a bronze statue — possibly a Mr Ludlow or Mr Abingdon. A granite slab war memorial, engraved with the names of the fallen, stood solemnly to the right. Four flowerbeds bordered the trio, while a pair of wooden benches offered the perfect vantage point for watching townsfolk go about their business. But since this was the dream of a five-year-old boy, The Market Square was also personalised with fantastical details and reminiscent of a scene from the Oliver Twist movie.

Wilson was standing in the shadow of the Clock Tower, turning full circle, his eyes agog, his mouth agape, taking everything in. He'd seen something like it in a film, on TV, about a boy with no mum, lost in London. Wilson stood in wonderment, he was in that movie.

Actors dressed in period costume were dancing across The Market Square in choreographed splendour. A dairy maid, carrying two milk churns sang "who will buy this wonderful morning?". Cheeky boys with no shoes and wearing tattered rags, stole handkerchiefs from each other's pockets. The square was drenched in sunlight and everyone appeared delighted to be there. Wilson's eyes searched for the Artful Dodger, but another familiar figure grabbed his attention instead. A glamorous, yet cruel looking lady with glossy black hair with a streak of ice-blonde. She was wearing red stiletto-heeled shoes, a slinky black dress and her sumptuous, white fur coat was speckled with big black spots. Ten Dalmatian puppies were yapping and running behind her. One of the puppies nipped at Wilson's shoelace and then scampered away. Wilson giggled as it stopped to bark at a troupe of penguins — he recognised the man with the sooty face, dressed in black, tap dancing with them.

From the far side of the war memorial, five of Wilson's school friends, dressed as Roman centurions, marched into view. They were heavily armed, with plastic swords and bows and arrows with rubber suckers on the ends.

"Come on Wilson, we're making a gang."

Wilson didn't need to be asked twice, but as he lifted his foot and turned to follow, The Market Square shapeshifted.

Wilson's vision became blurred, images fuzzy and detail indistinct. It was as though someone had shaken a snow globe and the snow was settling on an entirely different Market Square. Wilson knew he wasn't standing in a real snowstorm though, because the flakes were huge and not at all like snow. More like fluffy balls of cotton candy. They filled the air like drifting clouds. He held out his hand to touch one, but it passed through his fingers without sensation.

At the same moment he heard a sharp hiss, like steam being expelled under pressure and his field of view became further obscured by a pall of smoke. Wilson turned his head to locate the source and the air cleared. He was in touching distance of the enormous engines of a space rocket. Vapour billowed around coils of pipes and valves, suggesting the gleaming white rocket was primed for take-off, bang in the middle of The Market Square.

Wilson peered upwards. The Clock Tower was still there. But it had launched itself in an upward trajectory to match the colossal height of the rocket and a latticework walkway connected the two somewhere near the top. Black letters spelled out 'Apollo 11' but the middle 'o' was out of line and the American flag, positioned above the 'A', was upside down. Just as they were on the Airfix model in his bedroom. Through blasts of steam, Wilson could see two figures high up on the walkway. A Bratz doll was climbing into the landing module with Buzz Lightyear. Then something screamed past in a flash of blurred colour and a slipstream of warm air lifted him clean off his feet.

Wilson shook his head to correct his vision as the buildings framing The Market Square came back into focus. But now, hundreds of people were cheering from doorways and leaning out of windows waving an assortment of multi-coloured flags. To Wilson's right, beyond the rocket, a huge grandstand overshadowed the square. It stood five stories high and was bursting with banks of spectators.

The ground no longer consisted of stone cobbles. Instead, it was covered with a smooth layer of compacted, black plastic. Several narrow tracks, about four inches wide and lined with shiny silver metal were set into the surface. The tracks ran the length of the square from the Clock Tower back up to a bridge at the far end. The bridge was a rickety structure built from plastic drinking straws and branded with logos including Castrol Oil, Firestone Tyres, Richmond Sausages and Peppa Pig. Wilson got the distinct impression he was standing in the middle of a life-size Scalextric track.

A large sign with the words 'Starting Grid' hung below the bridge and alongside that, a traffic light holding on red. Directly beneath, Wilson could make out a row of cars. Each vehicle was fitted with the fat rubber tyres from Formula One, yet the bodies were like those that might be seen outside an amusement arcade, moulded in fibreglass. Just visible above the curve of a steering wheel, hidden within a crash helmet, Wilson sensed a determined driver – with eyes fixed firmly on him. Wilson could hear high-pitched, revving engines and the smell of burning oil made his nostrils sting.

It was at that moment, he realised the spectators had stopped cheering and were craning their necks towards *his* end of the track. Wilson then saw the traffic light flick from red to amber and a second later shift abruptly to green. At the sight of green for go, the crowd reignited as the bizarre collection of toy cars came hurtling down the metal tracks like missiles locked on target. Evidently, we all possess an innate desire for self-preservation, because without thinking, Wilson started to run as fast as his legs could carry him.

Climb on those hay bales and you're safe.

As he propelled himself, arms pumping like pistons, in the most frantic race of his short life, Wilson became aware that his legs were not following with the same urgency. He looked down. His right foot was hidden inside a huge felt slipper with the face of Mickey Mouse looking up. His left foot was wearing Goofy, and neither character seemed able to move. The hard plastic of the racetrack was turning into a lumpy, clingy jelly. Mickey and Goofy were frowning helplessly as both slippers sank deeper into a treacle blancmange. Wilson looked up, the cars were still on collision course. Eighty metres, fifty metres, ten metres away.

His ankles were almost entirely consumed. Wilson braced himself for the inevitable. Then somebody shook the snow globe and a blizzard of white flakes swirled across the square. As the flakes began to settle, the cars, the cheering fans and the syrupy tarmac all melted away and a new stage set was unveiled.

Someone tapped Wilson on the shoulder. He turned and immediately jumped back. An astronaut in a bulky, white spacesuit stood towering over him. Wilson could see his spoon-face reflection in the smoky glass visor. The astronaut was holding the lead for what Wilson presumed to be a dog. He couldn't be certain, because the four-legged creature was also wearing a spacesuit.

"Do you know where I can find the Burger King, young man?" The astronaut asked.

Wilson was about to say, "to infinity and beyond," when an enormous giraffe with a pink felt tongue ambled into view and started licking the top of the rocket. A seam along the top of the giraffe's neck had split open and white stuffing was spilling out. Some ham-fisted infant had pulled one of its ears off.

"Ten seconds and counting," announced the astronaut.

Then as if to create a suitable canvas for the explosive spectacle of a lift-off, an 'eclipse effect' passed across the square and daylight was replaced by dusk.

As Wilson's eyes adjusted to the gloom, he was surprised to find The Market Square now totally empty. It had morphed once again. Ornate gaslights cast an eerie glow on the fascia of the butcher's, the baker's, the candlestick maker's. The astronaut and the giraffe had taken off, exit stage left.

Wilson heard a bell tinkle, then after a few moments, a door creaked open. He followed the sound to his left and saw a candle splutter to life in a room on the first floor of an imposing looking building that signage identified as 'The Bank'.

Carried in the still air, Wilson could detect the faintest of voices and then the silhouettes of two figures appeared, side by side, framed by the window. One figure was small and round, the other tall and thin. Wilson shuddered as a flicker of candle light reflected from a pair of glaring eyes. Goosebumps rose on his arms and he felt a sinister chill in the air. The conversation between the figures continued with more whispering. All was fun before, but now Wilson was frightened. He didn't want to be taken by the child-catchers. The boy who gets eaten by the wolf. Cautiously, Wilson started taking small steps backwards, his eyes never moving from the two shadows in the dark room. Then he turned and ran.

The cloying darkness lifted as quickly as it had descended when a huge glowing moon rose in an indigo sky studded with planets patterned like glass marbles.

From somewhere behind Wilson, possibly to his left, but as often happens in a dream, from nowhere in truth, a party of schoolchildren walked past in a regimented single file. A stern faced lady, dressed in a matching tweed skirt and jacket brought up the rear. She was pushing a cast-iron bicycle with a basket overflowing with textbooks and appeared to be shepherding the children across the square.

The boys, who ranged in age from about five to fourteen, wore white trousers, white shirts and grey blazers with a large orange sun embroidered on the breast pocket. The girls wore pink pinafore dresses and hats in the shape of a Cornish pasty.

In the far corner of the square, to the right of the Clock Tower stood an elegant three-storey building, out of character with its neighbours. The walls were a creamy beige, while the window frames, louvre shutters and the entrance door were painted powder blue. The building resembled a French château. Window boxes were brimming with pansies and the letters wrought in a metal gate spelled 'L'École'. The singing children were being ushered in that direction, so with spirits restored, Wilson adjusted his stride to synchronise with the boy at the back and followed the class to school. He attended L'École for several nights and as a result, on the 29th October 2005, at 5.25 p.m., spoke his first sentence in French.

As you know, Wilson stopped speaking French in front of his parents after that extraordinary night in the family kitchen, but the visits to The

20

Market Square continued. As a result, the contents of Alex Armitage's imaginary filing cabinet did indeed begin to grow. The second folder relates to an episode that occurred during Wilson's final year at junior school, during an art and craft lesson.

Chapter 4

The sunflowers

"Today children, you're going to recreate a truly amazing work of art."

Mrs Hope, Wilson's Art and English teacher, pulled back the dust sheet draped over a wooden easel to reveal a framed print of one of the world's most iconic images.

"I present to you, *Sunflowers*. Van Gogh's masterpiece of Post-Impressionism, painted in oils, shortly before the end of his tragic life."

Mrs Hope believed that when it came to art, the best way to acquire technique was to imitate the experts. So, if the class weren't making plasticine versions of the sculptures of Henry Moore they were challenged to forge a likeness of a Banksy or a Rothko – but in poster paint!

"I do hope you followed my request last week for home study on the style of the Post-Impressionists, because today children, it's time to put that knowledge to the test. Take note of the various textures and the balance of light and shade in the composition. You have paper and brushes, so let's begin."

With that, Mrs Hope returned to her desk to mark a pile of poems handed in by Year Four the previous day.

It goes without saying that a limited palette of school-grade paint was hardly likely to facilitate even the slightest likeness to Van Gogh's *Sunflowers*, but in enthusiastic hands, the forging began.

Wilson was soon lost in his work. A mix of yellow with a hint of brown made an exact-shade replica of the burnt ochre Van Gogh used to paint the sunflower pot. A little more red with a touch of yellow gave the pot a feeling of depth and a blend of blue with white and green made the perfect hue for outlining the pot – just as Van Gogh had done. Even to a trained eye, the developing composition was beginning to look like a masterly, school paint portrayal of the real thing.

With a sparsely bristled brush, Wilson moved on to re-creating the rich complexity of the sunflower heads and the tangle of spidery petals that surrounded them.

Half an hour later, an uncharacteristic stillness descended on the art room and perceiving the absence of the normal din as the unmistakable sign of mischief, Mrs Hope put down her red pen, lifted her eyes from the wretched poem she was marking and surveyed the scene.

For some reason, the entire class had decided to abandon their work and, more significantly, their desks and had converged in the vicinity of Wilson Armitage. Much jostling and pushing was accompanied by whispering:

"Come on, let me see."

"No, you move."

"It's incredible."

"Class, what the devil is going on?" Mrs Hope rose from her desk and strode towards the scrummage surrounding Wilson.

"Wilson, what on earth are you doing in there? Class, move back, at once!"

Just as the irate teacher was about to reach the hub of the slowly parting children, Wilson clumsily dropped his brush in a pot of water causing it to tumble and release a sea of milky-brown opaqueness all over his artwork. In a split second, all the detail in his masterpiece had been flushed away.

Had he not been so absorbed in the challenge of faithfully replicating the twists and turns of the sunflower stems, Wilson would have noticed the interest the entire class was expressing in his artwork. In which case, he would have released the localised flooding earlier. Unfortunately, the teacher came close enough to catch a glimpse and in the brief moment before the painting was obliterated, what she saw, left her almost speechless. As speechless as if Van Gogh himself had sat at Wilson's desk and improvised his own poster paint, post-impression.

Later that afternoon, as Wilson was walking home from school, a classmate, a stocky, ill-tempered lad who'd made it plain he didn't like Wilson, appeared on his left shoulder. The boy's elder brother appeared on the right. Wilson was expecting the usual stinging slap across the nape of his neck. But not the solid punch in the face that sent a front tooth deep into his top lip. Nor the elbow to the stomach that left him, doubled-up and sprawling on the pavement.

"Smart arse freak." Spat the classmate.

Wilson stumbled to his feet and watched them high five each other as they crossed the road, giving the 'V' sign to a driver who was forced to brake sharply to avoid hitting them.

The punctured lip needed two stitches. Wilson told his mum he'd fallen and banged his mouth on a kerb.

It was not an isolated incident and questions were beginning to be asked in the Armitage household about the torn school shirts, mud splattered sweaters, the missing kit bag, grazed knuckles, facial scratches — all of which could not simply be passed off as Wilson being clumsy, a growing lad or a bit of rough and tumble in the playground.

Two months later, at parents' evening, Mrs Hope spoke with Gloria and Alex.

"I have to be frank with you both, I am a little concerned about Wilson. From being one of our outstanding pupils, he seems to have regressed quite markedly in recent months. He used to be the first to raise his hand, always with the correct answer, always happy to contribute in class discussion, but now he seems more hesitant. His work no longer shines like it used to. It's as though he's content with not trying. A lack of confidence I suppose. I can't put my finger on it. Wilson certainly has super potential but seems not to want to apply it, or rather, he prefers to mask it. For example, he created a wonderful version of Van Gogh's *Sunflowers* and then seemed to intentionally destroy his work by knocking a water pot over it. It was a superb piece for anyone, let alone a ten-year-old, quite incredible and I would like to see more of that from Wilson."

Alex agreed with Mrs Hope that Wilson, "does indeed have hidden potential that occasionally bubbles to the surface."

As the words left his mouth, he'd already started to open the filing cabinet. Behind a folder tabbed with the words 'Speaking French', he inserted a second folder labelled, 'Painting like Van Gogh'.

Chapter 5

Three years later

It was the move to a new secondary school that finally enabled Wilson to escape the bullying, petty jealousies and the 'freak weirdo' tag that had dogged his junior years. By the age of thirteen, he had become a fully fledged chameleon, effortlessly adept at blending in, with the pendulum of his life never swinging far from the median. And his camouflage had been perfect, until the day Gloria declared it was time to visit the charity shop.

"Girls, you have so much unwanted junk in your bedrooms. Those Bratz dolls have more clothes than Topshop and you don't play with them anymore. They need to be adopted by a new family. You too Wilson. We can't keep your old stuff forever. It's time for a tidy up."

Wilson and his sisters reluctantly followed orders and an hour later, after much foraging under beds and delving in cupboards, a collection of booty was piled in the hallway.

Alex returned home from shopping duties and promptly declared that he also had a loft full of old CDs, clothes and other bits and bobs well past their best before date.

"Ideal charity shop fodder Wilson, give me a hand with the ladders and I'll pass it all down." With that Alex bounded upstairs beckoning Wilson to get a move on.

As Wilson shuttled up and down the stairs, something half-hidden in a cardboard box caught his eye. He'd seen something like it before, a year or so earlier, watching a magician perform in The Market Square.

"What's this Dad?" Wilson held aloft the multi-coloured plastic block. It was a cube measuring about six centimetres and each face was divided into smaller squares of different colours.

Alex's head appeared from the open loft hatch like a tortoise emerging from its shell. He smiled on recognising the object in Wilson's hand.

"Goodness me, I'd forgotten about that. It's a Rubik's Cube. The best toy ever invented. You don't see them much now, but years ago, that was better than a PlayStation."

Wilson looked questioningly at the block as his father continued.

"The Rubik's Cube has six sides. You spin round the different sides, from left to right, and... here, throw it. It'll be quicker to show you."

Wilson tossed the cube up to his dad.

"At the moment all the squares on each face are mixed up. What you have to do is twist it, until you get all the same colours together. So all the small green squares are together, all the red, all the white and so on."

The verbal explanation was illustrated with much swivelling and rotating. Alex threw the cube back to Wilson.

"But what's the point Dad?"

"Well, the first point is to solve the puzzle, so that all six faces show the same colour. The second point is to do it really quickly. My best time was just under a minute but it took months to be that fast. Some genius in Japan did it in six seconds."

Alex returned back to the loft.

"Be down in a minute. Think I've just about unearthed everything."

Wilson sat on a stair and studied the cube.

All the colours must be the same on each side.

He rotated the top face ninety degrees and followed a yellow square as it vacated its position for a blue square. Simultaneously, a bewitching sensation, as if Wilson already knew how to complete the puzzle, shimmered through, or across, the surface of his brain. He turned away from the cube and by some inexplicable mental alchemy, an instinct, an intuition, was creating, unearthing, a step by step guide for his fingers to follow. Wilson looked back down to the cube and began twisting the different sides of the puzzle, two at a time. Just as the magician had done. His fingers were lost in a blur of motion as they followed the stream of instructions being transmitted to his hands. Nine seconds later, the sorcery ended with a final twist and sitting in the palm of his hand was the puzzle, all correct and solved, with six uniform sides.

"Wilson, just hold those ladders steady for me. I can't find anything else the charity shop will be interested in."

Wilson's wonderment at correcting the cube in a handful of seconds dissolved as an outstretched leg began searching for a foothold. Throwing the plastic block back into the box, he shifted the stepladders to the required position. With both feet safely on the floor, Alex tucked the ladders under his arm and headed for the garage.

"Bring that last box down will you son. I'm taking everything to Oxfam this afternoon."

"Lunch is ready kids!" Gloria was standing at the foot of the stairs.

The door to Megan and Kate's bedroom flew open and Wilson stepped to one side as the girls barged past.

"Wilson, you've got to leave for football soon and you need to pack your bag. Muddy boots are by the boiler, where you left them. Clean socks and shorts in the drawer. Can you also bring down any clothes that need washing."

As a result, Wilson forgot to carry the box downstairs for his father, which meant he also failed to undo his handiwork. Three hours later, Alex had finished topping up the local Oxfam shop and was just opening the door to leave, when he heard one of the ladies behind a counter say to a colleague:

"And look at this, a Rubik's Cube, with all the squares in the right place. That chap must be ever so clever."

Alex didn't turn around; he didn't need to. The cube was all mixed-up when he passed it to his son and somehow he'd managed to correct it without the need for practise.

A folder labelled 'Rubik's Cube' was filed away.

Chapter 6

The youth club incident

By the age of sixteen, Wilson had two best mates. Their names were Hoover and Teapot.

Hoover was very tall for his age and consequently, very skinny. He had fine, jet-black hair that couldn't be coaxed into any style other than the flat, straight look. His eyes shone mischievously and a permanent grin would stretch to laughter at the slightest comedic prompt. His gangling arms and legs looked out of proportion with the rest of his body and his coordination was terrible – as though he was breaking-in limbs for somebody else.

Inexplicably, Hoover was a musical wizard when it came to playing the drums. His oversized hands struggled to control a knife and fork, (his nickname came from an ability to vacuum-up food without much need for cutlery), but give him a pair of drumsticks and he'd turn them into magic wands.

Teapot was also into music. He played electric guitar with the same enthusiasm Hoover had for drums and two nights a week they would rehearse in Wilson's garage with the other members of The Girl Guides. Nick Storey was lead vocalist and Tom Archer played bass. Wilson felt sorry for Teapot for two reasons. The first, his nickname. The second, his mum.

Teapot was really called Graham Clarke, his nickname was a self-inflicted injury.

One afternoon, a few mates were gathered in Wilson's bedroom playing *FIFA World Cup* on the PlayStation when Graham Clarke declared that he wanted a nickname.

"What do you want a nickname for?"

"Cos it's boring being called Gray all the time."

"So what nickname do you want then?"

Hoover asked the question with little interest in a reply. Both eyes were glued to the TV screen and his clumsy hands were furiously rotating the toggle of a PlayStation controller. No matter what move he tried to make, his players either ran in the wrong direction or ran off the pitch. Everyone in the room found his man management skills hilarious.

Graham continued.

"I don't know. Something different. Could even be totally random."

Hoover was feverishly pressing buttons in an attempt to stop his star striker from running back to the dressing room. Wilson was transfixed by the comedy of errors and not really thinking when he said, "What? Like err, a... Teapot?"

And before Graham had a chance to tell Wilson to stop being bloody stupid, Hoover rubber stamped it: "Yeah, that's excellent. Let's call him Teapot!" The naming ceremony was over and from that moment onwards, much to his annoyance, Graham Clarke was referred to as 'Teapot', or informally, as 'Teaps'.

The real reason Wilson felt sorry for Teaps however, was down to his mum. She'd disappeared when he was just a baby, but Wilson didn't know the full story. Apparently, Vanessa Clarke, Teapot's mum, had been a successful business women and happily married. Then soon after giving birth to Teaps, she went to a meeting in London and never came home. Teapot's dad never understood what he'd done to drive his wife away. Over the years, the guilt took a toll on his mental well-being to the extent that his landscape gardening business collapsed and he'd turned to alcohol as an escape. Teapot and his dad lived in a small flat in the centre of Stockport and survived on Jobseekers' Allowance and Teapot's part-time work, stacking shelves in a supermarket.

Not that you'd think Teapot's life had been touched by ill fate.

He was good looking, had a small army of female followers on Twitter, wore his hair tied in a trendy ponytail and was forever flitting from one girlfriend to another. Gloria Armitage thought Teapot had a permanent air of sadness about him though.

"The sparkle seems to be missing from his eyes," she would say and be overly fussy whenever he called round.

At the time of the youth club incident, school exams were over and a "summer of football and *fräuleins*," as Hoover put it, was on the cards. To celebrate the end of the term, Bramhall Youth Club was throwing a Leavers' Ball and The Girl Guides had been booked to play.

The Youth Club booking was the band's first performance in front of an audience and the day was spent rehearsing and sound checking, plus order-taking and general roadying for Wilson.

Twenty minutes before they were due on stage, Nick Storey took a call on his mobile. Wilson and Teapot were standing at the back watching a boisterous audience stream through the entrance doors.

"Bloody hell," said Wilson, "there's about forty people here so far. The rugby squad are in and the tall girl Hoover fancies is there with a mate. My sisters are here as well. Don't bottle it Teaps or this could be very embarrassing."

Storey had walked to a far corner of the stage so none of the group could hear his conversation. When the call ended, the look on his face said it hadn't been good news.

"Archer's cried off."

"What?" They shouted in unison.

"What do you mean he's cried off?" Teaps asked.

"He said he doesn't think he's good enough to play. He's totally stressed and he's been sick."

There was a moment's silence as the news sank in.

"So, does that mean he's not coming... now, in a few minutes?"

"Yeah, that's exactly what it means Hoover, you muppet!"

The audience, which had swelled to over a hundred, was getting restless. Egged on by some of the rugby lads who'd managed to get served in the pub across the road, they began to chant, "What a load of bollocks."

It was all going disaster shaped.

Storey was about to tell the club manager the performance would have to be cancelled when Wilson turned his camouflage down a notch.

"Hoover, silly question, but is the bass player really essential? I mean, can't the band play as three rather than four?"

Hoover lifted his head, as if to say, "You haven't a clue what you're banging on about, mate," and then dropped it again.

"Alright then, look, Archer's guitar's there, so I'll stand in for him. You can't cancel your first ever gig. Come on, we don't have any other options."

Hoover turned to Wilson.

"What do you mean, stand in for Archer? Wilson, you've never played a guitar in your life. You think you can just pick up a bass and bang out a tune? No mate, not possible."

"Okay, okay. I was keeping it a secret. I've been having lessons on the quiet. It hacked me off not being able to play with you lot."

Hoover thought Wilson was joking.

"Are you any good?" Teapot asked, not sure if there was any sense in the question.

"No, well, not as good as Archer. But I know all the songs, I've heard you cock them up enough times. Besides, the rugby lot look like they're about to kick off if something doesn't happen soon."

Given the lack of alternatives, Hoover persuaded Storey to give it a go. "It's either play with Wilson or we do a runner, and that won't be easy, since I'm the one with a drum kit."

As Wilson strapped the bass over his shoulder and checked the tuning, the club manager apologised for the delay and the change of line-up, which now included the last-minute stand-in, Armitage Wilson!

The hall lights went out, the stage lights came on. "One-two-three" yelled Hoover and The Girl Guides launched into their set.

Although Wilson's playing ability was well above that of Tom Archer, he included plenty of duff notes in each song. His offer to stand-in was the only option to keep the gig alive and he knew better than to steal the limelight. But for that one night, he took a chance and enjoyed it. Those hours spent jamming in the basement music room of L'École had come in handy.

The next morning, Kate and Megan shared the news over breakfast, but for some reason, Dad didn't seem at all surprised by the revelation his son was a budding rock star.

Chapter 7

What's going on?

While those of a cynical disposition could dismiss the 'incidents' on the previous pages as nothing more than snapshots of innate talent; like a genius performing long division in their head or an opera singer always hitting the right note. Wilson however, was not born with a natural flair for triage skills and saving the lives of car crash victims. His extraordinary abilities were not a genetic windfall or a quirk of nature. The 'incidents' were actually mistakes. Careless mistakes, made on the handful of occasions when he dropped his guard and allowed a brilliant light, albeit fleetingly, to shine through the mist of everyday life.

Over the course of twelve years, from speaking French at the age of five, Wilson visited The Market Square at least once a week, sometimes for three or four nights in a row. In the early years, he was drawn to L'École and from his desk in Class 6a, dressed in a blazer with a flaming orange sun embroidered on the pocket, he was introduced to a number of languages in which he quickly became more than adept. It was as though in the course of a dream, Wilson could soak up the steady drip-drip of foreign words and then in daylight hours, trace the leak back to a full reservoir of vocabulary and grammar. Having dreamed a little, Wilson knew where to find the lot. In the same way, Wilson mastered a wide variety of other subjects on L'École curriculum. By clutching a twig of information during the night, he found it was connected to an entire tree of knowledge when he woke the next day. One night, having fallen asleep reading a school textbook about the Second World War, Wilson found himself at his desk in L'École facing Winston Churchill. The next morning, Wilson was not only able to call upon knowledge of vast swathes of the history of the war, he could remember — no, more accurately, he had access to, the full story of Winston Churchill himself. How Churchill had invented the first tank, the nation-rousing speeches and his political life. Everything experienced by Winston Churchill became a sort of flicker book that Wilson could refer to during waking hours, and open on whichever page he chose.

As Wilson grew older, his appetite for nocturnal experiences graduated to the full smörgåsbord available beyond the walls of L'École. Martial arts, skateboarding, speed chess, meditation, guitar lessons, flying helicopters, first aid training — every type of vocation and activity could be served-up and consumed from the limitless menu in The Market Square.

Now you'd think living such a life, with all that information crammed inside your head, not to mention the ever present paranoia, self-doubt and a self-identity issue, would drive you crazy. And why bother going to college when you can learn more at night school?

Well, for one reason, Wilson knew he wasn't normal and as a teenager he had no intention of appearing to be anything other than *completely* normal. The self-questioning as to the source of his abilities was constantly put to one side and left to be answered another day.

The second reason Wilson was able to lead a level-headed existence, was because all the knowledge acquired via his dreams wasn't actually stored in his memory. Just the links to it. It was as though once Wilson had dreamt a particular experience, the knowledge, the data, was then retained somewhere outside his actual, physical self. In a Pandora's Box perhaps. By keeping the box securely locked, Wilson could concentrate on being himself, with no distractions. Though he could mentally lift the lid on the box, whenever he wanted.

There's much to be explained and all will be revealed, but right now, we have to catch up with Wilson, as he is today, almost eighteen and just a few hours away from an unlikely rendezvous and a potentially 'game changing' event.

Chapter 8

Wilson has a dilemma

Thirteen years have elapsed since Wilson first arrived in The Market Square. The 'peas in a pod' are in the final year of their fashion course at Central St Martins. Broadband infrastructure interlaces the country, so Alex now spends his working week determining where the information superhighway will travel next. With three children *almost* flown from the nest, Gloria has a part-time job in a local charity shop and looks forward to her twice weekly yoga classes. A losing battle against the advance of grey hair has commenced and bifocals are never far from the tip of her nose.

"Don't worry, Mum, you've still got it" Wilson would observe, whenever Gloria complained about her favourite jeans stretching a seam. That also meant Wilson was probably after something; a lift into town or his mobile phone topping up.

As for Wilson, he went from junior school to Davenport Secondary and then to Stockport College where he's currently studying for A levels in English, Maths and Biology. He's the goalkeeper for a college football team and Hoover and Teapot are still close friends. He likes the music of Radiohead and Coldplay; and has never had a steady girlfriend, just a few unsteady ones.

As this chapter unfolds, we find Wilson lying on his unmade bed. He's just finished scraping dried blood from his fingernails with a nail file. The blood was from a girl in a car accident earlier that afternoon. Wilson was pleased, because a call to the hospital confirmed that Sally was going to be okay.

Empty crisp packets, crushed Pringles tubes, Coke cans, all the detritus of a teenage lad litters the floor, including wet towels and odd socks. On the wall facing Wilson's bed, a flat-screen TV is connected to a

PlayStation and although the signal to the TV is on pause and the image blurred, it clearly shows the cockpit of a helicopter. Wilson is staring at the ceiling with a perplexed look on his face. There's something he can't quite figure out. He has a dilemma.

The previous night, he'd arrived in The Market Square with the intention of seeking Mark Sampson's advice on the best winter tyres for his Vespa scooter. A travelling circus was snaking through the square and Wilson had to weave through a nose-to-tail convoy of animals and a troupe of acrobats. En route, a mime artist, with a white-face gesticulated towards his unicycle. Wilson soon got the hang of it and even managed a few words in sign language. Moving on through the melee, a clown in a baggy, striped suit taught him to juggle with five skittles and a magician showed him how to conjure a white dove from a wine bottle.

As Wilson stepped onto the pavement in front of Sampson's Motorcycle Workshop, two chimpanzees, walking upright and looking very business-like in pinstripe suits, sauntered past smoking bananas.

"I'm sure I saw Uncle Bill on Nat Geo Wild last night," said one.

"Who – uh, uh?" Questioned the other, chimpishly.

Wilson ignored the monkey business, pushed open the door and stepped inside the shop. It smelled of grease and spray paint and an impressive line-up of motorbikes and scooters with lots of gleaming chrome ran the length of the shop. At the far end, sitting on a work bench, was Mark himself. He was wearing oil-stained overalls, a torque wrench was protruding from a grimy fist and he was talking to someone.

Wilson closed the shop door, Mark looked up, smiled and beckoned him over.

"Hey Wilson, how's it going my friend? Haven't seen you for a while. Speak of the devil and the devil walks in. Was just chatting about your problems restoring that old Vespa with... erm..."

'Erm' was leaning against the seat of a Harley Davidson with their back to Wilson. Wilson had been too busy acknowledging Sampson to notice whether 'erm' was a him or a her, but as the customer turned to

Wilson, the swish of a ponytail followed by a pretty face confirmed the 'erm' was definitely a her.

"Hi, I'm Daisy, Daisy Meadowcroft."

She extended her hand.

For quite a few seconds nothing happened following the proffered handshake. It was as though Wilson's mental faculties had all scarpered and were peeking from behind a sofa somewhere, waiting to see what happens next. Wilson came to his senses and realised he was thunderstruck.

thunderstruck
adjective
  1. *completely taken aback; amazed or shocked*
  2. *(rare) struck by lightning*

Wilson had been hit by the rare version.

Daisy Meadowcroft was quite simply the most beautiful girl he'd ever seen. He was face-to-face with his dream girl and couldn't shake her hand, because his palms were too clammy. So, for some reason he stood on the balls of his feet to make himself look taller.

"Hi. I'm Wilson. Wilson Armitage."

"So I can't help you then?" Mark Sampson asked. He had an odd smile on his face as he headed off to a partitioned corner that stood for an office.

Wilson descended to normal height. Daisy really was lovely. She had chestnut highlights in her satin brown hair that Wilson guessed would reach her shoulders but for the ponytail. She had a perfectly proportioned face, with a soft roundness rather than a point to her nose and her olive skin had the sheen of a Mediterranean tan. No, even better, her silky-smooth skin was a shade of creamy butterscotch. Her lips and mouth were a work of art. She was slim and above average height; in fact, only a few inches shorter than Wilson, which may explain why he thought it necessary to try to look taller. She was wearing a cropped white t-shirt with the word 'HOAX' printed on the front, burgundy jogging pants and a pair of hi-top trainers. An assortment of bangles and bracelets jangled as she held out her hand.

"Hi, like I said, I'm Daisy Meadowcroft."

This time, Wilson took the outstretched hand. It was warm and soft and firm all at the same time. Then something like pins and needles ran the length of his arm. Wilson instinctively pulled his hand free.

"Whoa, what was that?" He shook the charge from his arm.

"Thought so," said Daisy. "I know you!"

"You know me?"

"Yes, I remember you from the school, L'École — you know, in the bottom corner of the square, behind the Clock Tower. It was a few years ago. We sat next to each other in French class. Didier had the desk on your left and I was on the right. We were only young. But I definitely remember you."

"Well, that's going back a bit. Sorry for not remembering you." Wilson paused and waited for an interesting follow-up sentence to enter his head.

"You've probably changed since then?"

This was not only, *not*, an interesting follow-up sentence, it made him feel as though he was still at an infant school. Daisy smiled, then replied.

"Yeah, of course I've changed, I'm not five anymore! Everything looks different as you get older. Even The Market Square. You've been coming here as long as I have, so you must have seen the way it can alter?"

She paused for a moment.

"Then you must've learned lots of neat things from this place?"

Daisy raised both eyebrows questioningly.

Wilson wasn't certain if Daisy was hinting that she knew the secrets of The Market Square.

"Oh yes, I know what happens here. More than you'd think."

There was a moment of uncomfortable silence but then the penny dropped and Wilson admonished himself for being overawed.

"Of course you know about The Market Square, because you're in my dream. My subconscious brought you here, invented you I guess and decided to call you Daisy – you're just a figment of my imagination!"

Wilson waited for his brain to instruct Daisy to praise his subconscious powers but she just laughed at him. The sweetest, syrupy rich laugh imaginable.

"That's a hell of a theory Wilson."

Her look of bemusement was tempered with pity.

"So what do you call someone who invents a girl just to meet them in a dream? Desperate? A sad loser?"

Daisy was now grinning and Wilson could see from her dancing eyes there was more to come.

"So, just supposing, if you invented me, I can jump around and do crazy things, because really it's you in control of all the jumping. And if I do this," – Daisy stepped forward and flicked the tip of Wilson's nose – "it's self-inflicted. Stop it Wilson. That's painful. You'll get a nosebleed."

Daisy was enjoying the moment.

"Wilson, why did you make me do that? No, why did you do that to yourself? Oh heck, it's complicated, this dreaming stuff."

Wilson's nose was definitely stinging, with real pain. He was bewildered and on the verge of trying to banish Daisy from the dream, in order to prove that he was fully in charge of what happened in *his* Market Square. Yet, at the same time he wanted Daisy to stay right there. In fact, a parallel line of thought was trying to fathom out what he'd done to bring Daisy to Sampson's workshop in the first place, how he'd been able to create her to look the way she did and how to do it again in the future.

"You're thinking of how to block me from this dream, aren't you?" Daisy asked, laughing at the same time. "But you can't seem to get rid of me. Even though I've been created by you."

More laughter flowed until Daisy finally took a deep breath and composed herself.

"Do you know why?"

Wilson had no answer and stood there entranced.

"Well, I'll tell you why. Because this dream is also mine. Well, it's shared actually."

"What do you mean, this isn't my dream? Of course it's my bloody dream."

Wilson was getting flustered and once again stood on the balls of his feet. But this time it didn't make him look taller, just a bit of a plonker.

"Do you remember a few moments ago, when you entered the shop and we shook hands? Did you feel a sensation, like an electric current running up your arm, just for a split second?"

"Yeah, 'course I remember. That's the first time that's happened — and I have some pretty vivid dreams."

"Good for you. But what was really happening at that moment Wilson, was you and me, crashing. My grandmother told me about it but I don't remember all the details; I was young at the time. Anyway, here in The Market Square it's possible. If you're a special person..."

Daisy started twirling round, making spidery movements with her hands, "...and have special powers."

Wilson's blank expression confirmed he was utterly lost.

"Okay Wilson, how can I put this? People like us find it easy to crash into dreams. It's like, it's like hijacking someone's thoughts."

Mark Sampson poked his head out from his office and considered correcting Daisy's explanation, but then thought better of it.

"So in theory then," said Wilson, trying to rationalise things, "although this is just a dream, I know that when I wake up tomorrow morning, I'll be in bed in Stockport and if I stick a pin in my thumb the blood will prove I'm real!"

He peered intently at Daisy, enjoying the moment before his checkmate move.

"So, the question is this: If me and you, meeting here tonight, is also your dream, that means there's also a real Daisy Meadowcroft, sleeping in her bed in a real house somewhere?"

Daisy removed her bobble, then tilted her head back to shake her tawny hair. She gathered it all together in one swift movement, twisted the bobble and pulled the new ponytail tight.

"I live in Macclesfield, it's about twenty minutes on the train from

Stockport, and when I wake up tomorrow, I'll stick a pin in my thumb if you like!"

Daisy held up her thumb and pretended to lick the blood, then she added.

"Want to meet for a coffee, in Starbucks, tomorrow night? The one on Deansgate in Manchester. My pottery class finishes at five so we could meet at seven. What do you think?"

Wilson's attention was lagging quite a distance behind.

"Wilson!" Daisy stepped forward to give his shoulder a gentle prod. "What do you think? Meet tomorrow? Coffee?"

To describe Wilson as in shock is possibly going a bit far, but he was certainly not all there.

"Err, yeah, 'course, Starbucks, at seven," he mumbled.

And that's why Wilson was in a dilemma. He was troubled by the concept of creating the perfect dream girl, only to then be invited, to meet her in real life. It touched on the surreal. Like sending a personal invitation to meet yourself.

He rolled off the bed, clicked pause on the PlayStation controller and with expert thumbs and fingers, proceeded to put one of the world's most advanced flying machines through its paces.

Chapter 9

Teapot's mum

After half an hour, Wilson paused the game for a second time as Teapot barged through the door shouting, "Black Hawk Down, Black Hawk Down." Teaps then proceeded to career around the bedroom imitating a stricken helicopter and rotating his arms to a 'pffuh, pffuh, pffuh' sound effect before crash landing on Wilson's bed. The amateur dramatics ended as he wrestled with an unresponsive joystick and declared, "I ain't gonna make it this time," then sat up and threw a pillow at Wilson.

"*Apache Pilot Pro,*" Teaps said, nodding at the screen. "Awesome. And you've got your captain's wings. They reckon if you get to that level, you could fly the real thing. I'm impressed."

Wilson's blank expression said everything he was going to say on the subject.

"But actually, it's your love life that you need to take off Wilson, not a helicopter. You need a girl, man."

"A girl man?" Wilson asked dryly. "Just because I'm fully on board with the LBGT movement Teaps, please don't assume I'm a signed up member. Think you've got me confused with Hoover mate."

Teaps laughed.

"Seriously Wilson, there's loads of smart chicks on that media course. Put yourself in the shop window. Let 'em know you're available. Hey, here's an idea. I could design a sign for you to wear round your neck at college, saying something like…"

"I strangled Teaps cos he was winding me up?" Wilson interjected, not in the least bit amused.

But Teaps was. In fact, he had a fit of giggles for a few minutes as he suggested a variety of messages that could be written on Wilson's, 'Sign of Love'.

Wilson wasn't in the mood for jokes, given his dilemma. Besides, there was something serious he wanted to broach.

Perhaps now is the ideal time?

"Teaps, can I ask you a question? It's kind of personal. And I don't want to make you feel uncomfortable?"

"Sure. Fire away."

Wilson placed the PlayStation controller on his desk.

"Do you ever think about what happened to your mum?"

A shadow crossed his friend's face.

"I know she disappeared — and I've always wanted to say I'm sorry for that — but it seems false, cos, I don't really know what happened."

"It's alright. I don't mind. It would be good to get it out in the open for once, to talk about, 'she who can't be named'." Teaps made the paraphrasing actions with his fingers. "To be honest, no-one asks me about her. They think it's too delicate a subject. It happened so long ago though and I was just a baby, I don't remember my mum."

Teaps deliberated over his next words.

"I only know life with Dad. I can remember our old house, when he had the gardening business, bringing me up by himself, finding the money for after school care and all that. But then the depression and the drinking started. There's nothing I can do to change things. I can't bring her back. If that was possible, Dad would have done it ages ago." Teaps took a deep breath and shrugged his shoulders. "It would be good to get my old dad back though. He's never given up hope she'll come back one day."

"Teaps, I don't want you to think I'm being nosey about what happened. I suppose what I'm trying to say is, I'm really sorry for how your life has been. I feel guilty mine has been so easy compared to yours and I never..."

Teapot was not listening. His eyes were looking straight ahead, fixed on some dim memory.

"My dad kept a scrapbook filled with old family photos. I flick through it sometimes to remind myself I did have a mum once. She was a babe, even if she was my mum. She was half-Italian and met Dad when

43

he was the gardener at her uni. Built her own recruitment business from scratch."

He turned to Wilson and a sad, grudging smile stretched his lips.

"She'd had enough of domestic life with Dad I guess. Or maybe it was postnatal depression. I was an awful baby apparently, crying all night, giving her no sleep. But Dad said it was only because I had colic.

"I blamed myself for a time. You know, 'cause she'd run off. But Dad said she never complained and would cancel a meeting if I'd had a bad night and stay at home to make sure I was okay."

Teaps hesitated.

"Then one day she didn't come home. She went to a meeting in London, won a new contract, had lunch to celebrate then left to catch the train back. The clients said she was in a great mood. But she never came home."

Teaps was sitting cross-legged on Wilson's bed, head stooped, peering down at his hands.

"It's one helluva mystery Wilson."

"But Teaps, surely there must have been an investigation; the police must have been involved?"

"Yeah, one of Mum's competitors told the police she was having an affair with the new client, and that was how she'd managed to win the contract in the first place. Blackmail was mentioned. When the police investigated, they discovered she'd used her credit card to take cash from her business account the day she disappeared and a few days later in Dover, at the ferry terminal.

"But after a month, they were no further on, so they changed tack and started searching for Mum as a missing person rather than a criminal on the run. But the newspapers weren't interested in a missing mum story, she'd had her fifteen minutes of fame. They preferred the headline 'shady businesswoman runs off with cash' rather than 'where's Mrs Clarke, loving wife and mother?'.

"Dad said the police also cocked things up. The case was passed over to some useless detective who used an old photo of Mum from her student days. So everyone was looking for a young hippy with blonde hair and not a businesswoman with long, straight hair.

"The duff copper lost some of the surveillance camera images from the train station. Then Dad found out that a lot of street cameras were out of order. They dredged the canals, searched empty buildings near the train station, rang the hospitals, but she was never found.

"In the end, the whole thing ruined Dad's life and I guess kind of ruined mine, compared to what it might have been. I'm sure things would have been much better for me and Dad if she'd been around all these years."

"I can't imagine what you've had to go through Teaps, it's just terrible" said Wilson, placing a hand on his friend's shoulder, "but things will get better, I'm sure."

"Yeah, I hope so mate, I really do."

They sat in silence for a minute or so until Wilson glanced at his watch and then leapt to his feet.

"Whoa, Teaps, sorry, don't want you to think I'm being insensitive, but I've got to go in fifteen minutes."

Wilson grabbed a clean white polo shirt from a shelf and fresh jeans from a hanger in his wardrobe.

"Why, what're you up to?"

"Contrary to my single man status Teaps, a flame of passion has been lit. Well, it's more of a spark really – I'm going to meet someone in town, for a coffee."

"You mean a date? With a real girl?"

"No Teaps, a real rabbit!"

"Excellent, come on then, spill the beans."

"Yeah, I met her in a dream and we..."

Wilson blinked and his cheeks erupted in a red flush.

"I mean, a drama class, a drama class about dreams, that's where we first met."

"What?" Teapot looked understandably confused.

"Yeah, I met her in a drama class. A workshop actually, at a college in Macclesfield, that I went to last summer. The story we had to act was all about a dream, that's where we first met. She gave me her number in the canteen afterwards and we kept in touch. She lives in Macclesfield. Probably won't come to anything."

Teapot wasn't convinced. He was also a little disappointed with Wilson's gibberish, particularly after revealing the heartfelt story about his mum.

Wilson felt the rift and decided to dilute the damage by playing the village idiot. So he jumped up and did a couple of awkward looking martial-arts-style kicks and hand chops.

"As from tonight, I'm in the game my man. I'm making my move Teaps, I'm making ma moves."

Teaps was a hundred per cent certain that Wilson was winding him up, but couldn't see the point in questioning the glaring irregularities in his ridiculous story, so let it pass.

"We're meeting for coffee in Starbucks on Deansgate at seven," said Wilson. "She's called Daisy, as in daisy the flower."

"Well, I didn't think it would be Daisy, as in Daisy the cow! Nevertheless, I'm sure love will blossom – kerrrching."

They both laughed.

"Anyway, good luck mate," said Teaps, "gotta shoot; working the late shift and then gonna eat with Dad. Tell me about it tomorrow. And thanks for listening about, err, you know who. Appreciate it."

With that, Teaps left Wilson's room, bounced down the stairs two at a time, shouted "See ya, Wilson's mum" to Wilson's mum and slammed the front door behind him. Wilson released a sigh of relief.

Chapter 10

In the mirror

Wilson took a quick shower, double-brushed his teeth and stood for a moment in front of the bathroom mirror.

"A blonde version of Ed Sheeran, without the tattoos," his mum had once said. Wilson wasn't sure if that was a compliment. However, as he studied his reflection, he wasn't inspecting the unruly cropped hair, stubby nose, green eyes or the sparse presence of sprouting bristles; he was looking beneath the surface and facing up to something more profound than a mirror's impression. Wilson was trying to see inside himself, to get a fix on the person staring back. This person who was able to dream about working in an A&E department and then somehow have the medical knowledge to help a dying girl.

For too long, Wilson had failed to admit what he was capable of, thinking that if he tried to ignore his strange gifts, they would go away and the whole dream thing would eventually stop happening. The phrase 'I'll grow out of it' had been a comfort blanket during his formative years. Now, after the heroics beneath the car, there was no escaping a confrontation with his adult self. It had all come to a head. He was nearly eighteen-years-old, mentally mature, yet still demonstrating the inexplicable ability to learn from a dream and carry the knowledge back to waking life. He was certainly not growing out of it.

You're going to have to get to grips with this. What you do is nothing about being clever or a child prodigy; it's actually a miracle, plain and simple. It defies explanation – and it's not going away.

He continued to silently question the person in the mirror.

Plus, if Daisy does turn up, it will be the equivalent of a ghost being captured and interviewed on TV. There's no law of nature able to explain how you can meet a stranger in a dream and then meet in real life. 'A-squared plus B-squared equals C-squared' won't matter, because there'll be a new, top trump law in town. If she turns up, it will be the tipping point, the point at which you'll finally have to confront this dream phenomenon and find an explanation for what exactly is going on.

As Wilson brushed his teeth for the third time, fifty per cent of him hoped Daisy would show, fifty per cent hoped she wouldn't and a further fifty per cent thought he was mad.

Intrigued by the implications of seeing Daisy again, he grabbed the scooter keys and zipped up his parka.

"Mum, just off into town. Need a book for college. Back about eight."

"But Wilson, what about something to eat?"

"I'll get a McDonald's or a Subway."

"Wilson, you know that food's not healthy."

"I know. I'll ask for extra lettuce. See you later."

"Be careful love, on that scooter. It's rush hour."

"I will, don't worry."

Wilson pulled up the garage door to reveal a fully restored, 1959 Vespa GS 150 – a classic 'mod' scooter complete with the essential stack of mirrors, multiple headlamps and bodywork painted like a Union Jack. The Vespa was Wilson's pride and joy.

With one kick the scooter fired up and ten minutes later Wilson was navigating his way through Davenport village heading to Starbucks in Manchester, with a seemingly zero per cent chance of meeting a figment of his imagination by the name of Daisy Meadowcroft.

Chapter 11

A pause, for background on the Vespa

Wilson first noticed the abandoned scooter from the top deck of the school bus. He'd just turned sixteen and for six months watched it continue to disintegrate, day by day, rusting and neglected in someone's garden.

At the time, he had no interest, in fact, no awareness of the world of scooters. However, a plaintiff cry must have registered, because Wilson spent several nights pottering about with Mark Sampson in his motorcycle workshop and not only acquired access to the skills of a competent mechanic but also a love of Vespas. With his newfound interest in two-wheelers, Wilson plucked up the courage to knock on the owners door and ask if the orphaned machine could be rescued.

"It belonged to my son," said the elderly lady as she pulled a ragged tarpaulin from the rusting carcass of metal and chrome. "He emigrated to Australia about ten years ago and though he promised to ship the scooter over, he never did. I'm surprised, because he loved his Vespa. He was obsessed with everything about the sixties and looking like one of those mods. Dressing like a mod, with the special hair cut, his black suits, the music and the scooter of course, was essential. Not that it looks like much now. I remember him going to Blackpool on it once, with all his pals, for some kind of Sixties revival thing."

Wilson knelt beside the decaying icon and pictured the machine in its heyday with all the headlights and mirrors.

I can bring this back to life, he convinced himself.

Three weeks later, following a conversation with her son, the elderly lady offered Wilson the Vespa free of charge, in return for removing the eyesore from her driveway and she wished him luck with the restoration.

Wilson nursed the scooter the two-mile walk home. As he wearily pushed a seized wheel bearing and two flat tyres up the driveway toward the sanctuary of the garage, Kate blocked his path.

"Are you starting a scrap metal business Wilson? Cos there's no way you're gonna be able to fix that. Dad will have a fit when he sees what you've brought home."

Using the last of his strength, Wilson eased the scooter into the garage like a hospital porter pushing a patient into surgery. He gently laid it to rest on its side, before shutting the garage door firmly in the face of his grinning sister.

"Well, see you in a few years Wilson," he heard Kate shout.

As Wilson surveyed the pile of dented and corroded metal, seized components and smashed headlights lying on the concrete floor, he couldn't help but think Kate may have had a point; perhaps he had bitten off more than he could chew?

From the day the Armitages moved to 7 Midland Drive, the garage had been the dumping ground for items that were either broken or no longer loved. Scanning the garage, Wilson could see an old pine table and four matching chairs, a stained mattress, plastic storage baskets filled with rusty tools and junk, a pair of step ladders and stacks of old paint tins. This was all piled strategically in front of the window at the back of the garage. The last thing he needed was a sister on a spying mission reporting back to Dad.

It took Wilson a day or so to dismantle the scooter into its component parts. He then spread these across the garage floor like a one-to-one scale 'build your own knackered Vespa' kit. He bought a book about rebuilding classic scooters, a couple of enthusiast magazines and printed off a bundle of pages relating to the technical aspects of scooter restoration from various sites on the web. Wilson then left this assortment of literature lying around the house to convince his dad that the restoration was being done in the old-fashioned way, with oil under fingernails and learning from mistakes. Questions like "Megan, have you seen this month's copy of *Scootering* magazine?" and "Mum, has the vinyl material for my scooter seat arrived from Amazon yet?" gave Wilson the necessary alibis.

To say that Wilson enjoyed the project would be an understatement. Hidden from the prying eyes of Kate and Megan, he dedicated every spare hour to the reincarnation of the fifty-year-old Vespa. Mark Sampson's tutoring in the basics of engine rebuilding, panel beating, spray painting and welding seemed to be amplified the moment Wilson pulled the roller door down on the garage. From knowing just a little, he knew where to find the lot. As though a step-by-step guide to restoring scooters was stored, or retrievable, in flicker book format in his brain and he was able to flick through it, chapter by chapter and follow the instructions on what to do. Plus, he had a genuine flair for the work involved.

Wilson's dad inadvertently caught sight of the Vespa halfway through the restoration (as bad luck would have it, on a night Wilson had forgotten to lock the garage door) and was amazed, not only by the work in progress but also by the sight of his sixteen-year-old son stretch-forming a side protection bar from a length of chromed steel tube. Though that was nothing compared to the afternoon Wilson wheeled the scooter out and asked his parents to open their eyes. Gloria gasped and grabbed Alex to help support her wobbling knees. She was looking at something brand new, very shiny and straight from a showroom.

"It's just beautiful Wilson, just incredible. I can't believe you did all that by yourself. It's... it's..." She was lost for words. "It's like a miracle on wheels Wilson."

Gloria was not wrong.

At the sound of the commotion, Kate stepped out of the front door, took one look at the scooter and declared, "Wilson, there's no way you made that!"

She then turned on her heel, took one step back inside the house and shouted, "Megan, I was right. Wilson did throw that pile of scrap away and he's bought a new one with his meatpie money."

Alex Armitage had to pretend to his incredulous wife that there was nothing remarkable about Wilson restoring an old scooter.

"I did exactly the same thing myself," he said, with fingers firmly crossed behind his back. "They look more complicated than they are. You see, you start with Lego, then move up to Meccano and soon after you have all the skills to rebuild a motorbike. It's a rite of passage for a growing lad, like your voice breaking."

"Wilson, it's just... wonderful," said his mum, who wasn't really listening to her rambling husband. Then she wiped a tear from her cheek with the back of her hand and tried to say, "I'm so proud of you," but it came out mixed with a sob, which only other proud mums can fully understand, so she simply turned round and went back inside the house.

Wilson on the other hand, *had* been listening to his father; in fact, he'd made a point of watching his dad's reactions very closely.

He did the same thing after playing with Meccano. What's all that about?

Though his dad knew zip about scooters, he did seem to know how to protect his son from a mother who would need a straitjacket if she'd understood the full implications of what she'd seen.

"Wilson, I don't need to tell you how impressed I am at what you've done here," Alex said when they were alone. "It's incredible. But I think you and I need to have a little chat."

They pushed the scooter back into the garage and returned to the house for their 'little chat'.

With two cups of coffee for company, Alex closed the lounge door and they sat on the sofa.

Wilson sipped his drink and waited.

"Son," began his father. Alex then scratched the back of his neck and sipped his drink. "What I said about building bikes being part of growing up was true. There's nothing remarkable about teenagers messing with scooters, dismantling them, tuning engines, doing them up. In fact, I had a mate at school, Charlie Smith, whose dad had a business renting out tractors and diggers and all kinds of..." Alex paused to reorder his words and to take another sip of his coffee.

"What I'm trying to say is that Charlie was messing around with machinery before he could walk. He worked with the mechanics who fixed JCBs and got involved in stripping down these huge great engines.

The point is, at sixteen, he'd been brought up doing mechanical stuff like that. One summer I helped him renovate a scrambler bike. His dad's workshop had all the tools and do you know what? Our project ended up a disaster! The engine constantly misfired, the gearbox rattled like it was full of rocks and after five minutes bouncing round a muddy field the back wheel fell off. Seriously."

Wilson was laughing.

"The point is, the best we could do at your kind of age turned out to be a complete dog's breakfast. But starting with a pile of rusty old scrap – in fact, an infinitely more knackered starting point than Charlie's bike – you've built that!" Alex nodded in the general direction of the garage. "A bloody jaw-dropping, retro perfection. And ignore Kate; I know you did it all by yourself because I saw you working away that night."

Wilson got the point. "Yeah, but you know I can be a bit of a perfectionist, and I had the magazines and internet for help. I bet Charlie Smith didn't have access to bike blogs in the 1920s."

"No, he didn't," replied Alex, too absorbed in thought to notice the dig, "and I agree, you can order parts and ask questions online. But you can't download expertise and bloody skill Wilson. You'd have to be a fully trained mechanic to do what you've done. Plus a welder and spray shop expert and Christ knows what else."

Wilson's father seldom swore, so to say the bloody word twice and now the 'C' word meant he was serious.

"So are you going to give me some answers or do I accept my son is a genius and call Mensa?"

Wilson finished the last of his coffee and put the cup down.

"Alright Dad, I'll tell you everything, but you've jumped to the conclusion I did it all by myself. Yeah, I made the Florida bars when you saw me that night, but bending steel pipe isn't that difficult. The truth is, I bought most of it. The original scooter was too badly rusted and bits were missing and I couldn't understand a lot of the expert advice on the internet. I bought most of the parts and a mate of Hoover's brother, who's a mechanic and into all the mod scooter stuff, did a lot of the work in his workshop and quite a bit here in our garage, when you were working away."

Alex Armitage sat back on the sofa, unconvinced.

Wilson hated lying and contemplated telling his father the real truth. Yes, he'd bought some of the parts — after all, he wasn't about to buy a lathe and start turning engine pistons from aluminium block, though he probably could have done — but the rest of it was all his own work. Then he did a quick mental run-through of how the 'tell the truth' story would conclude:

"So how do you like that for an explanation, Dad? I knew how to do it, because I dreamt I could do it. All of it: rebuilding the engine, fitting new brakes, the electrics, spray painting. No, I don't believe it either, but since it's the truth, you'll just have to accept it."

Wilson felt his bottom lip drop as he admonished himself for letting those stupid dreams once again get him into a stupid mess with no explanation as to why he was a goddam sleep freak. But he composed himself and stuck to the story.

"Yeah, it's the truth Dad."

Alex scratched the back of his head and darted to a different line of questioning.

"So where did the money come from then? That Vespa's not a pocket-money-sized project. How did you pay for it all?"

He folded his arms as if to say, let's see you wriggle out of that one then.

"I earned it from my internet business," came Wilson's robust reply.

There was a pregnant pause, which was quickly followed by Alex giving birth to a huge howl of laughter.

"What? You earn money from an internet business? Based where? In your bedroom? In the garage? Wilson, you are incredible!"

"No Dad, it's the truth, straight up — and you'll be proud of this."

And for the next twenty minutes, over a second cup of coffee, Wilson explained to his father how he had set up a website called Meatpie.com, basically a spoof search engine. The tag line was: 'Ask a silly question, get an even sillier answer!'

"We get loads of daft questions, me, Teaps, Hoover and a few others, and we reply to them with even dafter answers and post them all on Facebook. As some of them are really funny, we get lots of likes and referrals. And here's the crunch — we carry links to boys' toys and gadgets, the stuff lads buy online, and when they do, we get paid a commission. We made nearly three hundred quid last week."

In his office the following day, Alex checked out Wilson's website story and found that although his son's revenues from e-commerce weren't likely to worry the accountants at Amazon, they were more than sufficient to fund a scooter restoration.

Wilson was off the hook for his fundraising talents. However, the source of the skills required to restore a Vespa remained an open question that led Alex, once again, to the filing cabinet with yet another folder, this one entitled 'Vespa Restoration!'.

Chapter 12

Back to the journey to Starbucks

Wilson was scootering along the A6 and about to pass Stockport Infirmary, or to be more accurate, the still standing, Victorian wing with a frontage on the A6, when he felt the all too familiar sensation of déjà vu. That fleeting perception of having experienced a particular moment on a previous occasion. It was not uncommon for Wilson to have two or three such episodes a week. But this time the feeling was stronger. More substantial. As though he'd made this stage of his journey before: in the same place, same clothes, in heavy traffic with the hospital on the left. And this wasn't the usual sensation that dissipated in a second. This was a prolonged déjà vu that refused to vacate its moment in time and was accompanied by a thumping headache and blurred vision. Wilson felt he was driving the scooter looking through a helmet visor made from 3D vision glasses. With his sense of balance about to topple, he managed to guide the scooter across the bus lane before coming to a halt with a front tyre perched on the pavement.

He took a deep breath then unclipped and removed his helmet. His forehead carried a film of sweat and a fine mist fogged the inside of the perspex visor. Wilson peered back over his shoulder along the route he'd just taken, to the point where the déjà vu had started. He followed the traffic and pedestrians as they hurried by, oblivious to his discomfort. Then gradually, like a compass needle settling on the north, Wilson's eyes were drawn towards a huge mullioned window set between two ornately carved sandstone columns. It was the central, focal point that dominated the facade of the old part of the hospital building. The sun was low in the sky and although its rays defined the ornate brickwork of the building's Victorian architecture, the window was a dull plate of non-reflective blackness; as though Teflon coated.

A sixth sense was telling Wilson that someone was observing him from a room on the other side of the window and whoever it was, they were not wishing him a good afternoon. A feeling of ill will, like a telepathic warning, filled his head. Malevolence was being projected in his direction. Wilson tried to decrypt the message. Was he being threatened? Warned to stay away? Warned against doing something? The full translation wouldn't come. The subliminal communication continued to mesmerise for a few seconds more and then abruptly stopped. The slate blackness of the window evaporated in a burst of brilliant sunlight as a number thirty-seven bus beeped impatiently at the trespasser blocking its path.

Wilson shook his head in an attempt to restore order to confusion, pulled on his helmet, pushed his scooter from the kerb and steered the Vespa back into the throng of early-evening traffic. As he headed to the centre of Manchester, trying not to dwell on what had just happened, the headache abated, his self-composure returned, then came the fluttering of butterflies in his stomach. The moment of truth was less than five miles away.

Chapter 13

Starbucks on Deansgate

Darkness had fallen as Wilson stood face to face with the cube of concrete and glass, home to Starbucks on Deansgate. It was 6.55 p.m, and he was five minutes early. Reflections from streetlights and headlamps made it difficult to appraise the interior. Wilson cupped both hands against the tinted glass of a window and peered inside, like a submariner scanning the horizon through a periscope.

Is it wise to reveal ones self?

He couldn't see anyone who resembled Daisy.

The coast is clear, she hasn't arrived yet.

The usual menagerie of office workers, shoppers and students sat relaxing at booths and tables, chatting over frothy cappuccinos, while other customers stood in line, texting and Facebooking and waiting for their peppermint teas and macchiatos.

What will I say if she does actually turn up?

It was at that moment Wilson realised how totally unprepared he was for such a conversation. Butterflies were still flapping deep inside his stomach. His mouth was parched and he had the urge to run – very quickly indeed. To submerge and dive back into the night..

What the hell am I doing? This is totally stupid. I'm going mad. Believing that someone I invented in a dream might actually be alive. A real person. That something I dreamt, could influence the future.

That final, emphatic appreciation of the impossibility of being able to meet Daisy – in fact, the impossibility of Daisy existing at all – seemed to calm Wilson's nerves.

He pushed open the door and entered.

Usually, by 7.00 p.m. most Mancunians would be making their way out of the city centre, but on this occasion Starbucks was still busy.

Wilson queued patiently and considered the etiquette of only ordering for himself prior to Daisy's arrival. Should he wait? Order for two? He wasn't aware of a protocol for his particular situation. Surveying the crowded room, he also realised there would be nowhere to sit if Daisy did actually arrive.

I need to find somewhere quiet. We don't want people overhearing our conversation, so we can't share a table!

Perhaps over there would be best? Oh no, someone's taking those seats.

Is there a downstairs? Perhaps that would be less busy.

Wilson, does something so ordinary as choosing somewhere to sit really matter in the face of something so extraordinary as Daisy turning up?

Wilson's existential debate with himself would have made an excellent thesis for any philosophy student. Mind over matter. Potentiality or actuality.

One of the baristas called Wilson's attention.

"Can I help you?" The girl spoke with a Dutch accent.

"Caffè latte please, with an extra shot."

"Medium or large?"

"Middel tevreden," confirmed Wilson, his mind elsewhere. He handed over four pound coins. *"En hod de verandering."*

The waitress looked curiously at Wilson, he smiled in return and was about to continue the conversation when a shutter slammed down.

"Err, sorry. I mean, keep the change."

"Hey, but you speak Dutch. Great, you're my first Dutch speaking customer. I've only been here a week though," she said with a grin.

"Um, no, I don't really," stammered Wilson, "in fact, not at all – just got lucky with that. Probably heard it on TV, in a Heineken advert; that's made in Holland, you know."

Head down and blushing, Wilson took his coffee cup and headed for the sugar counter where he mentally kicked himself. It wasn't often he slipped up like that. First Teaps, now this. Daisy had him totally on edge.

He noticed two vacant stools by a small round table toward the back of the coffee shop. They would offer a good view of who was coming in and some privacy when, if, Daisy arrived.

Wilson sat down and checked his watch. Five past seven.

He poured out the contents of a sugar sachet and watched it slowly sink into creamy froth.

Will she, won't she?

He gave the coffee a stir and took a sip. Then he studied his reflection in an adjacent window. The crash helmet had not crushed his hair too much. He inspected his fingernails. Then checked the tip of his nose for coffee froth. Then discreetly sniffed his armpits.

All good.

Wilson checked the time on his phone: 7.10 p.m.

There was a missed call from Hoover and an accompanying voice mail from an hour earlier. He clicked 'play'.

"Wilson, it's Hoover. Teaps told me you're all loved up. So just a quick call to say I hope the dates going well and ask if she's got a tasty mate for me?"

Minutes ticked by. Sixty seconds followed by sixty even slower seconds. Another fifteen minutes dragged. Wilson sipped the lukewarm dregs of his coffee and kept an eye on the comings and not comings.

7.30 p.m. Only coffee grounds remained in his cup. Apparently, like tea leaves, they could also reveal the future. Wilson couldn't see any portents in the sticky patina staining the bottom of his cup; only a shape vaguely resembling Australia. And a bit of New Zealand. Possibly.

Starbucks was virtually empty and Daisy was half an hour late.

Guess that's normal for women. Treat 'em mean and all that. I'll give it a bit longer. Perhaps she's stuck in traffic.

7.35 p.m. During those last five minutes, Wilson had checked his watch and phone three more times.

7.40 p.m. The barista asked Wilson if he would like a top-up on the house? He was so lost in his own world she decided further questioning on the origin of his Dutch would be futile.

At 7.45 p.m. Wilson finally admitted that Daisy wasn't going to make an earth-shattering appearance. The whole notion had been ridiculous in the first place. He felt totally stupid for misleading himself, for even halfbelieving a meeting could have happened. Though not as foolish as the moment Hoover and two equally unwelcome mates, Denver and Sam, piled through the door.

"Well, well, well, look who's having a cosy bit of me time?"

Hoover could read in Wilson's woebegone expression and the single coffee cup that his date had stood him up.

"You're such a loser mate. I'm obviously gonna have to give you a few lessons regarding playing the ladies. You're letting the side down."

Hoover locked his long arm playfully round Wilson's neck and messed up his hair.

"Come on, get your hand in your pocket. You can buy us a brew and then tell us all about it."

So at 7.50 p.m., fifty minutes after Daisy was due to arrive, Hoover and his mates sat down and peppered Wilson with uncomfortable questions about the name and identity of the mystery girl, what would be his next move and which of the two Starbucks baristas was the fittest. Daisy Meadowcroft never arrived to hear the conversation.

An hour later, as Wilson made the return journey home, (which included a minor detour to avoid passing the hospital), he detected an abnormal clicking noise coming from the Vespa's engine. He disengaged the clutch and let the scooter freewheel. When he put the scooter back in gear, the tapping returned. Wilson knew exactly what it was. One of the nuts that held the clutch plate had come loose and was rattling around inside the housing. To open the engine and access the clutch, he would need the special spanner that only Vespa dealers were officially supplied with. Fortunately, he had made one during the restoration from an old wood chisel, which meant the repair would take only half an hour.

Wilson nursed the Vespa through the last few miles, jacked the scooter on its stand and locked the garage door. He stood in the fresh, evening air and shook his head.

Meeting Daisy was never going to happen!

It was only 9.20 p.m., but Wilson was tired. He knew why. Although he got plenty of sleep, eight hours at least most nights, he didn't actually get much *proper* sleep. Certainly not the kind that made you feel refreshed and recharged. The ever-present shadows under his eyes told as much. His personal trademark.

Wilson's mum greeted him from the kitchen door.

"You're back late, love. I was getting a bit worried. Have you eaten?"

"Yeah, had a Subway, with Hoover and the boys in town."

"The girls are back for the weekend; your dad's gone to pick them up from the station. There's a bowl of chilli in the oven if you want it?"

"No Mum, I'm good, really. I've got a problem with the scooter and need to get on the internet to find a fix."

"Okay, I'll bring you up a cup of tea later."

Gloria returned to the kitchen and left Wilson to climb the stairs, leaden footed.

His bedroom was in semi-darkness and the soft luminous glow from the grinning face on his alarm clock was reassuringly normal, exactly what he needed after an evening spent anticipating the decidedly abnormal. Wilson negotiated a path to his bed and flopped, deflated, on his duvet.

What an idiot. What a bloody idiot. Why on earth did I think for one minute she'd turn up?

Chapter 14

Words of wisdom

Twenty minutes later, as Wilson lay on his bed thinking about the grief Hoover and Co. would be giving him the next day, his father popped his head round the door.

"Hey stranger. Fancy a brew? Room service has sent up a cuppa and custard creams."

Wilson sat up, switched on his bedside lamp and took the mug and plate.

"Cheers Dad, just the job."

He took a couple of sips and dunked a biscuit.

"Got a minute?" Alex pointed at the stool by Wilson's desk.

"Grow florit," replied Wilson, trying to retain a mouthful of tea-and-biscuit mush.

"Haven't seen much of you recently, so I thought maybe we could meet for breakfast tomorrow morning?"

"Sounds like a plan, man."

Alex picked up the *'Making a Mint on eBay'* magazine on Wilson's desk.

"So how's the online empire looking?"

"Pays the bills Dad. Keeps me in Vans, the Vespa on the road – you know how it is, with all the sundries."

Alex quipped. "Yep, those ice cream sundries can add up."

Wilson forced a laugh, as though instructed to do so from a TV studio cue card. He wasn't in much of a mood for dad jokes.

"It's all going okay Dad."

"Good son, that's good."

Wilson had an easy relationship with his father and though the subject had never been formally raised, he half suspected Alex kept a memory bank of 'questionable' incidents relating to certain, inexplicably precocious, abilities. Speaking French at the age of five would have been the first deposit. Sure, over the years there had been the occasional lightweight probing, but nothing more. Deep down however, Wilson knew his dad would never draw a line under the matter without at least one earnest interrogation. Perhaps the moment had arrived.

"You seem to be pretty busy at work Dad. Mum says you've been promoted to more of a consultancy role, mixed in with cutting edge research; new office in London and all that. Sounds alright."

"Well, I wouldn't call it a promotion as such."

"Yeah, but better than laying cables in trenches across farmers' fields."

"True enough. But I stopped working on fibre networks years back. Everything is wireless now. Just computers and routers talking to each other through thin air."

"The never ending march of progress, eh?"

"It is, and part of my new role is to try to work out where we go next, how the internet can be developed further. More importantly, I have to figure out if the technology is all good."

Alex remembered an apt line from *Jurassic Park*.

"Our scientists were so preoccupied with whether or not they could, they didn't stop to think if they should."

Wilson laughed.

Alex paused for a moment.

"Take this new charging technology for example. You know, how you can put your mobile phone on, well, basically a metal plate and current flows through the plate to charge the battery, with no wires? It's mind-blowing. But the problem is, it could quite literally be mind-blowing. In the old days the internet used to flow down insulated wires, like water in a pipe. But now it's all around us in Wi-Fi networks, in the air."

Alex pointed to the flashing router on the wall beside Wilson's desk.

"Data billows out of that thing like smoke signals from a campfire and we have no control over where it goes. Your laptop can read the smoke signals, but the problem is, the smoke sometimes gets blown around by the wind. And I don't mean wind, as in a windy day, I mean energy fields that act like a wind to disrupt the Wi-Fi. How many times have you told me the internet is slow today? Well, quite often it's because energy fields are blowing the smoke around so much that your computer can't grab the signal. We have no idea where Wi-Fi goes once it's out there and no idea what it's reacting with in terms of all the other energy fields such as solar or magnetism."

Wilson was intrigued. He knew his dad's little lecture was going someplace and he was curious to find out where.

"But what's really worrying Wilson, is the fact that this new wireless charging technology, which uses magnets to charge the small battery in a mobile phone, will soon be used to charge huge batteries in cars and lorries. Think about it. We're using magnetism to transmit energy to charge batteries without a cable or a tube. So, what if some of that energy doesn't make it to the phone and gets sidetracked and then mixed up with smoke signals from that router? Plus, there's energy fields we know absolutely nothing about. We can see them on these highly sensitive monitors we have in the office. Just blowing the smoke around. It's not solar, or light or heat. So what happens when they all starting mixing together, in thin air? I'm not sure all that smoke is going to be good for our lungs, could even be mind-blowing, so my new responsibility is to set up various research programmes, to try and find an insight into what's happening. Then I have to report back to a government committee and the intelligence services people with a heads-up every now and again. No smoke without fire, as they say."

Alex leant forward to address his son, face-to-face.

"What I'm trying to say is that sometimes strange things happen and it's best to keep an open mind until we fully understand exactly what's going on."

With that, Alex stood up, picked up the empty mugs and headed out of the room. As he reached the door, he stopped and turned.

"And here's the funny thing Wilson. The name for one of the new open standards for wireless charging is pronounced 'Chee'. It's a Chinese word that refers to the life energy that exists in all living things. Life energy, charging batteries – interesting, eh? Talk whenever you want, son," he said as he pulled the door to, "I get this stuff."

Wilson lay back on the bed and exhaled, blowing slowly, all the air from both lungs.

Boy, that was cryptic. Strange things happen, no smoke without fire?

As he lay mulling things over, Wilson reached the conclusion that the day had been one helluva day. He didn't visit The Market Square that night or for the next few nights. The Market Square didn't seem to be open. That sometimes happened and secretly Wilson was pleased. He still hadn't got his head round the whole 'meet in a dream and meet in real life' conundrum.

Chapter 15

The supply teacher

A week after the chat with dad and no further encounters with Daisy, Wilson's arrived at the freshly inscribed milestone of his eighteenth birthday. It was the 18th October 2017. Wilson slid behind his usual desk at the back of Lab 2, opened his textbook and waited for the biology lesson to start.

At 9.40 a.m., as the class grew boisterous, an unfamiliar man strode purposefully through the door and announced that he was Mr Catlow, a supply teacher. The lesson that morning was being given by him because, funnily enough, Mr Edwards, their usual teacher, was having a wisdom tooth removed. A couple of quick-witted students laughed at the irony.

Mr Catlow was only a few years older than Wilson. He had spiky bleached hair, wore flared jeans, a Nirvana t-shirt and had an ear piercing.

"Now," he said, chalking out a long and complicated-looking mathematical equation on the board. "I thought this morning we would start by learning the maths underlying the genetic code for the human genome."

The same two students laughed for a second time, the others just groaned.

"Okay, I'll take that as a no shall I? Shame, because the way you solve the complicated bit just here is really ingenious," he said, pointing to a hieroglyphic like symbol in the middle of the equation.

Even more groans.

"Okay, only joking. I think Mr Edwards should be back tomorrow, so they've drafted me in just for today to give you a bit of extracurricular insight, some modern, off-the-cuff stuff. A bit of thinking outside the conker shell. Things we can't explain."

Wilson adjusted his seating position. *Think my dad has already given me this lecture.*

There was another minute of preamble before Mr Catlow drew the basic outline of a fish, a blob with a beak that could have been a bird and some squiggles that vaguely resembled a spider. He turned to the class.

"The natural world, the world of biology and plants and animals is a strange world indeed. Take this spider, for example."

Mr Catlow pointed to the eight-legged shape on the blackboard by way of illustration.

"How does this baby spider know how to build a web within hours of being born? Anybody know? Anybody?"

Hoover raised his hand.

"It has a knitting lesson from its mum, sir?"

Mr Catlow waited for the ripple of laughter to end.

"Good point, my learned friend. But when baby spiders hatch from eggs they are completely alone. Mum's not around to give knitting lessons and tiny spiders don't really have a brain, as such. Yet a one-day-old spider can build the most delicate and complex structure with which to catch an evening meal from the word go. And the spider doesn't even need to practise. It doesn't have a few efforts and declare, 'Mmmm, that's not so good, let me try another one'. No, it builds an amazingly intricate web, perfectly, with its very first attempt."

Mr Catlow paused and surveyed the class.

"So the question is, where does the information come from? Where's the blueprint stored? Where's the instruction manual? It's like you my learned friend," he said, pointing to Hoover, "being able to crochet a net with which to catch a rabbit, the day after you were born."

Mr Catlow then tapped his finger on the fish shape.

"And what about the salmon? Salmon are born in rivers and when they're about five inches long they get this sudden urge to swim out to sea, to feast on scampi. A year later, when they get the other urge – you know, to start a little salmon family – they find their way back to the very same river in which they were born. I get lost driving to the supermarket, so how can a salmon find its way halfway across the Atlantic Ocean and back home again? Only to swim down the river after spawning and start the process all over again. How? How is it able to do that? Where does the GPS come from?"

The puzzled-looking Mr Catlow gazed at the students; who remained silent and sent the puzzled look back.

"Finally, and even more interesting, is the cuckoo. Did you know the cuckoo is the only bird that doesn't build a nesting place? What mother cuckoo does is lay an egg in the nest of another bird, such as a blue tit or a robin. Robins are way smaller than cuckoos, yet they soldier on feeding the greedy cuckoo chick. And you know what happens then?"

The class had no idea.

"Well, once the mother cuckoo has laid the egg, she flies off to somewhere warm for a break. Then – and this is the good bit – when the baby cuckoo is big enough to leave home, it also flies off to join its real mum in Mallorca or Marbella for a family holiday. Then, a few months later, they all fly back to England and start the process all over again.

"The big question is, how does the baby cuckoo know where Mum and Dad have gone? They didn't leave a forwarding address. No tweets. Yet each year, young cuckoos fly thousands of miles with no sat nav to meet up with their parents. It's incredible. Almost like there's a network of instructions the cuckoo, salmon and spider can access, like a kind of naturally occurring Wi-Fi."

Wilson gulped audibly as Mr Catlow continued.

"A Wi-Fi of nature, an internet of past behaviours that animals can log into to understand what to do in the future."

"Sir, so if a spider wants to build a new home, does it log in to the world wide spiderweb?"

"Yes, yes, very amusing and not far off the mark."

Mr Catlow didn't allow the wave of laughter to drown out his next point.

"Professor Rupert Sheldrake, a famous biochemist from Cambridge University has an interesting theory about this. To put it in a nutshell, he believes that all the information a baby spider needs to build a web isn't stored in its head at birth, but held in a 'Wi-Fi of nature', or what he calls a Morphic Field. And the young spider is able to tune in to the Morphic Field that exists specifically for spiders and download all the instructions it needs to build a web."

It was a Eureka moment as the apple of Morphic Fields dropped into Wilson's head.

He abruptly stopped listening to Mr Catlow's lecture and his thoughts began branching out to join the dots between spiders, cuckoos, inexplicable abilities and himself. Mr Catlow's open window on phenomenal behaviours in the natural world had just provided Wilson with a view, a starting point, for an insight into his own extraordinary powers.

Could it be that in his sleep he was able to access a Morphic Field for dreams, from which *he* could download and acquire experience and skills? Like a spider able to access the knowledge to build a web when the need arose? On the face of it, the notion was little more than a combination of coincidental ideas, a blindly assembled pairing, like sporting red trousers with a green shirt. However, if a Cambridge University professor was sold on the shirt, Wilson was prepared to try the pants.

Though the word 'explanation' sounded insufficient for the task, too flimsy for the heavy lifting required, there had to be an 'explanation' for an ability to speak French at the age of five without tuition, not to mention all the other acquired 'competences'. The 'Wi-Fi of dreams' glowed like a single bulb in the darker recesses of Wilson's mind. A path that once looked impenetrable, with no obvious starting point, now had its first signpost.

Half an hour later, as a bell rang to signal the end of the lesson and students scooped up books and bags and trooped off to their next class, Wilson wrote 'Morphic Fields' and 'Sheldrake' on the back of his hand and headed for the college library.

Chapter 16

Wilson. In the library. With a computer.

The library was always quiet mid-morning so Wilson had no difficulty in finding an empty booth. He opened his laptop, checked to make sure Hoover wasn't going to suddenly peer over his shoulder, logged in to the college Wi-Fi and typed the words 'Morphic Fields'. Moments later the results came back.

'You are not connected to the internet. This page cannot be displayed because your computer is currently offline.'

"Not again," he sighed. "That's the third time the network's been down this week."

Wilson pushed back on his chair and considered complaining to the librarians idly chatting at the front desk, but he knew from past experience that banging his head against a wall would achieve the same result. So since he was in a library, the fount of all knowledge for the pre-internet age, he'd just have to go old-school and leaf through some books instead.

A search through index cards for anything by author 'Rupert Sheldrake' or the subject of 'Morphic Fields' came up blank, so Wilson walked over to the Science section and scanned book titles one by one. From a shelf labelled 'Psychology', he selected *Dreams Explained* by James Charlton. It was a thick, well thumbed paperback and fell open on an earmarked page that at first glance appeared to be describing an experiment. Wilson found a chair and started reading.

'In 2008, a research team at Johns Hopkins University School of Medicine monitored the REM sleep of eleven healthy participants in conjunction with images of their brain activity. The researchers found, that even when we dream, activity still occurs in the areas of the brain responsible for sight, hearing and movement.'

The text was accompanied by images of cross sections of a brain with hot spots picked out in orange. On the following page, the results of the experiment were summarised by the book's author in easy to grasp terms.

'In other words, if someone dreams of climbing a mountain, the brain behaves like they really are climbing that mountain. In real life, the brain sends messages, using lots of electrical energy, to move that hand, put a foot there and make sure you don't slip. But none of that happens in bed. You're not clinging to a rope. You're fast asleep. So here's an interesting question: we know where the energy goes when we really climb a mountain, but what if we only climb that mountain in a dream? Where does all the energy go then? For the person dreaming, the dream is as real as their perception when wide awake...'

Flicking quickly through the chapters, Wilson was intrigued and fascinated. Here was a textbook talking seriously about dreams, with scientific facts, experiments and research findings. He couldn't find a specific reference to 'learning from dreams', but in the A-Z at the back, under the letter D, he stumbled on 'Déjà vu. p. 62'. It was a surprise to find the subject included in a book about dreams.

He gave an approving nod to the definition of déjà vu:

'An unsettling feeling that a time or place is familiar, as if one had been there before, or that a new experience had been experienced before.'

But it was the following paragraph that really caught his attention.

'Other explanations propose the idea of a collective consciousness through which one is in touch with the universal experience of the human race.'

Wilson was taken by the notion of a collective consciousness and that somehow, déjà vu could be connected to what he'd heard earlier, in Mr Catlow's lesson, about Morphic Fields.

'It has been postulated that some déjà vu experiences are indistinct memories of past lifetimes. Another view, is that déjà vu is a psychic episode based on dream experiences that surface with the prompting of a situation or place when awake.'

Startled, Wilson read that last sentence a second time.

Although he couldn't fully grasp the implications of what he was reading, he felt certain his déjà vu moments were in some way connected to his dreams. But more importantly, a scholarly textbook was giving a stamp of recognition to dreams as a subject worthy of serious, scientific study. A second signpost perhaps?

"Old-school is so cool" he announced to the startled librarians as he left the library with a spring in his step.

The rest of the morning was taken by a double period of English and an afternoon of sport followed. Wilson was the first-choice goalkeeper for the college second eleven and as he walked across the muddy pitch, the team had gathered in a circle around their PE teacher, George Daley.

"It's the big one this weekend, lads. St Bede's away – as tough as it gets. So I want to put in a good session this afternoon. There'll be no point in playing a two-touch passing game. Their midfield general, the Grundy lad who plays in County's reserve team could probably beat us by himself, so our tactic on Saturday is to take him out of the equation. It won't be pretty, but our best chance is to fire in long balls and use Hoover's height to cause havoc in their defence."

Mr Daley paused for a moment as he searched for the embodiment of his masterplan. Then his jaw dropped.

"Hoover, what in God's name are you wearing?"

All eyes turned to the lanky figure of Hoover. While most of the squad were wearing tracksuit tops to keep out the cold wind, Hoover stood head and shoulders above them all in what appeared to be his mum's fur coat. It was like a cream-coloured, fluffy bomber jacket. Eight inches of hairy forearm protruded from each sleeve and it was zipped up from somewhere near his belly button.

"What have you got on?" Daley exclaimed incredulously. "You look like a bloody ostrich Hoover. We're supposed to be playing football not going to a fancy dress party."

"I know sir, but I couldn't find my trackie top and I wanted to make sure I kept warm and, err, you know, I don't want to pull anything, like

73

a muscle."

An outbreak of laughter was getting infectious.

"Not pull anything, not pull anything, you, you..."

Mr Daley was temporarily lost for words.

"Hoover, the only thing you'll pull dressed like that is Big Bird from *Sesame Street*. And what's with the odd socks?"

The team kit was all black. Black shirt, black shorts and long black football socks. Hoover was wearing one long black football sock and on the other foot, a short, thin, light-grey business sock that could have belonged to his dad. Half a shin pad was sticking out of the top.

"It's all to do with my sock drawer sir, and my mum. All my socks keep going missing. Seriously. I can't find my other football sock. Mum said she'd definitely put two in the wash but then only one came out. She searched everywhere but it just disappeared. So I borrowed a sock from my brother. He doesn't do any sport; he's a solicitor. And this was as close as I could get."

It took about five minutes for Mr Daley to retake full control of the Under-17s' 2nd XI and for the laughter to finally subside.

"Hoover, in the words of Roy Keane, 'fail to prepare, prepare to fail'. Now, take that stupid fluffy coat off and let's get started. Two circuits of the pitch to warm up."

Ninety minutes later, cold and mud-splattered, Wilson and company sat in the warmth of the changing room picking lumps of earth from the studs of their boots.

"If it's any consolation Hoover," Teaps confided, "my sock drawer is full of odd socks as well."

"Mine too," said Denver.

"And mine," said Wilson.

"I'm gonna get to the bottom of this," said Hoover.

"Wearing your mum's fur coat for training. That's so not right," said Iqbal, shaking his head.

Chapter 17

Coming of age

Wednesday 18th October 2017

Kate and Megan were home on a flying visit (something to do with a student fashion conference in Preston but more likely because Gloria pressed them to be back for Wilson's eighteenth birthday). So that evening, when Wilson arrived home from football training, Alex announced a plan to visit a favourite Chinese restaurant in order to celebrate the coming of age of his number-one son.

Wilson would have preferred to stay at home and continue investigating Morphic Fields but he could see his mum had been to the hairdresser's specially for the occasion and his dad was even wearing a suit! Plus, four or five gift-wrapped presents and a handful of cards were stacked in the hallway waiting for the trip.

The restaurant was busy, the atmosphere great and the food, top nosh. Table talk was dominated by Kate and Megan's gossip and Alex told all his favourite jokes, including the completely inappropriate one about the Chinese restaurant and the steak being rubbery.

Gloria had a gin and tonic too many and started waving at a well-known actress, who was with a male friend and trying to be as incognito as possible. Wilson prayed they wouldn't dim the lights and bring him a candlelit cake while the entire restaurant sang 'Happy Birthday'. Gloria was certainly in that sort of mood. The dinner had just reached coffee stage when she lifted the carrier bag onto the table and announced, "Present time".

Wilson opened the birthday cards. The first one was very amusing and not just because it said 'Now you are 14' on the front. The card was from Auntie Melinda, Alex's elder sister and his only sibling. Melinda was completely eccentric but somehow managed to hold down a top job as an editor at *The Sunday Times*. Inside the card was a book voucher for twenty pounds and a message that simply said, 'Happy Birthday, William'.

After the cards, Wilson opened the presents which included his first electric shaver, an excellent drip-feed battery charger for the Vespa, two pairs of matching socks, a mint-scented shower gel and a boxed set of three super-strong Belgian beers.

"Cheers," he said, "just the job. Thanks a lot everyone."

Wilson put the gifts and cards back in the bag ready for the return leg.

"So have you enjoyed your day then?" Gloria asked.

"Yeah, it's been great Mum, really good. Also had a very interesting day at college."

"Why, did they give you a balloon or something?"

Megan had obviously had a bit too much bubbly.

"No Megan they didn't give me a balloon. And before you ask Kate, they didn't make me stand on the stage during assembly either. No. It was interesting because we had this temporary teacher for Biology, some young boffin full of crazy ideas. He didn't bother with the textbook, told us all about strange phenomena in the natural world – how baby spiders can build webs, how salmon go back to the same river to spawn. He said that nobody could really explain how they do it. Has anyone heard about Morphic Fields?"

Kate and Megan turned to Alex for help.

"Interesting question son," so Wilson continued.

"Seriously, he told us about the possibility of this kind of natural Wi-Fi that animals log in to for guidance on how to do stuff, rather than being born with it or taught by their parents. You know, like how to build a spider's web. A baby spider isn't born with the instructions. It doesn't have a brain really. So it downloads them from what he called a Morphic Field. It was pretty cool."

Wilson was playing a game. He knew his mum and sisters wouldn't have a clue what he was going on about, but would his dad? After all, he was an expert in networks and Wi-Fi. Talking to his dad directly would raise an eyebrow, but under the cover of a family meal and his feigned wonder at the subject of the lesson, maybe Wilson had a chance to tempt his dad into spilling what he knew.

"Wilson, has this anything to do with your potato pie website?"

"Definitely sounds like something to do with Hoover," added Megan.

"Are you referring to Professor Sheldrake?" Alex asked.

Wilson gulped audibly for the second time that day.

"Yeah, I think that's the name he mentioned," he stuttered.

"Yes, I'm familiar with the work of Rupert Sheldrake. He's a really interesting fella. Treated as a maverick by some in the scientific community, but his ideas are... well, challenging and different, to say the least. Some people even think of him as a prophet. I once delved into his concepts as part of my doctoral research. Strange you should latch on to him Wilson."

"Wilson I think you're just winding dad up," suggested Megan.

"That's enough Megan, Kate, if you don't mind," said Gloria. "We're here for a pleasant family meal, no need for you two to gang up on your brother on his birthday. It's nice that he's curious about the wider world, rather than who's wearing what and what's in and what's not. Hey, it seems I am a poet and I didn't even know it."

Alex rolled his eyes and checked his watch.

"Come on Gloria, I think it's time to get the bill; it's getting late and we've all got an early start in the morning."

But before calling over a waiter, Alex kept his eyes fixed on Wilson for a moment longer than could be considered polite and that said everything about the importance of Morphic Fields.

Chapter 18

The Gateway

Wednesday 18th October into Thursday 19th October 2017

Later that evening, around 11.50 p.m., Wilson arrived at a Market Square hidden within a dense bank of fog; the corner of a flower bed and the base of the Clock Tower the only tell-tale points of reference. The smell of gunpowder, like spent fireworks the morning after bonfire night, flavoured the air. The thump of an explosion, muffled by distance, confirmed the peasouper was smoke and not fog.

Okay, interesting, so what's this all about then?

As Wilson considered his next move, a breeze ran across the square shepherding wooly blankets of white smoke in the direction of L'École. Moments later, as the swirling curlicues shifted and thinned to expose an avenue of clear space, Wilson caught sight of a far corner of The Market Square and it had quite literally been blown to pieces. A terrace of four pretty cottages and a bow-windowed shop had all been reduced to piles of rubble, like a desecrated graveyard, from which stumps of wooden beam and splinters of maimed furniture jutted out. An adjacent property was still standing, but had been torn open to expose a pristine interior, like the inside of doll's house. The air was clearing fast as a World War II tank flying an American flag trundled into view. The double bass of its mighty engine reverberated around the square and the steel tracks spat sparks as they grated over stone cobbles. A platoon of soldiers in camouflage uniform emerged from the shell of Sampson's workshop and following a hand signal, sprinted to the rear of the tank. They grouped together for cover and scanned the square nervously, as though expecting sniper fire at any moment. Two cameramen and a girl with a fur covered microphone clamped to the end of a three metre boom, followed the sound and action.

"And cut," shouted the director, through a loudhailer, "at ease men."

Wilson was on a film set.

The soldiers dropped their weapons and started chatting and sharing cigarettes. The director began a conversation with the leading man – the hero sergeant in Wilson's favourite war film. Then a curtain of smoke passed across that scene, exposing a different, though equally bizarre spectacle to Wilson's left.

In front of the (unscathed) bank building, mobile catering trailers were serving street food and refreshments to film crew and actors in a variety of familiar outfits and identities. There was a fuss at the food van closest to Wilson, where a sickly looking youth with scars and nicks all over his pale face was having difficulty eating a hot dog. His fingers were pairs of scissors and the hot dog was skewered on a thumb. A broad-shouldered man in a black cape and a skull cap with triangular flaps for ears, was trying to extract the hot dog when he sliced his finger on a bladed edge. Wilson grinned when the caped crusader turned to a cocky looking pirate with dreadlocks and black eyeliner and asked for a sticky plaster. A second superhero, in red Lycra with a spider motif on his chest was sitting on the floor. Black, sticky goo was seeping from knife cuts to each sleeve and as a result, his hands were entangled in elastic webbing.

Wilson was tickled by the sheer nonsense of it all.

What an excellent start to a dream.

The cameras were still rolling as the show continued.

A red sports car accelerated across the square and with a squeal of tyres, skidded through ninety degrees and roared off down a narrow lane on the far side of L'École. It was followed by a speeding black and white, NYPD cruiser with its siren on and roof lights flashing. A policeman was hanging out of the window firing a gun at the moving target in front.

Then a message came over a tannoy somewhere.

"Last call for Wilson Armitage. Re-make of *Ferris Bueller*, Set Three."

Wilson ignored the message. This was The Market Square in glorious technicolour inviting him to acting lessons. He couldn't help but smile.

An excellent day and now an excellent birthday night.

For some reason, Wilson's focus shifted back to L'École and the unfamiliar thoroughfare the cars had driven down moments earlier.

Haven't seen that before, I wonder where it leads to?

Skirting round the back of the Clock Tower, Wilson reached the far right corner of the square and stopped. To his surprise, the lane was less than a metre wide, more of an alleyway, and certainly not wide enough for a police car. Confused, Wilson turned to the Clock Tower to double check his bearings but he was in the right place.

The alley consisted of a red brick wall on the left, towering six metres or more in height. On the right, a featureless side elevation of L'École ran in parallel. They formed a narrow tunnel, at least eighty metres in length and starved of light. At the far end, Wilson perceived a thin, vertical strip of bright, vague colour, open countryside perhaps. Ignoring a feeling of claustrophobia, he began walking along the passageway. He felt like a white mouse scurrying through a maze, conditioned by The Market Square to respond with the expected behaviour. A final stride led to clear, open daylight and liberation, in a field full of poppies.

Rich, red flower heads atop slender green stems were swaying in a light summer's breeze, in every direction, for as far as the eye could see. Wilson cupped one of the flowers in his hand, it felt soft yet stiff, like velvet egg shell. A startled bee hovered out like a micro-drone, buzzed angrily and zoomed away. Wilson followed the flight path for a few moments, until his gaze landed on something far more significant and he was forced to squint into the glare of the sun.

Floating on the horizon, like a mirage, stood the shimmering facade of a truly enormous structure. It was some kind of palace or a magnificent hotel, with great stone pillars, a central colonnade and wings either side filled with rows of windows. Wilson was certain the colossal building had to be the intended venue for the next sequence of his dream. It was too far away and too indistinct to establish more by way of detail, so he decided to walk through the poppy field and move on to the next scene.

Strangely though, as Wilson took his first step, the building also seemed to advance towards him, to bridge the distance, as if impatient for his arrival. So as a result, after taking fewer than ten strides, Wilson found himself confronted by the monumental structure. Broad stone steps rose up beneath a vast portico supported on two rows of white marble columns. This central section reminded Wilson of the entrance to the British Museum in London, but on a much grander scale. The stone columns towered more than twenty metres above his head. The two wings, eight storeys high, featured row upon row of evenly spaced Georgian-style windows curving away to the horizon on the left and right. Craning his neck upwards, Wilson contemplated the battle scene sculpted into the triangular shaped pediment on the front of the portico. It seemed a one-sided fight: human warriors dressed in ancient battle dress were launching puny spears at the sky as fantastical winged creatures retaliated with bolts of lightning. In the centre, on a square panel of smooth stone, a mason had chiselled the words, 'The Gateway.' The deep impression of each letter was burnished with gold leaf. More than intrigued, Wilson was keen to investigate further.

Taking each step with two strides, he reached the top of the stairway and paused to take a breath in the shadowy, open area, beneath the portico. This atrium was the size of a small Italian piazza. Wilson expected the building to have the grandiose, revolving entrance of a luxury hotel, but was disappointed to be confronted by a pair of tall, featureless doors. They were painted a nondescript matt grey and appeared firmly shut with no handles or doorbell and no archetypal brass knockers, the least one might have expected on such a distinctive building.

Wilson stepped back and peered upwards. Fixed to the wall above each door was a tarnished brass plaque inscribed with feint lettering. He could just about read the words.

The plaque on the left stated: 'The Gateway. Visitors Only'.

The plaque on the right: 'The Gateway. Residents Only'.

Wilson walked up to the left door and pushed. It opened a few inches. He then applied his full weight and the door yielded more ground.

It's my dream and you can't get prosecuted for trespassing in your own dream, can you?

Wilson squeezed through the gap — and into the most astonishingly, cavernous room imaginable. It resembled the nave of a cathedral, but twenty times the scale. High above, shards of sunlight poured through the kaleidoscopic colours of stained glass set in stone mullioned windows. Particles of dancing dust created a rainbow of sparkling mist. The arched ceiling rested on a phalanx of interlocking, white stone beams, like the ribcage of a whale, aggregating to the size of a pinhead at the limit of Wilson's vision.

Wilson couldn't see much of the red marble floor because almost every inch was covered by enormous mounds of what appeared to be gold bangles. Undulating dunes of glittering jewellery completely filled the vast expanse of space. Hanging down, at regularly spaced intervals, was a white banner bearing a four-digit number. A 2017 banner hung directly above Wilson's head, followed by 2016 and they continued back in numerical order until he could just about read the banner for 1977. After that, the years became indistinct.

The volume of bangles stockpiled for 2017 was the smallest, but nevertheless, they were still spilling all over the floor around Wilson's feet. He bent down and picked one up. It was shiny and heavy and Wilson was certain it was solid gold. He turned the bangle over in his palm. It had a smooth, rounded profile but the inside face was flat and bore an inscription of some kind. His eyes strained to read the fine lettering which spelled out: 'Mavis Smith. 1947-2017'.

"That's a fresh one."

Wilson jumped at the sound of a high-pitched, childlike voice.

It rose and expanded to reverberate through empty space.

"Yes, freshly minted today," said a lower-pitched, though equally childlike voice.

Wilson turned to face the direction of the voices and as he did so, the bangle slipped through his fingers. His eyes followed the hoop of metal as it struck the floor with a soft tinkle. The bangle bounced once, rolled on its edge and came to rest against a pair of small, highly polished black shoes.

"Tut, tut, that was careless."

A second pair of shiny black shoes then appeared beside the first.

"Yes, yes, very inconsiderate."

Wilson's eyes tracked from the shoes up to two pairs of immaculately pressed black worsted trousers. Then two black snakeskin belts. Two crisp white cotton shirts. Two black silk ties. Two black jackets — and finally, one round bald head and one long and thin, bald head.

"Welcome to The Gateway," proclaimed Round Head, in the same high-pitched voice Wilson had heard seconds earlier.

"Yes, welcome," said Long Head, in his low pitch.

As Wilson studied the two individuals, he experienced a feeling of familiarity, the slight tremor of an approaching déjà vu possibly, as though he'd been in their presence before. Round Head was the shorter of the two. He was chubby and cherubic, a Tweedledum or Tweedledee. Long Head was taller and skinnier. His translucent skin was stretched taut over the sharp contours of his skull. He had the look of a creepy butler from an old horror movie. There was something about the pair that made Wilson feel ill at ease. They seemed comical, yet menacing at the same time. Like a cruel joke.

"Do you work here?"

"Yes we do," said Round Head.

"Indeed we do," said Long Head.

There was no trace of emotion on their faces, and although their voices had a childlike quality, the words were delivered in a stiff, formal monotone. Wilson scratched his head, for time to think rather than to relieve an itch.

"Cool place man," he said, acknowledging the building's dramatic interior and dazzling contents.

"This," said Round Head, "is The Gateway."

"The Gateway to what?"

"The Gateway to the Spirit World."

"And this," said Long Head, moving his outstretched arm in a slow arc to indicate the vast expanse of space around them, "is The Hall of

Extinguished Spirits."

"Wow," declared Wilson, politely following the imperious hand movements, "and is all this jewellery, you know, these piles of bangles, is it all real gold?"

"Indeed it is."

"Awesome!"

A silent moment slipped past and led Wilson to suddenly remember his manners.

"I'm Wilson, Wilson Armitage, by the way. Nice to meet you."

"We know who you are Wilson. We've been watching you. We've seen your trace. You're a number eleven. My name is Big Mac."

"And my name is Short Cake," said Long Head.

Are they having a laugh? The little guy's called Big Mac and the tall one's called Short Cake. Well, whatever!

"You're one of our butterflies Wilson," said Big Mac, "and when you flap your wings, a train gets derailed."

"Indeed," agreed Short Cake.

"Yes," continued Big Mac, "your unpredictability makes life more interesting. The Powers That Be don't like everything to run like clockwork, so they allow some elevens to cock-up the timetable. Happy birthday, Wilson."

That Chinese food, that's where all this is coming from.

"Okay, Mr Mac and err, Mr Cake, so what do you guys do then?"

"We are the Custodians of The Gateway," replied Big Mac. "The caretakers of this magnificent room, our Hall of Extinguished Spirits."

"Wow, that's quite a job, given the size of the place. And what's the story with the gold bangles? You've got millions of them."

"There are indeed millions Wilson, and each bangle represents an extinguished spirit."

"In other words, a dead person," added Short Cake.

It took a moment for Wilson to digest those last three words.

"So, no wonder it's so big then. It's like a Hall of Remembrance, but instead of a headstone you get a gold bangle?"

"Exactly," said Big Mac, "each bangle carries an inscription with the owners name and history."

Wilson stepped forward to retrieve the bangle resting against Big Mac's shoe.

"So this bangle represents the extinguished spirit of, let me see, Mavis Smith, and she lived from nineteen forty-seven until two thousand and seventeen. So that's why it's fresh, right? Because her spirit was extinguished this year."

"She moved on earlier this afternoon," confirmed Big Mac.

Wilson picked up three more stray bangles from the floor.

"This one says 'Emily Winters'. And the date shows nineteen fifty-two to two thousand and seventeen."

"Moved on last Friday."

"What about this one? It says... 'David Ellis'. Two thousand and nine to two thousand and seventeen."

"Ah. Yes. Quite sad. Just a child."

"And this one? This says 'Eric Murphy', from eighteen sixty-six to..." Wilson looked up at Big Mac. "He was over one hundred and fifty years old?"

"Mmm, an excellent choice Wilson."

"Are you telling me these bangles and the names represent people who've died, and their spirit has been extinguished and turned into gold?"

"Yes and no," replied Big Mac. "Yes, the bangles represent people who've died. But no, not all the spirit is extinguished. Only the outer layer, or Shell, which is kept as a golden memory of a life well lived. The Residual goes elsewhere."

"To the other side," added Short Cake, "to The Powers That Be."

It was entirely understandable that Wilson didn't understand a single word. Big Mac helped to clear up the confusion.

"Let me put it another way. We can never totally extinguish the Residual Wilson, because it's what you'd call, the soul. It's impossible to extinguish a person's soul. The soul goes on to eternity. But the protective outer layer of spirit, the Shell, lasts only until it has just three ounces of energy left."

"I think of the Shell as someone's will to live," chirped Short Cake. "At the end of the three score and ten, when someone has lost their will to live – or, for the less fortunate, when the will to live has been taken prematurely – the Shell delivers the Residual here. We extinguish the Shell to release the Residual, and three ounces of Shell are converted into three ounces of gold bangle bearing the owner's name. You see, spirit is energy and energy is spirit, and neither can be destroyed, only changed from one form to another."

"So, let me see if I've got this," said Wilson. "All the numbers, like nineteen ninety-nine and so on" – he pointed at the seemingly endless line of hanging banners – "are the years that the people died. The year part of their spirit, the protective Shell, was extinguished and turned into a gold bangle?"

"Indeed," said Short Cake.

Wilson had no idea from where his brain had conjured the source material for his dream. And more specifically, the bizarre conversation. However, determined to get to the bottom of it all, he continued.

"So how do the two parts of spirit find their way into here?"

"Through the Residents' Entrance," answered Big Mac, "the door that was on your right when you stood outside. You wouldn't have been able to open that door. After a person has died, the Shell brings the Residual to that door, to us, the Custodians. Only the Shell can open that door. Would you like to see the other doors?"

Before Wilson could answer, they shuffled off behind the steep slope of bangles from 2015 where two executive-style desks with matching chairs, were illuminated by two angle-poise lamps. Beyond the desks was a red-brick wall inset with three doors, similar to, but smaller than those at the entrance to The Gateway. A neon sign glowed above each door.

The first one read: 'Exit to Market Square.'

The second: 'Exit to Ghost World. Non-Extinguished Spirits Only.'

The third sign read: 'Exit to Eternity. Residual Spirits Only.'

To the right of the three doors, about twenty metres further along the wall, Wilson could also see a hole, the size of a serving hatch, roughly knocked through. Voices could be heard echoing up through the hole, as if workmen were busy a few floors below. On cue, somebody yelled in pain, as though they'd hit themselves on the thumb with a hammer. Even further along was another door, partly obscured by a ridge of bangles, with an illuminated, white box mounted above. Wilson presumed it had the words 'Fire Exit' printed on the front; it was too far away to see.

Referring back to the three doors Wilson considered the possible meanings of the neon signs. Big Mac gave him guidance.

"When a Shell is extinguished, the Residual is released and goes through the door marked Exit to Eternity."

"So what happens with the middle door then? What goes through the Exit to the Ghost World?"

"Spirits that are overweight, because they've arrived before their time."

"Simply put," interjected Short Cake with a macabre chuckle, "when a new arrival has not completely lost the will to live but is nevertheless, dead, they must go back to where they came from, through that door, as a ghost."

"A phantom," said Big Mac, "a thing that goes bump in the night. Either way, they go back for as long as it takes for the Shell to reduce its energy level to our management requirement of exactly three ounces. When the will to live is finally exhausted, they come back through the residents' entrance and we do our funky stuff. Extinguish and bangle."

"Indeed we do," nodded Short Cake, "and the more haunting they do, the quicker they're back. If they're happy to float like a shadow, wailing now and again, well, that won't burn up much energy, so they could be a spectre for hundreds of years. But banging on radiators with a saucepan, slamming doors, active stuff — takes lots of energy and they're back here sharpish."

"So," said Wilson, "the bangle for Eric Murphy, eighteen sixty-six to two thousand and seventeen, he went back to the Ghost World, didn't he? And then, when his outer Shell, his will to live, was fully used up, he came back here?"

"You learn fast, Mr Armitage."

Big Mac turned to his companion.

"I think our work is finished for the day, don't you, Mr Cake?"

"Indeed I do."

"One question though," said Wilson, "who are The Powers That Be?"

Big Mac supplied the answer.

"The Powers That Be know everything."

"Everything about The Gateway?"

"No, everything about everything."

"They like mischief and they love gambling," added Short Cake. "And they're watching you Wilson, and so are we. We've seen your trace."

"What do you mean, you've seen my...?"

But before Wilson could finish the sentence, the distinctive 'tring' of a hotel service bell echoed around the hall. Big Mac and Short Cake rushed forward, grabbed Wilson by the elbows and, surprisingly powerfully, lifted him off his feet and carried him toward the door marked 'Exit to Market Square'.

"You have to leave right now Wilson. A new resident has arrived," stuttered Big Mac, red faced and straining.

"Oh, I do hope it's a returnee from the Ghost World. They have such fun stories," said a breathless Short Cake. "It's truly been a pleasure to meet you birthday boy, do call and see us again."

They dropped him at The Market Square exit and hurried back towards their desks. Wilson was just about to leave when a thought stopped him in his tracks and he turned back. Big Mac was sitting at his desk, about to write something in a thick ledger with a chubby fountain pen.

"Sorry to trouble you, Mr Mac, but I have one last question."

Big Mac looked up. "Be very quick, young man."

"Can I ask if you have a bangle for Vanessa Clarke? Extinguished around nineteen ninety-nine?"

Big Mac peered over his glasses at Wilson. The light from the lamp cast an unpleasant shadow across his face.

"I checked the records earlier Wilson, in anticipation of your question. There is no bangle here by that name. And nobody by that name has gone through there." He pointed the end of the fountain pen at the Exit to the Ghost World. "So I suggest you conduct further enquiries in The Market Square. Now please leave, immediately, we have company. Good day, sir!"

Chapter 19

Squaring the circle

Thursday 19th October 2017

At 7.00 a.m., Mickey Mouse announced the new day by smashing a red mallet against a silver bell. Wilson slowly surfaced from his deep sleep, blinked and silenced the alarm with a well-aimed slap.

"Oooaaghh."

What a night. Where the hell did all that come from?

He combed a hand through his hair, rubbed his face and slowly opened both eyes. All the events and characters of the previous night flashed through his mind like slides on a carousel projector. Big Mac, Gateway, Bangles, Eric Murphy.

Wilson dressed, splashed water on his face and studied his reflection in the bathroom mirror. A smudge of dark shadow underlined tired eyes. He made a slow, plodding descent down the stairs and trudged into the kitchen where Alex was hidden by a newspaper. Kate and Megan were eating boiled eggs.

"Morning everyone," he mumbled, flopping onto a chair.

"Morning love. Sleep well?"

Gloria had her back to Wilson and was stirring something on the hob.

"Not really. Had a strange dream. Don't think that Chinese food agreed with me."

"Oh, what a shame – and after such a lovely night. Well, don't worry, I've made a big pan of porridge for breakfast. A good healthy start to the day won't hurt."

Gloria carried a bowl over and placed it on the table.

"Goodness Wilson, you look shocking, are you coming down with something?"

She placed a palm on her son's forehead.

"Well, you've not got a temperature. So it's nothing a restful day won't fix. I'll call college and tell them you're under the weather?"

"Nah, I'm okay Mum. I've got loads on. Plus, the Vespa's not firing properly so I need to sort it before an exam at ten."

"Okay love. Well just try and take it easy today then."

Gloria turned to her daughters.

"Girls, how are you getting on with those eggs? Would you like some soldiers?"

"Gloria, I'm sure the girls don't need any help to eat an egg." The newspaper shook as Alex chuckled away.

"Yeah, please mum," said Megan, "but not for Kate. She's modelling my outfits in the show next week and I don't want her big ass to get in the way of my needle."

Kate was laughing as she knocked the helmet off a second egg.

"You know what they say about dreams Wilson?" Came a voice from the other side of the *Financial Times*.

"No Dad, what do they say?"

"They say dreams are the gateway to another world."

Wilson thought there was extra emphasis on the word 'gateway', but perhaps he was just being neurotic, either way he lost his appetite and pushed the bowl of porridge to one side. Wilson didn't want the conversation with his dad to proceed a single word further.

"Gotta go folks, running late."

"But Wilson, you've hardly had any breakfast..."

"Gotta scoot, to fix the scoot. Catch you later family."

He grabbed his jacket and rucksack and quickly headed out to the garage.

"I do worry about that boy sometimes," said Gloria as Wilson closed the front door.

Wilson soon had the Vespa's engine drumming like Hoover and arrived at college in good time for the English exam. After lunch, he headed to the college library where he hoped the internet would be up and running. At an empty cubicle, he took a pen and paper from his rucksack and shifted his brain into first gear.

If you're looking for buried treasure, you need to know where to dig. At the top of a blank page, he wrote the words 'Morphic Fields'. As a concept, it sounded so similar to his dream experiences; the Wi-Fi of nature had to be worth exploring. Wilson considered his next move. *What is my hypothesis then?*

He chewed the end of his biro, sat back and mulled over the question. After three or four minutes, he leant forward and wrote the words 'Dream Fields' on his pad and circled them.

My hypothesis is that Morphic Fields and Dream Fields are the same kind of thing. A Morphic Field holds the instructions to create a spider's web. A Dream Field holds the instructions to restore a Vespa.

He drew a curved arrow to connect the two terms. It wasn't a revelation, but it was a start and for the next twenty minutes, Wilson stared at the words as cogs turned inside his head.

What other types of fields are there, he thought, going off-piste. Magnetic? Electrical? Gravitational? Yeah, they're energy fields.

Ding. Wilson had three cherries in a row.

Exactly, they're all energy fields! So Morphic Fields and Dream Fields could also involve energy!

His evolving clock diagram was now something like this: 'Morphic Fields' at twelve, connected to 'Dream Fields' at three, connected to 'Energy Fields' at six.

Now, what will square the circle? Where's my nine o'clock?

Wilson plucked his laptop from the rucksack, called up Google and searched on the phrase 'Morphic Fields'. A screen full of results came back and as expected, all the information revolved around Rupert Sheldrake. Wilson scanned down the links until a word in the following paragraph grabbed him by the collar.

'Sheldrake's morphic resonance hypothesis states that 'memory is inherent in nature' and that all natural systems, from spiders to orchid plants, inherit a collective memory from all previous things of their kind.'

The word 'memory' bounced around like a superball inside Wilson's head.

Memory is connected to Morphic Fields, and memory is about what's happened in the past. Dreams involve memories too. The past is a measure of time. So Morphic Fields and Dream Fields have something to do with time. It's all connected with time and things that have happened in the past!

It wasn't exactly another Eureka moment, but the notion of time, like the new kid in town whose parents own a sweetshop, seemed to warrant membership of the gang.

Wilson wrote the word 'Time' in the 9.00 p.m. position, put down his pen and studied the diagram. Not fully satisfied, he then added a new arrow, curving away from 'Time' at 9.00 p.m., pointing to the words 'Déjà vu', which he underlined, before once more placing the pen back on the desk and folding his arms.

Now that's what you call thinking outside the circle, he thought, looking at his handiwork, and it's all about time and dreams and fields and energy.

Energy. He played with the word in his mind. Like a kitten with a ball of wool.

What was it Short Cake said about energy last night?

He scanned through the still-lucid memory of his Gateway dream until arriving at the appropriate scene containing Short Cake's conversation.

"Spirit is energy and energy is spirit, and neither can be destroyed, only changed from one form to another."

Does that actually mean anything?

Wilson Googled 'energy can't be destroyed, only changed...' and was truly flabbergasted when the results came back.

"What the..." He exclaimed out loud. Then quickly ducked his head below the dividing walls of the cubicle. The energy stuff in his dream was a true fact, as quoted by Albert Einstein. Energy could neither be created nor destroyed, only conserved or changed.

How the hell did I know that, in order to dream it?

Wilson stared at his laptop screen in disbelief. Things were getting curiouser and curiouser.

At the centre of the circle he wrote the words 'Conserved and Changed'.

Wilson tried to fathom out how he could know, unknowingly, Einstein's theory of energy conservation and could only conclude it was similar to knowing, unknowingly, how to speak French.

It was all connected somehow?

A spider logs in to the memory of the natural world for instructions to build a web. Just as I log in to the memory of the dream world for instructions to speak in French.

Feeling he was on to something, Wilson once again reviewed the previous night's dream from the beginning, perhaps there were more hidden messages. He zoomed in, when the first gold bangle came into frame.

What does it say? Mavis Smith. 1947-2017. What if I...?

He keyed the name and dates into his laptop and pressed 'search'.

It took a few minutes to review every Mavis Smith in the list of results, but there didn't appear to be anyone who'd lived from 1947-2017. Searches for Emily Winters, David Ellis and Eric Murphy, also drew a blank. In fact, the Eric Murphy search returned absolutely nothing. Then it dawned on Wilson that there couldn't be any results for 'Eric Murphy, 1866-2017', because nobody lived to be one hundred and fifty years old. The only reason the spirit of Eric Murphy was extinguished in 2017 was because he'd supposedly been pottering around as a ghost for the majority of his years. Wilson deleted his search for 'Eric Murphy, 1866-2017' and quickly replaced it with 'The ghost of Eric Murphy, 1866'.

Google paused for a second, as though afraid to bring back what it had unearthed. No wonder, considering the brief summary in its search results.

'**Cleaning lady at Bramhall Hall reports yet another sighting of the ghost of Eric Murphy. Stockport Advertiser. June 2010.**'

It was one thing to learn to speak French in your dreams, but being introduced to the extinguished spirit of the dead — that was taking things to a whole new level. Wilson's index finger trembled slightly as he clicked the link and opened the full article.

'Eric Murphy, the genial ghost in residence at Bramhall's historic seventeenth-century hall, has once again made his presence felt — this time to Doreen Evans, part-time cleaner at the National Trust's Grade II listed property in Bramhall Park. According to records preserved at Manchester's John Rylands Library, Eric Murphy, the son of a blacksmith, was born in a worker's cottage on Lord Bramhall's estate in July of 1866 and died of tuberculosis in 1899. So frequent are the sightings of his ghostly apparition that Eric has become Bramhall Hall's most popular tourist attraction, particularly with Japanese ghost hunters, who...'

The article continued, but Wilson had read enough and folded his laptop.

"Jesus H Christ," he muttered, "what's going on?"

Looking up, he saw Teaps enter the library and head towards him.

"Hey Wilson. Hoover said you'd be here. What're you up to?"

Teaps grabbed a neighbouring chair and sat down. For some reason he was wearing sunglasses.

"Nothing much," mumbled Wilson. "Just trying to make sense of a puzzle."

"What kind of puzzle?"

"Errr, a kind of biology-slash-maths puzzle. A tricky one, involving energy."

"Need some help?"

"But you don't do maths, or biology."

"I know, but I like puzzles."

Teaps removed his sunglasses.

"Whoa Teaps, how did you get the black eye? Jeeez, let me see."

It was a textbook shiner. Red and swollen, with a touch of purple and yellow eyeliner to complete the effect.

"That. Is. A. Beauty! Girl trouble?"

"Long story."

"I'm listening."

"It was that 'b' word, Blamire. Warren Blamire."

Teaps kicked the desk angrily, disturbing the peace and quiet of the library.

"He has that pawnshop in town. The local drug baron, general thug – and unfortunately, the landlord of our flat. We fell behind with last month's rent, so yesterday he comes round havin' a go at Dad, calling him a waste of space and threatening to throw us out. So I flipped and it kicked off big time and I came off worse. He's a total nut job. Threatened to call the bailiff if we don't pay double, and interest, by the end of the month. Dad's been drinking quite a bit since then. No idea what I'm gonna do."

"Jeeesus Teaps, I'm really sorry. Couldn't you call the police or something? Do him for assault or..."

"No, I was the one who started it. The only reason he's not pressing charges is because I came off worse, says he enjoyed it and wants to do it again in two weeks, when he throws us out and on the street."

"What a lowlife! What're you gonna do?"

"Dunno. I checked the back of the sofa but we're skint mate. Was thinking of asking the council for temporary accommodation, for a homeless place. I've no idea. Could try for another shift, stacking shelves, but that's peanuts. Need to find nine hundred quid, like yesterday. Fancy robbing a bank?"

"Funny you should mention that Teaps, but no, I'm totally against crime. We could kill him though."

"Now you're talking. What I could do with a pair of pliers and a hammer."

"Teaps, I've got some savings. I could let..."

"Forget it Wilson. I only told you because you asked me about my black eye. Thanks man, if I get really desperate, I'll let you know. I need to sort this by myself. No idea what we'll do if we're thrown out. It could be the last straw for Dad. You know, he might do something he'd, we'd regret and..."

"Okay, stop; it won't come to that. I'm gonna help. We had good sales from the website last week, so I can give you all that. It's about three hundred quid. I can pay you early before we get the payment through."

"Thanks mate, it's a start. But I'll need a fair bit more."

Teaps grabbed his bag and pushed the chair back under the desk.

"Gonna check on Pops. See you tomorrow."

"Yeah, see ya Teaps. And let me know if I can do anything to help."

Wilson tore the top sheet from his pad, folded his diagram, zipped it safely in the side pocket of his rucksack and slowly followed Teaps out of the library.

Chapter 20

The torn pocket

Thursday 19th October into Friday 20th October 2017

It was midnight and a funfair was in town. The Market Square was a merry-go-round of carnival rides and glowing neon. Music from an accordion rose and fell rhythmically with the motion of a fairground carousel as visitors, drawn like moths to bright lights, flitted between attractions, fast food vendors and 'try your luck' stalls.

The Clock Tower, now masquerading as a quarter scale replica of the Eiffel Tower was bedecked in strings of giant fairy lights. One moment they glistened like ice crystals, the next, they were racing round latticed steelwork, red pulse, chasing green, chasing blue. Roving searchlights swept lazy arcs of full beam over the heads of the crowds as though searching for a suspect on the run. Fleetingly, they would illuminate the jagged, jerky flight path of what appeared to be a giant bat flying camouflaged against a soot black sky. The stroboscopic light show strained Wilson's eyes as he searched for a second sighting and confirmation of the fact.

"Head down sonny!"

The instruction, in ultra-sound, was felt rather than heard and Wilson instinctively ducked. A broad wing, thicker than school satchel leather, flapped inches above his head with a sharp crack, like a crisp bed sheet being shaken. The cargo of passengers, all holding on for dear life, shrieked with laughter as the bat buckaroo'd off into the night.

Yeah, that's definitely a bat. With a pink bat nose and fine black fur - but a bat the size of an elephant!

The bat was tethered to the Clock Tower by a thick cable and a roller-coaster style carriage was saddled to its back.

The passengers were whooping and waving and having the time of their lives.

Health and safety would have a field day with this.

Wilson followed the stomach churning spectacle until the darting and diving became less extreme and the bat eventually folded its wings and settled upside down on the statue of Mr Ludlow (or possibly Mr Abingdon). Dizzy, grinning passengers pushed away their padded restrainers and stepped, somewhat unsteadily, back on to solid ground.

A neon sign read: 'The Bucking Bronco Bat Ride. You gotta be batty to try it.'

Awesome.

Someone tapped Wilson on the shoulder. A circus ringmaster in top hat and tails, striped waistcoat, tight white pants and knee-length black leather boots, was grinning beneath a splendid, waxed moustache.

"Care to trunk-wrestle the elephant my friend?"

The sweep of his arm and a wink drew Wilson's attention to a baby elephant sitting on a three-legged stool in front of a small wooden table. The elephant raised its trunk and trumpeted a few notes before bringing the tip of the trunk to rest, with a meaty slam, on the tabletop.

"Trunk-wrestle? What does that mean?" Wilson was confused by the word pairing.

"It's the same as arm wrestling – but the elephant has to use its trunk because clearly, it doesn't have any arms." The indignant ringmaster was stating what he believed to be the obvious.

Wilson let out a burst of laughter.

"Oh, that seems fair enough then."

"It's only a pound and if you win, you get fifty quid back. Good odds, eh?"

Wilson had to straighten his face for a second time.

"Out of interest, has the elephant ever lost?"

"God no. Never."

"Then you must make a lot of money from this attraction?"

"Oh yes, a fortune!"

Wilson wasn't sure if it was all a spoof and a camera was following for TV entertainment. He compared his outstretched arm with the elephant's trunk, which was thicker than his leg.

"Well?" The ringmaster enquired.

"Maybe later," said Wilson, having quickly reached the conclusion that there could never be a good outcome from wrestling with an elephant. He started to take steps backwards.

"Gonna check out the flying bats over there, so half an hour..."

But his last sentence didn't register. The ringmaster was pitching his challenge to three teenage girls eating candyfloss.

As Wilson turned and headed towards the Clock Tower, a subliminal thought was left straggling some way behind. It soon caught up though and tapped him on the shoulder. Wilson stopped in his tracks and looked back.

The three girls talking to the ringmaster were identical triplets. Same eyes, nose, mouth – every facial component exactly the same. But one was tall, one short and the other had red hair. Stranger still, Wilson couldn't be certain they were girls. Sure, they were dressed like girls, but they were also genderless. And not teenagers; maybe older, possibly younger. The more Wilson studied their facial features, the less he could pigeonhole them as this age or that, boy or girl. As Wilson watched, a couple in their thirties also stopped to listen to the ringmaster's pitch.

Hold on a minute, those two are identical as well.

That observation was then followed by something more seismic, as it dawned on Wilson that the matching pair 'snapped' with the trio.

Five identical faces?

Wilson scanned the crowd. Everyone was the twin of somebody else. A child in a buggy had exactly the same facial features as the parents, who in turn looked like the five teenage lads on Wilson's left. The only clues to their likely age and gender were the clothes they were wearing and their physical size. The matching 'face mask' effect wasn't disturbing however; the carnival atmosphere didn't foster a feeling of unease. So Wilson overcame his initial shock and continued moving in the direction of the Bucking Bronco Bat.

The crowds became congested as Wilson gave way to a girl, sized about four-years-old with parents sized about thirty-years-old. The girl was carrying a fluffy bear. The Koala shook Wilson's hand with a lifelike paw and said "G'day mate," as the family brushed past. Wilson watched the family walk away and dissolve into the same face crowd.

"Well you certainly stand out," chimed a familiar voice.

Wilson slowly turned to face the source and after a semicircle, Daisy Meadowcroft was standing directly in his line of sight, waving and smiling from her lovely Daisy Meadowcroft face.

Wilson felt a mallet hit his sweet spot and his head went kerching.

"Wow. Daisy. Hey, is that really you?"

"Yes Wilson, it really is. But let's not start the 'whose dream' debate again."

Daisy reached for his arm. "Come on, we need to talk."

She navigated a path through a sea of same faces, towing Wilson in her wake, and pulled up alongside a ticket booth for the 'Catapult Gliders'.

"Well, hallelujah," she said, releasing her grip, "found you at last. Are you enjoying all the fun of the fair?"

Wilson struggled to reply. Daisy had returned to his dream, he was surrounded by hundreds of people all with the same faces, a gigantic bat was flying all over the show and he'd just escaped from an arm-wrestling elephant.

"Err, I think I'm good," not really certain if that was true. "I really wasn't expecting to see you again."

"Why not? I was sure I'd meet you. It was inevitable."

"Well, you know, I'm still not convinced that you're not just a figment of my night-time imagination."

"Wilson, you've got to stop with that. I told you, when we first met, we have special talents and..."

Daisy made those spidery movements with her fingers.

"...magical powers, remember, our last conversation? Duhhh?"

"How could I forget?" Wilson was still puzzled by the reality of the figure standing in front of him.

Daisy was wearing denim dungarees over a white t-shirt, cream

101

coloured trainers and Wilson had to admit:

She looks fantastic. With the same chestnut hair with tawny highlights, deep brown eyes, petite nose, perfect lips and butterscotch skin. But now she's even more perfect.

Then he snapped out of his trance.

"I've thought about that night, every day since it happened. I went to Starbucks, like we agreed. I waited for ages and felt a total idiot when you didn't show up."

Daisy frowned. "I know. It wasn't my fault though. It's a long story. But hey, I've got all night to explain."

She looked over her shoulder at the ticket booth for the Catapult Gliders. A crabby faced old man sat hunched inside counting ticket stubs.

"Have you tried this ride? It's better than anything at Alton Towers."

Wilson hadn't really taken in his surroundings, he was too preoccupied taking in Daisy, but as she spoke, he tried to fathom out the appeal of Catapult Gliders. Beyond a barrier fence, Wilson could see a slowly advancing line of 'carriages'. Each was about four metres long and represented, in a simplistic way, a jet plane with an open cockpit, a cigar-shaped body, broad delta wings and a stumpy tail. They reminded Wilson of the toy gliders his father had bought him as a child. The kind they would play with on the beach – little plastic jet-plane gliders that could be launched with an elastic band and after a series of loops would land, nose first, in the sand. Beyond the creeping line of gliders was some form of launch strip, like the short runway on an aircraft carrier.

"Come on," said Daisy, pulling Wilson along by the arm, "there's no queue. I'll explain on the plane."

The man waved them through the turnstile without looking up and mumbled that they should "take the next red one." They climbed the steps to a wooden platform, alongside which a red glider was inching along. Wilson clambered into the cockpit, offered a steadying hand to help Daisy on board and locked the padded bar that held them both securely in their seats. The plane had no instrument panel or controls.

"Prepare for take-off," came a tinny voice from a speaker in the footwell.

The glider continued inching to the end of the platform where it slowly juddered through a ninety-degree arc, lurched forward and then stopped, dead centre, at the start of the runway. A series of heavy mechanical clunks shook the carriage, as though something was locking itself on the nose of the plane, followed by the stretching creak of tension being applied. In the distance, the runway rose to the height of a three-storey building and then abruptly stopped, like the end of a ski jump.

"How do we fly this thing?"

"Wilson, it's not a real plane, it's a fairground ride. It's in your dream. Nothing bad can happen. You're still going to wake up safe and sound in the morning, even if we crash. Anyway, I've been on this one before, it's wicked."

Daisy patted Wilson's knee then gripped the handholds on the restraining bar. "You're so going to enjoy this."

Then, as the word 'this' was released from Daisy's smiling lips into the indigo-blue expanse of the night, Wilson was catapulted into said, indigo-blue expanse, at approximately seven hundred miles per hour. For a few seconds Wilson wasn't able to breathe. He couldn't do anything actually. Couldn't move, couldn't see, couldn't think, couldn't even couldn't. He was aware of the sensation of moving forward rapidly, like entering a tunnel on a rocket-propelled train, then zooming upwards, even faster and all his peripheral vision becoming a blur. Speeding like a bullet. Then coming to his senses.

Daisy was laughing and screaming and oh-my-Godding and punching his arm, then jerking forward and laughing some more, then banging her feet on the floor.

"Oh my God, oh my God! What an adrenaline rush. Wilson, how good was THAT?"

Wilson didn't fully understand what the 'that' was. He was trying to reply, but he suspected his mouth had shifted to a new position on his face. His palms were superglued to the grips on the sides of his seat and his knuckles were white.

"What... the... the," he stammered. Daisy threw her head back and hit the padded cushion and cried with laughter. Like their first night in the motorcycle workshop, she had tears running down her cheeks.

"Daisy, that, that was..."

His faculties returned to normal as he loosened his grip and blood began to flow back to his hands.

"That was the best thing ever! I mean, how incredible was that? Just unbelievable. Totally awesome. Err. Where are we?"

Wilson cautiously peered over the side of the plane into a void of clear air. Far below he could make out the glowing neon of The Market Square and the laser-like beams of roving light darting around the Clock Tower − searching for an elusive bat.

"Daisy, we're about a mile above the ground and we're flying with no controls *or* parachutes."

Daisy's head bounced off the restraint for a second time.

"No Wilson, we're not flying, we're gliding. We've been fired from a catapult and now we're slowly gliding back down. Incredible, isn't it?"

"Yeah, I guess so," he said, peering into the night. "It's really, really, indescribable I guess. In fact, awesome."

They sat in silence as the warm night air streamed through their hair and the glider slowly descended in a gentle curve.

"The loop-the-loop bit was the best."

"What?" Wilson exclaimed. "We looped the loop?"

"Yeah, immediately after we launched. It's the first thing that happens."

"If you say so, I don't remember too much about it. One moment I was down there and the next, I was up here. Phenomenal."

After shaking his head in disbelief for a final time, Wilson began to relax and enjoy the experience. Best of all, he was sitting next to Daisy.

"Daisy, this is incredible. And whether it's my dream or your dream, who cares? I wish we could do this all the time. When I said that I'd been thinking about the first night we met every day, what I really meant was, I've been thinking about you every day since we met."

Wilson turned away, the result of a sudden rush of sadness.

This is stupid! She's not real. Not flesh and blood. Not going to be around tomorrow morning when I wake up. This is all a dream.

Daisy put a hand on his.

"Wilson, I know you're a real person, in real life, I mean – that you exist in flesh and blood, you have a family and a job, or you go to college or whatever. So you have to believe me when I say I'm also real, just like you. I do live in Macclesfield. Dad's a painter and decorator, Mum's a nurse and my brother's in the army."

The glider continued its slow descent as the hubbub of people and music increased in volume. Wilson caught the unmistakable aroma of hotdogs and onions.

"Okay Daisy, so if what you say is true and you do exist, then why did I spend an hour hanging around Starbucks looking like a fool in front of my mates?"

"That's what I wanted to talk to you about Wilson. It wasn't my fault. I left college and caught the ten past six train. But it broke down and we had to get a bus back to Macclesfield and... anyway, it was eight o'clock before the new train arrived and I had no number, no way to get hold of you. I'm sorry. I've been searching The Market Square ever since."

"Well, you've found me now. So I guess I'll get over it."

"That's the spirit," said Daisy. "What doesn't kill us can only make us stronger. Speaking of imminent death, how far off the ground are we?"

"About twenty miles."

"Wilson you liar." Daisy checked for herself. "Three minutes to touchdown."

There was a brief silence before Daisy asked, "Have you been here recently?"

"Yeah. I had a really odd dream a few nights ago. I met these two crazy guys who told me all this weird stuff about energy and spirits and ghosts and it all turned out to be true. We were in this huge building called The Gateway. Search me what it all meant, but there was something about the whole thing that..."

There was a terrifically loud bang, a screech of brakes and a bone shaking judder as the glider landed. The restraining bar lifted and a voice from the speaker announced, "Thank you for flying with the Catapult Gliders today. Have a safe onward journey and do fly with us again."

As they passed the ticket booth, Daisy complained to the crabby man about the lack of a drinks service on the flight.

"What next?"

"Well," said Daisy, "since the dream is still young, why don't you go and win a fluffy bear for me?"

"Err, not a good idea. I think they bite. But what the hell, yeah, let's check out the other rides. If there's anything half as good as the gliders, I'm going for it."

"Make sure you don't lose me in the crowd though," said Daisy.

"Oh very funny. Hey, did you ever see that video with George Michael and Mary J. Blige?"

"No, why?"

"It's exactly like this dream."

Wilson smiled foolishly and gave Daisy a clumsy hug. He wanted to know if she was solid and warm and full of bones. And she was.

They linked arms and paused in front of the 'Dart Birds Game'. This involved adjusting the wings of a bird with a pointed beak, like a paper plane, before launching it at a moving target of floating balloons. Wilson presumed the aim was to pop a balloon and win a koala bear. He could see the bears munching leaves in a tree at the back of the stall.

At the next stall, the ducks involved in 'Hook the Ducks' didn't seem keen on being hooked with a long metal pole. They quacked and flapped and kicked up all kinds of fuss. The 'Pin the Tail on the Donkey' was just as cruel, given that the donkey was real and a blindfolded size-nine-year-old was attempting to pin the tail in the donkey's eye.

In the distance a gigantic, Ferris wheel was slowly rotating beneath an umbrella of exploding fireworks.

"Fancy a go on the London Eye?"

"Sure do," said Daisy. "But first, we've definitely gotta go and check that one out."

Daisy pointed to a rickety, metal staircase that spiralled around a cylinder shaped structure that was panelled with wooden planks. It gave the impression of a beer barrel, six storeys high. A turnstile barred entry to the 'The Ten-Mile Drop'.

The ticket booth was unattended so they forced the turnstile and raced each other up the creaking, iron stairs. At the top, the stairway opened onto a metal-plate platform with a birds-eye view over the entire funfair. A red door at the far end of the platform was the only possible entrance to The Ten-Mile Drop so Wilson and Daisy gave it a push.

The door swung open to reveal a round, dark room with a clear glass floor and a ceiling studded with twinkling star-lights. They searched each other's faces for a suggestion of what to do next. Daisy took the initiative and shoved Wilson through the doorway.

"It's only a dream. Be a man, you scaredy-cat."

Wilson edged gingerly out onto the glass, peered downwards and quickly stepped back to safety.

"Well, that wasn't much of a ride, was it?"

"Daisy, do you know what you see if you walk out onto that bloody glass?"

"Err, a ten-mile drop maybe?"

"Exactly, a ten-mile drop. Straight down. Whooosh. Ten miles."

"Yes, I know Wilson. I get it. And I presume that's why they call it the Ten-Mile Drop. So you get the idea in advance."

Daisy followed Wilson, a small step at a time, back through the door and out onto the glass.

"Whooaaa," said Wilson.

"That is a long – way – down," said Daisy.

Wilson felt his knees would buckle. So they both gazed down through the glass floor on hands and knees.

Far below, a mosaic patchwork of green, gold and brown was dappled in shadow and sunlight.

"They're fields," said Wilson.

Around the edges of the glass, they could see the surface of the earth curving away and the jagged outline of snow-capped mountains. Wisps of cloud drifted by, as though a steam train had passed beneath their feet seconds earlier. Then someone pulled a lever and the glass floor wasn't there anymore.

Wilson was plummeting downwards with nothing more than ten miles of cool, fresh air between him and the ground.

"Wilsonnn!" Daisy was yelling. "Wilsonnn. This is so great."

She was almost within touching distance as they hurtled earth bound at breakneck, break-leg, break-everything speed. Wilson reached for Daisy's hand, then an arm, both arms and then they were facing each other − locked together in freefall, like skydivers. The roar of air drumming through their clothing was louder than a loose tent flap in a hurricane.

"Is this supposed to be happening?" Wilson yelled as they plunged earthwards.

"Yeah. That's why it's called the Ten-Mile Drop."

"But I thought we'd just look at the ten-mile drop."

"So did I. But this is ten miles better, don't you think?"

Despite the blast of rushing air, Wilson noticed that Daisy's mouth and cheeks weren't stretched and rippling − as might have been expected.

"It's just a dream Daisy," he yelled.

"I know, Enjoyyyyyy."

And with that, she released herself from Wilson's grip and careered away, tumbling and spinning ever downwards.

"Yahoooo," cried Wilson, to no-one in particular, "I'm a bird − I can flyyyyyy."

A few minutes later, as the quilt of gold and brown began to define itself as crops of wheat and ploughed fields, the rate of descent declined. The ten-mile drop ended with a cushioned landing on a conveniently placed haystack. Daisy had been half-swallowed by the hay and it took a few minutes of giggling and pulling to get her feet back on solid earth.

"Bet they don't have that one at Alton Towers either," said Wilson.

"Thank goodness," said Daisy, pulling stalks of straw from her hair. "I'd live there if they did."

"Phenomenal ride," said Wilson, looking directly above. All he could see was blue sky and wispy clouds; no evidence of a glass ceiling.

"How do you beat that?"

"Don't know Wilson, but I think we should try. We may never get the chance to dream here again. Come on."

A plastic banner with the word 'EXIT' had been fixed to a hay bale and beneath it a red arrow pointed to a metal door half-camouflaged in the straw. Daisy pushed the door open and they stepped back into the buzz and spectacle of a funfair at night.

Firework rockets were still exploding above the Ferris wheel at the top of the square. Wilson plucked the last stalk from Daisy's hair and tentatively put his arm around her shoulders. Daisy hooked her thumb in the back pocket of his jeans. A few stitches along the side seam gave way, leaving a ragged edge hanging down.

"When does the dream end?" Wilson asked.

"Dunno," said Daisy. "When we wake up, I suppose."

They walked along in silence with the flow of the crowd, enjoying the sounds, the lights and the smell of greasy burgers and fresh popcorn, until they eventually arrived at the Ferris wheel.

It was modelled on the London Eye, but smaller and without the pill-shaped passenger pods. Around the axis, the words 'Ferris the Catherine Wheel' shone with incandescent light. The white spokes of the wheel were thick, iron girders studded with rivet heads and rows of glowing bulbs. Black tubes, the size of wheelie bins, were fixed around the circumference at two metre intervals. The wheel was rotating at idling speed.

Same-faced workers in yellow jackets were organising the boarding process. Some were buckling passengers into a combination of harness and rucksack while others were helping passengers clamber into the black cylinders. As the wheel crept forwards, black tube after black tube was being loaded, locked and lifted high into the sky.

"But nobody is getting off. Look." Wilson pointed at a section of the wheel that was approaching the loading platform. "All those black tubes are coming down empty. Where are all the previous passengers? How did they get out?"

"Yeah. It's strange Wilson. And they can't see anything anyway, apart from the inside of a black tube. Not much of a ride is it?"

"Come on, let's go."

Daisy stifled a yawn.

"Yep, let's go. I'm tired."

They were just about to turn away when a tinny, trumpet fanfare sounded and the lights running the length of each enormous spoke started to flash.

Scores of spectators, standing three deep along the perimeter fence, all hushed in anticipation of the ride commencing.

Daisy and Wilson felt subterranean vibrations throb with increased power as the wheel slowly, but very visibly, increased in speed.

"Look, it's started," said Daisy. "Let's wait a minute and see what happens."

As the spokes picked up speed, the black tubes glided past the now empty loading platform. Every now and again a hand would wave from one of the tubes and give an indiscriminate thumbs-up to nobody in particular.

Wilson chuckled.

"How can they tell if they're waving at their friends? They haven't a clue who they're waving at from inside those tubes and everybody looks the same anyway – apart from you and me."

"Wilson, shush." Daisy kicked his shin. "I'm watching, I think something's about to happen."

The wheel continued to accelerate as the steady hum of an underground motor rose in pitch.

And then Wilson got it. The name of the ride: Ferris the Catherine Wheel.

"Daisy," he whispered, "it's not a Ferris wheel. It's a Catherine wheel. Like the ones on Bonfire Night. You know, you nail them to a wooden post and then light them, and they spin round, spitting out sparks. This is a giant Catherine wheel."

By now the wheel was revolving so quickly it had become a spinning disc of concentric circles of light and colour.

"So what happens with the black tubes?"

"Well, I don't think this one spits out sparks. I think this one spits out..."

"Passengers!"

As Daisy spoke, a cannon fired at the apex point of the wheel.

Instinctively, they looked upwards.

High in the sky, each resounding boom was accompanied by an exploding firework rocket high above their heads. The visual spectacle and the boom after boom followed by another sixty booms left them both speechless and their ears ringing.

The wheel rapidly slowed and within a minute was back to rotating at snail's pace. Fine plumes of white smoke drifted from the black tubes as they scrolled past at eye level.

Then, as though a conductor had tapped his baton for audience participation, everyone standing around the perimeter fence suddenly began cheering and waving at the pitch blackness of the sky.

Daisy saw them first.

"Look Wilson, there." She was pointing and jumping excitedly. "And another one over there and there and there."

Wilson saw them too: one, three, five, a dozen, dozens of bright-red parachutes all gently drifting down to earth.

Then Wilson was cheering and high-fiving and hugging Daisy.

It took a chaotic ten minutes for passengers to be repatriated with family and friends, a task made complex by the fact they all appeared alike.

"Fancy a go?"

"No, another time. I'm getting a bit tired now."

"Daisy, you're in a dream, how can you be tired?"

"I don't know Wilson, but I am."

The last passenger to land was a size-eleven-year-old girl who was instantly mobbed by proud parents. Then the lights all over the wheel were switched off and the glow from the illuminated words expired.

"Looks like the show's coming to an end Daisy. What shall we do now?"

"Wilson, I was just thinking about what you said, about being tired in my own dream."

"And?"

"Well, what if my being tired and yawning in a dream is a sign that I'm about to wake up in real life? You know, like the opposite. If I wake up, I won't be here anymore. I'll just disappear and you'll be here by yourself, until you wake up, or also stop dreaming, or whatever."

"Daisy, I've no idea. I don't know what's going on myself. In fact, I'm still not sure if you're real."

Daisy reached out for Wilson's hand and wove her fingers between his.

"Meet me at Starbucks."

Wilson rolled his eyes and tried to pull away.

"Seriously, I want us to try again. One more time. The stuff I told you about the train is true. You can check it for yourself. It really did break down. From tomorrow I'm away on a Geography field trip in Ambleside, but I'm back next week and I'll be waiting for you in Starbucks on Deansgate at seven o'clock, next Friday."

She shook him by the shoulders.

"Daisy, I don't know. I'll have to think about it. I..."

Daisy saw the look of confusion and kissed him on the cheek.

"Did that feel like a figment of your imagination Wilson?"

"Mmm, not so sure. Can you try the other cheek."

She pushed him away and scowled.

"You'd better be there next Friday or you'll be in such..."

Daisy stopped mid-sentence. Colour began to drain from her face and lips, her hair, her clothes. Her presence was diminishing to a sepia-tint, a monotone hologram, a translucent shadow of her former self. Seconds later, incredibly, she was no longer there. Daisy had dissolved right in front of Wilson's eyes. He swept his hand through clear air; through the space in which she'd just been standing. Daisy had dissipated, evaporated, like morning mist.

Then Wilson felt tired, increasingly tired. He tried to stifle a yawn, but the yawn fought back. Like Daisy, he started to dissolve, to reduce to a sepia tint, a monotone hologram, the translucent shadow of his former self. As his spectral, particulated presence finally departed The Market Square, Wilson was no longer a face, in the same face crowd.

Chapter 21

Hoover's crazy idea

Friday 20th October 2017

Wilson woke the next morning feeling as though a lifetime of Valentines Days had all arrived at once. It was 7.30 a.m.

For thirty-five sumptuous minutes, like a child slowly savouring each spoonful of a favourite dessert, he relived the dream of the funfair and the clear-as-day memories of Daisy Meadowcroft.

Warnings from his mother of being late for college and no time for breakfast finally coaxed him from his duvet. After a quick shower he slipped into a clean shirt, belted his jeans and tucked his wallet into a back pocket. He felt the tear in the side seam and inspected the damage.

"Wilson, you're going to be so late. What are you doing up there?"

Fast forwarding through the dream he watched himself and Daisy emerge from The Ten-Mile Drop. He plucked stalks of straw from her hair. They strolled along for a few yards. Then he put his arm around Daisy's shoulders and she tugged at...

"Daisy tore the pocket. In my dream. No, that's impossible!"

Somewhat puzzled by the pairing of physical damage with an event in a dream, he checked the frayed edge of denim a second time and then went downstairs for breakfast.

Gloria was wiping down a worktop as Wilson entered the kitchen.

"Morning love. You'd better get a move on. Me too. I'm opening the shop this morning. What do you want for breakfast?"

"Nothing Mum. I'll grab something in the canteen. I'm not hungry."

His mother tutted by way of reply.

"Mum," he said, "you see these jeans I'm wearing, my old Levi's?"

"Yes love, I do. I can see them because you're wearing them."

114

"Yeah, sorry, I know. What I mean is, when did you last iron them?"

"Those jeans? About three days ago – no, the day before yesterday, I did the ironing in the afternoon. Why?"

"Can you remember if they had this tear in them?"

He showed her the torn flap of fabric.

"No, they didn't, or I'd have put them to one side for stitching. You probably caught it on something. Don't worry, they can be repaired."

"Are you sure it wasn't there two days ago?"

"No Wilson, it definitely wasn't. Now will you at least eat some cereal and then get yourself off to college?"

The morning's classes passed uneventfully and at 12.30 p.m. Wilson headed to the college canteen where he ordered chicken and chips, a slice of lemon meringue pie and a can of Fanta. He saw Hoover sitting at a table, head and shoulders hunched over some papers and Wilson went to join him.

"Alright mate," he said, sliding the food tray on the table. "How's it going?"

"Fair to middling," replied Hoover. He was sketching something out on an A4 notepad and engrossed in his work.

Wilson tucked into his lunch as brief snippets of gossip were exchanged regarding various posts on social media, the new girl in Hoover's geography group, the weekend's football fixtures and Teaps's black eye. But Hoover wasn't fully engaged in the chitchat. He was more focused on the paperwork spread out on the table.

"What're you doing there then?" Wilson asked, spearing chips with his fork.

"Designing a website mate."

"Excellent. For any particular reason?"

"Yeah. To find my missing football sock."

Wilson nearly choked on a chip and a shot of Fanta bubbled-up inside his nose.

"To do what? To find your missing sock?" He asked incredulously.

"Yeah, I'm gonna show know-all Daley that it's possible for socks

115

to go missing with no explanation. Everyone knows it's true. And I'm designing a website to prove it. Wilson, how many single socks have you got in your sock drawer?"

"Quite a few I'd say."

"There you are then. My website will help you find all the missing halves of the pairs."

Hoover made a few more notes and doodles as Wilson turned to the lemon meringue pie.

"And I've already got the domain name" he continued.

"So what's the site called then?"

"Missingsock.co.uk."

"Hoover, you're having me on."

"No I'm bloody not."

Hoover peered indignantly at Wilson through his drape of fine, black hair.

"I've done some research and every lad I've spoken to in this college has told me he's missing socks. And some of the teachers too. Mr Franks told me he has more single socks than pairs."

"So?"

"So, the interesting thing is this: all the lads told me they've also found single socks that aren't even theirs. Imagine that. You lose a sock and you gain someone else's. That's not right, is it mate?"

"No, it certainly isn't mate," said Wilson, hoping nobody was listening in on the conversation.

"So my idea is that I help people find the sock they've lost, by taking a photo of the one that's left – they can't take a photo of the exact sock that's missing, cos it's gone missing. So they upload the photo of the partner of the missing sock, plus photos of any socks they've got that don't belong to them. And my website matches 'em up. And you get your lost sock back."

"Genius," said Wilson.

"I know," said Hoover. "My brother's doin' computer programming at uni and he said he'd build the site for me, no problem. That's why I'm working on the layout and words."

"And where do you make money with this vital public service then?"

"I don't mate. It's the thought that counts – and proving a point!"

He returned to his site plan and continued scribbling.

"Well, good luck with that then. Let me know when it goes live and I'll do some uploading."

"Yeah, no worries mate." Hoover didn't look up.

Wilson contemplated a further comment but then shook his head, grabbed his bag and headed for the library. His next class was at 2.00 p.m., so he had exactly an hour for more digging.

The library was quiet and Wilson headed for a corner cubicle where he opened his laptop, typed 'Macclesfield Reporter' and tapped 'enter'. He clicked the link to the newspaper's home page and watched it load. There was a search box in the top-right corner and Wilson paused for a second before deciding on 'Macclesfield train disruption'. A moment later a handful of abbreviated results came back. The most recent was from three weeks earlier and began with: '**Falling leaves disrupt Virgin train service from London...**' The entry beneath was from six weeks prior to that: '**Virgin train service to Euston breaks speed record**'. Wilson leant forward and scanned down the entire page. There was nothing relevant. Daisy's story was a fabrication which he'd obviously made up, just as he'd made *her* up. The rip in his jeans was just a weird coincidence. It was probably something he'd done himself, unconsciously, during the day, only to be reminded of in a dream during the night.

"I'm going mad" he muttered.

Wilson pushed back on the swivel chair, put his hands behind his head and studied the library ceiling. An interlocking grid of suspended panels and row upon row of fluorescent lights hanging from thin steel cables.

"Wait a minute."

He jerked back to the laptop screen with a new line of enquiry.

Maybe I need to be more specific?

Wilson clicked back to Google and typed in 'Bus service for broken down train, Macclesfield, October 2017' and tapped the return key.

A flood of results flowed down the screen and still there was nothing relevant. He clicked 'next' to call up a second page of results, not expecting any kind of revelation, but then a single line caught his eye. It was an extract from a Facebook post: 'Bus service replaces broken train. Another night of mayhem at Macclesfield train station.'

It was from a girl called Jessie Evans. Wilson read the recent posts until he came to a message with a picture. A photo of a broken-down train with an engineer inspecting the undercarriage. Jessie had captioned the photo:

'Thanks to the muppets who run Macclesfield trains, missed a concert last night. Waited hours in freezing cold in middle of nowhere. Fat Controller should be sacked.'

Goodness, she's not happy.

But Wilson was. He was bordering on ecstatic.

He grabbed his phone, opened Twitter and keyed in '#macclesfieldtrainmayhem'.

A flurry of tweets came back, all warbling about the problem with the train that night and how the breakdown had caused this difficulty or that disappointment. A tweet from the Stoke Sentinel newspaper blamed it on bad weather caused by Storm Ophelia.

Wilson blinked and stared at the screen of his phone in utter astonishment.

So Daisy was actually telling the truth.

Wilson struggled to contain his jubilation.

I couldn't have heard about the breakdown because it wasn't in the news. The train had actually broken down. I couldn't have known about that, and it was just as she told me. And Daisy tore my jeans, which means she's real. Daisy is real. Daisy exists.

Losing all awareness of his immediate environment – and most of his inhibitions, Wilson leapt to his feet and with a broad grin, proclaimed: "it's true, Daisy Meadowcroft exists and I proved it, here, in this library. She's a real person and lives in Macclesfield." Then he raised his arms, messiah-like, and declared to the entire library: "She's got blood in her thumb, just like me."

Wilson was asked to leave the library after his unwarranted outburst, an instruction he was more than happy to follow. He spent the rest of the day in a state of enlightened bliss.

"You alright, Wilson?" Teaps popped the question as they sat in an English class a couple of hours later.

"Yeah, why?"

"Oh, no reason in particular."

After the English class, as Wilson made his way down a corridor toward a biology lab, he heard someone behind him shout:

"A real person lives in Macclesfield."

This was followed by:

"And she's got blood in her thumb."

Which in turn, led to more ribbing and banter.

Wilson didn't turn to face the culprits. Instead he leapt and punched the air, then raised a middle finger. He was in a great mood. He'd discovered a kindred spirit, a really pretty one and together they were going to lay bare the mystery of The Market Square.

Over tea that evening, Wilson spent an hour catching up on the latest news and gossip with his mum. Like the story of how Mrs Abbott had asked her son, who was an electrician, to fit a new plug socket in the charity shop, only for Mrs Green to then sell his valuable toolkit for fifteen pounds when he went to buy a sandwich. How Cybil had discovered an old Dickens hardback in the books section, which she then proceeded to auction on eBay for two hundred pounds but gave every penny back to the shop! Then she moved on to how Kate and Megan both had boyfriends who were law students and wouldn't it be weird if the boyfriends were also twins! She also suggested that Alex was doing more swanking about in London and hobnobbing with MPs in the House of Commons, than actual work.

"Something to do with a select committee reporting on mobile phone networks – at least that's what he tells his gullible wife."

Gossip over, they launched into a ten-minute session of 'Film Quiz', which basically involved reciting classic movie one-liners and challenging each other to name the movie. Gloria was a wonder woman at the game but Wilson's line from Jurassic Park, gleaned from his Dad, had her stumped. Wilson was leading by a single point at the end. An end that came with the same closing line.

"Now that is a tasty burger."

Wilson didn't need to say, *"Pulp Fiction."*

He rose from the kitchen table and gave Gloria a hug. "Got some homework to do, Mum. Thanks for tea."

He was walking out toward the hall when an inkling, a random thought, made him stop and turn. His mum was folding a tea towel and quietly humming to herself. The mum who had carried him for nine months and then delivered him into this world. A vivacious, lovely, middle-aged lady who ran a charity shop. That was Wilson's mum, and Teaps didn't have one.

"Mum, where was I born?"

"That's a strange question Wilson. Funnily enough, you were born in the same hospital, in fact, the same ward as your dad – here in Stockport, in the infirmary, Ward 3B. It still exists but it's an old people's ward now. Mrs Bushel, a lovely old lady from the shop was in there for a while, but she died a couple of weeks after they moved her to an old people's home. Why do you ask?"

"Oh, no reason. It's just that... Ah, nothing important. Love you Mum," said Wilson, as he pulled the kitchen door behind him and bounded up the stairs two at a time.

"Love you too," said Gloria.

Chapter 22

Questions need answers

Night of Friday 20th October 2017

As Wilson entered his bedroom, his mobile phone rang.

"Hi Hoover. How's it going?"

"Good man, good. Listen, can you do me a favour?"

"If I can."

"Can you send me some photos of your single socks? Remember, you said you had a few. I need to get them over to my brother; he's started to build the website."

Wilson paused for a second, slightly irritated at the stupidity of what he was being asked to do.

"Let me get this right Hoover, you want photos of all my odd socks, so that you can put them on your website and wait for someone to find a match, just to prove to George Daley that socks have the power to go missing all by themselves? Is that right?"

"Yeah, that's exactly it. Oh, and if you find a sock that isn't yours, you know, like you don't know where it came from, send me that as well. So send me two folders, one with your odd socks and one with other people's socks if you have any."

"Hoover, are you serious? I thought you were messing about."

"No, I'm deadly serious mate. This missing sock thing is a real mystery. Like a conspiracy theory. It's too big to ignore without trying to find an explanation."

"Well I can't do it now. It's late."

"Come on Wilson, my brother can only work on this at night and he's ready to start. I've sent him the words and some of my sock photos, but he needs more for the test site. Why, what else are you doing, texting that imaginary girlfriend?"

"Very funny," scowled Wilson. "Alright, give me half an hour and I'll bang something over. But don't tell anyone I'm in on this – just helping out a mate with mental issues."

"Cheers man, soon as you can." Hoover rang off.

Wilson looked apologetically at his undies drawer.

I don't believe this!

Nevertheless, he spent ten minutes identifying mismatched and partnerless socks and taking photographs, which he then forwarded on to Hoover. In total, he had six orphaned socks, including a very smart green sock with a Ralph Lauren 'Polo' logo embroidered in red. These socks had been a Christmas present that he'd only worn once, before half of them went missing. He was not expecting repatriation via Hoover's website. Wilson also discovered a blue-and-white-striped sock that absolutely didn't belong to him, so he took a final picture and sent it to Hoover with a fingers-crossed emoji. Then he sat at his desk and his thoughts returned to Daisy.

The torn pocket of his jeans, the discovery that Daisy's train had really been delayed, the very fact she visited The Market Square – this was already a chain of events so implausible that the next link, meeting Daisy in real life, well, why not? However, the torn pocket was also troubling because the tear was a sign of actual, physical damage. Somehow, during the course of a dream, in which Daisy's thumb had loosened a few stitches, the same thing had happened to the real Levi jeans lying on his bedroom floor. The notion first brought to mind a horror movie, then an even more sinister possibility followed.

Perhaps his assumption that Daisy existed was wrong and he really had made the tear himself! And had subconsciously heard about the train problem in Macclesfield and woven it into the dream with Daisy. Maybe he had some kind of personality disorder, schizophrenic even? It was a shattering possibility. But then a split personality wouldn't explain how he had been able to master so many skills – the languages, flying helicopters, playing the guitar – simply by dreaming about them. He certainly hadn't learned to speak French in the conventional way, for that would have required a teacher and lessons and there was no evidence for that. The truth was, he could speak French and he'd learned it in a dream. Full stop. Which meant he wasn't schizophrenic and there had to be an alternate explanation for the torn pocket and the train.

This controlled, rational thinking about highly irrational events reassured Wilson and allowed him to consider a number of other related questions.

Was The Gateway part of The Market Square? There was no golden bangle for Teaps's mum; did that mean she was still alive? And should he meet Daisy, how was the dream world connected to the real world. How was it possible to bridge the gap?

Would his clock diagram reveal the answers? Wilson needed the hour and minute hands to point the way.

Chapter 23

Tick, tock

During a night of restless, dreamless sleep the questions on Wilson's mind continued to nag for answers and he woke the next morning with a headache. He tried to escape the self-interrogation by ducking under his duvet but an image of Big Mac tracked him down. Thinking back, Wilson recalled The Gateway dream had felt different to The Market Square's usual manifestations. With its darkly comic characters and revelatory content, that experience had felt more serious and profound, like a different species of dream.

Also, was it just a coincidence that it occurred on my birthday? Could my birthday, my eighteenth birthday, coming of age and all that, be a factor?

Wilson reached for his phone and searched: 'Significance of 18th October 2017'.

The first result came from Wikipedia.

'October 18th is the 291st day of the year in the Gregorian calendar. There are 74 days remaining until the end of the year...'

Wilson skimmed through the rest of the article. Although October 18th had been significant over the centuries – famous battles, major earthquakes, Edison generated electricity in 1878, the BBC was founded in 1922 and so on – nothing in the listings gave any insight into his particular quandry.

Daft idea, he decided, tossing the phone to one side.

After a minute of further contemplation, he revised the plan.

Maybe I should be looking at the day I was born, 18th October 1999, rather than the day I turned eighteen. My real birthday!

He reached for the phone: 'Significance of 18th October 1999'.

Once again, Wikipedia failed to enlighten and pages one and two of Google results brought the same disappointment. However, on page three Wilson saw a link with the title: 'Mybirthday.ninja. October 18, 1999. Birthday facts.' Intrigued, he clicked the link.

The page loaded under the heading: 'Here are some snazzy birthday facts about 18th of October.' The snazzy facts included Wilson's age in dog years, which celebrities shared his birthday and again, all the major events. But under the heading 'What does my birthday, October 18, 1999, mean?' Wilson read:

'Your birthday numbers, 10, 18 and 1999, reveal your Life Path number as 11. It is a master number that represents intuition, idealism and invention. You have the potential to be a source of inspiration and illumination for people.'

Okay, that's more like it, now what the hell is a Life Path number? Google had the answer.

'The most important number in your 'numerology' chart. Your Life Path number reveals a broad outline of the opportunities, challenges and lessons you will encounter during this lifetime.'

Wilson double clicked 'numerology'.

'Numerology is a belief in the divine or mystical relationship between a number and one or more coinciding events. It is often associated with the paranormal, alongside astrology and similar divinatory arts.'

As Wilson's eyes moved over the words, his attention lagged some distance behind, still dwelling on the word 'paranormal'. It soon caught up however, as he read the following:

'Numerology... was the origin of the theories of electromagnetism, quantum mechanics and gravitation.'

In other words, energy fields.

He clicked a link to www.numerology.com:

'...the 11 symbolises the potential to push the limitations of the human experience into the stratosphere of the highest spiritual perception, the link between the mortal and the immortal, between man and spirit, between darkness and light, ignorance and enlightenment.

This is the ultimate symbolic power of the 11.'

Then he followed his search steps back to the words 'divinatory arts'.

'Divination, from the Latin, divinaire, to foresee, to be inspired by God.'

Understandably, it took a while for Wilson to pull together the disparate threads of information he'd just read and then weave only the relevant strands.

So my Life Path number, the number eleven, is a special number that links me to the paranormal, to divination, the spirit and is connected with energy fields. What the beeep?

Wilson grabbed his rucksack, unfolded the clock diagram and jotted down the above conclusion. He then put the paper back in his rucksack. It was Saturday and that meant one thing, football.

After breakfast, Wilson cleaned his boots, prepared his kit bag and checked the time. He had an hour to kill and the master number '11' still glowed like an ember, or the mark of a branding iron, in his head.

He returned to the search history stored on his phone and read the following sentence twice, to make sure he had it clear in his head.

'...the 11 symbolises the potential to push the limitations of the human experience into the stratosphere of the highest spiritual perception, the link between the mortal and the immortal, between man and spirit, between darkness and light, ignorance and enlightenment.'

Do I have that potential?

Wilson recalled all the sequences from The Gateway dream and fast-forwarded to the conversation in The Hall of Extinguished Spirits.

"The soul is the Residual spirit, it goes elsewhere."

"To the other side, to meet The Powers That Be."

There was an obvious connection between the supposed power of the number 11 and the narrative in a dream. From ignorance to enlightenment. Wilson grabbed a pen and double-checked the formula for calculating a Life Path number.

No point in getting too excited if the sums are wrong.

My date of birth: 18th October 1999

Month

October is the 10th month of the year.

10 reduces to 1 plus 0, which equals 1.

Days

My day of birth is the 18th.

18 reduces to 1 plus 8, which equals 9.

Year

My year of birth is 1999.

1999 reduces to 1 plus 9 plus 9 plus 9, which equals 28.

28 reduces to 2 plus 8, which equals 10.

Then 10 reduces to 1 plus 0, which equals 1.

Now add the 1 and the 9 and the 1, and the result is 11.

The master number 11.

No question about that, I am a number eleven.

Wilson then performed the same calculation for his twin sisters and his mum. His sisters were both eight and his mum, a six. He made the calculation for his dad.

Wilson wasn't surprised his father was a number eleven, a master number, just like himself. He'd left that date until last, for just that reason.

Dad was born in the same hospital as me, knows there are things that can't be explained. He studies energy and information networks, I gate-crash them and we're both connected by the number eleven.

Wilson's imagination then raised the alarming possibility that his father might also have visited The Market Square.

Wilson laughed at the thought, but not for long, because the disturbing recollection of something Big Mac had said, wiped the smile off his face.

"We know who you are Mr Wilson. We've been watching you. We've seen your trace. You're a number eleven."

Stop! No more. This is seriously freaking me out.

Wilson grabbed his bag, scooter keys and left for the football match.

Chapter 24

How time flies

In the build-up to a 'potential' rendezvous with Daisy, Wilson avoided all further thoughts of magic numbers and a Wi-Fi of dreams. He needed all his faculties fully focused in readiness for Friday. Wilson didn't journey to The Market Square once that week and he was glad. The last thing he needed was more cryptic revelations from the dynamic duo in The Gateway.

Wilson didn't journey to The Market Square once that week and he was glad. The last thing he needed was more cryptic revelations from the dynamic duo in The Gateway.

Wilson's dad was working away in London. His sisters were busy at college planning a big fashion show and his mum was fully occupied with charity work. That meant Wilson could keep his head down and focus on being your typically average college student.

Here are the main stories of the week.

Wilson's Monday was taken up by an event called 'Getting Ready for Work'. This involved a morning of talks and presentations by an employment agency explaining how students should prepare for job interviews, what to wear, how to write a curriculum vitae and other issues along the same theme.

Monday afternoon was slightly more engaging and involved a Career Path Assessment; the purpose of which was to help Wilson choose a suitable vocation based on the answers he gave to a bunch of questions. After Wilson's tick boxes were processed, the results came back and the college careers lady told Wilson that based on various metrics his ideal career would be that of a physiotherapist or a plumber.

As Tuesday arrived, Wilson continued to contemplate the still-possibly-fictitious Daisy Meadowcroft, on a Geography field trip in Ambleside, tramping across the fells searching for interlocking spurs and oxbow lakes.

The big highlight of Wednesday was the global launch of a new, indispensable, cutting-edge website called Missingsock.co.uk. Hoover Facebooked and Tweeted absolutely everyone and by 9.00 p.m. had a collection of twenty-nine single socks, all looking for a partner online. 'Only the perfect match will do' was Hoover's snappy strap line. Iqbal managed to diversify the entire business plan by uploading a lost glove.

Thursday dragged by with nothing noteworthy to report, but then Friday finally arrived.

Chapter 25

D-day

Friday 27th October 2017

Wilson was in the students' common room drinking coffee and counting down the minutes. He'd gone there for peace and quiet and to steady his nerves in preparation for the drive to Manchester. Hoover and Teaps were playing pool with Hoover's younger brother and Eddie Spinner. Spinner was renowned as the college drug dealer, a lowlife and the lad whose name was always called last when picking sides for football. The last thing Wilson needed was an invitation to play a frame of pool. Any refusal would require an explanation, and any explanation would have to steer way clear of Manchester city centre and the second coming of Daisy. The merest scent of a fib and Teaps would be all over it like a rash. Plus, the presence in the common room of Hoover brought back the jarring frustration of his last trip to town. Wilson wasn't religious, but that didn't stop him looking up to the ceiling and muttering:

"Please God, don't let them see me get stood up again."

More of a certainty however, was the likelihood of Spinner wandering over once the game was over.

One night, at a party at Iqbal's house, Wilson smoked a joint for the first time. He'd drank too much cider and Spinner had told him the weed would make him relaxed and more confident with the girls.

"Everyone does it man. It'll help you chill Wilson."

So Wilson took the joint, inhaled, held his breath for a moment, exhaled, coughed, and coughed some more. Then his brain exploded. Whether it was the combination of drink and drugs or just the strong weed, Wilson had no idea. But he did know there was no relaxing and no chillin' out. Wilson's head was a volcano about to erupt and minutes after taking a puff, he passed out.

Two hours later he woke up on Iqbal's bed with a million fairy lights twinkling inside his head. He staggered downstairs and stumbled home, much to the amusement of everyone at the party.

So the general opinion was that Wilson was a lightweight when it came to 'extracurricular activity', as Hoover put it. But Wilson knew the reality was more to do with the way his brain was wired. A brain that didn't take kindly to finely tuned neurones being short-circuited by a spliff. Wilson also knew that Spinner hadn't given him the joint to be friendly; he'd supplied with the unspoken understanding that Wilson would be buying weed from him in the future. It would only be a matter of minutes before the pool game was over and Spinner would come creeping over with his predictable, smarmy, "Hey, Wilson, amigo, qué pasa?"

Wilson grabbed his Vespa keys, helmet and parka and made for the door. He'd rather be early and sit in Albert Square watching the pigeons than deal with Spinner and Inspector Hoover.

"See you at footy tomorrow lads," he shouted. "Elvis has left the building."

"Hey Wilson, wait, we've finished, Hoover's just potted the black with his elbow. Where're you going?"

But Wilson was gone.

Chapter 26

Will she, won't she?

As the A6 dropped down into Stockport, Wilson remembered to turn left and take the detour around the back of Stockport Infirmary.

Tonight's not the night for any déjà voodoo.

He arrived in Manchester city centre at 6.30 p.m., parked his scooter in a bay on Bridge Street then walked across Deansgate and up to Albert Square near the junction with Cross Street. He picked an empty bench facing the town hall, sat down and checked the time on his watch: 6:38 p.m. Then the date on his phone: Friday 27th. Correct, just as arranged. Twenty minutes to go.

But twenty minutes to go to what? Twenty minutes to crushing disappointment? Twenty minutes until the psychiatrist is called?

At that moment, sitting alone on a damp wooden seat, about to repeat the embarrassment of a few weeks earlier, Wilson felt strangely deflated and hollow.

Yes, he had his family, friends and compared to so many others – Teaps, for example – had a great life. But observing the people hurrying across the square with purpose, feeling the pulse of a major city at rush hour, he felt lonely and lost. A stupid lad with crazy dreams, foolishly wishing for a miracle to happen; desperately needing someone, another outcast, a tightrope walker, to lead him from his always walking on egg shells existence. In a moment of weakness, all the pent up, straitjacketed feelings of alienation and self-doubt wrestled free and charged into his head like Orcs into battle.

You're going mental mate, goin' mad, losin' it.

The needle on a safety valve was touching red.

The dam was about to burst its banks.

The lid was coming off.

Would Daisy be his salvation, his sanity? She had to exist. Must exist. She would be his lifeline and if needed, he would be hers.

Words from a favourite Coldplay song, 'The Scientist' came into his head. He silently sang them from beginning to end, amazed at how poignant and pertinent the lyrics were.

'I was just guessing, at numbers and figures, pulling the puzzle apart.'

Every line captured his predicament perfectly and in doing so, took the edge off his agitation.

Come on, pull yourself together you idiot.

He was going to be ten minutes early, but set off back down Bridge Street in the direction of Starbucks anyway.

Turning onto Deansgate, he joined the headlong rush of commuters heading home. The fine drizzle lubricated their walking pace. The Starbucks sign was glowing like the Pole Star as Wilson felt around his mouth and nose for anything that shouldn't be there. He paused at the corner of the building, almost asking his vision to bend ninety degrees in order to see if Daisy was inside, then took a deep breath to prepare himself for either of two possible outcomes.

"This is it."

The coffee shop was warm and welcoming. The alchemy of fresh coffee aroma, the musk of damp clothing and the cosy, subdued lighting had a calming effect. The place was busy, but not so busy that Wilson wasn't able to quickly scan the room and see that Daisy wasn't there. He perched on a stool and double checked for a second time.

No, she's definitely not here.

There was a queue of about six or seven people waiting to order but all were taller than or as tall as Wilson.

None of those can be Daisy either.

Then he moved on to the female form standing at the milk and sugar dispenser. She was wearing a long black coat with a turned-up collar, ankle boots, bobble hat, fixing a coffee or hot chocolate; Wilson couldn't tell. His eyes remained fixed on the back of the girl. Whatever she was doing, she was certainly taking her time about it. A wooden stirrer was deposited in the bin. Cup in hand, she began to turn, to reveal flushed cheeks, pink lips, a button nose, then she looked up and saw Wilson. For a split second, time stood still. Then the coffee mug slipped through Daisy's fingers as Wilson started to run. His crash helmet bowled across the floor, striking a table leg and knocking froth from a fresh cappuccino. But that didn't matter, nothing mattered, because Daisy was in his arms. Her bobble hat fell off, strands of chestnut hair were tickling his nose and he was intoxicated by her scent of fresh vanilla. With all the Orcs fleeing left, right and centre, Wilson was trying to say 'we did it'. Daisy was lifted clean off her feet and he was spinning her round and she was laughing and trying to say 'I told you I was real'. She was warm and full of bones with butterscotch skin and blood in her thumb and Daisy Meadowcroft, the girl he'd met in a dream, truly did exist.

"Now there's two of us," he whispered into the soft pink shell of her ear.

It took a few minutes for Daisy, speaking in Danish, to explain to the manageress that Wilson was a best friend whom she hadn't seen for years; that she was sorry for dropping the coffee mug and they would go and sit at the table in the corner with two fresh coffees and not cause any further fuss or trouble.

Wilson's eyes never moved from Daisy throughout the conversation.

"Bloody hell," said Wilson as they sat down. "Double bloody hell."

"I told you I'd be here Wilson. Absolutely no problems with the trains tonight."

Wilson gazed into Daisy's eyes; they danced when she smiled. He placed his hand on hers.

"Sorry I doubted you, but I can't believe it," he said. "I mean, I really, really can't believe it. I don't know what I would've done, what would've happened, if you hadn't come here tonight. And then if I'd met you in The Market Square again... You really have saved me Daisy. Saved my sanity."

They sat in complete silence for the next minute, hand on hand. Wilson kept his head down, manfully trying to hide his tears.

"Wilson it's alright. I'm here, I'll always be here, always have been, in this real world." He released a deep, body-shaking sob.

"Wilson, I think we were meant to find each other. Some weird magnetism has drawn us together, like it was planned to happen. My grandmother said this was possible and I never doubted it. No need to be sad. It's not a bad thing."

"I'm not sad Daisy, I'm happy — in ways I can't begin to describe. And I'm trying to come to terms with the fact that I met someone in one of my crazy dreams, who also shares those crazy dreams, the only person I know who does in fact, and she's flippin' sitting here next to me, now, in real life. That's where I am at the moment."

He brushed a tear from his cheek. "That's not a tear of joy, it's the tear of a miracle."

"Yeah, it is kind of a miracle. But now you know: in our world, Wilson, miracles actually happen. Accept what we do in The Market Square as inexplicable, but also true and let's build from there."

"I'm glad I've found you Daisy."

"Me too Wilson," she said, without having to think.

They spent the next hour talking about all the things a boy and girl usually reveal on their first date. (Though on this occasion, certainly in theory, the term 'blind date' could also have been uniquely applicable). Family, friends, phone numbers, birthdays, likes and dislikes and favourite bands were all ticked off the list. It felt necessary to do this groundwork, to give the relationship a conventional footing. But all the while, the main item on the agenda, The Market Square, was simmering away on a hot plate somewhere in the background.

Strangely, however, they both knew, without the need for words, that Starbucks was not the place to broach the subject of The Market Square. It was simply too huge a part of their lives and too private an issue to dissect in the open forum of a coffee shop. Besides, the guys on the adjoining table kept listening in to their conversation.

Daisy held her second coffee cup with both hands and took a sip.

"Do you ever think about dreams Wilson, you know, their meaning, their purpose? Because even top scientists don't understand them, or even which part of the brain is responsible."

Wilson got the message. They would cover some neutral ground.

"Yeah, I do. And what amazes me is how we can just invent a dream in our heads, like a movie, with characters and a story, all invented on the spot. The most powerful computer in the world could never do that. Yet we do it every night, no problem."

Daisy took a second sip, a light in her eyes was twinkling. She placed the coffee cup down.

"Okay try this for size. Do you know we spend more time, in our lives, dreaming, than we do eating? No, don't laugh Wilson, it's true. I read it in a book. The average person sleeps for eight hours each night, which is a third of a life, right?"

Daisy muttered her way through some mental calculation.

"So twenty five years of our time on earth is spent fast asleep. And do you know how long we spend dreaming? Six years. Six years! We only spend four years eating. So what does that tell you?"

"Err, that dreaming is more important than eating?"

"Correct Wilson. But if you go into a bookshop, the cookery or food section will have stacks of books, while the psychology section, probably just a single shelf, will only have a couple of books about dreams."

Wilson stretched out his legs. He was relaxed and fully at ease with the amazing girl who had miraculously entered his life, a nocturnal soul mate, a like-minded companion. Wilson locked his hands behind his head, sat back and laughed at the cameo performance of Daisy burbling away. The living embodiment of his salvation.

"Also Wilson, dreams have meaning."

Daisy repeatedly tapped a painted fingernail on the table top. As any girl insistent on a close friend hearing what she has to say might do. "And a snake in your dream can have a double meaning. Good and bad. It all depends on the colour of the snake. Apparently."

As Daisy entertained Wilson in Starbucks, in The Gateway, an entirely different conversation was taking place.

"Ah, I see our friends have finally crossed the Rubicon," said Big Mac.

"They certainly have," said Short Cake. "Do you think The Powers That Be are aware?"

"If they're not, they soon will be."

Chapter 27

After-dinner chat

Wilson and Daisy were the last customers to leave Starbucks and as they made their way to Piccadilly Station, the voyage of discovery continued with animated chatter under the cover of Daisy's umbrella.

"Have you got a boyfriend Daisy?"

Wilson wanted a feel for the terrain. For where he stood. Would he be standing on anyone's toes?

Daisy smiled. "Just friends, nothing serious. And you?"

"Same situation. But I have been engaged three times. Still not found the right one yet."

"Yeah, my second divorce is just going through. I'll probably lose my vinyl records in the settlement."

They huddled together on a platform pock-marked with puddles, waiting for Daisy's train to Macclesfield.

"Be careful driving back Wilson; the roads will be slippery after all this rain. Don't want our friendship to end on the same night it started."

"Don't worry, I'll make sure my headlights are on. The Vespa had five the last time I counted, so I should be visible."

Wilson paused for a second, then continued.

"So where do we go from here then? I mean..."

Daisy inched closer, slipping her hands inside Wilson's parka pockets for warmth.

"Erm, I go that way on the train and you go that way to get your scooter."

"Daisy yeah, I know. But seriously. I mean, what do we do now? I've spent the last few weeks hoping for this moment and now it's here I don't have a plan for part two."

"Look Wilson, what's happened to us is off-the-scale crazy. But it's happened, nevertheless. I've got your mobile number and you've got mine. So we can meet in Starbucks every day if you want, forever. That's set in stone. We found each other in a dream and now we can share our strange secret together. Daisy gently flicked the tip of Wilson's cold wet nose.

"Remember that night we first met?"

Wilson smiled and nodded. How could he not remember. Daisy continued.

"As for The Market Square, maybe it won't continue to happen, all the learning stuff; it could stop tomorrow. But I think we've been given a unique gift, a strange gift, and we should accept it for what it is and not think too much about what's happened, or why us, or try to rationalise it, cos then I think we'd both be sectioned. Let's go with the flow and see where it takes us.

"Whatever happens Wilson, I exist, you exist, and if The Market Square closes down, because they have to build a supermarket on it, then good; we found each other and we can lead our lives knowing we don't have to appear in some bizarre freak show every night. But for now, let's enjoy it. We may never get the chance again to do things nobody else can do — well, nobody I know. We may grow out of this whole, ability to interact with dreams thing, or it will be taken away, or the wormhole closed and we'll become just the same as all the other ordinary people."

Daisy's train was pulling into the platform.

"Here's a thought," she said, not wanting the night with Wilson to end, "let's try to reverse the dream and see if we can meet in The Market Square again, tonight."

"Wow, that's a cool idea, I'm definitely up for that. My dream or yours?"

Daisy rolled her eyes. "I'll text you later." She turned to board the train.

"No, text me now. Text me now from the train. Just to double-check I've got the right number."

"Wilson, you've double-checked five times already. It's my number. Speak later."

Then Daisy was waving through a window, finding a seat, pretending to text, laughing and then waving again as the carriage moved away. Wilson stood watching it pick up speed. Daisy was leaving him. As the train curved round a bend and disappeared from view Wilson once again felt vulnerable and alone, his emotions fully exposed. What if the entire night had been nothing more than a dream? His phone beeped with an incoming text: 'Drive carefully, Wilson. See you tonight, D.'

It was 9.40 p.m. when Wilson arrived home. As a precaution, he'd once again taken the detour round the back of the hospital. Alex and Gloria were just coming to the end of what appeared to have been a romantic dinner for two, with candles, tablecloth and flushed cheeks. As Wilson entered the dining room, not surprisingly, he was in a buoyant mood.

"Well, this is all very cosy, looks like you two are out on a first date. What's the special occasion? No, wait. You're not pregnant again are you Mum?"

Gloria giggled, her cheeks blooming a rosier shade of pink at the very thought.

"But you're drinking wine, so you can't be pregnant. Hold on, I've got it; you're going to be a grandmother?"

Alex joined in the laughter and passed Wilson a glass of red wine.

"You're very chipper this evening son, have you won the lottery or something?"

"No, just wondered what the special occasion was?"

"There's no special occasion and as far as I'm aware, your sisters aren't pregnant." Alex checked his watch. "However, it is Friday night and still early, so there's definitely time."

"Alex!" Gloria shrieked. "That's a terrible thing to say about your daughters."

She threw a napkin at him.

"I know, I know, what a terrible father," said Alex dropping his head in mock shame. His shoulders shook as he laughed in silence.

Gloria ignored her husband and turned to Wilson.

"Are you hungry love? I saved you some lasagne and garlic bread. It's in the oven, still hot."

"Yeah Mum, that'd be great. I'm really peckish."

Gloria cleared up two empty plates and left for the kitchen.

Alex sipped his wine.

"How was London?" Wilson asked.

"Errm, interesting, I guess. But those MPs and that committee are bloody clueless. How about you? How was your week?"

"Errm, interesting. But those teachers in that college are also bloody clueless."

They toasted each other with the clink of wine glasses. A liquid high five.

"Actually, it was a top week. I met a girl" said Wilson.

"I thought you had a girlfriend. Steff Green. Walter's daughter? The champion swimmer. Sorry, no, I get those two confused. I mean the sister, Natalie. The netball player. Or am I thinking of..."

"What are you two gossiping about?" Gloria placed a dinner plate in front of Wilson.

"Wilson was just telling me about a new girl he's met."

"Oh, but what about Stephanie Green? I thought she was –"

"Mum, time out. You're as bad as Dad. Steff's family moved to Wales about six months ago."

"And Natalie?"

"Mummm, stop! Natalie was her younger sister and she had to move to Wales as well. Given that she was only fourteen!"

Wilson held a forkful of lasagne suspended in mid-air as he pictured Daisy waving goodbye from the train.

"No, this one's different Mum. But I don't want to say too much. Tonight was the first time I've really, err, spoken to her. Though on the other hand, it also feels like I've known her for ages. It's kind of weird. Anyway, we'll have to see where it goes. Let's just say I like her and we have quite a lot in common."

"Oh Wilson, that's so lovely. There's no need to rush into things. Let nature take its course."

Wilson continued with his meal and the wine as his parents returned to their tête-à-tête on the latest news from the twins, the possibility of renting a flat in London and the revelations behind a cousin's divorce.

Soft-focus images of Daisy and Catapult Gliders and same-faced people descending on parachutes floated around his head. During a lull in the conversation and with a second glass of wine a motivating factor, Wilson asked his dad if he knew anything about numerology.

"I've been reading about it, the power of numbers and I discovered that you're a number eleven Dad. I mean your Life Path number is eleven, one of the master numbers."

"And if my memory serves me correctly Wilson, so is yours," replied his dad.

"What?" Asked Gloria, looking from husband to son. They'd lost her at the mention of the word numerology.

"Ah, it's nothing love," said Alex, placing his wine glass down. "Just a bit of pseudo-science that Wilson's picked up from college."

Alex abruptly stopped speaking, as though someone had whispered something troubling in his ear. Slowly and very deliberately, he began tracing his finger around the rim of his wine glass, enticing a high-pitched, wavering tone to float around the dining room.

"This could be the song of a siren, couldn't it? Hypnotic... enticing... impossible to resist... drawing you in. At the same time, something dangerous... likely to end in disaster... lurking under the surface, like an old wreck, dashed against the rocks."

Alex frowned at his wife.

"This wine glass is singing to me Gloria. It's singing a warning, a beautiful, dark, enchanting message. It's saying, 'Alex... Alex... tell your wife to stop drinking so much red wine'."

Alex started laughing furiously, tickled not only by his tale of the unexpected but also by the response of an infuriated wife flicking a fully loaded tea towel. He had to excuse himself and went to the loo, chuckling away. Gloria went to make three mugs of coffee and when she returned, the conversation sobered up and Alex revived the earlier subject matter.

"We suddenly seem to be having some interesting conversations about unusual subjects Wilson. First Morphic Fields and now numerology?"

Alex paused.

"I can see how you arrived at Sheldrake's ideas from your biology class. Off-grid, for sure, but brightens up a dull day for a bored teacher. But how did you land on numerology? I mean, I can't see that being on any syllabus. Well, unless you've switched to an A level in the supernatural."

"What?" Gloria was lost again.

Wilson intervened. "It's okay Mum, nothing sinister, just that I..."

Fully aware that the wine was affecting his judgement, he continued nevertheless, into uncharted territory.

"It's just that I had a dream the other night and it was mad, sort of eccentric and bizarre. It was on the night of my birthday. I think I told you. Probably caused by the Chinese food. But it was so vivid, as though being eighteen had something to do with it. Can't explain why. Anyway, the next day I searched on the internet to see if my eighteenth was a special or significant date. I don't know what I was thinking; just seemed there was a connection. And do you know what I found out?"

"What?" Asked Gloria, for the third and final time.

"Absolutely nothing. A few bits about famous battles and pop stars with the same birthday, nothing unusual. But then I did a search for my actual birth date. The day I was born. And to get to the point, the search results threw out a load of amazing stuff about this 'power of numbers' theory called numerology. It said I was a Life Path number eleven and that this was a big deal. So I checked the birth dates of the twins and you two, and guess what? Dad is a number eleven also, and he was born in the same hospital and in the same ward as me. Strange coincidence, don't you think, Mum?"

"Well love, I don't know what to think. Sounds like you've been at the Ouija board to me."

From the corner of his eye, Wilson sensed Alex was observing him and listening with profound interest, but he didn't return the attention.

"Don't worry about it," Gloria continued. "I'm sure it'll all come out in the wash. You can discover everything's connected on the internet one way or another. Anyway, I thought you were going to a birthday party at the rugby club tonight?"

"Nah Mum. It'll be a late one, with the inevitable Jaegerbombs, drinking games and money for the taxi. Besides, I don't really fancy it. It's the big game tomorrow; Stockport Grammar at home. So gonna watch a bit of TV and have an early one. 'Night folks."

Wilson felt his father's stare sear the back of his shirt as he left the dining room.

"I don't know what to make of Wilson sometimes," said Gloria, brushing crumbs from the tablecloth. "You know, I still think about that night he spoke French when he was little. He can... he... I really can't put my finger on it. He just seems different to other lads of his age, like being interested in this numberology nonsense."

"Oh it's nothing. I think he's just got an overactive imagination love."

"Yeah, I'm sure you're right. Funny that you already knew he was that number eleven though?"

Gloria was oblivious to the significance of her comment.

Chapter 28

Reversing the dream

Friday 27th into Saturday 28th October 2017

Wilson entered his bedroom and stood with his back pressed firmly against the closed door. What he'd just confessed to his parents probably wasn't that smart and his heart rate agreed. Under the influence of two glasses of wine, he'd linked The Gateway dream with numerology, brought his father into the equation and mentioned the existence of Daisy.

The latter point, the outing of Daisy, albeit fleetingly, had been a spur of the moment decision; completely unrehearsed, spontaneous and by definition therefore, a stupid mistake. A slip-up that normally would never have got past his internal censor, the sentry at the gate who'd monitored and tempered Wilson's behaviour since his junior school days.

Let's not draw attention now Wilson, there's a good chap. Don't want to cause a scene with one of your episodes. Putting your head over the parapet. Upsetting everyone with those tricky talents of yours. Probably best not to mention Daisy either at this early stage in the relationship. It might not come to anything you know. She's not exactly the girl next door type.

As Wilson's heartbeat returned to normal however, he realised he actually didn't care about the disclosures he'd made over dinner. For far too long, the slightest deviation from his behavioural norm had brought feelings of guilt. The mental equivalent of a slap across the legs for showing off. Now, the straitjacket had been removed. Meeting Daisy was living proof he wasn't a castaway on his own crazy island and it brought the confidence and impetus to think he could finally get to the bottom of what was going on. If that meant ruffling his dad's feathers and kicking the apple bucket or whatever that correct saying was, just because he'd spoken about numerology, then what the hell, he was going to do it.

Wilson opened his phone and scrolled to the new entry in contacts: 'Daisy Meadowcroft. 7 Cedars Lane, Macclesfield. SK10 13N.'

I'm sure she said it was near The King's School.

A Street View search confirmed the house was there, exactly as described: the middle cottage in a row of five with a black door. Wilson entered the digits relating to Daisy's birth date into the calculator tool. Her eighteenth was only a few days away. He wasn't in the least bit surprised to find that her Life Path Number was an eleven.

If we do meet later, must remember to ask her where she was born.

He suspected he already knew the answer.

Brushing his teeth, Wilson wondered whether Daisy would be able to smell toothpaste on his breath. He couldn't begin to answer such an abstract question, but just to be safe, he sprayed a double helping of deodorant under both arms, checked his hair and climbed into bed.

It was only 10.25 p.m. Wilson switched on the TV and watched the local news. Then he tried to relax with a chapter of *The Count of Monte Cristo*. His phone beeped with a text from Daisy.

'Hope you made it home safe. Getting sleepy over here in Macc. See you in an hour or so. Fingers crossed. D. P.S. How will I recognise you?'

'I'll be waiting by the Clock Tower – with a box of chocolates.'

'Wilson, you're a KEEPER. See you there. 'Night.'

A few minutes later Daisy texted again.

'This is going to be so cool if we can do it!'

'Cooler than cool!'

Like an excited child on Christmas Eve – waiting for sleep to send the all-clear signal to Santa – Wilson couldn't seem to nod off either. He started thinking about the parallels between himself and Edmond, the main character in his book and the girl he travels the world to find. His mind wouldn't switch off. For two hours he tossed and turned. Then the 'what ifs' arrived. Questions came out of the darkness thick and fast, almost rolling like film credits down the screen of his closed eyelids.

What if The Market Square isn't there?

Or I can't find Daisy because there's a street party and the Clock Tower isn't there?

What if Daisy doesn't look like Daisy?

Or she doesn't recognise me? Or we see each other but we can't speak?

The more he tried to sleep, the more frustrated and wide awake Wilson became. He checked his phone. No more messages and it was 12.50 a.m.

She's been waiting for hours. Probably thinks I've stood her up. She could be searching for me and doesn't know I'm still wide awake in bed at home.

At last, as Mickey's gloved hands pointed to 1.25 a.m., Wilson's eyelids began to flutter and he finally arrived in The Market Square where a sporting event was in full swing.

The cobbled surface of the square was covered entirely by a layer of lush, green grass and reminiscent of a school playing field. A running track, six lanes wide, had been marked in white lime and ran the hundred metre distance from Sampson's, top left to L'École, bottom right. Wilson was aware of athletes and spectators but didn't stop to take in the finer details. He could see the Clock Tower and sitting alone on one of the benches was Daisy. She'd been waiting from the moment Mickey pointed to 11.55 p.m.

Daisy waved as she saw Wilson make his way across The Market Square and ran to meet him halfway. They stopped a yard apart.

"Hey, you remembered."

Wilson felt something in his hand and looked down. It was a box of Thornton's chocolates tied with a red ribbon. He looked up at Daisy, smiled and shrugged his shoulders.

"The thing is, I don't even know where the Thornton's toffee shop is. How crazy is that?"

They walked back to the bench where Daisy tore into the chocolates.

She passed Wilson an Orange Cream and with a mouthful of Caramel Crunch declared that they tasted just like the real thing. Daisy's comment confused Wilson. He was about to say, "but they are the real thing, why wouldn't they be?" then realised he was sitting by the Clock Tower in a dream and that it would be impossible to give Daisy a meaningful reply.

It was a glorious summer's day and honeybees murmured contentedly as they gathered nectar from patches of clover. Huge, yellow butterflies — a species Wilson knew with certainty would never be found in any reference book — chased each other chaotically through the warm air. The Market Square was fielding an athletics meeting and the hub of activity appeared to be focused in the bottom-right corner, in front of L'École.

"It's a school sports day. Well, sort of." Daisy confirmed.

In front of L'École, serious looking athletes in running kit were stretching and warming up with short sprints, star jumps and bunny hops. Some were covering impressive distances jumping with both feet in a sack. Others shuffled through hoops and ran zig-zags down a line of small plastic cones.

Dispersed amongst the competitors Wilson also identified the other unmistakable sign of a sports day: overly enthusiastic parents. Summer dresses and flat shoes for the mums and short-sleeved shirts and khaki pants for the dads. Some parents were holding hands with their children, doing their best to stop them running off.

The children, who were actually fully grown athletes and certainly not school kids, were nevertheless, extremely agitated and excited.

Wilson and Daisy watched as a tall man with impressively toned muscles, wearing a tight-fitting, lycra running suit, sprinted powerfully away from L'École.

"Roger, come back this minute and do as you're told!"

The athlete, who had the stature and bearing of Usain Bolt pulled up the moment he heard his name and jogged back.

"Sorry Mum."

As Roger came within striking distance, the petite lady in the flower patterned dress seized his arm and gave him two stinging slaps across the back of the legs.

"Stop running away." Her arm was raised fully upright but her accusing finger still fell four inches short of his nose.

Roger stamped his foot on the grass three times, folded his arms across his chest and looked as though he was about to cry.

"Oh it's definitely a sports day" said Daisy, giggling at the spectacle.

"Certainly is and I'm sorry I arrived so late. Took me absolutely ages to get to sleep. I was still awake at half past two."

"Really? I was only sitting here waiting for a few minutes."

Wilson paused for a moment, searching for an explanation.

"No idea how that works! But at least we reversed dream travel. We're clearing hurdles by the minute."

"And breaking all records" said Daisy.

They both laughed, at ease in their familiar, surreal world and their developing friendship.

"Seriously though Daisy. Do you ever wonder what this place is, what it all means? Where we are exactly?"

"Funnily enough, I was thinking that exact same thing earlier, when I was lying in bed. I remembered what my grandma once told me."

Daisy hesitated for a second.

"Quite a few years back, Grandma was very ill in hospital. We went to visit and a doctor asked Mum if he could speak to her in private. So when I was alone with Grandma, she beckoned me closer and started whispering. I think she was on medication because everything came in a bit of a jumble but basically she told me she knew I came here to The Market Square and she told me that she'd also visited many times. Which came as a bit of a shock, to say the least. She described The Market Square as a place through which dreams travel and she said that people like us could absorb all the experiences and memories held in those dreams. Something called crashing was okay but straddling was more serious, I think she might even have said it was dangerous. Also, there were lots of people like us and I shouldn't feel strange or find it disturbing. It helps me a lot to know that my grandma's been here."

Daisy stopped speaking and Wilson sat quietly sifting through the nuggets of information like a prospector panning for gold.

"Hey, do you want to see something really weird, something I discovered how to do?" Daisy suddenly had a mischievous look on her face. Wilson needn't answer; she was going to show him anyway.

"Listen, you arrived here with this sports day thing going on, but I don't think I created this dream just because I was here first. I think it was arranged in advance, for both of us. I don't think we control what happens here. It's somehow preplanned. Maybe all the people here are also in their own dream and The Market Square facilitates it. Do you get what I mean?"

It was a thought provoking notion.

"I think so. You're saying we don't control, through our dreams, or at the start of a dream, what The Market Square will be like when we arrive here?"

Wilson wasn't sure if he'd explained himself properly or even come close to teaming up with Daisy's thoughts.

"Yeah, but here's the trick: I know how to influence what happens once we've arrived. To continue with the sports day theme, my hockey teacher at college is called Gwen Burton. She's nearly six foot tall and has ginger hair always tied up in a bun. Can you see anyone here who looks like that?"

Wilson cast his eye over the sports field.

Roger the sprinter and another five impressively muscular athletes had taken starting positions on the running track. Each was holding a spoon with an egg balanced on it. Parents lined the length of the track baying encouragement.

Wilson couldn't see anyone even remotely similar to the unmistakable description of Mrs Burton, though he did notice someone that could have been Mo Farah practising for the wheelbarrow race.

"Nope, can't see your hockey teacher anywhere."

"Okay, well watch this."

Daisy scrunched her eyes shut tight, seemingly searching inside her head for something, then after twenty seconds, they burst open.

"Now look. She's probably wearing a navy-blue tracksuit with the name 'Burton' in white letters on the back."

Wilson searched the sports field again. Roger had dropped his egg and his mum was delivering another slap. His gaze stretched the length of the running track and down at the far end, near a table laden with trophies he noticed the word 'Burton'. It was written in white letters on the back of a tracksuit worn by a tall lady, with red hair tied in a bun and she was carrying a hockey stick.

"There," pointed Wilson, "she's there. Standing by the finishing line with her back to us."

"Yep, that's her. Always looks exactly the same."

Wilson turned to Daisy, amazed. "How did you do that?"

"I pulled her in. I closed my eyes, imagined how she looks, how I see her at college, concentrated really hard and then pulled her into my dream, this dream. I actually think that's what crashing is all about, but I've no idea how to explain it. Cool trick, huh?"

"Bit more than a cool trick."

Wilson peered at Mrs Burton, who was now in conversation with a parent, then looked back at Daisy.

"Phenomenal!"

"Give it a go," said Daisy. "Pull someone in. Just close your eyes and imagine someone you know really well, one of your best friends, someone who stands out; imagine how they usually dress, how they normally look, how you remember them. Focus for a minute and see if you can bring them here. Try it."

Wilson, while not fully certain of what he was being instructed to do, tried nevertheless. He thought of Hoover. Tall, awkward, hair drooping over his eyes, black hoodie, black skinny jeans. Wilson concentrated on the picture in his mind, then opened his eyes. Hoover was easy to spot.

"Is that him over there?" Daisy was pointing in the right direction. "That guy in the black hoodie, acting a bit like Basil Fawlty, he definitely stands out."

Wilson was highly amused by Daisy's observation, but it was true, Hoover was there, mimicking one of a pair of stumbling athletes as he practised alone for a three-legged race.

"Daisy, that is so cool — let me try it again."

Before Daisy had chance to consider the ramifications of pulling three people into the same dream, Wilson had an image of Teapot in his head. Long hair, medium height, good-looking, white t-shirt, denim jeans, white trainers. He concentrated, then opened his eyes. Teaps was standing directly in front of them both, five metres away, lifting a beanbag from the ground.

"Who's the new addition? That guy who's just turned up?"

"Another best mate," said Wilson. "We call him Teaps."

"Ah, so that's Teapot, the friend you told me about in Starbucks. You're right, he is good-looking."

"Mmmphhh" scowled Wilson, playfully pinching Daisy's leg as he rose to his feet.

"Where're you going?" Daisy grabbed his arm.

"I just want to say hello."

Wilson slipped out of Daisy's grasp and walked over to Teaps.

"Hey Teaps, welcome to The Market Square. Everything okay?"

Daisy was now by Wilson's side.

"Wilson, I'm not sure this is such a good idea. I never speak to the people I pull in."

Teapot appraised Wilson as though they'd just bumped into each other in a supermarket.

"Hey Wilson, fancy meeting you here."

"Teaps. Dude. Welcome to my dream." Wilson stepped forward to pat him on the shoulder.

Daisy cried out "No Wilson, I don't think you should touch..."

She stopped, open-mouthed, as the physical effects of what appeared to be an electric charge took hold of Wilson's body. His arm shook and every hair on his head momentarily stood on end, as though brushed with static.

All activity in The Market Square came to an instant standstill. A female athlete, in full stride, with both feet inches above the ground, was suspended in mid air — freeze framed in action. The vibrant hues of the square, the emerald green grass, the vivid lycra outfits were now masked behind a yellow film. It was as though Daisy and Wilson were viewing The Market Square through the coloured cellophane of a toffee wrapper. Roundels of red, purple and green cellophane then flared across the yellow film, like droplets of coloured oil landing on water. Then the translucent roundels started to float free, growing bigger, becoming more distinct, three dimensional, fully rounded orbs, like giant baubles from a Christmas tree. And clearly visible on the convex surface of each bauble a picture was reflected, a moving image, like a home video. A red bauble played a clip of Teaps running across a school playground. As it floated past Wilson's right shoulder, the bauble grew larger, became transparent and then popped, like a soap bubble. A green bauble advanced, depicting Teapot stacking supermarket shelves. That too popped liked a soap bubble as it drifted past Wilson's head. More flying baubles materialised, each growing in size as they hovered towards Wilson and Daisy and all portrayed different scenes from Teapot's life: Teapot at different ages, swimming, running, singing; now as a toddler playing Lego with his dad, and there, right there, as a baby, in the arms, of his... mum!

Daisy had seen enough. "No, you have to stop." She tugged at Wilson's arm and pulled his hand free from Teapot's shoulder.

The baubles scattered and dissolved as power returned to The Market Square and the sports day came back to life in full colour.

Wilson was confused and dazed as Daisy led him back to the bench. He wasn't in any pain, but his head felt strange, like pins and needles were rippling over the surface of his brain.

"Wilson, I've never touched or spoken to anyone I pulled in. What happened just then?"

"We saw his past Daisy. All the scenes from Teaps's life. Did you see them?"

"Yeah, I saw it all. But I don't think you should have touched him."

"I saw Vanessa, his mum, with Teaps when he was just a baby. It was... she was so real. How did that happen, just from touching him?"

"I can't tell you, I've no idea. But it's a dream Wilson, just a dream."

Daisy started to yawn. A long, deep yawn.

"I think I'm leaving Wilson; I'm feeling tired. I'm going back to bed. Text me tomorrow when you're up. Don't forget."

Then Daisy faded away into her hologram shadow and in seconds she was gone.

Wilson stood up, stretched out his arm and rotated his shoulder. There didn't seem to be any physical damage. The hand he'd placed on Teaps's shoulder wasn't injured and there were no red marks. He turned full circle, but Teapot and Hoover and the hockey teacher were nowhere to be seen.

Wilson sat back on the bench and for some reason the words of Mrs Hope, his old art teacher, came into his head:

"Before class next week, please conduct some home study on the style of the Post Impressionists."

He recalled those nights he'd entered the craft room at L'École for painting lessons. Could one of those teachers have been Van Gogh himself. Had he pulled Van Gogh into his dream in the same way he'd made Hoover and Teaps appear? Winston Churchill too?

As Mickey's gloved hand pointed to 5.30 a.m. Wilson began to feel tired. His image dissipated into a pixellated hologram, a translucent, grainy shadow of his former self and he was no longer dreaming in The Market Square.

Two familiar characters had been watching the sports day and were thoroughly enjoying the comedy antics, until the dream crashers arrived that is. A few seconds after Daisy and Wilson departed, a short conversation began.

"I think we have a problem." Said Big Mac.

"Indeed we do." Said Short Cake.

"Shall we?"

"We shall!" Short Cake confirmed.

Then the Custodians of The Gateway strode across The Hall of Extinguished Spirits to the door marked 'Exit to Eternity' and hurried through to consult with The Powers That Be.

Chapter 29

The big match

Saturday October 28th 2017

First thing next morning, Wilson sent Daisy a text.

'Need to talk about last night – don't understand what happened. I can come to Macclesfield later. How about pizza or KFC – you choose – 7.30 p.m.?'

He was in the kitchen eating toast when his mum entered.

"Morning Wilson. Did you sleep well?"

"Morning Mum. Yeah, I'm good. There's tea in the pot."

Gloria poured herself a mug and sat at the table stirring in sugar.

"So what's your plan for the day? Your dad was up at the crack of dawn to go fishing. Said he was off to bag a salmon."

"Yeah, heard that one before, yet to see the evidence. I'm gonna have a lazy morning, tidy my room, football this afternoon and then I was thinking of going to see Daisy. You know, the girl I told you about last night."

"The girl you met yesterday from Macclesfield. Yes, I remember; I do listen to you occasionally."

"I invited her for a pizza or a KFC."

"Wilson, you didn't suggest fried chicken! It's not exactly the place to sweep a girl off her feet. Pizza sounds much better. There's a really nice place on the road that runs past the train station in Macclesfield. Think it's called Fabio's. It's one of those proper Italian places, with all the recipes handed down through the family and a real oven where you can watch pizzas being baked. We went there last year for the shop's Christmas party. Think I ordered..."

"Mum, I got it. Fabio's. Near the train station. Daisy's not even said if she can make it yet. Just an idea for now."

"Have you got money?"

"Mum! There's no guarantee I'm going yet. And yes, I've got money. A meatpie transfer arrived yesterday, so I should be able to do some sweeping off the feet. I bet she prefers a KFC though."

"Well, if your night's a success, why don't you invite her round for lunch tomorrow? I'd love to meet Daisy. It's the first time in ages you've spoken more than a few syllables about a girl."

"Yeah, she's different Mum, definitely different. Let's see how tonight goes though."

Wilson downed the last of his tea and went upstairs to tidy his room. He'd just deposited a bin liner full of crisp packets, empty cans and scooter magazines in the bin at the side of the house when Daisy texted back.

'Hey W. Yep, made it back to bed. Bit tired now though. Just finished playing hockey. Mum wants to go to the Trafford Centre. But yes — pizza tonight. Where? Fabio's? Fab place. KFC — no chance. 7.30 p.m. Fabio's. Opposite the train station.' The message was signed of with a thumbs up emoji.

'Okay — see you there.' Two thumbs up.

"Was that Daisy?" Gloria had been watching Wilson from the kitchen window.

"Mum, it's like living with Agatha Christie. Yes, that was Daisy and yeah, you're right, absolutely no fried chicken. She recommends Fabio's."

"Ha ha — female intuition you see. I'm liking that girl more by the minute. In fact, do invite her round for lunch tomorrow. I think we'll have a lot in common. Could even teach her some of my surveillance skills to keep an eye on you."

"Alright Mum, let's see how it goes tonight."

Wilson put his phone in his pocket and went back to his room. There was an item on the agenda before the Stockport Grammar match.

He needed to go back to the early days of the internet and look for something that happened in 1999. He wasn't sure if Google even existed then.

'Vanessa Clarke. Missing person.'

Wilson clicked 'Search'.

He needn't have worried, the story of Teapot's mum was online for all to see, archived on a number of national newspaper websites.

The Times and *Daily Telegraph* reported the story objectively.

'**North West woman disappears after a meeting in Mayfair**' read the headline from *The Times*.

'**Mystery prevails after businesswoman disappears in London**' from the *Daily Telegraph.*

Wilson read both articles and the story was just as Teaps had outlined:

Vanessa Clarke travels to London on the first train from Stockport. Tells her husband she'll be back on the 3.30 p.m. from Euston. She has a meeting room booked at The May Fair Hotel and spends the morning in the hotel preparing. At 11.30 a.m. the prospective clients arrive. She wins a big recruitment contract worth over £140,000 a year and celebrates with champagne and sandwiches. At 2.30 p.m. she leaves to catch the return train – and is never seen again.

The Times carried a grainy picture of Teaps's parents with Teaps as a baby and a picture of his mum as a carefree student with long blonde hair.

He then read other articles from the tabloid newspapers, all of which featured the same poor-quality images and said pretty much the same thing, but with more sensational headlines.

From the *Daily Mirror*: '**Stockport businesswoman accused of IBM bribery scam**'.

From *The Sun*: '**Blonde bombshell bribes client for £140,000 pay day**'.

One of the articles printed by the *Daily Mail*, referred to 'a police line of enquiry that had not ruled out a change of identity and a false passport'. Another, from the *News of the World,* referred to '£2,000 taken from a cashpoint in Dover by someone fitting Vanessa Clarke's description'.

The Dover cashpoint and the false passport angle was of significance to the police who, according to the *Daily Mirror,* 'were working closely with the Gendarmerie in northern France'. After a week or so of declining media coverage though, the investigation appears to reach a cul-de-sac and the story withers on the vine.

It's all exactly as Teaps explained it. It really is a complete mystery.

Wilson recalled the night of The Gateway dream.

Big Mac had said there was no bangle for Vanessa Clarke in The Hall of Extinguished Spirits and that nobody by that name had gone through the door to the spirit world.

Wilson continued adding links to his chain of thought.

So if Big Mac was telling the truth and there's no bangle for Vanessa Clarke... then is it possible she really could be alive? And Teaps still has a mum somewhere? I brought Teaps to The Market Square and witnessed episodes from his past life, so maybe I could also bring Teaps's mum to The Market Square and do the same thing. If she is still alive and I can see episodes from her past life, then maybe I can discover what happened to her!

Wilson knew there was no logic to the chain, but it did seem to be linked together with a degree of sound reasoning, given the revelations of the night before. He closed his laptop and grabbed his kit bag.

It was a bright, mild, autumn afternoon and perfect for football as Wilson arrived at college for the local derby with Stockport Grammar. He caught up with Teaps and Hoover and another team-mate as they walked across the car park towards the changing room.

"Alright Wilson, you up for it?" Tom Kelly played in the left back position. Wilson fell into step.

"Yeah, I'm good. A bit knackered. Couldn't get to sleep last night, and when I did, had this mad dream about a school sports day."

"Oh yeah, did you win anything?" Hoover asked.

"No, it was really odd. There was an egg and spoon race and a wheelbarrow race, like from infant school, except it wasn't kids in the races — it was all these top athletes."

Hoover laughed at the picture forming in his head.

"And the winners were standing on a podium and being given paper rosettes and this sprinter, called Roger, who looked like Usain Bolt started crying cos his mum told him off."

"Wilson, you're losing it mate," said Teaps.

"Yeah, you're probably right. Funnily enough Teaps, you were also in the dream, with Hoover. Don't you remember it? You were picking up beanbags."

Now they were all laughing at the idea.

"And what was Hoover doing?"

"Oh, I don't remember now. He was just there somewhere, out on the periphery, not doing anything in particular."

"Sounds exactly like Hoover."

Hoover aimed a kick at Tom, who kicked back.

"No Kelly, it sounds like your game plan for this afternoon; out on the periphery, not doing anything in particular."

Then Tom started chasing Hoover round the car park, trying to get another kick in, while Hoover pretended to be carrying an egg on an imaginary spoon.

Wilson seized his chance.

"Yep, that was a real crazy dream last night Teaps, because it's kind of like... weird when you see someone, like your best mate, in your dream and you talk to them, like last night. You know what I mean?"

Wilson studied Teaps to see if his friend recognised the underlying question, which was: *do you remember anything about being with me in a dream last night – the sports day, my hand on your shoulder, strange visions etcetera?*

But Wilson's subterfuge wasn't necessary.

"No, I didn't dream about anything last night. In fact, don't think I ever dream of anything. Well, other than of torturing Blamire – now that would be my kind of dream."

Wilson was relieved. It made things a lot less complicated.

"Think we have a chance this afternoon?"

"Yeah, we beat them last year, three-nil I think," said Wilson, happy to change the subject, "and it's gonna be another clean sheet today. Come on mate, changing room's open. Let's get ready and warmed up. We need to be focused."

Five minutes into the match, Wilson noticed something odd. Standing amongst the usual bunch of hardy perennial parents who supported the Second XI, rain or shine, was a face he'd never seen in the crowd before – his dad!

What's he doing here? Mum said he'd gone fishing!

But there was Alex Armitage, intently watching the game, with his hands tucked in the pockets of his fishing jacket. When play was safely at the other end of the pitch, Wilson took a sideways glance.

It's definitely him. Still got his wading jacket on. And wellies!

Moments later:

Now he's talking to Toby Renshaw's dad!

Then, after a fairly decent save that brought applause from the home fans:

He's just given me a thumbs-up.

Wilson didn't know what to make of it. He could count on the fingers of his muddy glove the number of times his dad had watched a match.

Something's up, was the only conclusion he could draw.

Wilson failed to save a penalty with ten minutes to go but when the final whistle blew, Stockport College 2nd XI deserved their two-one victory against the local rivals.

There had been five soccer matches that afternoon and although the area around the entrance to the changing rooms was congested with parents and players, Wilson couldn't avoid noticing his father beckoning him over for a word.

"Hey, Wilson, what a match. That was bloody great. Shame about the penalty."

"Yeah, he sent me the wrong way. But we won, that's the main thing."

"I really enjoyed it. Might apply for a season ticket."

The bonhomie seemed false to Wilson.

"Well there's no waiting list Dad. Anyway, thought you'd gone fishing. Off to catch a salmon."

"Yeah I've been, but the river was up, so I decided to call it a day and come and watch the match." Alex paused for a moment. "Plus, I wanted to have a word. It's something I don't want your mum to be involved in. Meet you in the canteen when you're changed? It'll only take five minutes. What do you want, coffee or tea?"

"Err, tea Dad, two sugars. See you in there. What do you want to talk about, the one that got away? Cos that'll take more than five minutes."

"No, it's nothing to do with fishing son." Alex's mind was elsewhere.

Wilson was towelling his hair dry when Hoover, being Hoover, shared his thoughts with half of the changing room.

"Wilson, was that your dad watching us before? I've never seen him here, ever."

"Yeah, he was supposed to be fishing. But now he wants a quiet chat in the canteen."

"Bet he wants a divorce from Gloria." Hoover was rummaging in his bag for deodorant, oblivious to the hand grenade he'd just lobbed on the floor.

Teaps was so startled he half thought he was missing the joke.

"Bloody hell Hoover, that's a bit spicy. Where did that come from?"

Hoover then tried to put the pin back in.

"Well, you know Wilson, your dad's away a lot. Just sayin', that's all. That'll be why he wants to speak to you away from your mum. It happens. My dad was a right old..."

"Hoover, it's alright mate. I get your point. I'll find out in a minute, won't I, when I speak to him?"

Wilson took his time gathering his belongings, his mind was elsewhere and clearly he'd grabbed the wrong end of the stick. The very idea that his dad wanted to talk about divorce hadn't entered his head until Hoover had suggested it. Wilson had been anticipating an uncomfortable chat about the birds and the bees, probably at the behest of his mum. He'd told her about Daisy and how she was special, so his mum now wanted Alex to emphasise the need to wear a condom and all that nonsense. Thinking about it, Hoover's theory was far more likely.

The noisy canteen was packed with lads huddled together drinking soup and eating pies and groups of parents sharing news over tea and coffee. Wilson quickly spotted his father sitting alone at a table for two. He dropped his kit bag and crash helmet on an empty chair and sat down opposite.

"Cheers," he said, sipping the sweet tea, "just the job. Needed that sugar rush."

Wilson studied his father's face. His cheeks had lost that fresh air glow, they looked washed out, his skin blanched and his eyes had acquired a dull, matt quality.

"So what's on your mind Dad?"

Alex placed his drink on the table and quickly looked round the canteen. Wilson sensed his father was nervous and didn't want to be overheard.

"I might be about to make a terrible mistake here son, so forgive my reluctance to get to the point. I'm trying to convince myself I need to do this before I do it."

Alex paused.

Wilson waited for the inevitable. His knees were beginning to shake beneath the table. His mouth and lips dry, despite the tea.

"I'm going to say something to you in a moment son, just a couple of words. If they mean nothing to you, absolutely nothing, then I want this conversation to end, right here, never to be discussed. Just forget it ever happened. Okay?"

"Okay Dad, I can..."

"But," continued Alex forcefully, "just bear with me. If what I'm about to say does mean something, then tell me with a simple yes or no. No need to think about it. The question is easy and you'll know if the answer is a yes or a no."

Things were moving too quickly for Wilson to work out how to respond. It was obvious the question related to where Wilson would

162

live: yes to live with Dad, or no, because he preferred his mum. But what about his sisters?

"Dunno Dad. I'd have to think about it. It's not as clear-cut as a yes or no. You can't just spring this on me right now, here at college, away from Mum and Kate and Megan. We have to discuss this together, as a family. Does the other woman you've met live in London?"

Alex's jaw dropped.

"What are you blabbering on about Wilson? What other woman in London?"

"The one you're divorcing Mum for" replied Wilson.

Alex's face was a picture. Like the picture of a respectable middle-aged man being confronted with the details of his secret life as a male stripper. Then he roared with laughter, so loudly in fact, that virtually every other conversation in the canteen abruptly stopped and all the students and parents turned to Wilson and his dad. Alex sheepishly waved at everyone and then turned back to Wilson and whispered:

"I'm not getting divorced Wilson, you silly bugger. Why would you think that? I mean, who told you that?"

"You did Dad. The secrecy of this little chat here in the canteen, away from Mum; that you're about to make a terrible mistake; that I have to choose yes to live with you or no to live with Mum."

Alex kind of laughed. But it wasn't a real laugh, because this laugh also involved him covering his face with both hands before massaging his temples and breathing deeply down his nose. He brought his face close to Wilson's.

"No son, this is not a conversation about a divorce. It's even more of a game changer. The answer is a simple yes or a simple no, and the question is: do you visit The Market Square?"

"Yes," said Wilson, without having to think.

Alex Armitage sat back in his chair, put his hands behind his head and looked up to the canteen ceiling. Wilson looked down to the canteen floor and gripped the sides of his chair to steady the tremor in his hands.

Though it was only a few seconds, it seemed an eternity had passed before Alex turned his attention back to Wilson and said:

"Thanks son. Thanks."

Initially, Wilson felt as though he'd been accused of a shocking crime. He was embarrassed by what he'd just confessed.

"How did you know that, that I've been there Dad?"

But then Wilson saw the flip side and a weight lifted slightly from his shoulders.

"More to the point Dad, how do *you* know about The Market Square?"

"It's a place in a dream Wilson, a place you only visit at night. Somewhere I suspect you've been exploring for a long time – I've had my suspicions over the years. I think you're old enough for us to have this conversation now, but away from your mum – she knows nothing about this. Don't worry, we're talking about the same place."

"But Dad, this is incredible? Do you know how it works, do you ever go there, do you...?"

"Shhh, keep your voice down." Alex checked over his shoulder again. "Wilson, we're not discussing a visit to Legoland. We're talking about a place that if people knew existed, what happens there, would send most of them crazy. Or get you expelled and me locked up."

"Jesus Dad, you knew all along. But why tell me now? Why didn't you say something when I was younger?"

"Yes, I could have done that, but I couldn't see any problems with your behaviour, or in your life. I suspected you visited The Market Square, I kept all the mental notes, but there didn't seem to be a need to let the cat out of the bag before now."

"Dad, it's more than letting a cat out of a bag don't you think?"

"What I'm trying to say is that..."

Alex paused for a moment.

"I discovered The Market Square when I was about fifteen. Those night classes were the reason I was able to get into Cambridge University in the first place. And in my final year I met a few other people who'd also been there. Like this Indian guy, Pavrel. We went to an air show for vintage planes one afternoon and the big attraction was this famous old biplane but they couldn't get the engine started. All these anorak types were under the bonnet and Pavrel went over, took a look and told them what they were doing wrong. They thought he was some kind of young prodigy. It was only when he said he was at Cambridge University studying aero-engineering they decided he was just some brainy student. But he was actually studying Ancient Greek. Anyway, we were at a party later that night and after a few beers the truth about our shared secret came out."

Wilson knew his face carried a look of utter amazement but there was nothing he could do to change it.

"But like I said Dad, you could have told me this when you were certain I visited The Market Square."

"Possibly. But I stopped going after my years at Cambridge and I'm hoping you will. I got the gist of what it was: a funnel for dream energy."

Wilson couldn't believe his ears.

"Look Wilson, we don't fully understand the workings of the brain. We know the areas for speech and hearing and so on, but it could be that some unmapped areas are also involved in processing unknown forms of energy. Dreams, for example. I accept that The Market Square exists, but what is its purpose, its potential. I prefer to measure temperature with instruments and science rather than just diving into a swimming pool and saying, 'Yeah, it's bloody hot'."

Wilson ran a hand through his hair, confused by what he was hearing.

"Wilson, you've got to stop going there. That's what I came to tell you. The Market Square is more than just an inexplicable phenomenon and until we understand more – its power, how the place can exist, its purpose, the potential dangers – you have to block it out of your life. Stop looking for explanations that will only drag you further in. Morphic Fields, numerology – stop probing into all that stuff."

"But I met a girl there Dad."

"In The Market Square? And?"

"And I'm meeting her for a pizza in about an hour, in Macclesfield."

"You did what? You met a girl in a dream, in The Market Square and now you're meeting for pizza!"

"Yeah. It's the girl I told you about last night. She's called Daisy and she lives in Macclesfield."

Wilson's dad wasn't sure he'd heard correctly.

"You met a real girl in a dream, in The Market Square and then you met in real life, yesterday?"

"Yeah Dad, yeah, exactly that."

"Christ," said Alex shaking his head, "I need to think that through."

"But what does it mean? How is it possible?"

"I've no idea Wilson. I know that many number elevens can access dream energy but I thought that was just a passive acquisition process, I don't think, didn't think, what you've just told me was possible."

"Well it is Dad, because it happened."

Alex stood up.

"I honestly don't understand what you've done. Let me think and we'll speak again. Nothing in front of your mum though. Love you."

"You too Dad."

Alex stood up, pushed his chair beneath the table and walked out of the canteen, acknowledging familiar faces en- route to his car. Wilson ordered another tea and sat contemplating the totally unexpected conversation he'd just had with his dad. In twenty four hours his life had completely changed and it was definitely fate, not free will, that was dealing his cards.

It was dark as Wilson flicked down the visor on his helmet, kick-started the Vespa and set off to meet Daisy for pizza.

Chapter 30

The Eager Beavers

Saturday October 28th 2017

Wilson found Fabio's without too much difficulty. Macclesfield train station was well signposted and the restaurant frontage glowed like a homing beacon in the dark. The interior of Fabio's was candle-lit and quiet, Daisy was waiting at a table for two in a corner towards the back.

She was wearing a burgundy, woollen fitted dress in a sleeveless style that revealed her lovely, slender arms to perfection. The polo neck accentuated her pretty face and plum-shade lipstick. Her hair was held in a bun by long, ornately carved hairpins jutting out at all angles. She looked stunning, like a movie star.

"Wow" said Wilson, by way of a compliment. He was over-awed and over-nervous and never once took his eyes off Daisy.

"I like those chopsticks in you hair."

Daisy gazed up at Wilson, then fell into hysterics. She couldn't release any laughter though, because a mouthful of red wine was blocking the way. So she clamped her lips shut, covered her mouth with a napkin, made some frantic, whimpering sounds and flapped her free hand up and down as though it were sign language for laughing one's head off.

Wilson slipped back into his coat and using his thumb and the questioning look on his face mouthed "Should I go out and come back in again?" Which caused Daisy to jump from her chair, shove Wilson to one side and leg it to the ladies'.

It took Daisy a few minutes to regain her composure and apply fresh lipstick and mascara. She was still giggling as she walked back to the table, now looking like an off-duty princess.

"How's a poor girl ever going to cope with you?" Daisy asked, slipping back into her seat. Wilson became conscious of the fact he was still in the same clothes he'd worn to the match. He hadn't 'upped his game' by at least wearing a fresh shirt.

"Sorry Daisy, didn't think to put smarter stuff in my bag. You look like a fashion model and I..."

"Wouldn't want you any other way. You look great. Perfectly normal. But with a few cute differences."

So Wilson relaxed, ordered drinks and placed a hand on Daisy's just to reassure himself that she was still full-fat, flesh and blood.

"What a day! In the space of twenty-four hours I meet you in Starbucks, reverse back into a dream, meet you again, bring Hoover and Teaps into the same dream, then take a peek at his past life. I see his mum. Whom I've never seen before. Then my dad tells me he's a fully fledged number eleven and the cherry on top, we beat Stockport Grammar two-one."

"No girl will ever accuse you of boring table talk Wilson."

"I mean, I should be in shock after all that. But the cherry on top of the other cherry is my dad also telling me he knows about The Market Square! I've been looking over my shoulder to see what's coming next."

"What?" Daisy exclaimed. "Your dad knows about The Market Square?" She cast an anxious glance round the restaurant then lowered her voice and leant low over the table, closer to Wilson.

"Your dad's been to The Market Square?" She almost hissed the words in disbelief. Wilson was about to reply when a party of middle-aged women, all wearing t-shirts with the words 'The Eager Beavers' emblazoned on the front, lurched noisily into Fabio's to celebrate a hen night. The increase in background noise meant Wilson no longer had to concern himself with being overheard.

"Yeah, he came to watch the match, which is strange in itself. But then in the canteen, after a bit of a misunderstanding, he told me he knew about The Market Square. He said he stopped visiting after a while and I should do the same."

"Wow, what a revelation. That must have come as a shock."

"Just a bit. I think something I said to him last night over a glass of wine may have acted as a catalyst."

"Or maybe, it could be an hereditary thing Wilson. I mean, you and your dad. Me and my grandma. Just imagine if we all met in The Market Square..."

She snapped a breadstick for the dramatic sound effect.

"God, can you imagine? My brain hurts enough as it is, trying to figure out what's going on. For all these years I've been completely alone with this weird secret and now I find out there's a big gang of us, including my bloody dad. And I'm sure numerology is involved, but no idea how. What's your birth date again?"

"Eighth of November nineteen-ninety-nine. I'm eighteen in just over a week. A bit younger than you. I like roses. Favourite colour blue."

Wilson took out his phone, talked Daisy through the calculation then waved the result as though it was a vital piece of evidence.

"See, look, you're an eleven."

"Actually, I'm an eight. But after pizza, I, err..."

"Daisy, this is serious. Where were you born?"

"Stockport Infirmary."

"Which ward?"

"Not a clue. Maternity ward I guess?"

"Ward 3B I bet."

"Rings a bell, but not for me, for Grandma. My uncle John who works for the NHS is trying to get her transferred to 3B. She's in a hospice in Bournemouth so it's better if she's closer to us, and my uncle says Ward 3B has the best record in caring for terminally ill, old people."

Two pizzas and a salad arrived and they ate in silence for a few minutes, chewing things over.

"You know," said Daisy, "if Gran has sat by that Clock Tower and also lived to her age, well, I don't think The Market Square can be all that dangerous. Can it? And what's the big thing about being an eleven? In fact, what is an eleven?"

Daisy helped herself to a piece of pepperoni from Wilson's pizza.

"To be honest, I've no idea, but I've read about a few things that sound really relevant."

Wilson then outlined the concept of Morphic Fields as a Wi-Fi of nature and his idea of the equivalent for dreams and how the conservation of energy could make this possible.

"But this is also related to time, because in just a few days, even hours, we know how to do stuff, like fly a helicopter."

"Or drive monster trucks. Archery to Olympic standard?"

"Monster trucks Daisy. Really?"

"Yeah, I can even play jazz flute."

Wilson wasn't at all surprised.

"But the number eleven Wilson? How and where does that fit in?"

Daisy was munching on a strip of raw carrot dipped in garlic mayonnaise.

"I don't really know, I just stumbled upon it. I had this dream on the night of my birthday, it felt different, in a place called The Gateway. This enormous building where these two odd characters live, or work. Anyway,because the dream was so intense, I checked the significance of my date of birth and came across numerology, which has connections with energy fields and spirituality. Most important was the Life Path number, and depending on when you were born, it can be super-powerful. How was it described?..."

Wilson stopped and searched for the words.

"That's it. People with the number eleven have the potential to be a source of inspiration and illumination for others — and numerology also has links to the paranormal."

"Wow. So you think that, because the number eleven is a big deal in the numerology world. Which is somehow connected with energy and the paranormal. And because it seems this Life Path number eleven also connects you and me and your dad, then that means... what, Wilson?"

"I don't know! I just think they're all connected somehow. I think all these puzzle pieces will eventually make a full picture. I just don't know how to pull it all together, to join the dots."

Half an hour later the waiter came over to ask about dessert or coffee.

"I'm too full," said Daisy, "but I'd love a caffè latte."

"Just an espresso for me" said Wilson.

Then he remembered his gift.

"Oh I forgot. I bought you a present Daisy."

"Oh great. I love presents" she said, scrunching up her nose and clapping her hands like an infant. "What is it, what is it?"

Daisy's exclamation caught the attention of a very tipsy Eager Beaver who turned on her chair and declared:

"Oh look Chanelle, how romantic. Me and Pete were like that once."

With all eyes now turned in his direction, Wilson made a fuss of searching for something in his jacket pockets.

"He's a bit young to be popping the question if you ask me" said Chanelle. "He only looks about seventeen."

"Daisy, when I said a present, I don't want you to think..."

"Get on with it love, or she'll be off with your mate" boomed Chanelle, thereby inviting the attention of the diners on surrounding tables.

Daisy was enjoying Wilson's blushes and slight discomfort.

"Look, it's no big deal Daisy. Just my way of showing" – he dropped his voice to a whisper – "my appreciation for being here, you know, in my life."

"Bloody hell, we're all falling asleep, get on with it lad."

Wilson coughed nervously, reached for Daisy's hand and spoke in a loud, clear voice:

"Okay, I know it's not much, but it's the best I can do. Daisy, I want to ask if you'll share the rest of..." He glanced at the now silent, wide-eyed, open-mouthed Beavers. "...if you'll share the rest of this bag of wine gums with me?"

The words "They're my favourite" and "I wouldn't share a packet with anyone else" were lost in the face of Daisy's laughter and the groans and insults from the Beavers – plus the flying napkin that accompanied them – all aimed at Wilson.

"This means something Daisy. So don't laugh! This is important, a milestone. I know for you that bag contains only wine gums, but to me, they're like tiny, moulded pieces of jelly friendship."

"Oh Wilson, they're beautiful. But wait a minute, aren't these...?"

"Yeah, yes, they are" said Wilson, following where Daisy was heading with the lines to the Britney Spears song.

"But I thought the old lady dropped them in the skip when they ran out of date?"

"Well baby, I went down and got them for you."

"Awww Wilson, you shouldn't have."

Daisy then finished the rest

"Oops, I did it again..."

The Eager Beavers, recognising the chorus and being in a giddy mood, all joined in and then sang it for a second time.

Five minutes later, when the mood had calmed down, Wilson was sipping his coffee as Daisy checked her watch.

"Mum'll be here soon and there's something I want to talk to you about Wilson. Something important. I know you said your dad stopped going to The Market Square and thinks you should do the same. I half agree with him. We were lucky enough to meet there and if I never go back, I'm more than happy. Maybe we *should* close a door and put all this craziness behind us – have a normal future and lead ordinary lives. But before we do, I was thinking, what if we exploit it, but in a good way, one more time?"

Wilson sensed Daisy wasn't speaking totally unrehearsed as she continued.

"There was a time, a few years ago, when I used to do loads of bad things in The Market Square. I'd think about people I didn't like at school, girls who were bullying me – and I'd imagine them in The Market Square and inflict all sorts of punishments on them to get my own back. That's probably how I learnt to bring people, or pull people, into my dreams. Then other nights, I'd be a total hell-raiser. I'd jump off the Clock Tower and other crazy stunts like that, because I knew nothing bad would happen. Though I did wake up one morning with a sprained ankle.

"Anyway, forget all that; it's in the past. What I'm trying to say Wilson, is that now we've met and before The Market Square closes or ends for us, shouldn't we use it to do something good? What happened with your friend the other night, when we saw the baubles with clips of his life – couldn't we try to do that kind of thing again? But this time try to use the flashes of the past in a good way? Expose people traffickers for example, drug dealers, criminals, dodgy politicians. See the secrets in their lives. Use what we discover in The Market Square to expose crime or help people? I don't know what exactly. I feel we have this amazing gift and it can't only be for amusement."

Daisy paused and held one of Wilson's hands with both of hers.

"Wilson, I don't care about Morphic Fields and magic numbers and explanations for what we do. I think it would be good to try to forget about The Market Square. But before we stop, let's try to use it to do something good. Just one memorable thing."

She glanced at her watch again.

"Mum'll be outside; I have to go. I've had a lovely time. But think about what I've said Wilson, please. I don't want to go to The Market Square tonight. I'll try not to anyway. So don't wait up for me."

"Okay, no problem. When shall we?... Oh, Daisy, I forgot. Mum's invited you round for lunch tomorrow. She wants to meet you."

"Wow! Yeah! I'd love to. Text me in the morning with the address and I'll see if I can get a lift over."

Daisy said goodnight to the waiter, shared a joke with the Eager Beavers, gave Chanelle a hug and left the restaurant.

173

file 11

Chapter 31

The Gateway II

Saturday October 28th 2017

It was almost 11.00 p.m. when Wilson arrived home. Gloria was in bed but a bead of light from the box-room-cum-office told Wilson his father was working.

"'Night Dad," he called tentatively.

Wilson waited on the landing but there was no answer.

Lying in bed, he reflected on the previous twenty four hours and the revelatory events that had dispersed self-doubt in every direction. During the course of one day, he'd gone from the brink of neurotic disorder to discovering an incredible, like-minded partner, a father who shared his secret plus the seeds of an explanation for their unique abilities. For the first time, Wilson was looking forward to sleeping without any apprehension or concern for what new revelation the next morning would bring. From now on, The Market Square could be acknowledged completely, unquestioningly and accepted for the phenomenon it was because Wilson was no longer alone. As he began to drift off, something Daisy had said earlier played on his mind like the words on a scratched record: "try to do something good... help people if we can."

Two hours later, Wilson was standing in a field of bright-red poppies. The dream was dressed in the mantle of a hot summer's day and the hazy outline of The Gateway shimmered on the horizon. After taking no more than five or six paces, Wilson stood facing its colossal, imposing facade. He paused for a moment to once again contemplate the ancient battle scene carved in the pediment of the portico set high above his head. He climbed the broad, stone steps and stood in the shadow of the atrium. The nondescript entrance doors still resembled emergency exits. Wilson pushed the 'Visitors Only' door and slipped inside.

Nothing appeared to have changed in The Hall of Extinguished Spirits. The mountains of gleaming bangles stretched away, seemingly for centuries and once again, the cavernous interior took Wilson's breath away. The hillock of bangles beneath the 2017 banner had grown; more had been added since his last visit.

A high pitched voice carried through the hall.

"Well, well. If it isn't our good friend Mr Armitage, dropping by to say hello." It was Big Mac. "We were waiting for you."

"You've been summonsed" said Short Cake.

The two custodians revealed themselves to Wilson's left. They were standing by the mound of bangles designated as 2015, dressed exactly as he remembered from their polished black shoes to their shiny, bald heads. On this second meeting though, their facial features seemed more sternly set, a degree colder, as though they were distracted or irritated by something.

"We need to have a chinwag. About your mischief."

Wilson was prepared for the verbal joisting.

"Funnily enough" he said, "I was hoping I'd meet you two again. I wanted to say thanks for telling me that whole conservation of energy thing. Saved me a lot of library time."

"Yes! Energy can never be destroyed and all that," said Big Mac, waving a hand dismissively.

"Yup. Thanks for the insight fellas."

"Well, you've been a busy boy Wilson. A very, busy boy." Short Cake's words were delivered in the cool monotone of a headmaster about to get to the point.

Wilson tried to take the chill from the atmosphere.

"You can say that again, what with meeting Daisy and then coming back to The Market Square to meet her again and then the numerology stuff and Dad's confession. All a bit of a whirlwind really."

"Oh, beautifully put Wilson. As though a butterfly had flapped its wings and created a storm and then snow, cold white snow had fallen on the Amazon."

Big Mac dropped the humorous lilt and took three steps towards Wilson.

"But that's not right, is it? The Amazon's a rainforest: the Amazon doesn't want snow. It's unsettling. It disrupts our forward planning. What do we call this unsettling Mr Cake?"

"We call it mischief, Mr Mac."

"Exactly! So much so, we had to visit The Powers That Be. Through the Exit to Eternity. Where we were firmly reprimanded for being negligent!"

"Well, I'm sorry if I... flapped my wings too hard. But to be honest, I don't have a clue what you're wittering on about."

Wilson saw the opportunity for a tactical move. He'd gained an insight the last time he was in The Gateway – about the conservation of energy, so perhaps he could do the same again.

"So what does crashing and straddling mean?"

"Goodness me Wilson, they certainly threw away the mould when they made you."

Big Mac turned to Short Cake who nodded approval to continue.

"Crashing is when you trespass in a particular type of energy field and straddling is when you trespass in two or more – with a foot in both camps, so to speak. We've seen your trace Wilson and you're one of the most accomplished straddlers we've ever seen. That's why you still have your permit to enter The Market Square.

"The Powers That Be find you very entertaining Mr Armitage. And to finally get to the point, we brought you here to warn you that when the roulette wheel stops spinning and the chips are down, the betting will end. And I have no doubt, that end will bring tears."

"After they let you make the last, throw-o'-the-dice," added Short Cake.

Wilson wanted to glean as much as he could from the dynamic duo before he woke up, but while their comments made him sound enigmatic, he was struggling to make sense of their verbal nonsense.

Maybe when I revisit this conversation in the morning, perhaps everything will be clearer.

"What exactly do you mean when you say you've seen my trace?"

Big Mac paused before replying, as though calculating how much of a secret he was prepared to divulge.

"Wilson, all the things you've done, all the places you've been, all the things that have happened in your life, they all leave a trace and we can see them."

"Like watching a home movie of the complete life and works of Wilson Armitage. Farts and all" added Short Cake with a knowing wink.

"What? You mean you can see everything I've ever done. Every conversation. See where I've been, what I've been doing. Everything?"

Wilson was startled by the notion.

"Everything" said Big Mac. "You leave a trace for us to follow. Everybody does. You just need to know where and how to look."

"In which camp to put your foot" confirmed Short Cake.

"I, err, don't understand" said Wilson, blushing at the thought that what he'd just heard could actually be true.

Short Cake looked down at Big Mac and once again gave his consent to continue divulging.

"Okay" said Big Mac. "Take this instant right now, with you standing there, us standing here and nobody moving. Let's call that a single moment. And let's say we seize that moment."

From behind his back, Short Cake produced a Polaroid camera and smartly took a snap of Wilson. He passed the instantly processed, square print to Big Mac.

"That" said Big Mac, passing the image to Wilson, "is your here and now, captured forever. A bundle of light photons, energy, captured in time. So if we take a second photo..."

Short Cake passed Big Mac a second Polaroid snapshot.

"This second image has captured the next moment. The next bundle of energy. And this is the third, this is the fourth, this is the fifth and sixth, seventh, eighth, fiftieth, two thousandth. And if we put them all in a line, we would have this."

Wilson was directed to the floor where thousands upon thousands of Polaroid prints stood on edge, about a centimetre apart, snaking around the piles of bangles – like a queue of thin white dominoes about to fall back and knock each other over.

Wilson bent down to pick one up. It was the same as the first picture Short Cake had taken. He picked up another, then another. They were all the same, apart from miniscule differences. In one picture Wilson's mouth was very slightly open; in the next it was closing; after that it was closed.

"That" said Big Mac, gesturing to the regimented line, "is your trace. The first one always exists and the last one always exists, because each moment is made of energy and energy can never be destroyed, so it is always there. Any moment from time always exists."

Short Cake bent down to pick up one of the snapshots and then threw it in the air.

"That one is out there."

Then he picked up another and threw that one in the air.

"And that one's out there. And that one. And that one."

And in seconds the air was filled with a blizzard of Polaroid pictures.

"An ever-growing album of instant snapshots of your life is out there. There's a trace for everything and for everyone. An energy field of your own personal history."

Big Mac snatched a Polaroid as it flew past his nose then the photos all fluttered to the floor and evaporated as the hall reverted to its solemn, silent self. Big Mac passed the Polaroid to Wilson without looking at it. It portrayed him standing between two jumper-goalposts on the playing field at junior school.

"All your past life is out there Wilson, every second of it, in tiny bundles of time energy that will never be lost" said Big Mac.

"So when we saw you meet Miss Meadowcroft at Starbucks," said Short Cake, "and then watched you conjure Mr Teaps and the traces of his life, well, we were obliged to inform The Powers That Be."

"They don't usually like their butterflies flapping so well" explained

Big Mac "creates too much of a storm. But for some reason they like you Wilson. They're excited to see where you're heading with this. So we brought you here to warn you, in the strongest possible terms, against further mischief, but also, paradoxically, to give you permission to continue."

"Game on" said Short Cake, rubbing his hands with glee.

Big Mac interlocked his fingers and cracked all his knuckles.

"I think that's all the issues resolved" he said, turning to go back to his desk.

"Indeed" said Short Cake. "Come, The Market Square is this way."

They beckoned Wilson to follow and he remembered just how physically persuasive they could be.

"Wait, wait just one second. Sorry."

Wilson wanted to glean more, to stay in the narrative of the dream for just a few seconds longer.

"So what is déjà vu? I mean, how does it work?"

"Well give that man a coconut!" Exclaimed Short Cake. Big Mac nudged him in the ribs.

"That's very good Wilson. Very good. And very easy to explain, because this... this is déjà vu."

For a second time, Wilson's time trace photos assembled on the floor in a long curling column, like the ribs of a paper snake.

"Look at your time trace Wilson," said Big Mac pointing to the Polaroid at the head of the snake. "This snapshot at the very front represents the instant reality of the here and the right now. But see what happens when a wind blows — and by wind, I don't mean a summer's breeze: I mean the wind caused by other energy fields."

"Smoke, as your father describes it" said Short Cake.

"Here's what happens" said Big Mac.

Wilson watched transfixed as an imaginary breeze caught hold of a tight loop of Polaroids lined up a short distance behind the very first one, and in doing so brought photos from the past to a new position, ahead of the front. Like the leading coil of a sidewinder snake slithering forward and for a moment being fractionally in advance of itself.

"So the past is blown in front of the future" said Wilson, amazed by the visual analogy. "We experience the feeling of déjà vu because the instant reality of the here and now is briefly overtaken by the past. So we feel something that has already happened to us. We experience the same thing twice."

"Indeed" said Short Cake, "just for a fleeting second. And only when the wind is blowing in the right direction. That is déjà vu. Question answered. Time for you to go now."

With the same brevity and strength demonstrated on his first visit, Big Mac and Short Cake then transported Wilson, feet dangling, past two executive desks and two angle-poise lamps and out through the exit to The Market Square.

"Do heed our warnings Mr Armitage, our retribution can be swift and brutal."

Wilson sat gathering his thoughts on a bench by the Clock Tower.

Neat explanation for déjà vu.

Looking across the empty market square, fluttering photos still flying around his head, Wilson's thoughts turned to Teaps and the coloured bauble that portrayed a moment in time with his mother.

Can I do it without Daisy here to help?

Wilson closed his eyes and once again set to work building the doppelganger of Teaps: with the same swept-back-hair and ponytail, the dark eyes beneath thick eyebrows, wearing torn jeans and trainers, playing his guitar with The Girl Guides in his garage. When Wilson's mental imaging was complete, he studied the body-double for flaws, like an exhibit in Madame Tussauds, then he opened his eyes.

He'd done it. Teaps was sitting on the bench opposite, playing his guitar.

Wilson half expected an audience to be applauding or a brass band to march past in celebration.

Bloody hell. It really works and I can do it without Daisy.

He walked across to his friend and knelt on one knee.

"Hey Teaps, it's me, Wilson. How's it going?"

He was strumming chords for the song 'Wonderwall'.

"It's good Wilson. It's all cool man."

Wilson sat on the bench to steady himself then reached forward and placed his hand on Teaps's shoulder. A jolt of energy once more surged along his arm as The Market Square paused on freeze-frame behind a yellow cellophane screen. Coloured baubles began to appear, each one reflecting traces of Teaps's life. Wilson focused on a bauble in the middle ground depicting him playing football on the beach with his dad and as it drew within touching distance, Wilson noticed that something peculiar happened. The images on the surrounding baubles and those following, all changed to portray a similar scene, from the same holiday — as though they'd all switched to the same channel. There was Teaps building a sandcastle, flying a kite, Teaps wearing armbands and paddling in the sea. It seemed that by selecting one specific moment in Teaps's life, neighbouring baubles would then be instructed to re-tune to the same time frame.

Wilson scanned each bauble as they glided by.

Teaps at school. *No, too recent.*

Camping two years ago. *Too recent.*

As a Cub Scout. *No.*

Teaps in the arms of his dad. *Yes.*

Wilson stayed with this latter bauble then turned to those on either side, drilling down into a specific period of time.

Teaps in a highchair being fed by his dad.

Having a bath in the kitchen sink.

Crying in his cradle and his mum picking him up.

That's the one. Stay with that.

The baubles were coming thick and fast.

Teaps being bottlefed by his mum.

Being christened with his mum and dad.

Teaps with his mum on a bed.

With his mum, laughing.

In each image, Vanessa was wearing her long blonde hair loose or fixed with clips. Wearing lipstick or no lipstick. Always a pretty, smiling face. But the pictures were fuzzy and indistinct. Wilson was acquiring only the basic outline of Vanessa. Would it be enough?

He lifted his hand from Teaps's shoulder who was oblivious to what had just happened and continued strumming the guitar as The Market Square re-emerged from behind its yellow mask. Wilson closed his eyes and tried to picture Vanessa, but it was difficult; he didn't have a strong image on which to focus and the most memorable, with Vanessa bottlefeeding, wasn't sharp. Mentally retouching made no difference. After seven unsuccessful attempts to bring Vanessa Clarke to The Market Square, Wilson was thoroughly demoralised and Teaps's mum was nowhere to be seen. He sat for a while, listening to his best friend play a medley of Oasis songs until he dissipated into a diminishing shadow and made his way back to bed.

Chapter 32

The wedding photo

Sunday 29th October 2017

Wilson was dragged from deep slumber by a sharp knock on his bedroom door.

"Are you hibernating in there Wilson?"

"Why? What time is it?"

"It's half past ten. I know it's Sunday and you're allowed a lie-in, but I wanted to know if you spoke to Daisy about coming for lunch? If it's not too much trouble, can you tell me in the next half hour? We're having roast lamb."

Wilson reached for his phone on the bedside table: 10.37 a.m. He'd been out for the count and missed three texts and a call from Daisy.

He sat up, rubbed his eyes and opened the text messages.

'Morning Wilson. Am I still invited to meet your folks?' That was at 9.20 a.m.

'Wilson, sorry to trouble you, but an answer anytime soon would be good. My mum said she can give me a lift, but I need to tell her soon.' That was at 9.55 a.m.

'Wilson, you're not really creating a good impression here in the Meadowcroft household – text me – NOW.' That was 10.15 a.m.

"Jesus."

He threw back the duvet, texting at the same time.

"Mum, yeah, she's coming," he yelled down the stairs. "What time's good?"

The simultaneous text read: 'Daisy sorry, yes, – come, 7 midland drive, stockport, sk7 6tf. Blue garage door. Text back.'

"About one o'clock if that's okay, I hope she's not a vegetarian."

"No Mum, she'll be fine. Roast lamb will be good."

Wilson hurriedly dressed, sent another text to confirm the time and popped his head round the kitchen door on his way out.

"Mum, gotta dash out for an hour. Daisy's mum's dropping her off about one-ish. I'll be back, but I need to see Teaps."

"What, right now?"

Gloria was peeling potatoes.

"Yeah, I've gotta see him about something – an English textbook I need. Won't be long."

"Well make sure you're not late love. I've told your dad to be back from fishing early. He says he's really keen to meet Daisy."

"Yeah, I'm sure they'll have loads in common. Mum I have to go."

"But you've had no breakfast Wilson."

"Mum, I'm good. Be back as soon as I can."

Wilson didn't have long to organise his plan. If you could actually call what was racing through his mind a plan. As the door to the garage rolled up, his phone bleeped.

'Don't know what's happening with you. Will be there for 1.00 p.m. Expecting more than a bag of wine gums – sports mixture might do it. Luv D.'

'Great' was all he had time for by way of reply. Five minutes later, the scooter was on full throttle as Wilson headed down the A6 towards Stockport town centre. He braked as the red-brick wall and the cast-iron railings of the hospital grounds came into view. Wilson pulled into a side street, jacked up the scooter and took off his helmet. He then walked back to the A6 and followed it for a further fifty metres until he reached the perimeter of the hospital.

The second Wilson arrived at the wall, his head started to ache. He continued walking, the pain steadily increasing, until he stood beneath the huge window that dominated the front of the original part of the building. A prolonged sensation of déjà vu swept over him, just as it had during that first trip to meet Daisy. The throbbing migraine intensified, his vision became distorted and blurred. Dizzy with pain, Wilson grabbed the railings for support and forced himself to continue peering up at the window. Like trying to spy land from a pitching boat, his eyes were failing to lock on their shifting target. The glass carried a slate grey tint and seemed to swallow light rather than reflect it. The odious feeling of familiarity with something unpleasant, something he couldn't identify made Wilson nauseous. Then two dark shapes, like back-lit shadows in a puppet show or on a Chinese lantern passed across the window. One figure was small and round, the other, tall and thin. Wilson managed a weak smile, his intuition confirmed.

I knew it. I knew that's where they were based.

Wilson's legs finally gave way and he slumped down with his back against the wall. The sickening ache in his head made him retch. A string of spittle stretched down from his mouth and coiled on his crash helmet. Wilson took a huge breath and forced himself to stand upright. He pushed himself away from the railings and staggered back up the pavement towards his scooter. As the headache eased, he turned and gave a beaming smile and a big thumbs-up to the two characters Wilson knew were watching from on high.

Wilson sat recovering on his scooter for a full twenty minutes. He wiped clean his mouth and helmet then turned the scooter away from the hospital and followed the back streets down to Mersey Square and the centre of Stockport. Teaps lived in a flat opposite a pub and Wilson had a good idea of where it was.

As he parked the scooter opposite The Sun and Unicorn, Wilson checked his phone. It was 11.20 a.m. He didn't have long and he wasn't certain he was in the right place. He dialled Teaps's number.

"Hey, it's me, Wilson."

"Hey. How are you pal? All okay?"

"Yeah, I think so. But listen. Sorry for calling you a bit random like, I've got a slight problem."

"Right," said Teaps. "Hit me with it."

"Listen mate, I left my English Lit text book in my locker on Friday and I've gotta answer those three questions on the war poets for Monday morning or I'll get a major bollocking. Wanted to know if I could borrow yours?"

"Yeah, 'course you can. I've just finished with it. The one on Sassoon is a killer, but yeah, the book's here. I'll text the questions to you if you want, or screen grab the page and WhatsApp it."

"I was gonna call round and collect it. I'm in Stockport anyway — just passing your flat in fact, I think."

"You're what?"

"Yeah, had to buy some, er, weedkiller for my dad, from the garden centre. So just on my way back, I'm near where you live, so I could grab the textbook, like now and then scarper. Only take two minutes."

"But Wilson, I, err..."

"I'm already here, outside the pub."

"Sun and Unicorn."

"Yeah, I'm looking at it."

"Wilson, it's really not the ideal time."

Wilson sensed all was not right, but he had a plan to help his best mate and that sometimes required cruel love.

"Teaps, come on, help me out here. Just let me borrow the book. I can't work from WhatsApp; wouldn't be authentic."

Teaps went silent for a moment, then gave up on further protest.

"Okay Wilson. Shabby, dark green door, just opposite the pub. Looks like it's been kicked in a bit. Ring the bell and I'll let you in. But Wilson, Dad's not good right now so it'll have to be quick."

"Okay mate, fully understood. In and out, no worries. Be there in a mo'. In fact, I think I can see the green door."

Even on a Sunday morning at — he checked his watch — 11.25 a.m., Wilson knew he was in a dodgy bit of Stockport. He put the edge of his hand against the pub's window and peered in. The place was busy and the customers weren't sipping coffee.

Wilson crossed the road and pressed the cracked plastic buzzer. After ten seconds, he heard footsteps and an ill-fitting door scraped open.

"Sorry mate, I appreciate your help."

"No worries," said Teaps. He looked stressed and tired.

"Dad's in there, I think" – he motioned to the pub – "topping up last night's bender and my shift starts in an hour. Don't really want you to meet him, so need to be quick. I'll show you what I've written."

Wilson followed him up the bare, wooden steps of a creaking stairway and into a dingy flat.

"Sorry mate, not much to look at, but it's okay for Dad and me."

The lounge-cum-kitchen had a tiny sink with a single tap, a small oven with a two plate hob connected to a Calor Gas bottle and a rickety-looking table teamed with two odd chairs. There was no fridge, a carton of milk stood in water in the sink. The lounge area was furnished with two threadbare armchairs parked in front of a bulky old TV. Wallpaper that had lost its pattern years ago, was peeling from the walls and there were dark patches of damp in the corners of the ceiling. In a corner, a fold-out bed was freshly made and standing to one side was a small desk with a lamp shining on an open textbook.

"We call it the Blamire Hotel."

"Ah, it's not so bad. You've seen my room, it's not much better. And Megan's... well, wipe your feet as you leave."

"Does the job, I guess. We're waiting for a council flat. Told them how unhealthy this place is, but we have to wait. More urgent cases apparently."

Teaps walked over to his desk, switched off the lamp and collected the textbook for Wilson.

"Here you go. The Sassoon question is tough, but the other two, well, call me if you need some inspiration."

Wilson needed more time.

"Can I use the loo? Dying for a pee. Bit difficult to stop once I'm on the scooter."

"Sure. It's not the Savoy, but everything works, just about. It's down there, past Dad's room, at the end."

He nodded towards a passageway that Wilson hadn't noticed.

"Two ticks, as they say."

"Would offer you a brew, but I think the milk's off."

"Nah, I'm good. A quick leak and I'm away."

Wilson took a few steps down the narrow corridor and saw the door to the toilet at the end. Which meant the door on his left, the only other door, led to the bedroom of Teaps's dad. The flimsy door was covered with wood-effect, plastic veneer. It swung open at the slightest touch.

Wilson put his head around the door and peeked inside. The room was neat and tidy. The bed had been made and although the bedspread looked a little frayed, it was clean and the room smelled of air freshener. There was a plush, plum-coloured rug on the floor and a bedside table on which a framed print of Teaps and his parents stood. Loose photos were scattered with a degree of symmetry over the glass surface of a dressing table.

Wilson stepped inside the bedroom and studied the pictures. The images were the same as those he'd seen in The Market Square: Teaps being bottlefed, Teaps in his highchair. But there was a new one too: a close up of Teaps's mum and dad on their wedding day. That image was sharp and clear with the figure of Vanessa Clarke in a flowing, white wedding dress captured in high definition. Wilson slipped the photo inside his shirt, taking care not to crease it, then repositioned everything to fill the empty space. He pulled the door to and walked back.

"Much better. I needed that. Wouldn't have made it back without an emergency stop. Anyway, best be off. Mum's cooking lunch; have to be back for..." Wilson checked the time. "Bloody hell, quarter past twelve! I'm late. Dad's waiting for his drill bits."

"Thought you said he needed some weedkiller?"

"Yeah, that as well. Gotta go; he's waiting."

Wilson headed for the door.

"I'll give you the book back tomorrow."

Teaps followed.

"No panic. Like I said, call me if you get stuck. Shame you can't stay longer. You could have seen Dad's shrine to Mum. He keeps her bedroom just like it was, in the old house, for when she comes back."

As Teaps opened the door that led out to the stairs, Michael Clarke, Teaps's dad, lurched in, took two unsteady steps and stumbled to the floor. The stench of alcohol arrived a second later, followed by the stocky, doorway-filling figure of Warren Blamire, their notorious thug landlord. Eddie Spinner followed him into the flat.

"Hey, Wilson, qué pasa?" Spinner, as always, looked uncertain and sheepish.

"Shit" said Teaps.

The four upright bodies virtually filled the flat. Michael was curled in a ball at their feet. His shirt and pants were stained and damp in places.

"Don't worry son," he slurred. "Everything will be okay. Just like the golden days." Teaps went to help his father to his feet but Blamire kept him pinned him down with his foot.

"See this excuse for a man Spinner? He's a waste of space. All because of the demon drink. Can't be trusted."

Teaps sprang up and went to shove Blamire away.

"Get your foot off him, you lowlife thug."

But Blamire was expecting the move and grabbed Teaps by his hair, spun him round and clamped a hefty, tattooed forearm around his neck.

Although Wilson hadn't spent many nights learning martial arts in The Market Square, he was certain Blamire and Spinner wouldn't be much of a problem, even in such a cramped space. But he was aware of the stolen property tucked inside his shirt and if that got damaged or fell out during a scuffle, how would he explain the theft to his best friend?

No, best not. That would only make things worse.

"Listen girlie" said Blamire, his ugly mouth inches from Teaps's ear, "me and Spinner, we're like the third emergency service. A Sunday service. Helping those who've lost their way. So I'm telling you, if I see that, that..." He looked down on Michael with undisguised contempt. "If I see that numpty spending my rent money in The Unicorn again, it won't just be my size eleven that's gonna be making the point."

Then Blamire pushed Teaps away.

"Now, I don't know who that lanky piece of piss is" he said, pointing to Wilson, "but you're lucky he's here, cos I don't want no outside grief.

If I don't have my five grand in the next couple of weeks, things will turn a bit sour for you and that muppet you call a dad. Two weeks, five grand. Come on Spinner."

Blamire clattered down the narrow stairwell making as much noise as he could to emphasise the threat. Spinner took off without looking back at Wilson or Teaps.

"Come on Dad, let's get you to bed."

"She's still alive you know" mumbled Michael, as Teaps helped him to his feet.

Wilson felt utterly helpless. His best friend was in a horrendous fix and all he could do was stand there and watch the misery unfold.

"Can't you get any money from social services to help? Disability allowance or something?"

"He's not disabled Wilson, he's an alcoholic and clinically depressed. He doesn't want to be helped. Look, you'd better go" he said, gesturing to the door. "I'll be fine. Just another day in paradise, eh."

"You sure?"

"Yeah, he'll sleep it off and I need to go to work."

Wilson turned to leave.

"Hey Wilson, what about that?"

Teaps was nodding at the textbook on the table.

"Oh the book. Forgot all about. Cheers mate."

Wilson checked the time as he fired up the Vespa. It was 12.30 p.m. Half an hour to go. He checked the wedding photo was secure inside his shirt and thought briefly of the pain he wanted to inflict on Warren Blamire, pain which involved a number of bone fractures and some tendon damage. Then he set off for home, taking a detour round the back of the hospital.

Chapter 33

The Sunday lunch

Sunday 29th October 2017

Wilson arrived home on the stroke of 1.00 p.m. and opening the front door, heard a familiar voice coming from the lounge. Daisy was already there, talking to his mum! He carefully retrieved the wedding photo from inside his shirt and placed it between the pages of Teaps's textbook then made his entrance.

Daisy was sitting on the sofa. She was wearing blue jeans and a white jumper and her hair was in the same style as the previous night. She looked amazing.

"Hey, Daisy, wow, you're here already; a bit early, but that's great, you've made it all the same. Sorry I'm late, had to go to the DIY store for some, scooter parts... and this textbook."

Daisy cocked her head to one side with the hint of an uncertain smile on her lips – as though unsure of how to respond to the antics of a naughty but amusing child.

"Yeah, I've met your mum, she told me all about your bad habits, so I'm leaving now."

Daisy pretended to get up to go. Wilson's mum started laughing.

"Ooh Daisy, stop with that. He'll have an uncontrollable tantrum and we'll have to call the ambulance again."

"Okay, very amusing. Sorry I wasn't here when you arrived. Sorry Mum, for not doing the introducing. Had to go and see Teaps. Needed to borrow this."

Wilson held the book in the air as though it was something priceless and irreplaceable, like the Rosetta Stone. Daisy's look of bemusement returned.

"Three pieces of prose analysis to complete. The war poets, Sassoon and er, Vidal. Needs to be done by tonight."

"Are you alright love?" Gloria was somewhat bemused.

"Yeah, 'course. Why wouldn't I be?"

"I don't know son. You seem to have been acting a bit odd this morning. Like you're up to something. Anyway, I'll leave you to it, need to check on the lamb. Dad's gone fishing but promised he'd be back just after one, so I'll have dinner ready for one thirty if that's okay."

"Sounds and smells perfect, Mrs Arm..."

"Please, call me Gloria," she said, patting Daisy on the shoulder.

As she left the lounge she badgered Wilson. "Ask Daisy if she wants a cup of coffee or something. She's our guest remember."

Wilson closed the lounge door, sat down next to Daisy and with his voice on minimum volume, excitedly started to bring her up to date with the events of the last twelve hours.

"You won't believe what I found out last night Daisy, from Big Mac and Short Cake. I was in The Gateway again and they told me all about the time traces and déjà vu and how straddling involved different energy fields. They said that only people with a pass could visit The Market Square and that we're up to mischief. The Powers That Be know this and I'm sure Big Mac and Short Cake are behind the hospital window and..."

At that point, Daisy stopped him by putting her finger on his lips.

"You lost me after the first sentence. Who are Big Mac and Short Cake again?"

"It's complicated, and I'm trying to tell you all of this before Dad gets back. We can't talk about this at the dinner table. I had to tell you, share it with you. It's incredible. It's starting to make sense; I think I get it. I'm joining up the dots. And then there's this."

Wilson leafed through the textbook, retrieved the photo and gave it to Daisy.

"I tried to bring her in last night."

"Who?" Daisy still wasn't following.

"Last night in The Market Square, I tried to bring in Vanessa, to find out what happened to her, to use The Market Square to do something good, just like you said. But I struggled to build a clear image and I couldn't bring her in. So this morning I took this wedding photo from Teaps's dad's bedroom. Look, a sharp picture."

"Wilson, stop, calm down. I'm not following you."

A car pulled into the driveway.

"Damn, Dad's here. We can't talk now. What time do you have to leave?"

"My brother said he'd collect me at four. I have to text him. He's at the Trafford Centre."

"Okay, soon as lunch is over I'll make some excuse to go for a walk and once we're out of the house we can talk properly. I've got an idea, like an experiment and if it comes off, we'll be using The Market Square to do something really good. I need you to help though, because if I do it, but don't remember all the bauble images then..."

"Stop Wilson, stop. Okay, 'course I'll help you. Let's try to do something good. Explain it to me again, later."

Alex Armitage had caught his first salmon of the season that morning, a twelve-pound cock fish and as a result, was in a buoyant mood. If there was a veil of awkwardness hanging over the conversation between three of the diners, it didn't show.

The first course was accompanied by Alex's painfully detailed account of 'the one that didn't get away'. It began with how he'd been fishing in Goose Pool on the River Ribble with the river at seven inches, ideal conditions, when a big salmon had jumped towards the far bank. Then how he'd used a 'double Spey' to put the fly – a fly he'd tied himself called The Usual Suspect – right on the nose of the salmon. Then an almighty struggle followed until he finally netted the monster, only to return it to fight another day.

Alex then explained, in excruciating step by step detail – the techniques involved in tying his Usual Suspect fly and the intricacies of the Spey cast, which to Daisy's untrained eye, was similar to fighting Darth Vader with a lightsaber. Alex was just about to launch into a summary of the best salmon rivers in the UK when Gloria said:

"Alex, I think that's enough fishing talk for today. I'm sure there are a couple of other subjects under the sun we can discuss. Though probably not with the same level of mind-numbing detail."

Daisy felt sorry to see Alex's enthusiasm curbed so abruptly.

"Well, maybe one day Wilson and I can go with you. I'd like to try it. An afternoon by a river, surrounded by nature – sounds really nice. How many salmon do you normally catch?"

"Two or three, if I'm lucky. I might fish twenty, maybe twenty-five times each season, for about five or six hours each trip."

Daisy did the maths.

"So that's about... maybe sixty salmon each year. Sounds great. I'd definitely like to have a go with the old Spey casting." She waved her arms around like Darth Vader, simulating Alex's casting technique.

But Alex was shaking his head.

"No Daisy, that's not two or three salmon every time I go fishing, that's two or three salmon each season. Some years I don't catch anything at all."

"But you still go twenty times each year, for five hours each time, and all that travelling and petrol and the Spey casting and then catch... nothing?"

Daisy found the idea that someone could go fishing for a year and not catch a fish absolutely hilarious, and though it was probably rude, she couldn't help but break into a fit of the giggles. It was so infectious that Wilson, his mum and then his dad came down with it moments later. Daisy tried to make a joke along the lines of the usual suspect always being the wrong suspect, but couldn't get the words out for laughter.

So I guess you'd call the lunch a success. There was plenty of small talk about Daisy's family. What her mum and dad and brother did, her college subjects, was she going to university, who were her best friends, any pets? All the obligatory subject matter that needs to be covered when parents 'A' are first introduced to girlfriend 'B'. So all in all, it went off smoothly and the elephant in the room by the name of 'The Market Square' was kept well hidden behind the aforementioned veil.

It did slip once though, when Alex asked Daisy where she and Wilson had first met. But Alex recovered pretty quickly and repeated the question, so that, "and where did you first meet?" became "and where did you first eat?" Which Gloria thought a very bizarre question. She let it pass though, as Daisy quickly launched into an amusing story about Fabio's restaurant and a packet of wine gums. Gloria was hoping that she would get to see more of Daisy.

"How are you getting home Daisy?" She was loading pots into the dishwasher.

"Oh, my brother said he would pick me up in an hour" she said, checking her watch. "He's out shopping with his kids."

"Oh, that's nice."

That was the cue Wilson had been waiting for.

"Think we'll go for a walk Mum, before Daisy has to go. I'm totally stuffed; need to walk off that second helping." He gave his stomach a series of theatrical pats. "Fancy going down to the park Daisy? I'll show you the ducks."

"What a lovely idea Wilson" said Gloria. "I'll put some of that stale bread in a bag for you."

Wilson rolled his eyes.

He and Daisy quickly donned coats and scarves, took the bread and headed off.

"Be back in about half an hour" Wilson yelled, before closing the front door and setting off for the park.

"Well, that seemed to go alright, all things considered. Thanks for coming Daisy and meeting my folks. Gives everything a feeling of normality, like feeding ducks."

He raised the bag of crusts and they both laughed.

"But things aren't normal, in fact, far from it. Come on, we haven't got much time and we need to talk."

Wilson dropped the bread in a neighbour's wheelie bin and when they were about a hundred yards from home, they sat in a draughty bus shelter and Wilson began.

"Like I said earlier Daisy, it's incredible, really incredible."

"Okay, well look, we don't have much time, so why don't you start by telling me what's involved in the plan to do something good?"

"Daisy, I went to The Market Square again last night. I saw Teaps and his mum. Before that, The Market Square was a different place. I think I told you there's this huge building, The Gateway, with a Hall of Extinguished Spirits filled with the spirits of dead people, which have been changed into gold bangles, like jewellery bangles, with their names on and the date they..."

"Wilson, you're losing me again. I..."

"Sorry, what I think is that The Market Square is like an access point to the energy in people's dreams. Dreams don't just evaporate; the energy of the dream survives. In The Market Square we can log in to all this energy, all the dreams of everybody. The trace of this dream energy, like time itself, the living past, is always out there."

Daisy shifted position and Wilson sensed she was getting frustrated with his foggy theorising. She checked her watch.

Wilson took one of her hands in both of his.

"Look, our Life Path numbers – the special number eleven that you and I have, and my dad – and Stockport Infirmary and The Gateway and The Market Square – they're all connected. I don't know how exactly, but they're all connected. Two nights ago, when you showed me how to bring Teaps into my dream, well, I did it again last night."

"Wilson, my brother's going to be here soon."

"I know. I'm nearly at the point; just bear with me. That thing we did with Teaps, when I put my hand on his shoulder, touched him and then we saw those images of his life – they were his time trace, the energy of his past. Like dream energy, always out there. But it's not dream energy, even though we experience it in a dream. It's another type of energy."

Wilson paused.

"When I touched him, that was straddling. I had one foot in a dream energy field and the other in a different energy field of Teaps's past experiences, his time traces. I could sense them both. That's why I was able to see his mum, because as those baubles came towards me, we were viewing all the events of his past life. It seems that everything he's ever done — everything that everyone has ever done — is recorded and stored on some super memory chip of time. You and I, in The Market Square, can access this... this memory bank. Do you follow what I'm saying?"

"I think so. But what happened last night, when you brought Teaps to The Market Square?"

"I focused and focused and eventually I could see loads of stuff with his mum on the baubles — the christening, Teaps being bottlefed. I held onto the image of Vanessa in my head and then I tried to bring her to The Market Square. But my memory of how she appears on the baubles, wasn't sharp. I tried and tried but couldn't make her appear."

"But I thought you said that Vanessa... that the police said she could be dead, never found."

"Yes, but she doesn't have a bangle. Big Mac told me that. He said I had to look in The Market Square. So I kind of borrowed this from Teaps."

Wilson once again presented the wedding portrait.

"Look, this is his dad and his mum on the day they got married. I want to go back to The Market Square again tonight and try one more time to bring in Vanessa using this better image of her. And I want you to help me. It's an experiment. To test my hypothesis about the energy fields. Look, you said you wanted to try to use The Market Square to do some good. And I think finding out what happened to Vanessa is something we should try to do. A good thing. Tonight."

Daisy studied the smiling bride and groom.

"Wilson, I... I... yes, okay. I don't understand half of what you're telling me. And I need to get back. My brother will be here. But hey, since it's only a dream we're talking about, what harm can it do? So, yeah, let's try."

Daisy stood up and was about to head back when Wilson put his hands on her shoulders.

"Daisy, you have to want to go, to want to meet me in The Market Square. And if we bring Vanessa in and we see the trace of her past, take in as much as you can. Try to remember all that you see, what

197

you experience – memorise everything as it flashes by. There could be clues, information we can use. If my theory, my experiment works and Vanessa is alive, maybe we can find out where she is."

"So that's what straddling means?"

"Yeah, that's Olympic-standard straddling."

Chapter 34

The Rolling Stones concert

Monday 30th October 2017

Wilson arrived in The Market Square to find himself at a pop concert — something like a scaled down version of the Glastonbury Festival.

Olde worlde buildings had been replaced by a new worlde of marquees, tents and food vendors. The jangle of a lead guitar and the thump of drums came from musicians on a raised platform that filled the bottom end of the square. Wilson was too far away to identify the band. But then he recognised the melody and the words, 'If you start me up, if you start me up I'll never stop!'

Wilson's route to the Clock Tower looked impenetrable; blocked by a human wall of fans. Plastic glasses half-filled with beer occasionally flew into the air followed by raucous cheers. Raised hands held out mobiles to capture selfies. Girls balanced on boys shoulders, sang and clapped and waved their arms in time with the music.

How the hell am I going to find Daisy in that lot?

He could see a clock face and the pinnacle of the tower about thirty metres to his right and two lads clinging precariously to their bird's eye view.

She'll be near the benches Wilson concluded, before forcing his way into the densely packed crowd.

After a few minutes of argy-bargy he reached an open patch of space near the flower beds and the war memorial. Daisy waved and smiled as he approached.

"Have you seen who's playing?" She nodded her head in the direction of the music.

"Yeah, I know, great isn't it. The Rolling Stones, awesome."

"Want to go on and join the band? We're allowed."

Wilson realised that what was about to happen was beyond his wildest dreams. Beyond anyone's wildest dreams.

"But listen Daisy, seriously, only two songs. Ten minutes at the most. We're here to find Vanessa, remember?"

Ten tunes later, Wilson Armitage on bass guitar and Daisy Meadowcroft on jazz flute were centre stage, the new members of The Rolling Stones and loving every minute.

Nobody can ever take this memory from me, even if it's only in a dream, thought Wilson, looking down on The Market Square filled to capacity with cheering, singing, waving people. As the sun dipped behind L'École, the lighters came out.

Jumpin' Jack Flash, it's a gas, gas, gas.

Wilson turned to Daisy and mouthed a simple instruction: "Come on. We need to go, now!"

They slowly retreated from the limelight, to the side of the stage, and handed the bass and the flute back to a stage hand. They scrambled down a set of metal steps, through some heavy black curtains and along an empty corridor before coming to a door with a notice saying 'Rock Stars Only'. They opened the door and stepped into a changing room. Four electric guitars were resting against a wall. A clothes rail was filled with leather jackets, colourful silk shirts, black satin pants, scarves, a feather boa and a black suede Fedora hat. Two bottles of Jack Daniels, a half-empty bottle of Moët Champagne, glass tumblers, two packs of Marlboro Lights and a half-eaten kebab littered the table which stood beneath a dressing mirror bordered with white light bulbs.

"Daisy, I don't know how much time we've got, but we need to do it soon. We have to bring in Teaps's mum."

From the stage above, the muffled thud of drum and bass continued. Someone ran down the corridor shouting "Security."

"So I guess this will have to do."

"What? In here, now?"

"Yeah, here, now. Or we'll run out of dream time. Plus, we'd never find her out there anyway."

Wilson sat on the edge of the table, closed his eyes, pictured the wedding photo he'd borrowed and zoomed in on the face of Vanessa Clarke. The broad smile, the pale complexion, the blonde hair in ringlets.

He focused and focused and then opened his eyes. Nothing.

"Damn. She won't come."

Wilson tried again, concentrating harder, for almost a minute.

Still the same negative result.

"Why's it not happening? We did it with Teaps and Hoover." Wilson turned forlornly to Daisy for an answer.

"I don't know Wilson. Maybe it's because you never met her. Or you can only bring in your friends. Or we need to be out in The Market Square, or maybe she's..."

"No, she's not dead. I know it; she's not. There's no bangle." Wilson refused to accept Daisy's line of thought. "You have a go at bringing her in. Remember the wedding photo; happy, smiling face, blonde hair. Try Daisy. Maybe you're better than me. A woman to woman thing."

Daisy was about to say something negative, but then closed her eyes.

There was a knock at the door.

Wilson opened it a fraction and peered through the crack. A man with a clipboard was talking into a tiny microphone projecting down from an earpiece.

"Two minutes, final call."

"Okay, err, thanks. We're ready," said Wilson. He closed the door and turned back to Daisy.

Vanessa Clarke was sitting in the chair, dressed in a long flowing bridal gown with her blonde hair in ringlets, gazing wistfully at her reflection in the mirror.

"Daisy, you genius! You did it!" Wilson was both elated and amazed.

"Is that her? I mean, really her?" Daisy was also questioning her stunning achievement.

Vanessa was reaching for the Champagne bottle and a glass.

"Yeah, absolutely. She looks just like her photo."

Wilson slowly and gently placed his hand on Vanessa's shoulder.

"Yes, I'll be ready in a minute, love," she said, looking up at Wilson.

But there was no power surge. No electrical impulse ran along Wilson's arm.

He raised his hand and again placed it back on Vanessa's shoulder. But still nothing. No baubles and no visions of the past.

He turned to Daisy in frustration. "It's not working. Her traces won't come."

Daisy took a step forward.

"Move, let me try. Maybe I have to do it because I brought her here."

Daisy rested her hand on the shoulder of a complete stranger, sitting in a white satin wedding dress, sipping Champagne, in a dream.

Then the music stopped and a transparent curtain of yellow cellophane was drawn across the room. A small, red bauble emerged, followed by a green bauble and in quick succession, white, silver and blue baubles. To the eyes-wide-open astonishment of Daisy and Wilson, floating towards them, reflected in traces of the past, were the events that led to the disappearance of Vanessa Clarke. And all was revealed.

Chapter 35

Mystery solved

Vanessa Clarke was in a state of euphoria as she left The May Fair Hotel and headed north towards Euston station. The short presentation had been a huge success. The new IBM contract meant promotion to the Premier League of executive recruitment and she needed fresh air to clear her head of the Champagne bubbles. As she walked through Berkeley Square, with its swanky offices, famous restaurants and luxury car showrooms, Vanessa smiled at the thought that one day, her name would be on a polished brass plaque at the entrance to one of those buildings.

Whether it was the bubbly, or a momentary urge of devil-may-care, it's impossible to say: but as she passed the shop frontage of Nicky Clarke, hairdresser to the rich and famous, she decided that the mumsy, long blonde hair reflected in the window needed an upgrade, in keeping with her new status.

Vanessa was lucky; the salon had just received a cancellation and was told if she came back in fifteen minutes, a cut and colour with the head stylist, 'wouldn't be a problem'. Vanessa didn't bother to ask the price on the principle that if you had to ask, you probably couldn't afford it. However, she knew the Nicky Clarke understudy would be expensive and serious cash would be required.

Vanessa Clarke avoided using a credit card whenever possible, paying with cash revived memories of her childhood in Naples and the old-fashioned ways of her father. "Only hard-earned cash in your pocket is virtuous and honourable" he would insist, like it was some Mafia coda. En route to the nearest cashpoint, Vanessa's reflection called out again, this time from the window of an upmarket, clothes shop.

Isn't that old Marks and Spencer raincoat a bit drab? Wouldn't you prefer to be wearing this lovely new camel coat instead? Classically cut, calf length, lambswool and cashmere mix...

Her raincoat wasn't that old and it certainly wasn't drab, but she was sold on the camel coat. She withdrew £1,800 in cash from her business account. *This one's on the company,* she decided and ten minutes later walked back to the hairdressing appointment wearing her new, luxury acquisition. Later, the Marks and Spencer raincoat, now gift-wrapped in a posh box, was discovered by a homeless woman sleeping under cardboard in a backstreet doorway.

As Vanessa sat waiting for the Natural Light Ash Brown colour to take effect, she reached for her phone and was about to text Michael to say she was taking the later train when she decided against it. The business win and makeover would be a big surprise.

So the woman who walked out of the salon did not look remotely like the woman who walked in. Vanessa's long blonde hair had been transformed to ash brown, in a classic short bob with a tousled, blow-dried finish, 'to give it a contemporary new take', the stylist had said. With the IBM contract, new hair and a cashmere coat, Vanessa Clarke felt fantastic. It was one of the best days of her life and as she headed for the train station she didn't have a care in the world, other than arriving home to her son and husband two hours later than originally planned.

As she approached the junction where Davies Street meets Mount Street, Vanessa felt something go pop, deep inside her head. She momentarily stumbled before quickly regaining her balance. She felt nauseous and confused and stood for a few minutes with her shoulder against a lamp post, waiting for the sensation to pass.

Vanessa Clarke had just suffered a mild ischaemic stroke caused by a combination of three glasses of Champagne, seven hours' sleep over the previous two days, an inherited condition that involved a narrowing of certain blood vessels in the brain and most significantly, a tiny clot of blood. The blood clot had lodged itself deep in her hippocampus and for two minutes had restricted the flow of oxygenated blood to a cluster of cells involved in speech and memory. The area of tissue damage was tiny, but also irreparable and catastrophic, like a permanent crack across the M6 motorway.

In layman's terms, the hard drive, the storage part of her brain, was still good, but her mental operating system couldn't access it. Which meant Vanessa Clarke was no longer able to remember anything about herself or her past. The memories were still there, but she could no longer retrieve them, or, more importantly, tell anyone who she was. She had been mentally mugged. The victim of a random act of violence on the streets of London.

The well-heeled residents of Mayfair objected to overt evidence of police surveillance in their gilded borough. So, a paucity of functioning cameras meant the blonde figure of Vanessa Clarke in the old navy-blue raincoat being monitored from The May Fair Hotel to Hay Hill was lost, as she entered the environs of Berkeley Square. Three days after Vanessa was officially declared missing it was discovered that scaffolding, hurriedly erected on the morning of her disappearance, had blocked the field of view of the camera observing the street with the cashpoint. The camel coat shop was closed when the police conducted door-to-door enquiries and the girl on reception in Nicky Clarke's (who hadn't been working on the day of Vanessa's disappearance) stated confidently that she had "checked the appointments book twice and they had no customer by the name of Vanessa Clarke." The footage on every police camera along the route from Berkeley Square to Euston was pored over, painstakingly, for blonde hair and a blue mac, but to no avail. Vanessa Clarke had simply disappeared.

Of course, the camera at Hay Hill, which captured the last known image of Vanessa, was the focus of most attention. But with over sixty thousand people and eleven thousand vehicles passing each day, the police constable given the task of studying the tapes could be forgiven for not noticing the smart-looking businesswoman with short brown hair, walking back toward The May Fair Hotel — in the opposite direction of Euston station.

In a state of extreme confusion, Vanessa Clarke retraced her footsteps back up to Stratton Street, where she momentarily stopped outside the entrance to The May Fair Hotel. She then continued on to Piccadilly, through Green Park and down to Victoria coach station, where she boarded an overnight Country Express coach to Inverness.

She handed the driver a handful of notes as she mumbled the word 'Stockland'.

Her eyes were glazed and the driver detected a stale scent of alcohol on her breath. He smiled as he gave her the one-way ticket and change for a twenty-pound note and slipped the rest of the money in his back pocket. Vanessa made her way unsteadily to the back of the coach where she slumped in a seat and fell asleep, totally hidden from view.

Eleven hours later, as the coach made its way through the early morning traffic in Inverness, Vanessa was still sleeping. The coach turned into the bus station, reversed into the allotted parking bay and twenty-two weary passengers disembarked. As the last of the departing passengers stepped down from the coach, a shifty-looking lad, who had been sitting three rows in front of Vanessa, took a few steps backwards and silently lifted the attaché case belonging to the well dressed lady, still sleeping in the corner at the back.

She must be on something, he'd been thinking for the previous two hours, and it takes one to know one!

So this scoundrel – who specialised in transporting, twice weekly, two kilos of cocaine from Dover to Scotland – left Inverness bus station, with a case holding over four hundred pounds in cash and all the documents that could be used to identify the presumably pissed-up, drugged-up woman at the back of the coach. The two envelopes, one containing a new credit card and the other, a slip showing the PIN number, were an unexpected bonus.

The credit card was used a few days later in Dover to make a maximum cash withdrawal of £2,000 and then passed to the courier's contacts for use on a return journey to Paris. The attaché case containing a mobile phone, driving licence and a signed IBM contract, was weighted with a brick and somewhere between Dover and Calais, found its way to the bed of the English Channel.

The driver winked at the courier as he departed the coach with the case and after a coffee and a cigarette he helped Vanessa from the coach.

"Go and get a cup of tea love" he said. "It'll make you feel better."

"Grazie," she mumbled.

The driver handed his coach keys in at the station office then scarpered off to the nearest pub with the wad of stolen beer money burning a hole in his grubby pocket.

Confused, disorientated, unable to remember who she was, not knowing where she was, Vanessa walked slowly from the station down Margaret Street towards the river until she came to a small park overlooking the Ness Bridge, where she sat on a bench and waited.

She had been sitting in the rain for five hours when a lady walking a dog brought to a policeman's attention the poor soul sitting in the park 'totally drenched' and 'not quite all there'.

"Come on love, let's get you checked out and dried off," said an ambulance man, as he helped Vanessa into a wheelchair.

"Grazie" she mumbled.

In the ensuing investigation, nobody made the connection between the blonde businesswoman missing in London – who had absconded to France, suspected of fraud, with the well-dressed lady found bewildered in Inverness - who'd lost her mental faculties and could only mutter a few words in Italian.

The people running social services for that part of Scotland secretly believed she'd been abandoned on their doorstep by a relative who couldn't cope. Or she'd been brought over from one of the islands, where dementia services were limited, by a family who would rather not see her, than see her not cared for. Either way, the end result was the same: whoever the mystery lady was, she needed twenty-four-hour care and the health authority for Inverness had a duty to provide it.

Of course, the two people who could have intervened, the drug courier and the coach driver, both had a vested interest in keeping schtum – especially the coach driver, who was told by his accomplice, "jist keep yer trap shut, or yeee'll be havin' a wee accident!"

So for almost seventeen years, Vanessa Clarke had been a virtually mute resident of the South Kessock Care Home. She had a lovely room looking out over the Beauly Firth, but she had no idea of where she was, no idea of who she was and neither did anyone else. That is, until the night Daisy Meadowcroft brought her to The Market Square.

Chapter 36

So, what now?

Monday 30th October 2017

"Daisy, I can't just walk up and say, 'Hey Teaps, my girlfriend discovered what happened to your mum. She's alive and she's been in a care home in the north of Scotland for seventeen years' can I?"

There had been a flurry of texts between Wilson and Daisy all that morning and after Daisy was threatened with having her phone confiscated during a pottery class, they agreed to speak at lunchtime.

"I know that Wilson. We can't be seen to be involved in this. Teaps has to find out for himself. But first, we need to be certain that the woman we saw in The Market Square is in a care home that actually exists in that part of Scotland and she really is Vanessa."

"Daisy, there is a South Kessock Care Home. It was the first thing I checked this morning. It's owned by a big company and overlooks the sea. The lady will be there and she's Teaps's mum. We both know that."

"But we have to confirm it. I mean, we can't just send a random anonymous message saying who she is and where her family are. Or can we?"

Daisy paused and then corrected herself.

"Maybe Wilson, maybe that's exactly what we do. Just reveal her location anonymously. It couldn't be tracked back to us."

"I know, I was thinking that. But if I was Teaps, it would tear me up to discover that perhaps someone had known all these years and they'd never said anything. I'd go crazy trying to work out who it was. So I don't think that's how we do it.

What if we help someone, perhaps a doctor or a nurse, someone working at the home, to discover Vanessa for themselves. We just have to point them in the right direction. Crop the face from the wedding photo, and then leave it on..."

"But Wilson, there would have to be an explanation of where the photo came from. Anything that leaves a trail can be followed, and as you said, Teaps would go crazy if the trail led nowhere and he was left in the dark. He has no mum for virtually all of his life, then someone leads him to her and he doesn't know who, or why, or why they waited all this time. No, that's not the... wait, wait, I have an idea. What if Vanessa leaves the trail herself? What if she does something that suddenly reveals a vital clue?"

"Like what?"

"Like her name, scrawled on a piece of paper beside her bed?"

Wilson fell silent.

"Then, maybe, when one of the nurses or a cleaner goes into her room, they see the name, and it's like she's written it, subconsciously.

"They'd take it to a supervisor or a manager, and if we're lucky, they'd have the nous to do an online search. And once they found out that someone by that name went missing all those years..."

"Daisy, you're a genius. That's exactly the way to do it. It'll be like she's trying to send a message, to tell them who she is. A cry for help."

"Exactly. Nobody would ignore her name if it was written five times on a piece of paper. Or even better, if she just wrote, 'I am Vanessa Clarke'. Or just, 'Me, Vanessa Clarke'."

"Yeah, that would definitely do it, and nothing suspicious about it. All we need to do is find a way to get to Inverness, get into the home, leave the note and then get back to Stockport, without anybody knowing about it."

"Mmm, that's not going to be so easy." Daisy's enthusiasm for the idea was waning slightly. Wilson however, wasn't daunted by the challenge.

"Daisy, I think only one of us can go. I know you found her and maybe you want to see it through, but he's my mate and knowing his mum's there..."

"Wilson, are you crazy? This isn't a bloody movie. There's no way

I can go to the north of Scotland; I get lost walking in the garden. You need to go alone, as soon as possible – like tomorrow. And if you go by yourself, we reduce the, 'someone might find out what we're up to' factor by fifty per cent."

"Yeah, you're right. I have to do this by myself. Tomorrow. Daisy speak later – I've got a trip to plan."

Wilson checked his college timetable for the next day and began planning schedules and alibis.

No classes after 3 p.m. That's good.

Now, where can I say I'm going to be all day?

A university visit?

No, they'd want to know which uni, which course. Not credible.

Hospital appointment? Curious lump on my leg?

No. Too personal, too lumpy!

Broken Vespa?

No. Wouldn't cause me to be away all day.

Jury service?

Giving blood?

Charity work?

Prince's Trust?

Prince's Trust. That might do it!

Wilson talked through a potential scenario.

"Sir, I won't be in tomorrow morning – until sometime after lunch, at the earliest. I have to go to the Prince's Trust Open Day in Manchester Town Hall with my dad and mum."

No, no. Too forceful.

"Sir, is it okay if I go by myself to the Prince's..."

But what if he says no? Don't give him the chance to say no.

"Sorry to trouble you sir, but my mum has asked me to ask you if I can help her tomorrow morning. She needs help with an exhibition stand for Oxfam, at the Prince's Trust at Manchester Town Hall. The guy who was going to help hurt his back and she just called to ask if I could ask you for permission. She'd be really grateful. It's for a worthy cause, plus I'd find out about all the beneficial work the Trust does around the world. It wouldn't be four hours wasted."

Bang on.

"Wilson, that is a very public-spirited gesture and you're a credit to your parents" said Mr Finch, his English tutor an hour later. "I'll leave notes at reception for tomorrow morning's double English. What else will you be missing?"

"Err, just one biology class and maths, sir."

"Well, let Mr Edwards and your maths tutor know and tell them I've said it's okay on this one occasion. Highly commendable Wilson. You've climbed a rung on the ladder of my expectations and you'll be pleased to know, you're now on rung one."

"Ha ha ha, thank you sir. Excellent joke."

Old buffoon.

But that was the college alibi sorted.

Now, how the hell do I get to Inverness and back in a day? How far away is it anyway? I know it's bloody miles.

'Trains to Inverness from Manchester. Search.'

The earliest train I can catch is the 6.14 a.m. from Piccadilly. Gets me to Inverness for 13.29 p.m. So would have to be up at 5.00 a.m. and sneak out of the house. Gulp.

I'd have to invent some reason for being up so early.

Okay, worry about that in a minute.

Two changes, Edinburgh and Perth.

And it's a hundred and forty-one quid.

What about the return?

The 15.51 p.m. from Inverness gets me back at 23.28 p.m. Half eleven in Manchester. Back home for nearly half twelve in the morning.

One change.

Another hundred and forty-one quid!

That means I've got two hours and twenty-two minutes in Inverness to get to the home, do what I need to do and get back to the station.

Wilson studied a Google map for the north of Inverness.

'Inverness to South Kessock. Search.'

Eight minutes by car, one point four miles. So I've got two hours and twenty-eight minutes. Will be cutting it fine, but doable.

Now, how do I persuade them to let me into the South Kessock Care Home?

Wilson spent twenty minutes researching the home and its range of services. South Kessock was renowned for the quality of its residential care for those suffering with dementia. As Wilson understood it, you could ring a care home, tell them a relation was suffering from dementia, that you were looking for a bed in the area and often they'd let you visit to see the facilities.

Wilson dialled the number.

"South Kessock. How may I help you?"

"Hi, it's, err, yes. Sorry to trouble you, I'm ringing about my father. He's suffering from dementia and my mum is struggling to cope and my sister, Daisy and I are, err, we think we need to start looking for a home for him. Dad's doctor told us that South Keswick, I mean Kessock, was, is, a very good home and I wanted to know if I could come and visit tomorrow, at two o'clock in the afternoon?"

"I'm so sorry to hear that. What stage of dementia is your dad at?"

"Oh, he's at an advanced stage. Forgets things all the time. Walks around mumbling about energy fields and a place called The Market Square."

"Well, I'm so sorry to hear that."

"Yes, he's certainly on a downward path."

"Well, we'd be delighted to show you round. Whom shall I say will be calling in then?"

"Just myself. Mum's too upset to contemplate all of this. So there'll only be me."

"Yes, but what name shall I say?"

"Oh, err, I'm Frank. My name's Frank. Mr Frank Spencer."

"Okay Mr Spencer, we'll look forward to seeing you tomorrow afternoon then. Thanks for calling. Goodbye."

"Goodbye."

And that was it, Wilson was in. Now all he had to do was come up with some reason he'd be out of the house by 5.20 a.m. and back around

12.30 a.m. the following morning. He paid for the train ticket by maxing out his credit card and went off to his biology lesson.

He bumped into Teaps in the corridor en-route. He'd been in a fight. There was crusted blood on his skinned knuckles, he had a fat lip and the purple-blue flush of a fresh bruise was swelling on his cheekbone.

"Teaps, what's gone on?"

"You'd better ask Spinner, the slimy little bastard. All the time I thought he was a mate, well, he was spying on me. Watching to see if I was spending money, buying clothes and stuff. Then telling Blamire I was wasting cash when I should be paying our debts. Well, he won't be doing that for a while."

"Why, what's happened, where is he?"

"He's in an ambulance. I just put him in an ambulance."

Then Teaps wiped his eyes with the sleeve of his jacket and tears started to flow. He put his head on Wilson's shoulder and all his frustrations came flooding out, right in the middle of a college corridor.

A girlfriend came over and tried to console him. Students walked past, concerned, but reluctant to get involved for fear of being caught in collateral damage. News of the fight had spread quickly.

After a minute, Teaps stopped crying, composed himself, wiped his eyes and blew his nose on his torn and blood speckled t-shirt.

"I've had enough Wilson. I'm at the end of my tether."

Tears were brimming over the rims of his eyelids.

"Dad was rushed into A&E. He was peeing blood and he'd collapsed in the flat. I was there on the ward all night. They say he'll survive, but only if he stops drinking. But I don't think he can. I can't stop him — I've tried. And when we got home earlier, that little bastard was there in the street spying and laughing at me. So I just lost it. Think I broke his jaw and his arm. I'm going home to check on Dad before the police come. Text you later. See ya, Wilson."

And before Wilson had time to say anything, to suggest Teaps come and live with him, bring his dad, even for just a few nights; anything to help his best mate, who was clearly losing it — he'd walked out of the revolving door of the college and away.

Wilson couldn't concentrate in the biology lesson — and certainly not on dissecting a rat. "Looks like the work of Jack the Ripper," said the class technician as he put the mutilated corpse of Wilson's Rattus norvegicus back in the freezer later that afternoon. Not surprising really: Wilson had carved out a plan that in principle, would allow him to travel to Inverness and back, all in one day, without alerting too much suspicion. After hearing of Teaps's problems, his scalpel was blunt.

When Wilson arrived home, there was a note waiting for him on the hall table. Another divine intervention, without a doubt.

'Wilson,
Have gone to see your auntie Rita. She's slipped a disc again, so have to help and stay the night. Dad's in London — back tomorrow. Fish pie in the fridge. Call me if you need me.
Love, Mum X
P.S. Lock the front door when you go to bed!!'

"Half a miracle, anyway," Wilson muttered as he scrunched up the note, *I'll worry about explaining the late return on the trip back.*

Wilson called Daisy and brought her up to speed with Teaps's fight, the Prince's Trust excuse and his good fortune at being able to slip away the next morning, under the radar.

"Wilson, I hope that lady in the home really is his mum. But what do you think will happen when she's identified? What if she wants to stay there? What if we make the whole situation worse?"

"I know. I was thinking about that. It's like we're using a dream to change what happens in the future, like a butterfly beating its wings and causing a snowstorm in the Amazon rainforest."

"No Wilson, that's bullshit. It's like playing God. We're in charge of that lady's destiny, manipulating her future because we think it will be good for her and I don't know if we should."

Wilson didn't know what to say.

"But then equally Wilson, if I was Teaps, I'd want someone to find my mum and I wouldn't care what happens after that."

Daisy's voice trembled. "It makes me cry just thinking about it."

She paused for a sniffle.

"Please make sure you text me from the train, especially on the way back."

"I will."

"And don't go to The Market Square tonight. You need some sleep."

Wilson had to laugh.

"Daisy, what do you think we're doing when we're in The Market Square? We are asleep."

"You know what I mean, just try and have a normal dream. Oh, and I forgot to tell you, they're bringing my grandma up from Bournemouth tomorrow and taking her to Stockport Infirmary. She's not got long and needs to be close to family. I'm going to see her, so if I don't text back immediately, I'm not ignoring you."

"Okay, I think I'll survive."

"Goodnight and good luck."

"Oh Daisy, wait. Which ward will she be in?"

"3B, I think. Why?"

"Nothing. Tell you another time."

"Okay, goodnight."

"'Night."

Wilson ate the fish pie and watched an hour of TV. He was double-checking train times when his phone beeped. It was a text from a number he didn't recognise.

'Wilson, buzz me back if you can.'

Wilson pressed redial. Teaps answered after two rings.

"Hey Wilson, it's me. I'm using my dad's phone. You won't believe this."

"Are you okay? What's happened?"

"Spinner's not pressing charges. The police came round and told me I was lucky, cos I could have been done for assault. Spinner told them he provoked me and got what he deserved. Pretty sure Blamire's behind it. Probably didn't want his pet dog spending too much time with the coppers, given the extra-curricular activities."

"Jesus, that's a relief. You must have done some damage."

"Yeah, a fractured arm and jaw and a broken nose. He won't be in college for a week. And I smashed my phone."

"Christ, remind me not to get on your angry side. You're like the Incredible Hulk."

"Wilson, I've never hit anyone in my life. I'm a writer, not a fighter."

"Could have fooled me."

"Nah, it was just the spying stuff, but mostly my dad. He's losing it and taking me with him, today was a low point and I just snapped. Now he's in bed, with his arm around a bottle of JD, the surrogate wife. The drinking's not likely to stop and I'll lose him soon. Maybe it's for the best; then they'll be together. Think that's what he wants."

"Teaps, don't speak like that. We need to get you some support. There must be help groups who can get involved. You can't live with this pressure and the money problems and college; you'll have a breakdown."

"Yeah, you're right. Anyway, just wanted to let you know I'm not in a cell for the night, so I'll see you tomorrow."

"Oh wait, I forgot. I won't be in tomorrow – well, not in the morning. Helping mum with a charity thing for the Prince's Trust."

"Okay mate, no worries. Say hi from me."

"Will do Rocky."

"Very funny. See ya."

Wilson was in bed for 10 p.m. He read the first three chapters of *To Kill a Mockingbird* and spent some of the night dreaming of Jem and Atticus and Boo Radley in Alabama – and not The Market Square.

At 6.14 a.m., as Wilson slipped into seat 23B with a bacon baguette and hot coffee, a shrill whistle trilled along the platform and the Virgin West Coast train slowly pulled out of Piccadilly station, heading north, to Scotland.

Chapter 37

North

Tuesday 31st October 2017

Wilson slept for the first hour of the journey but woke as the train skirted Morecambe Bay and the comely hills of the South Lakes came into view.

Wilson was no country boy; he hardly knew a starling from a grayling, but was captured by the beauty of the scenery. The undulating hills, lush green valleys, grazing sheep, the purple heather, the ploughed fields and the endless trails of dry-stone walls — it was a new world to Wilson and he was touched by the unblemished purity. A natural revelation.

A few miles short of the Scottish border, the train charged over a bridge spanning a wide river in which a man stood alone, fly fishing. He was at one with his surroundings, absorbed in the peace and tranquillity, the ever changing light and the appropriateness of The Usual Suspect on that day. There was something ethereal about the whole thing; both spiritual and sublime. Wilson understood at that moment, the catching of a salmon was not the point. The real pleasure, was in just being there. Waist-deep in a river with a memory trace as old as time itself. He realised what he'd been missing and vowed not to turn down the next invite from his dad.

An hour or so later, he sent a text to Daisy to say all was running smoothly and he was on a platform at Edinburgh station waiting for the train to Perth. Then a text to his mum to say he'd survived the night 'home alone', the burglars were all in custody and he'd be back late, because he was going to see a band with Hoover.

After the Perth train, he caught the connection to Inverness and at

13.29 p.m., bang on schedule, he walked out of the station and climbed into a waiting taxi.

"The South Kessock Care Home please." Wilson tried to make the request sound as routine as asking for the nearest KFC.

"Aye, that'll be the one up on Kessock Road then."

"Yeah, near the bridge, overlooking the sea."

"So what brings a young laddie to South Kessock?"

Wilson was nervous and didn't really want to get into a conversation. Then the stark reality of his situation and lack of planning, suddenly struck home. He was about to try and pull off the acting performance of his life: in the role of an anxious son, in a dementia care home, in the north of Scotland and needed a script and to practise his lines, quickly.

"Yeah, my dad's not so good. He's got advanced dementia so Mum's asked me to check out a couple of care homes because she really can't cope anymore."

"You're not from round here, are you lad?"

That's a point. The home probably wouldn't be interested in talking to someone whose dad lives in Stockport and not in Scotland.

"No, but both my dad and my mum are from Inverness. They were born here and they're thinking of moving back. Mum's got family here – her sister's here – and they all want to be back together for my dad's... well, you know, as he declines."

"Aye, that's dementia. We're all living too long. Used to call it old age; now we've got fancy medical terms for everything. How old's yer dad?"

"He's forty-eight."

"Och, that's no age for a man to be taken in."

"Err, I mean, he was forty-eight when he was first diagnosed. He's seventy-two now."

"And he's got a son who's a mere slip of a lad like you? Achhhh, it's all part of the plan of the Almighty up there."

The taxi driver appealed to the heavens, stroked a set of rosary beads dangling from his rear-view mirror and mumbled a few words in a thick Scottish accent.

For the next five minutes, Wilson refined his story, part of which relied on the memorising of a few street names on the southern fringes of Inverness.

The taxi pulled to a halt outside a sprawling, two storey, red-brick building bordered by manicured flower beds. Wilson paid the fare, paused for a moment to admire the stunning sea view, filled his lungs with fresh, salty air then pressed the visitors' bell.

A lady emerged from a side office and opened the door.

"Hi, I'm Wilson. Err, Frank Spencer Wilson. I spoke with someone yesterday, about my dad and a viewing. He's got dementia."

"Oh yes, Rosie said you'd be calling in. Perfect timing; they're on lunch. Take a pew and I'll call Celia, the duty manager."

Wilson took a seat in the reception area. Music was playing in the background and a plate of iced buns had been placed incongruously on a small side table. The place smelled of cabbage and bleach.

"Hi, I'm Celia Green, duty manager for today."

Wilson stood up to shake hands with an officious-looking lady wearing a black suit and carrying a clipboard.

"Fill this in and I'll take you for a swish round."

She pushed the clipboard and a pen into Wilson's hands, "I'll be back in five," then she pressed four buttons on a keypad and departed through a door.

Wilson sat down and flicked through the questionnaire. Name, date of birth, address, name of doctor, surgery address, NI number, current medication – and a lot of additional questions he really should have anticipated. The time was exactly 13.56 p.m.

Just under two hours. Should be enough.

He fudged answers to some of the questions, left one section completely blank and sat waiting for the duty manager to return. It was 14.11 p.m. The duty manager reappeared five minutes later and reviewed Wilson's paperwork. Her initial look of scepticism was turning to a frown by the last page. Wilson was prepared for the light interrogation that followed.

"So, Mr... Frank... Spencer. Rosie told me you're here about your father. He must be very young to have dementia. You can't be more than eighteen?"

"Yes, that's true. But he's not my real dad, he's my stepdad. My mum's real though."

"Well, thank goodness for that."

Wilson jaw tightened as he sensed Celia Green not only wanted to get this over and done with asap, but she was also clearly suspicious of his story and certainly the false name.

"I mean, my dad died and then my mum married an older man, called Alex. Anyway, now he's got dementia and Mum's struggling to cope and needs my help. There's only me and my sister Daisy, but Daisy's away at school, training to be a doctor, so they've sent me to check the place out."

The duty manager raised an eyebrow.

"Where does your father live?"

"Ah, that's the thing you see. He lives in England, in Stockport, with my mum, but he was actually born in Inverness. Mum also. Her sister lives in Inshes, on Culloden Road. Near Inshes Wood. And they want to move up here for family reasons. And so I'm here, you know, to see if Dad would like it."

"We have no funded places I'm afraid."

"That's no problem. Mum's first husband, my first dad, er, real dad, was a football player for Stoke City and so, anyway, she's got money. And err, we think this may be the perfect place. If I could just, you know, have a quick look round. Check out the standards. Then Mum and Daisy can come another time."

Celia Green skimmed through Wilson's completed form for a second time, then lifted her eyes and tilted her head. She was evaluating the anomaly that went by the highly implausible name of Frank Spencer. Wilson ran through the likely ramifications of her deliberations taking a turn for the worst. These involved a local policeman ringing a startled Gloria Armitage for confirmation that her son was not in college, but visiting a care home in Inverness because his stepfather had dementia. And an urgent phone call being put through to Alex, deep in the House of Commons, from a wife seeking clarification on her husband's mental well-being.

Fortunately, the duty manager decided against dialling 999.

"Okay, Mr... Spencer. Follow me."

They passed through the security door and entered a long corridor with small bedrooms leading off. On the wall outside each bedroom was a picture frame and beneath the frame, a small aluminium name-holder. Each frame held a montage of family photos depicting happier times from an earlier life.

The duty manager was striding off in front, pointing to this and pointing to that, rota this and prescription that.

Some of the rooms were occupied, but the people in the rooms didn't bear any resemblance to the people in the picture frames. The people in the photos were young and full of life, wearing flared pants and tank tops, drinking beer and dancing at parties. The people in the rooms were grey and shrunken. They were lying in bed in colourless, washed-out nightclothes, propped up with pillows, stroking strands of greasy hair, hypnotised by the movement on silent TV screens. Horribly alive in their other world.

"And this Mr Spencer, is the dining room" said the duty manager, pointing out the obvious in a cursory manner. Vanessa would be about fifty, fifty-five at the most, remarkably young compared to the other residents. After weighing-up each diner, Wilson concluded that nobody even vaguely resembled Teaps's mum.

"Looks very nice – friendly, clean, organised. I think my dad, my stepdad, would like it here. Just out of interest, what's the average age of a resident here?"

"Well, dementia is one of those illnesses that can strike at any time but I'd say the average is roughly eighty and we'll have a resident for about twenty months, maybe two years."

Celia gave Wilson a look that said she was bored and the tour was over.

"Mr Spencer, I really must get back to the office. If you want to bring your mum and sister, call again. We can have a more detailed chat when you're all together."

The duty manager was heading back down the corridor.

"Yes, I'll do exactly that. I'll be back. Looks great," said Wilson, ambling behind her.

He stopped to check his watch. It was 14.35. *Just over an hour left.* He still had time, but the duty manager obviously didn't. He had to find a reason to stay longer, an excuse to do more looking.

"Who's been here the longest? You know, exceeding all expectations, outliving everybody? I'd like my stepdad to be like that."

"Well, in that case Mr Spencer — and it's strange you should ask — we have our very own mystery woman. An Italian princess, waiting for her handsome prince to come to the rescue."

"Gosh, who's that?" Wilson asked, trying to sound only mildly interested, though his heart rate was beginning to climb.

"Funnily enough, she's right here. We call her Alice."

The duty manager took two steps back and pointed into one of the bedrooms Wilson had walked past earlier. The picture frame was empty but the word Alice was just about legible on a strip of card inside the name plate.

"Quite the little enigma is our Alice."

Wilson peered tentatively into the room. It was clean and tidy with no TV. Just inside the door, sitting in a tatty, high-backed armchair was a lady who, on first impression, appeared much younger than the other residents. She was wearing a tweed skirt that had lost most of its colour and her clean, white blouse was fraying at the cuffs.

"Hello," she said, looking up at Wilson in the doorway.

The hair was now more of a creamy grey than a honey blonde, nevertheless it retained a silky sheen. Fine age lines creased the skin around her lips but her green eyes were shining like light beams bouncing off a rippling sea. Vanessa Clarke was definitely still alive!

"Alice is a bit of a strange one. No family, no friends. She was abandoned in a park here in Inverness. It was all well before my time. Apparently, her family who lived on the Isle of Lewis or Harris, can't remember now, couldn't cope and just dumped her. And she's been here ever since, for seventeen years. We don't think she's got dementia like your father. We did at first, but she's not deteriorated since the day she arrived. Completely lost her memory though. She can say 'hello' and a few words in Italian, but that's it. There used to be a big Italian community on the Outer Hebrides, just after the war, so we think that's where she's from."

Teaps's mum was smiling, looking up at Wilson.

"She's not incontinent, can feed herself, needs no medication and she's no trouble. There's nowhere better to put her in the area, so she's become a bit of a fixture here."

Wilson knelt down and touched the hand of the long-lost, forever-loved and never-once-forgotten mum of his best friend — found at last. He looked into Vanessa's eyes and smiled. It really was her.

Wilson stood up and coughed to check his vocal chords hadn't gone all mushy.

"Right, well, thanks for showing me round."

He put his hand on the pen and paper in his pocket.

"Just need to use the loo, if that's okay. Long journey back. Think I saw a toilet sign back there."

"Yes, but that's a residents' toilet. The nice visitors' toilet is this..."

But Wilson was off, heading back toward the dining room and the duty manager was not going to stop him.

"Okay Mr Spencer, use that one if you must. I'll be in reception, just press the buzzer."

Wilson ducked into the loo. There was no lock on the door. He fished out the pen and sheet of paper in his jacket pocket and using his left hand scrawled a spidery, 'My name is Vanessa Clarke'. He tore the paper until it was about the size of a cigarette packet and put the pen and scraps back in his pocket. Then he flushed the toilet and stepped back out.

He walked down the empty corridor towards reception and checked over his shoulder. The coast was clear. He ducked into Vanessa's room.

"Hello," she said, as Wilson dropped to one knee and clasped her hand.

224

"Look, I don't know if you can understand me, or if you can hear what I'm saying, but you're not called Alice. You're called Vanessa, Vanessa Clarke. You have a husband, Michael and a son called Graham. And they love you and miss you and we're going to get you out of here."

Vanessa looked through Wilson as though some vague, distant familiarity with his words had triggered a memory, a recollection, that was now calling her attention.

"Graham." The two syllables were released as barely a whisper.

"Yes. He's coming to get you. We all are. All the cavalry."

Wilson pulled the scrap of paper and pen from his pocket and placed them both in Vanessa's lap.

In the lap of the gods!

He kissed her on the forehead, squeezed her hand and then strode briskly down the corridor, through reception and out into warm, afternoon sunlight and a fresh, liberating breeze, flavoured with seaweed, almost strong enough to taste.

Waiting for the taxi, Wilson reflected on the building in which Vanessa Clarke had been held as a prisoner for seventeen, lost years. He thought of Teaps and his dad and all they had missed as a family apart and his emotions gained the upper hand.

"Jesus" he exclaimed, trying to stop a lump rising to his throat, "it's like watching *It's a Wonderful Life* on Christmas Day."

An hour later, Wilson was on the train heading south with mission hopefully accomplished. There was just one station change on the journey back, but he hoped a more seismic change was also in motion.

225

Chapter 38

South

Tuesday 31st October 2017

'DAISY. WE FOUND VANESSA. ONE HUNDRED PER CENT. WE DID IT!'

Wilson didn't want to tempt fate, so he waited until the train had left the station before he sent the text message.

Twenty minutes later, he was still waiting for a reply.

He checked the BBC website for any breaking news. There was no startling headline. Not surprising really, because the train was only about fifty miles out of Inverness. Wilson was fidgety and experiencing something of an anti-climax after his heroics; like a commando waiting to be debriefed after a successful mission. With Daisy's help he'd pieced together the mystery of Vanessa's disappearance, used dream power to trace her to a care home in Scotland and then travelled to Inverness to leave a secret message. But now, as he was stealthily making his way back home, totally incognito, the blue touchpaper seemed to have gone out.

However, after a further half an hour, the hypnotic, clickety-clack of the moving train began to placate Wilson's understandable impatience and he dozed off.

The ping of a message an hour later woke him with a start. He read the lines from Daisy and replied:

'Yep, mission accomplished. Can't speak on the phone — train packed. On my way back. Inverness is a long way! But enjoying the views. You okay?'

A minute later she text back:

'All good. Just off to see Grandma at SHH. Well done. Fingers crossed. luv D'

'Text later. W x'

Wilson had noticed the word 'luv' in Daisy's message and so signed off his reply with the more expressive 'x' rather than a thumbs-up emoji. He saw it as a small, yet significant step forward in the evolution of their relationship.

Wilson checked the time. Another six hours to go and a platform change at Edinburgh. His mind started to wander.

No messages from Mum. That's good. No suspicions. Looks like I might just get away with it. With luck I'll be back for quarter past twelve. A reasonable time to get back from a night out with your mates — having watched a local band, for example. Actually, the hour's not the issue. I'm eighteen; my folks won't be bothered if I'm home at quarter past three. It's the lie that's the point. You tell lies, you get found out and no one can ever find out about this little trip. When Vanessa Clarke is discovered it could be huge local news, maybe national news and there's no way anyone can connect it with us.

Wilson slouched down in his seat, pulled up his jacket collar and urged the train to continue eating up the miles. The final leg of the journey was completed under the cover of night. Station after station flew by with a sudden phhuuuuddddummm and a blur of lights. Wilson had completed a stack of college coursework during the seven hours travelling up to Inverness, but now, with nothing further to read and no countryside to contemplate, he was left gazing at himself in the carriage window. He studied the reflection of the old lady opposite as she nibbled at a homemade cheese sandwich and the grandson, as he played Candy Crush on his phone. The refreshments trolley came and went. Passengers wobbled and lurched in the direction of the loo. Then they wobbled and lurched back again. Unstructured thoughts floated through Wilson's mind. Thoughts about energy and the time trace of a fast-moving train. Would it create more Polaroids? Polaroids closer together? Or thinner Polaroids? As he peered through the train window and into darkness, Wilson's consciousness, his perception of that very moment, slipped anchor and took a new mooring in a different channel of cognition. It was a slight but very palpable shift. As though he was thinking with, or from, a new part of his brain. Like the office for certain, *special* mental operations was located in a different room, through a door he'd never opened before. Wilson sensed this 'side room' held a kind of reference library, his Pandora's Box and then, quite bizarrely, the image of a river flowing *backwards* came to mind. At that moment Wilson's psyche no longer seemed to reside within his own body. It had taken wing and was flying above the river, but the river wasn't flowing down to the sea, it was flowing in reverse. One Wilson was tracking the current back upstream, over pools and rapids and the swirls of eddies, like a duck flying home to roost, while the other was sitting with his eyes closed, on a speeding train, in an altered mental state.

When the river divided into two tributaries, the flying Wilson chose the path of the smaller and followed its winding journey up a steep valley overgrown with trees. At the head of the valley, as the canopy of green thinned out and the last tree standing surrendered to moorland, the river was already reducing to the size of a narrow stream. Forging on, shedding rivulets and runnels along the way, it eventually diminished to the merest trickle as it ran between carpets of lichen and moss, and finally arrived back at its source, between rocky crags on a moorland fell covered in heather.

The dimly lit train carriage hurtled through the wet night. As it roared into a tunnel, the sudden thump of displaced air brought Wilson back from his out-of-body experience. The old lady had fallen asleep. The grandson was still playing Candy Crush. The lights in the carriage made rain streaks sparkle on the window. Wilson followed the translucent path of a single raindrop as it meandered then rushed, down the glass. For the raindrop; this single, living cell of liquid, this embryo of a river, the journey to the sea was already in motion. Then a totally new cognition presented Wilson with the mental image of a Scrabble board superimposed on window glass, set against the lamp-black night. The words 'energy field' were spelled out in a vertical line of tiles. Ten letters spelling 'the gateway' then dropped into position across the top – with the first 'e' in energy taking the role of the second 'e' in 'the gateway'. More letters fell into place, inter-linking like the answers to a self-fulfilling crossword puzzle. 'Dream', 'eleven', 'time', 'numerology', 'residual' and many other words from the lexicon of The Market Square all found a niche on the board and in so doing, spelled out the epiphany Wilson had been seeking. The explanation had been there all along - he just hadn't been looking for it from the perspective of the side room.

As the train pulled into Piccadilly station Wilson had his theory, a theory that could explain how the dot of meeting a girl in a dream could be connected to the dot of meeting her in real life. On his scrabble board, the words 'The Gateway' carried the most points.

Chapter 39

Home

Wednesday 1st November 2017

It was quarter past twelve in the morning when Wilson eased the Vespa into the garage and pulled down the door. A light was shining from the lounge and through the window Wilson could see Alex sitting on the sofa, reading a book illuminated by a table lamp.

"Hey Dad. You're up late. Everything okay?"

The breezy greeting from the hallway rang hollow and Wilson sensed the trepidation in his own voice, a trace of guilt possibly, as he closed the front door.

"Yeah, just catching up with some recent papers and research findings."

Wilson entered the lounge as his father looked up from his book.

"Mum's in bed. Your auntie Rita's tired her out. How was the concert?"

Wilson downgraded the trepidation to apprehension.

"Oh it was great! One of Hoover's mates plays in the band and we went backstage afterwards. That's why I'm late. Anyway, pretty tired myself, so I'll be off to bed. 'Night Dad."

Wilson was just about to make good his escape.

"So what's all this about missing socks then? And a website that Hoover and his brother have been working on all night?"

Wilson stopped in his tracks.

"Oh that? It's just a crazy idea of Hoover's. You know what he's like. He believes there's some kind of missing sock conspiracy and by building a website with pictures of odd socks — you know, people's missing socks — he can repatriate them."

"Yeah, it's a great idea. Won't work of course. But I like it! I told Hoover I'd upload some photos of my own. I thought Gloria was hiding mine on purpose to wind me up. I didn't realise it was actually a global phenomenon."

Alex closed his book.

"But Wilson, that's not what I meant. My question wasn't about the website. It was about something far more bizarre than a website for missing socks. It was a question of how Hoover and his brother could be working together, tonight, at Hoover's home, when he was also with you at a concert? Now, a website that can explain things like that — that'd be huge, don't you think?"

Wilson slumped in an armchair. He was angry and tired and didn't want a stupid mind game with his dad, who was gloating because he'd managed to trip him up.

"What did you do Dad? How did you find out?"

"Ah Wilson, you know..."

"Dad, shut up. What did you do?"

"What? What did you say Wilson?"

"I said, what did you do? Tonight! To find out? I'm not playing games Dad and I haven't got time for your Sherlock Holmes routine.

"Something important has happened that no one can ever know about, even you. What did you do?"

Alex paused for a second, sensing from the tone of Wilson's voice, and the look on his face, now was not the moment to be acting like a sitcom dad.

"Nothing son. You're safe. Look. All night your mum's been worried about you. She said she sensed something was happening; that you weren't at the concert. To be honest, I felt exactly the same. So I said I'd call Hoover's dad and without blatantly noseying, ask him if Hoover was with you at a concert."

"Dad. Jesus, you..."

"Wait Wilson, wait. Look, I know Hoover's dad. I used to go fishing with him. So I called him up about two hours ago on the pretext of asking him about catching carp in salmon rivers. I'm sure he thought I'd lost the plot. Anyway, I didn't mention the concert but during our conversation Hoover came to the phone and told me about his sock project. I didn't drop you in it. I told your mum you were in town with Hoover. So nobody knows what you've been up to today — including me!"

"I can't tell you."

"Why not? I told you I'm here to help. Remember our conversation in the canteen?"

"Dad, what does The Market Square look like?"

Alex started wringing his hands. He was about to speak, but stopped. Then he said in a clear and certain voice. "The Market Square can be anything son. Just like a dream."

"I know Dad. But what does it look like? You know what I'm asking. What does it look like?"

Alex paused again and shook his head. He was buying time as his eyes followed the pattern in the carpet.

"Why Wilson, why are you asking me that?"

"Because I want to know."

Alex held his breath for a moment that seemed to fill a minute.

"The Market Square has a Clock Tower."

Wilson flipped; tiredness and his mental state momentarily getting the better of him.

"Bloody hell Dad! So you've really been there! You've known about that place for years and never thought to give me help or support? Have you any idea how it messes up your head. You think you can grow out of that as a passing phase? Seriously? I so wanted to bloody well grow out of it. I thought I was becoming a bloody schizophrenic — until I met Daisy."

"Wilson, language! And volume: your mum's in bed."

"I really don't care Dad! And you should have said something a long time ago."

Wilson paused and then addressed his father with no trepidation whatsoever.

"You're a coward Dad! You chose a career outside your daft swimming pool metaphor, because you were too scared to dive in and get wet and..."

"Wilson, yes, okay, you're right, I can see that; but for good reason. When I met your mum and the twins came along, I decided to stop going to The Market Square because deep down I felt there was a possibility it could actually be dangerous. I had a family and a wife. I didn't want it to jeopardise my personal life, my children or my home. Then you came along, a master number and I knew there was a chance you'd discover The Market Square. I just hoped you wouldn't find it, or you'd blank it out after a while and stop. But I guess a part of me also wanted you to go there — to explore, to learn, to find out more about the energy."

"Just stop a second." Wilson leant back on the sofa and took a deep breath. "That is so messed-up."

Wilson raked his fingers through his hair as he sought to compose himself for what was about to follow. Then he leant forward, eye to eye level with his father and declared in a calm and even voice.

"I'm going to stop swearing now Dad, because in about ten seconds, I guarantee, it'll be your turn.

"You know how you just said you wanted me to explore, to find out more about the power of The Market Square? Well I did. I conducted a little experiment, which is why I was late home. But the good thing is, the experiment was a big success.

"Daisy and I did a bit of detective work and we discovered something quite astonishing. So I had to go to Scotland. I had to visit a care home today, in a very nice place called South Kessock. It's near Inverness and it's where I found a lady by the name of Alice. She'd been there for seventeen years. But she's not really called Alice, believe it or not, she's actually called Vanessa. Vanessa Clarke. In other words, Teaps's mum!"

There was complete and utter silence as the full meaning of Wilson's words registered. Alex's response was understandable, all things considered.

"Son, have you been taking drugs?"

"No Dad. It really was, I mean, is, Teaps's mum. Something happened to her when she was in London, I think it might have been a stroke. So she lost her memory and travelled all the way to Inverness, where her bag was stolen and nobody could identify her because she'd changed her hair and spoke Italian."

"But I thought she was dead or she'd absconded to France..."

"I know Dad, but that's not true. She was in a care home in Scotland all along, for all those years And that's where I've been today. To find Teaps's mum. Who is so definitely alive!"

Wilson was right, Alex did swear a couple of times when he heard that last sentence.

Chapter 40

Talking into the night

Wednesday 1st November 2017

Alex made two mugs of coffee and returned to the lounge for round two of revelations.

"Bear with me Dad, this explanation's going to jump about a bit and I'm still not sure I've got everything clear in my own head."

Wilson continued.

"You know I can speak quite a few languages, fly a helicopter, right — in fact, if there was one parked outside, I'd take you up to visit Vanessa."

Alex smiled at the notion.

"So Dad, The Market Square is where you access all this information, but it's also a chicane, where other forms of energy converge. Now, put those facts to one side and consider Morphic Fields. Morphic Fields are thought to be based on a memory of actions right; that animals can access, like a Wi-Fi of nature."

Alex nodded.

"So a baby spider logs in to this 'Wi-Fi of nature' to access the instructions on how to build a web left by billions of other spiders before it. Those instructions must be a form of energy, because they don't get destroyed. They're always out there. Like internet Wi-Fi, which is also energy?"

"It's a microwave actually, son. But yes, it's made of photons, which are essentially small bundles of energy."

"Okay Dad, so if our internet Wi-Fi is an energy field, let's assume the Wi-Fi of nature is also a type of energy field."

"Yes, I'll go with that. If it exists, of course, but..."

"Dad. Dad, just give me two minutes and I'm done. A few weeks ago you told me about unknown types of energy. Well I think a Morphic Field and a dream energy field are two of those unknown types. And when we dream all that dream energy somehow flows into The Market Square. My laptop takes the energy in a Wi-Fi signal and builds a web page. In The Market Square, I take the energy from dreams to learn to play the piano. From all the people who have ever dreamt of playing the piano or their piano lessons. They leave a trace. I can access the data, I can feel it, that's our special gift — mine and Daisy's and yours I guess. But there's even more to it. It can take six months to get your head round a new language, but I can reach the same level after just six nights in The Market Square. And this is the thing, this came to me on the train today. Learning a language involves time. And time, this very moment, me and you drinking coffee, leaves a trace, a little package of energy on a Polaroid snapshot of right now. And a million, billion nows, altogether, make the past. And all those traces, everyone's trace, the energy of time also runs through The Market Square."

Wilson paused for breath and leant forward to monitor his father's facial expression as he came to the final point.

"Are you still with me?"

"I'm with you so far son. Go on."

"In The Market Square, all those Polaroids can be pushed even closer together, like compressed data, like the zip files on my laptop. So you can experience, or absorb, more of the past in a much shorter time. In The Market Square, you can access the energy of past dreams to find piano lessons. And if you combine that with a time energy field, you can zip-up weeks of tuition and store it in a file that I can download in minutes. That's what we did, to find Vanessa."

Wilson knew his father was keeping pace.

"Daisy logged in to the Wi-Fi of dreams and found Vanessa in her wedding dress. She crashed that dream, to bring her into The Market Square. Then once Vanessa was there, Daisy accessed the time energy field, straddled the two, and we saw everything unfold, right in front of our eyes. We saw all the traces of her life pass by in minutes."

It took a moment for Alex to reply.

"Wilson. That, that is just the most incredible thing I've ever heard — anyone has ever heard. If what you're saying is true... I don't have the words. It's incredible. We believe in the space-time particle and we're getting close with the Higgs boson, but this could be the biggest scientific finding ever. Every physics book, every science book would have to be rewritten, maybe even the Bible!"

"Funny you should say that Dad. You see, rescuing Vanessa was easy, we used dream energy to find her and then time energy to look through her trace, then a trip to Inverness. But something makes it more complicated, mind-blowing, as you'd say, because I think there's another type of energy."

"I'm mind-blown enough son."

"Dad, here's a question: how did I know Vanessa wasn't dead?"

"You mean, how did you know she was still alive?"

"Yeah, how did I know she was still alive?"

"A lucky guess, a hunch."

"No Dad, it wasn't a guess. How did I know Vanessa Clarke was still alive even before Daisy and I brought her to The Market Square?"

Alex was struggling to follow the logic.

"I've no idea son."

"Someone told me, that's how. I don't know who these characters are, but they told me about another type of energy. The energy of the human spirit. And they told me — in a dream, in The Gateway — that Vanessa's spirit had not been extinguished, because there was no gold bangle and I'd find her in The Market Square. Big Mac — who works for The Powers That Be and knows all about ghosts — told me that Teaps's mum was still alive. And while we're on the subject, I think The Market Square is actually in Ward 3B of Stockport Infirmary and I know exactly how déjà vu comes about, because Short Cake — who also works for The Powers That Be — told me."

Alex Armitage said absolutely nothing, then rose to his feet and went directly to bed. Unsteady on his feet, both hands held the bannister as he climbed the stairs. One of the effects of having your mind blown.

Chapter 41

Any news?

The first thing Wilson did when he woke the next morning was check BBC North West on his phone. There was no story about Vanessa Clarke. He checked BBC Scotland. The same.

A text message arrived from Daisy.

'Hi W. Sorry I went silent on you last night. Major issues with Grandma, but she's in SHH, comfortable. Going to see her again later. Any news? D x'

'No, nothing yet. Thinking maybe a dozy cleaner binned the paper. Please God no. Don't think they'll let Frank Spencer back in that place. Call you later. W x'

'Frank Spencer?'

'He's from some old comedy programme Dad watches. His name just popped into my head. I'll explain later.'

Teaps and Hoover were eating cheese toasties as Wilson crossed the college canteen to join them. All appeared normal.

"How's it going, boys?" Wilson asked, his eyes searching Teaps's face for a sign of news.

"Fair to middling," said Hoover, through a mouthful of hot cheese; a blob of which was dangling from the end of his chin like a creamy cocoon.

"We've got six hundred socks now."

"Any matches?"

"No. We had a false alarm from Ecuador though. Same colour, same pattern, but wrong size. The guy in Cardiff was an eight and the guy in

Ecuador was a twelve. Not even close."

"How are you Teaps? All okay?"

"For now, yeah. Dad was alright when I left him, nursing a hangover, but let's see what this afternoon brings. And I've got no phone at the moment; Spinner's nose broke it."

"How was the Prince's Trust thing?" Hoover asked.

"What Prince's Trust thing?"

"Yesterday, Town Hall, your mum, charity, day away from college."

"What? Oh that. Err, yeah, I met the Prince."

"Riiiiiighttttt. As if" said Hoover.

"No way" said Teaps.

"Way" said Wilson.

"Bollocks" said Hoover.

A bell rang to signal the next period of classes and herds of students, saddled with bags and backpacks filed out of the canteen and trailed across the recreation square.

"Like wildebeest crossing the Serengeti" said Hoover, who was heading to the same part of the college as Wilson.

Teaps's IT room was in a different building and Wilson watched him walk away, joking and chatting up one of his ex-girlfriends. Perhaps the dozy cleaner had binned the slip of paper after all.

Nobody told Wilson that half an hour into his Computing class, Teaps was passed a note asking him to report urgently to the Principal's office, but when Wilson arrived home later that afternoon, he found out. The seismic change had arrived. Magnitude 7.9 on the Richter Scale.

Gloria came rushing into the hallway as Wilson was halfway out of his jacket, grabbed his arm and dragged him into the lounge. The TV was on.

"Isn't it just the most incredible thing Wilson, the most incredible, unbelievable thing."

His mum was weeping into a damp lace hanky.

Wilson removed the other half of his jacket and threw it on the sofa.

"It's a miracle Wilson, that's the only word to describe it. A miracle for that blessed boy and his poor father."

Wilson's mum was sobbing uncontrollably.

The image on the TV was of a reporter standing outside a red-brick building, the tail of a police helicopter was jutting into the shot. Directly behind the reporter stood a sign that read: 'The South Kessock Care Home'.

Wilson sat down on the sofa. His mum joined him — still sobbing — and put her hand on his knee. They listened to the reporter.

"I'm standing here in South Kessock, a quiet, peaceful suburb just a few minutes from the centre of Inverness in the north of Scotland. You can forget biblical stories of turning water into wine, because yesterday, in the building behind me, a real miracle occurred, witnessed by the staff of the South Kessock Care Home."

The screen then cut to a photo of Vanessa from around the time of her wedding. The reporter continued as a voiceover.

"Seventeen years ago, Vanessa Clarke, a successful businesswoman from Stockport, left the family home to attend a meeting in London and seemingly walked out of the lives of her husband and her one-year-old son forever..."

Wilson's mum didn't know whether to be happy or sad, to laugh or cry, so she did both.

"...around the same time, this lady, known only as Alice..."

The screen switched to a grainy picture of care home residents enjoying Christmas dinner. The face of a smiling Alice was circled in red.

"...was found sitting in a park in Inverness, cold, alone, with no knowledge of who she was or where she was. That is, until late yesterday afternoon when a nurse made an incredible discovery."

Cut to the interview recorded earlier with the nurse.

"Well, I was taking Alice her afternoon cup of tea. She always has it in her room. She's such a lovely lady; never any trouble. So, I placed the cup on her bedside table and I was just about to leave when she pulled at my skirt and I turned around, and..."

The nurse hesitated for a moment and wiped a tear from her eye.

"Yes... and she pulled my skirt ever so gently."

She paused again but needed the back of both hands to wipe away the tears this time. Wilson's mum was listening intently and copying her actions.

"And then I looked down, and she was, like, looking up at me and, you know, she was crying..."

The nurse was really struggling to contain her emotions.

"And then she slowly handed me a scrap of paper and on the paper she'd written, 'My name is Vanessa Clarke'. So I ran and grabbed the duty supervisor and then... and then... Sorry, I have to stop... it's hard to believe."

Now Wilson couldn't stop *his* eyes watering.

The screen switched back to the reporter who was standing with two men, still outside the home. One wore a suit and the other was a policeman. The interviewer turned to the camera.

"I'm joined here now by Vincent Machonachie, company operations director for the South Kessock Care Home and Sergeant Derek Jordan, the duty officer with the North Caledonia Constabulary yesterday afternoon.

"Gentlemen, thank you for joining me on this truly amazing day. We've just heard from the nurse who found the note, Staff Nurse Trisha Sedgwick. So Vincent, can you tell us what happened next?"

"Well, it started with a call from Celia Green, around 5 p.m. yesterday afternoon. Celia told me there'd been an incident and they weren't sure how to deal with it. She wouldn't say anything over the phone, so of course I came down immediately. At first I thought it was all a prank. But when Celia took me to her office and showed me the story on the internet about Vanessa Clarke, and a photo, we realised *that* person was also *our* Alice. The facial similarity, even with the passage of time, was striking – plus, how else would Alice know about Vanessa Clarke? We didn't even know she could write."

"So what happened then?"

"I called the police and spoke to Sergeant Jordan."

"Sergeant Jordan, good afternoon. Talk us through what happened next."

"Well to be honest, when I got the call, the message was like gobbledygook. I thought Vincent had been on the whisky. So I rushed down here, and they told me the whole story. Then I got on to Scotland Yard, who sent us the incident and missing person files and for the next few hours we tried to make sense of everything, and we're still doing that now."

"I understand that Vanessa's husband Michael and also her son Graham are here right now?"

"Aye. We had their address on record and at lunchtime, a police helicopter picked them up and brought them straight here."

"What did they say? Who broke the news to them?"

"It was funny actually. My colleagues in Greater Manchester told me the lad thought they'd called to arrest him. Anyhow, they told Graham and his father there'd been a sudden development in the search for Vanessa and asked for help with enquiries. We have to be careful though. While it seems likely that Alice and Vanessa are one and the same person, we won't be a hundred per cent sure until we get the DNA test results back."

A second policeman then came into view and whispered something in Sergeant Jordan's ear. Sergeant Jordan smiled and cleared his throat.

"Err, I've just been told by my colleague that Alice's DNA was a one hundred per cent match with the boy's. So we can now say with certainty that Alice is Vanessa Clarke."

Cheering could be heard in the background. The camera scanned the perimeter of the care home. There was a battalion of photographers, TV cameras, mobile broadcasting units and people, hundreds of people, waving at the cameras.

"Bloody hell," said Wilson. "I never thought all this would happen."

"Me neither. Though I did pray for it, I really did," said Gloria, not fully appreciating Wilson's point.

The reporter had his finger on his earpiece.

"I'm being told that the father and son – that is, Michael and his son, Graham – are coming out in a second to give a quick interview."

The film editor switched to a different camera focused on the entrance to the care home. The door was pushed open by a policeman as Teaps, his dad and Celia Green emerged to face TV cameras and journalists shouting questions.

Wilson could see from the puffy eyes that Teaps had been crying.

"I'd just like to read this prepared statement, if I may," said Celia.

"The staff and management of South Kessock Care Home and myself, would personally like to say..."

A reporter put his microphone in front of Teaps, who had his arm round his dad's shoulders and a camera instantly zoomed in. Celia Green was jostled to one side.

"Mr Clarke, tell us about the emotions you're feeling right now. Can you put them into words?"

Michael was standing tall and straight with his shoulders back and at first Wilson didn't recognise the person he'd seen cowering at the feet of Blamire.

"All I can say is that my son and I never once doubted that Vanessa would come back. She loved Graham with everything she had and she would never have left him. I told everyone that at the time and I knew we'd find her one day. We never, ever, gave up hope."

"Is there a chance we'll get to see her?"

"No, I don't think you'll ever see her. When Graham and I take her home, we won't be letting her out of the house ever again. She's back for good this time."

Then Michael had to stop because he was too emotional to speak so the reporter turned to his son.

"Graham, how does it feel to have your mum back?"

"It's just incredible. I was only a baby when she disappeared so I don't really remember her. But of course, I missed not having a mum, like my friends. And I always felt she was still alive, just like my dad said. He never once stopped willing her to come back to us, praying for it. The pain almost ruined his life, but I think we'll be just great now and that's the main thing."

Then Teaps hugged his dad and someone ushered them back inside the home and the door closed.

"So there we have it, a modern-day miracle. A missing mum back in the arms of her loving family after being lost for seventeen years. Questions will be asked as to why the stories of the two missing women, Alice and Vanessa, were never pieced together, and no doubt there will be a full inquiry. But for now, as the night falls on the beautiful Beauly Firth, this is Felix Armstrong for BBC Scotland saying a miraculous good evening from the South Kessock Care Home."

"In other news now..."

Wilson switched the TV off. He sensed that a moment for quiet reflection and the curative powers of a cup of tea were needed. Gloria was still staring at the blank TV screen.

"You were back late last night love. Your dad and I had a funny feeling about you, like something was wrong."

"Nah, the gig just went on a bit. And then I got chatting to Dad for an hour or so."

"I know. I don't think he went slept well last night. Then he was up and off for the early train again. He'll be shattered. Do you think he's heard about Graham?"

"Oh I'm pretty sure he will have Mum. Certain in fact. I'll go and make you a cuppa. I think you might be suffering from shock. I know I am."

"Think of it Wilson. That poor woman, trapped in that place for seventeen years, almost like a hostage. Why didn't she say something, tell someone?"

"I don't know Mum. I've no idea."

"It's a scandal. She never got to see her baby grow up."

As Wilson waited for the kettle to boil, four hundred miles away, more steam was rising. Having been snubbed on national TV, Celia Green was thinking through the previous day's events. She was putting two and two together and it was adding up to eleven and a visitor by the name of Frank Spencer. It was too much of a coincidence that a resident, who had never communicated in any way and with no visitors for seventeen years, would suddenly write a help note on the same day she'd been the focus of attention for a suspicious young lad.

Celia picked up the phone and dialled Sergeant Jordan.

Chapter 42

The hiccups

Thursday 2nd November 2017

That night, and into the morning, Wilson and Daisy celebrated the incredible result of their detective work.

The Market Square was wearing its dancing shoes and authentically attired in the guise of the magnificent ballroom at the top of Blackpool Tower. Cobbles had been replaced with a sprung floor of mahogany, oak and walnut. A domed ceiling, decorated with finely detailed frescoes and faux-neoclassical plaster relief, arched over the entire square. The twinkle from three, magnificent crystal chandeliers reflected jewels of light from a rotating mirrorball. The buildings on the perimeter of the square had all been remodelled to feature at least one theatre-style box jutting out over the dance floor at circle level. Each box held an audience of five or six people, all dressed in splendid Edwardian costume. The music, which rolled and cascaded around the entire Market Square, came from a wonderfully ornate and authentic Wurlitzer pipe organ taking centre stage on the far side.

"*Strictly's* in town," said Daisy as Wilson arrived to join her.

The dance floor was a quadrangle of long, flowing dresses, feathered hats, black tie and tails and elaborate waxed moustaches. A rotund, pompous-looking man with a flushed, red face and bushy whiskers strode over and with a polite bow, enquired as to "the possibility of mademoiselle honouring me with the pleasure of the next waltz."

Daisy took the man's pudgy, pink hand and curtseyed, which Wilson thought was completely over-the-top. She was wearing a voluminous pink hoop skirt, long white gloves, black Doc Martens and her hair was in finely coiled ringlets. Daisy pulled her tongue out and winked at

Wilson as she twirled across the floor.

Somebody tapped Wilson on the shoulder and he turned to be confronted by a lady, standing at least a foot taller than himself. Her gown was made from blue silk with white lace around the edges. A bustle protruded from the back, creating the impression of someone hidden beneath her skirts. She had the waist of an egg timer and the bodice of her dress, stretched like a corset, was tailored with all kinds of fancy trimming and embroidery. A monocle was wedged in one eye and her hair had been braided and then pinned to form an elaborate stack, from which some of the braids were tumbling free. She reminded Wilson of a praying mantis or, more accurately, a gorgon.

"You really can't just stand there ogling" said the Medusa with a haughty, plummy accent, "it's not polite."

She took Wilson's arm and with surprising force, dragged him onto the dance floor. The button-fronted breeches Wilson was wearing were far too tight and gave him a wedgie. The frock coat was too big and the cravat pinched his neck. Nevertheless, over the course of the next hour, under the expert tutelage of Medusa, Wilson managed to master the timing and footwork for the waltz, the samba, the paso doble and the tango.

"She was good fun, in a matronly sort of way" he said to Daisy as they sat drinking Champagne in their own private box. They were looking down upon the graceful choreography of what Daisy identified as 'the foxtrot'.

"I feel like the Queen," she said, as bubbles tickled and fizzed somewhere inside her nose. She raised her Champagne flute and they toasted the liberation of Vanessa Clarke.

"Do you think we'll have hangovers tomorrow?"

Wilson started laughing.

"You know what Daisy? I never considered that. It's a great thought though. However much we celebrate, we'll still be totally sober when we wake up in the morning. What an excellent place this Market Square is.

"Another bottle then my dear?" Wilson asked, playfully adjusting the cravat.

"For sure... err, I mean yes, my dear Lord Armitage, that would be truly delightful" said Daisy, giggling and hiccuping as Wilson departed to find the waiter in charge of their Royal Box.

"But not a bottle Wilson" she called after him, "get one of those big magnum thingies and make sure it's the most expensive. In fact, get two!"

Chapter 43

Smile, you're on Sky News

Thursday 2nd November 2017

Wilson woke early to the ping of a message from Daisy.

'Wilson, have you seen it? The news? Teaps is everywhere. The front page of the papers, on breakfast TV, he's all over social media. He's gone viral!!'

Wilson sat up in bed, clicked a 'news' app on his phone and waited.

The first chunk of data delivered a photo of Teaps and his dad. They were smiling and had their arms around each others shoulders as they stood outside the South Kessock Care Home.

Then came the headline: 'Husband and Son Reunited with Missing Mum After 17 Years'.

Wilson knew the story of course, but the online report carried much more detail than the TV broadcast the previous evening. There were links to the old coverage about Vanessa going missing in London and the subsequent police search. One report from a local paper in Inverness talked about a woman who had 'probably been abandoned by one of the crofting families on the Outer Hebrides'. A policeman from Inverness had been interviewed that morning and was quoted as saying, 'we made enquiries at the time, but in the absence of any evidence or other possible line of enquiry, the investigation was eventually dropped'.

When asked if it was true, as suggested by a source inside the local police, 'that the case was given a low priority because the woman had impaired mental faculties', he said hospital tests at the time had proved inconclusive and there would be a full internal investigation. The statement was accompanied by a photo and from his facial expression, it appeared that Assistant Chief Constable Simon Montague was not chuffed to find himself in the spotlight. There was no mention of the current whereabouts of Teaps and his parents, but Wilson was certain they wouldn't be back in their dingy flat opposite the pub. He checked a few other media sites, Twitter was abuzz with the news.

As Wilson ate his breakfast, his mum was sitting in the lounge watching *Good Morning* on TV. The presenters were interviewing a vicar from Romiley, who was outlining the pastoral care and time for healing that Mrs Clarke and her family would need over the coming months and years.

Gloria was still sobbing and simply said, "goodbye son" as he left for college.

Wilson had a sense of foreboding about the day ahead; the discovery of Vanessa had been meticulously planned, but the aftermath was completely out of his control. There was a major plus point to be thankful for though, because even after downing two magnums of Moët with Daisy, he'd woken with a perfectly clear head.

Twenty minutes later, Wilson eased on the brake of the Vespa and indicated to turn left into the college car park. A security guard in a hi-vis orange jacket barred his entry through the gates and informed Wilson that the car park was closed for the day and he would have to find a space further down the road. Wilson drove past the college grounds and glanced through the railings. The aftermath had arrived. The car park was rammed full with outside broadcast vans, reporters and cameramen. After about three hundred yards, he managed to find a gap for the Vespa, then he walked back to the gates, showed his student pass to the hi-vis man and entered the college grounds.

Sky News, BBC, ITV, Channel 4 and French and German TV broadcast vans, with logos on the sides and aerials on the roof, filled every bay in the car park. A Japanese TV vehicle was parked with two wheels on the steps leading to the college's main entrance, in front of which, Mr Proctor, Teaps's personal tutor, and Miss Patel, an English teacher, were being interviewed.

Wilson skirted around the back of the melee and made for the common room, but he was confronted by another pack of eager reporters grilling anyone and everyone, on the subject of Graham Clarke.

"Did he ever mention his mum or talk about her?"

"How did he get the nickname Teaps?"

"Woz 'ee ever down or, 'ow you say, melancholeee?"

"Who are his best friends here at the college?"

Wilson retreated deeper into the hood of his parka on hearing the last question and searched for a different route to the sanctuary of the common room. His phone vibrated on silent and he tapped the screen. It was the unknown number from the other night.

Teaps's dad. It's Teaps!

Wilson turned from the scrum and headed for the empty tennis courts on the periphery of the college grounds and well out of earshot. He answered the phone on the move.

"Hi, it's me, Wilson."

"I know Wilson. I've just called you."

"Mate, it's incredible! Just unbelievable! How are you? Your mum, your dad? The cameras are all over the college. You're on TV. You're famous man. Viral. My mum's not stopped crying since she heard."

"I know. It's a miracle."

From the hushed tone of his voice, Wilson suspected that Teaps was trying to speak without being overheard.

"I haven't slept since I... Awww, man, I still can't get over it. I was calling to let you know everything's okay."

"Thanks pal. Wasn't worried, obviously. But I was waiting to hear from you. So how is your mum? And your dad? What did you think when you saw her in that room? Will she get her memory back? Does she remember you? Where are you now?"

"I can't really speak. We're at a private hospital near Chester. Dad's become a changed man, virtually overnight, he really has. Don't tell anyone where we are though, even Hoover — especially Hoover. Some agent from *Ok* magazine wants an exclusive on the story and we've to keep everything secret. But the main thing is, my mum's here. She's back after all these years. I can't believe it. Look, I gotta go. I'll text you later when I've got a minute."

The call over, Wilson and Teaps picked up where they'd left off.

For Teaps, that was sitting in a private room with his dad, watching his mum sleeping. As he did so, it struck him as odd that Wilson knew his mum had been in a room, and that she had memory loss. How did he know? A doctor had only just told them about that!

"We can see from the scans that some years ago Mrs Clarke suffered a small but severe stroke that damaged cerebral connections to her memory. Probably around the time she went missing in London. We don't believe her memory has been wiped clean as such, because the damage was limited to the neural networks that govern retrieval, rather than memory storage itself. With cognitive therapy at the time, those connections might have been restored, but in my professional opinion that's not likely to be possible after all these years."

Wilson meanwhile, had headed back to the common room where he was cornered by a reporter after being pointed out by a girlfriend of Teaps.

"Jan Smith, Sky News. I understand you're Graham Clarke's best friend. What do you think of the news?"

A microphone was thrust in front of Wilson's face and the intrusive lens of a camera followed.

"It's, err, it's just sensational. The best news ever."

"Did Graham ever think he would see his mother again?"

"Err, I dunno really. We spoke about her sometimes. I know his dad never stopped believing that she'd come back. He knew she hadn't run away or anything like that."

"Where is Graham now?"

"I don't know. He couldn't tell me."

"He couldn't tell you? So you've spoken to him then?"

"Yeah, really briefly, but he, err... I don't know where he is."

"Is it true that Ok magazine have offered a million pounds for an exclusive?"

"I can't say. I'm just so happy his mum's back. I gotta go. Thanks."

Wilson pushed the microphone and camera away and forced his way through the doors of the common room – where he then caught sight of himself pushing the microphone and camera away. He was following his own footsteps via a TV mounted on the wall.

"It's like déjà vu" shouted Hoover, waving him over.

Hoover was sitting with six or seven others, watching the story unfold on TV. Spinner was with them; his arm was cradled in a sling and one side of his face was a swatch book of purple and yellow bruising.

"Thought you were in hospital Spinner?"

"Discharged myself didn't I, when I heard about the commotion and the good news."

"You're the news mate, and it's all bad news" said Wilson.

Hoover's long arm stretched out to keep Spinner in his seat.

"Leave it out mate" he said looking at Spinner threateningly. "In fact, don't know why you're here with us anyway. Go and sit over there, in the naughty boys' corner. Go on, clear off."

Spinner got up and trudged away.

"What a low life" said Hoover.

Wilson sat on the vacated chair and watched the images on TV. He couldn't hear the voice-over for all the din in the common room. The screen was showing a photo of a happy Mr and Mrs Clarke on their wedding day, but the caption underneath was referring to an internal investigation within the North Caledonia Constabulary.

"I'd have said there was more chance of one of your socks turning up than this happening" said Wilson.

"Wilson, do you want to go and join Spinner over there in the naughty boys' corner... Oh, what the hell does he want now?"

Spinner had hobbled back over to thrust a mobile phone into Wilson's hand.

"It's Blamire. He wants a word."

Wilson put a finger in one ear and pressed the phone to the other.

"Hello?"

"Hey, Winston, how are you my friend? It's me, Blamire? The good-lookin' fella, the landlord for your friend Teaps and his muppet of a dad. We had a discussion in the flat the other morning."

"I know who you are."

"Well, I was just thinking, about all of this bein' a bit of a turn-up for the books. You see, there I was at home last night, readin' the kids a bedtime story, when me missus shouts me to come and see what's happening on TV. Can you believe it, there was the muppet and son, complete with a mum. All happy families again."

"Listen Blamire, can you get to the point?"

"So, when I heard this morning this rumour see, that some gossip mag' me wife reads is gonna fork out a million quid for the exclusive story, it got me thinking! So I alerted my pet hyena and told him to get out of his sick-bed and back to school, cos he could learn how to make a bit of bunce."

Wilson turned to Spinner.

"And then, a couple of minutes ago, when you let slip about your chat with our Mr Teaps, I thought maybe you could pass him a personal message about interest on the interest. Like my little phrase Winston? Interest, as in, on top of the five grand he owes me, and interest, as in, he'll be a rich lad in the next couple of weeks from all the stories in the papers. So tell him the interest on the interest now makes what he owes me eight grand, and he's got two weeks. Or his mum'll be missing him for another seventeen years. I'll be in touch."

Then the call was over.

Wilson stood up with purpose and headed over to Spinner to hand the phone back. As Spinner took it, Wilson grabbed his thumb and bent the knuckle down into the palm. Spinner winced in pain but didn't scream out. Wilson wasn't applying that much pressure, just enough to let Spinner know he was being serious, to shut up and listen.

"Spinner, whatever Teaps did to you the other day, you deserved, because you're a slimy rat."

Wilson exerted a bit more pressure and Spinner felt it.

"If I see you in this common room again, you won't be getting out of hospital, full stop. You'll have a permanent bed somewhere, a bit like Teaps's mum — you know, Teaps, your friend? Tell Blamire not to use his little dog to deliver his messages, get him to call me himself. You've got my number pusher-man."

Wilson gave the thumb a final squeeze.

As Spinner squealed and everyone in the common room turned to the source of the distress, Wilson was heading back to Hoover.

"What was that all about?"

"Nothing. Just giving Spinner a message to pass on to someone."

A different directive then came over the college tannoy system.

"As a result of the current media interest in the college and the major disturbance to our schedules, there will be no further classes. The business of education will resume as normal tomorrow."

For the next hour, Wilson and company sat around drinking coffee, watching the news, laughing at Wilson's crap TV interview technique and generally speculating on what the future held for Teaps. They didn't see Spinner slouch off, but Blamire got the message. Wilson's phone beeped with a text.

'Winston. Tough guy. Will be in touch. Still eight grand. Don't care where it comes from. Blamire.'

Then his phone beeped again. Wilson was sufficiently wound up to fight fire with even more fire, but the text message was from Daisy.

'W, going to Stockport this afternoon to see Grandma. Want to come and meet her? Don't worry, will only be me. No parents etc. D'

Wilson had a free afternoon and he was definitely interested in meeting Daisy's grandma. After all, she knew about The Market Square. Plus, there was another reason he wanted to go to Ward 3B.

'Yeah, 4 sure. What time?'

'Three thirty at the main reception.'

'Okay.'

Then Wilson had second thoughts.

'No, meet at the entrance to the main car park, in front of the new bit of the hospital. By the information boards.'

'Err. Okay. D X'

Chapter 44

Ward 3B

Wilson arrived at the hospital with five minutes to spare and passed the time reading the information boards. One board was for the purpose of navigation and directed visitors to Reception, X-ray and Outpatients. The other carried details of the NHS Foundation Trust and the history of the site.

The hospital consisted of a new state of the art structure, clad with panels in calming, pastel shades and a crumbling red-brick building, from the Victorian era, that had to be retained because of its Grade I listing. The old section had frontage to the A6 and a facade featuring three enormous windows, one of which Wilson knew only too well.

The new building housed the core of the hospital's services. The old building, half propped up with scaffolding, provided palliative care for the elderly and terminally ill. Daisy's grandma had a bed in Ward 3B, a ward Wilson suspected was home to certain energy fields and déjà vu headaches.

Daisy arrived and gave him a hug.

"Thanks for coming Wilson."

"No, I wanted to come, I wanted to meet your grandma."

"Well she's not really with us anymore, it's just a matter of days. They've stopped feeding her and it seems cruel, but there's no quality of life. Mum's been here since she arrived from Bournemouth, but she's gone home to shower now and change, so I want you to meet Gran, before she leaves us. She's called Gwendolyn."

They walked to reception hand in hand.

"Have you seen Teaps?"

"No, but I spoke to him briefly. He's with his mum at some kind of special hospital. He said everything's good."

"The story's never been off the news. Even Mum was going on about it. I didn't tell her Teaps was your best friend."

"To be honest, I just want it to blow over now. It's strange. Although we've done this incredibly good thing, made a miracle like they say on TV, it actually freaks me out."

Wilson stopped and turned to Daisy.

"Do you think we've been playing God? We made something happen that maybe, wasn't supposed to. We held Vanessa's future in our hands and decided what happens next. All the repercussions that follow, like me nearly breaking someone's thumb, are a result of our actions."

"Yeah Wilson, I've been thinking that as well. But then I thought it could also be God who showed us The Market Square in the first place, and how to look back in time to find Vanessa. Maybe God wanted her to be found and we had no say in it.

"I don't know much about philosophical stuff, you know, free will and fate and all that, but I know I'd do it again. And if I was in the same situation as Teaps, I'd want someone to do the same for me, to find my missing mum. I wouldn't worry about playing God, I'd just want Mum back."

"Yeah, I know Daisy, it's great that we rescued her, but what if we cause a chain of events so bad, it turns out she was better off, everyone was better off, when she was in the nursing home. Does that make sense?"

"Wilson, I get your concerns, I really do, but right now we're here to see Grandma, so can we talk about this later."

Daisy wrapped both arms round one of Wilson's as they carried on to the hospital entrance.

"Wilson you're a good person. That's all you need to know."

They walked through the hospital reception area and down a long, wide corridor. Other corridors led off at intervals, to Maternity Ward 7, Coronary 1 and Neonatal 5. Wilson and Daisy kept walking until they eventually reached the point where the steelwork of the new hospital was grafted to the red-brick of the old building. They made a ninety-degree turn beneath a sign pointing to Ward 3B and Wilson immediately felt the pressure of a vice closing on his head. As he took the next few steps, a tidal wave of déjà vu arrived, his head started pounding violently, as though a bare-knuckle boxer was trying to thump a hole from inside his skull. After another three steps Wilson collapsed on the floor and threw up.

"You've probably picked up the stomach bug that was sweeping through town last week. Lots of water and you'll be fine" said a doctor, having checked Wilson over. Wilson and Daisy were no longer in sight of Ward 3B. They were sitting in an empty waiting room just off the main corridor.

"Daisy" said Wilson, still looking green around the gills, "I have to tell you something."

"That wasn't a stomach bug was it?"

"No it wasn't. It was caused by this place."

Wilson paused to get his thoughts in order and sipped water from a plastic cup.

"Daisy, I don't think it's a random coincidence that you and I were born here, my dad, and possibly your grandma too. I also don't think it's by chance our birth dates align, we're all a number eleven and we all visit The Market Square. My dad described the Clock Tower; he's definitely been there."

Wilson started to laugh at how ridiculous he was sounding. But Daisy wasn't laughing.

"For years I've been coming past this hospital and every time, I'd get a slight feeling of déjà vu. An impression I'd been here before. Recently, it's started to become painful, like the most powerful déjà vu mixed with a migraine, but stronger. That's what happened just then, when we turned the corner to Ward 3B and I think I know why."

"Go on" said Daisy.

"This analogy came to me on the train the other night. When I was at junior school, we went to Saddleworth Moor with a teacher. It'd been raining and we followed a trickle of water running between the pebbles. The trickle merged with other trickles and became a small stream, then a beck and eventually we came to a road, where all this gushing water was directed into a concrete tunnel and under the road, to prevent any flooding.

I think that when we dream, all the dream energy merges and flows together, like a beck. Every moment we live, every trace, also combine to make another beck. And in some places, they meet. So there's this gushing flow of energy that needs to be channelled through a pipe, to avoid flooding. I think that tunnel is in the corridor outside 3B.

"I also believe, to end the analogy, that we can put a foot in a beck of dream energy and feel people's dreams flow by. At the same time, we can put the other foot in a beck of time energy and straddle both. We combine dreams with the time traces of people's lives, their past and that's how we found Vanessa. Somehow, in that corridor, the two becks merge together and the energy flow is so strong and deep it makes me feel ill. I don't know why it didn't affect you in the same way though."

Wilson sat back and emptied the plastic cup.

"Wow" said Daisy.

"You need to be my wading stick."

"Your wading stick, what the hell is that?"

"Dad uses one to steady himself against the current when he's fishing in a river. You didn't feel anything when we turned the corridor to 3B, so I want to try walking down there holding on to you. Like a wading stick."

"You certainly know how to flatter a girl Wilson."

They left the waiting room and headed back down the corridor and stopped at the 3B sign and the ninety-degree turn.

Daisy held Wilson's arm.

"Ready?"

"Ready" said Wilson.

They turned the corner and faced the doors of 3B, just thirty metres away. This time however, there was no excruciating headache, no superstrength déjà vu, no nausea. Wilson could sense prickly spikes of energy in the air, all around him, like a tangible static before a thunderstorm, but it was no longer debilitating.

"Let go, just for a second."

Daisy slowly lifted her hand from Wilson's arm – at the same time his legs buckled, he winced with pain and began to retch. She quickly grabbed his arm and Wilson steadied himself.

"Thanks" he whispered. "Keep going."

They walked arm in arm with Wilson gazing down the corridor toward the glass and wood-panelled swing doors of Ward 3B. He closed his eyes and slowly moved his head from side to side and then up and down as though blindly searching for something.

"Wilson" whispered Daisy "why have you closed your eyes?"

"Because, now I can see everything."

He urged Daisy onwards, still shifting his head from side to side. As they slowly advanced, Wilson stretched out his arm as if reaching out for an invisible, floating object that only he could see in front of his face. Daisy looked over her shoulder to make sure nobody was following them, men in white coats possibly? They resembled an elderly couple shuffling towards a geriatric ward.

When she turned back, Wilson had a white plastic rocket in his hand, like a toy model from an Airfix kit. He stopped walking and scratched the transfer, a stars and stripes flag, that had been positioned on the rocket upside down. Wilson smiled at a distant memory, his eyes still firmly closed. Then, as though distracted by a different floating object, he let the rocket slip through his fingers and fall to the floor. It zoomed off past Daisy's leg. She turned to monitor its progress but it was nowhere to be seen. Then Wilson had a small doll in his hand. He was playing with the stringy little toy, all arms and legs and platform shoes. He let the doll drop to the floor and again it flew past Daisy's leg. But this time she followed the journey as the doll disappeared into thin air – it seemed an invisible current, a transparent river had carried it away downstream and a strong undertow had pulled the helpless toy beneath the surface.

Wilson opened his eyes.

"Take me back Daisy" he whispered hoarsely. "I'm very tired. Need to go back, now, quickly."

She kept her arm firmly entwined around his as they turned and trudged back up the corridor, around the ninety-degree turn and out of sight of Ward 3B. Daisy slowly released her grip on Wilson's arm. He collapsed to the floor, as though someone had just stolen all of his bones. A few minutes later a doctor and two nurses from A&E came flying down the corridor quickly followed by a porter pushing a trolley bed.

Chapter 45

They never thought of that

Friday 3rd November 2017

"So, Sergeant Jordan, like I say, it's all too much of a coincidence. Alice is here for seventeen years without a single visitor, then this nervous young lad turns up with some cock and bull story about finding a home for a step-dad who lives in Stockport. While he's here, he shows a lot of interest in Alice and then two hours later, she miraculously writes a message to say she's really called Vanessa Clarke, who also happens to come from Stockport."

Sergeant Derek Jordan was taking notes, not convinced that the heartwarming elation of the last few days could ever warrant a police investigation. However, having been snubbed live on TV, the duty manager had grabbed a bone and she wasn't letting go.

"So I'm not buying it! Something strange was going on with that lad and in my opinion he knew about Alice being here and knew where she was from and what happened to her."

"But Celia, I thought you said the boy looked about sixteen. That means Alice, sorry, I mean Vanessa, was already in South Kessock before he was born. Not sure how he could have influenced much back then, given that he was just a glint in his dad's eye."

Celia Green was not amused.

"Look, I don't know what he was up to. All I'm saying is that, that lad, Frank Spencer, or whatever he's really called, was involved in this and it's your job to find out how."

The sergeant closed his notebook, clipped his pen in his shirt pocket and stood up.

"Well Celia, in the absence of an obvious crime I'm not really sure how to go about this, even if the boy was involved, strikes me he's done the family a big favour in bringing them all back together again. Think he deserves a medal, not a police enquiry."

"But what if he'd known she was here, for a long time? Or he was part of a trafficking gang - maybe his dad was involved years ago and they left her here, alone, knowing the family were looking for her, thinking she was dead? Maybe he could have acted earlier? That would be wrong wouldn't it, a crime possibly? Obstruction of something?"

"Yeah, okay. Look, maybe you've got a point, let me think about. I can see there's a strange coincidence. Let me have a word with the chief, get his take on it. It does all seem a bit odd, the chain of events. So thanks for bringing it to my attention Celia, I'll take it further, I promise."

Sergeant Jordan was heading out of the building when he had an afterthought.

"Celia, are there any cameras in the home, maybe on the car park, something that might have caught his image?"

"No, I thought of that. But we don't have any."

"Shame, would help if we had an image of young Frank."

With that the sergeant said goodbye, left the building and climbed into the police car parked directly in front of the South Kessock Care Home.

"Frank Spencer eh," he said, smiling at the thought, "he's certainly got a sense of humour."

When Sergeant Jordan arrived back at police HQ, he popped up to see the Assistant Chief Constable's secretary and asked for a quick ten minutes with the boss.

"Leave it with me, I'll see if I can find you a slot," she said, "but he's still full on with the media after the Alice discovery, you know, given his role in the case at the time."

"Yeah, I've seen he's getting a fair bit of stick, but it's actually the Alice thing I want to see him about."

Half an hour later Sergeant Jordan's conversation with the Assistant Chief Constable was coming to and end.

"I'm not sensing a major misdemeanour here Derek, but as you say, it would be nice to know the full story. It does seem massively coincidental. Don't think we need to go about it mob handed though. Where are Vanessa's family from again?"

"Stockport, sir."

"And where did the laddie say he was from?"

"Same place, Stockport."

"And the boy, Frank, didn't have a Scottish accent and looked too young to drive you say?"

"Yes, that's what Celia Green at South Kessock told me."

"Well sergeant, he's not likely to have ridden his bike all this way. So driven by someone? There's a good possibility. But it'd take a lot of man hours to check that out, so let's start with a train. Probably from Manchester. Make it discrete Derek. Not sure what we're dealing with here and that family have suffered enough at the hands of the North Caledonia Constabulary, let's not compound their distress. No media mention okay. Keep it under the radar in fact, just between you and me, on the off chance this thing has legs. Get a description and start with the train station, trains to Manchester, just platform footage. You said the receptionist at the care home thought he'd arrived in a taxi? Well try and track down the driver. If you get a match on anything, get back to me."

"Yes sir, I'm on it. I'll check the phone records at the home also, the receptionist said the boy called the day before to make an appointment, perhaps he was careless with a mobile number?"

Later that evening Sergeant Jordan was studying two black and white images. One showed a young man in a parka sitting on a south bound platform at Inverness train station. The other showed the same young man leaving Piccadilly station on a Vespa scooter. The registration plate of the Vespa was clearly visible. It belonged to Wilson Armitage of Midland Drive, Stockport, Cheshire.

Chapter 46

Ward 7

Friday 3rd November 2017

When Wilson woke he was still in the hospital but in the new building, in a bed on Ward 7, also known as the Intensive Care Unit. He had a drip in his arm and he peered groggily around the room. There was Daisy, there was his mum and over there, his dad. He couldn't keep his eyes open.

The following day, when able to sit up in bed unsupported and with enough energy to stay awake for more than five minutes, a consultant doctor gave his verdict.

"Quite extraordinary. You're a very lucky young man, young man."

Wilson's eyelids felt like two manhole covers.

"You've had a catastrophic neutralisation of plasma electrolytes. Basically, the positive and negative ions in your body were neutralised somehow, so pretty much every system shut down. Like you had a flat battery. If we hadn't got to you as quickly as we did, I shudder to think what the outcome would have been. The old ticker doesn't run so well on a flat battery. You probably had just enough juice to keep it going. The only other time I saw something remotely like this was in a farmer who was hit by lightning, and he didn't make it, poor chap. No idea what you've been up to. Burning the candle at both ends, no doubt; what we call a toxic lifestyle, eh? But I wouldn't do it again if I were you.

"Anyway, all the tests indicate you're getting back to normal. We'll keep you in for a few more days of observation, keep you plugged in to our machines, make sure you're fully charged and then all being well, you can go home. Cheerio."

Wilson fell asleep again.

Chapter 47

Home time

Tuesday 7th November 2017

Four days later, Wilson was given the all-clear and permission to go home. Daisy arrived at the hospital with a half-eaten bunch of grapes and the latest copy of *Scootering* magazine.

"Some of the pages are stuck together," said Wilson, as he tried to thumb through it. And half the grapes have been eaten!"

"Well, I've no idea how that could have happened on the bus. Anyway Wilson, stop complaining. The doctor said you're not at death's door anymore. I'm going to see Gran in half an hour and it's so handy having you both here. Like having two birds in a bush, or whatever the proverb is."

Wilson laughed weakly, coughed and told Daisy he wasn't sure if he had the energy to cope with her in such a bubbly mood.

He couldn't remember much about the last few days, just vague recollections of blurry comings and goings. His parents being at the bedside with Kate and Megan. Fleeting glimpses of Daisy and Hoover. He could recall a few snatches of conversation and some anxious words from Gloria.

"It's all the excitement of his best friend finding his mum; it must have been too much for him" he could recall her saying.

Apart from that, everything was just a hazy memory from the moment he turned the corner and started walking towards 3B.

Daisy helped Wilson sit higher in the bed and adjusted his pillows accordingly. They made light conversation for a few more minutes until it seemed timely for Daisy to broach the subject.

"You had your eyes closed all the time, but what could you see?"

Wilson sank back into his pillow and for a moment stared blankly into space, looking for words to explain the inexplicable.

"Daisy, it was just the most incredible experience. As though I was standing in a wind tunnel facing this strong breeze, but it wasn't a wind that was blowing, you know, like air rushing past. It was a billion pictures, impressions from my life, your life, everyone's life, the world was flowing past at a million miles an hour. It's impossible to convey with words, because I didn't see anything visual to describe. I was feeling the pictures, rather than seeing them. It was as if my brain could build an image from the signals, the data it was receiving, but without my eyes needing to be involved. This torrent of energy, these particles of moments, were rushing down the corridor and I was standing in the middle of it all. I could feel them brushing past my hair, passing through my body. Like when you put your tongue on the end of a battery and you get that burning buzz. That sensation was inside me. There was this impression of energy all around, zooming past me and through me. I could see it, sense it, when I closed my eyes. It almost fried me though, there was too much, it was too strong and too powerful."

Wilson turned to Daisy and reached for her hand. All colour had been blanched from his face by the effort of recollection.

"You weren't my wading stick. That analogy was wrong. You were my lightning rod, cos I think through you, some of the energy was kind of earthed and you lessened the damage."

"Okay, stop Wilson. We can talk about this another time, when you're stronger."

She popped a grape into his mouth.

"But one last question. Do you remember the toy rocket and the little doll?"

"What?"

"The ones you plucked from thin air, like a magician."

Wilson's weary eyes briefly glimmered with a look of bemusement.

"Yeah, vaguely, now you come to mention it."

"And when you let go of them, they just flew away and disappeared again. It was a great trick."

"I don't fully remember Daisy. But whatever I did, it discharged my battery pretty quickly."

"Well, making a plastic model suddenly appear out of nothing and then making it disappear again, I can understand how that would be a bit draining. Anyway Dynamo called again. He wants to meet up and pick your brains about conjuring an elephant out of thin air."

"Oh yeah, are the flowers from him?" Wilson asked, nodding at a sorry looking bunch of daffodils in a vase on the window ledge.

"No, they were delivered two days ago. We don't know who sent them, but there's a card."

Daisy walked over to the small bouquet.

"It says, 'From me and the missus and the boys, hope you get your strength back soon, Blamire.' And he spelt strength with no 'g'."

"I know who that is Daisy and you can chuck those fly-traps in the bin."

There was a soft knock followed by Wilson's dad popping his head around the door.

"Taxi service?"

It took Wilson about ten minutes to get dressed and the final hurdle of pulling a sweater over his head left him panting for breath. His dad pushed him to the car in a wheelchair.

"Don't go on the A6 Dad" Wilson said as they pulled out of the car park. "Can you go the back way, please?"

They had been driving in silence for ten minutes when Alex broached the inevitable, "want to talk about it son?" There was no pressure or sense of urgency in his voice.

"Not right now Dad. But I know what happened."

"Me too. Catastrophic neutralisation of plasma electrolytes caused either by lightning or inhaling too much smoke. Didn't I ever tell you about the dangers of smoking?"

"Yes, you did Dad, you certainly did."

Wilson started laughing and coughing.

"It all goes through there Dad. All of it. Through Ward 3B. You should get some of your monitors in there. Some really powerful ones."

"I will Wilson. Your mum would love that."

They sat in silence for a while, enjoying the reassuring normality of a car journey in heavy traffic.

"Listen son, I'm just glad you're okay. Plus, I'm still trying to get my head round what you did for Teaps. This is what happens if you smoke; you nearly kill yourself, but on the plus side, you can find missing people. Just don't do it again son, please, for your mum's sake."

Chapter 48

Birthday girl

Wednesday 8th November 2017

The next morning, Wilson felt a little stronger, sixty per cent charged and his mum served breakfast in bed.

"Just so happy to have you home love. Two miracles in the space of a week."

When she finally stopped fussing, tidying his room and chattering to herself, Wilson managed to get a word in edgeways.

"It's Daisy's birthday today Mum — she's eighteen — and I haven't had a chance to buy her anything."

"Well, are you up to a trip to the Trafford Centre?"

"Think so. Let me have a shower and we'll go."

Wilson suddenly remembered his phone.

"Mum, what happened to my phone?"

"Oh, it's downstairs on the bureau love. Your dad brought it back from the hospital the night you were admitted. Do you want it?"

"Please Mum."

She scurried downstairs as Wilson went to take a shower.

When he returned from the bathroom, his phone was on the bed. Seventeen missed calls from Teaps and lots of 'get well' messages. Also a couple of nasty ones from Blamire.

Teaps had been waiting anxiously for his calls to be returned.

"Wilson, what happened to you man? Called you about a hundred times. How come you were in hospital?"

"Nothing — it was a false alarm. Think I was a bit run-down and then I got a stomach bug in the hospital, so they kept me in."

"Wilson, you were in Intensive Care for three nights and your dad told Hoover's dad there was a moment when it was touch and go. Said you had absolutely no energy, no strength left in your body."

"Think that's a bit of an exaggeration. Anyway, I'm alright now. More to the point, what's happening with you? Bring me up to speed."

"Phew, don't really know where to begin mate. As Alex James would say, it's been a bit of a blur. The most important thing though is that Mum's okay. Physically fine. She can speak a little bit, about things that happen during the day. She knows what she had for breakfast. It's just the old memories that have gone. She doesn't really remember us — seems to sense that we're her family, that I'm her son, but can't explain why or how."

Teaps then paused for a moment before continuing with a flat timbre to his voice.

"Wilson, I've got to ask you something. Something that struck me as strange."

"What's that?"

"Well, when I spoke to you, on Dad's phone, the morning after we found Mum, remember? I called you and you said, "What did you think when you saw her in that room? Will she get her memory back?" Wilson, how did you know she was in a room or that she'd lost her memory? Nobody knew that. Not even me and my dad, not until the doctor told us. But you knew she'd lost her memory."

"Well, err... I don't really remember what I said in all the excitement. Probably meant 'that home' when I said 'that room', and I heard on the news that she had some impaired mental abilities and I presumed that it was to do with memory. Yeah, and my mum said it. I remember now — she was watching the news on TV and she said your mum's memory must have gone. Think it's cos she works with all those old people, she has experience of this type of thing. Anyway, what does it matter? It's not important. Where are you?"

"We're still at this private hospital place near Chester, but everyone knows we're here. It's been in the papers. Cameras and TV wagons have been camped outside all week. But some amazing things have happened.

"First, the council got in touch to say they'd put us at the top of the housing list now that Mum's back and needs care.

"Plus, a few – quite a few actually – of Dad's old customers have been calling, asking if he's interested in going back to do their gardens for them.

"And there's some really unbelievable news. When Mum went missing, she had some junior partners in her firm, really loyal girls she'd trained up to become her associates. When Mum went missing, they carried on running the business thinking she'd come back. As Mum was never pronounced dead, the company stayed in her name. The associates told Dad at the time, but he was so upset he said he wasn't interested and they could keep the business. The publicity and mystery of her disappearing brought in loads of new clients and now they employ forty people. They've even got an office in London! Mum was allocated chunks of profit every year and it turns out she's pretty wealthy now. There's certainly enough to avoid a return to the Blamire fleapit.

"Oh and finally, *Ok* magazine wants to do a UK exclusive when Mum's up to it, plus some other magazines. Dad's found an agent to deal with it all.

"The best news though, is that I've packed in my job at Morrisons."

Wilson started laughing.

"I'm so happy for you mate, I really am. What will you do about college?"

"I'm taking a gap year. Might not even go back. I want to spend all my time with Mum for now. Dad's asked if I'd like to get involved with his landscaping business, but to be honest, I think recruitment and the London office is more up my street."

"Okay, well keep in touch, and if you need any help with anything..."

"Yeah, will do."

"Say hi to your dad – hey, and your mum! Sounds strange saying that."

"Yeah, I know. See you Wilson."

"See ya, man."

The yell from an impatient mother brought Wilson back to earth.

"If you want to go shopping for Daisy's present, we need to go now. I haven't got all day."

"Be down in a minute."

Wilson read Blamire's texts, then deleted them.

An hour later, they were both standing in the ladies' clothing section of Selfridges. Wilson had no idea what size Daisy was.

"I don't know if she's an eight or a ten or a twelve, Mum. Actually, no, I'm sure she's an eleven."

"Wilson, there's no such thing as an eleven!"

"Oh, I'm pretty sure there is Mum."

Since clothes were clearly out of the question, Wilson bought Daisy a fine gold chain necklace with a St Christopher pendant, a pair of black suede gloves, a book entitled *A Guide to the Meaning of Dreams* and a big bag of Midget Gems. His mum wasn't sure about the last two presents but was okay with his choice of the jewellery and gloves. She made him drink two bottles of Lucozade Sport in the car on the way back.

At about seven thirty, Daisy and her mum, Frances, popped round. Gloria and Frances had been introduced during Wilson's time in Intensive Care. They sat chatting and drinking tea in the kitchen while Daisy ripped open her presents in the lounge with Wilson.

Daisy loved the necklace, she said the gloves fitted, 'like a glove', she playfully hit Wilson with the book and then started eating the Midget Gems.

"Sorry we couldn't do anything better for your birthday Daisy. The doctor said I need early nights and lots of rest, and to be honest, much as I'd like to ignore doctor's orders, I still feel absolutely knackered."

"Wilson, shut up. I'm eighteen years old now, an adult. You can take me to Fabio's next week and I'll interpret all your dreams with my new book."

"Sounds like a plan."

"Speaking of dreams Wilson, I don't want to go back to The Market

Square again. It doesn't feel right anymore and it scares me. I enjoyed the dancing the other night, but it's not real. I want normal relationships like everyone else and I want to get drunk and feel the hangover the next day. Let's try to stop. We did a good thing there. Let's end on a high. You said we have the power in our brains to close it down. Let's really try. I was worried and I really missed you when you were in hospital Wilson. A lot."

"Me too — I mean, I didn't miss myself a lot — well, I did actually, but I also..."

Daisy thumped Wilson on the shoulder and tried to force a black Midget Gem into his mouth, then up a nostril. He retaliated by tipping a handful of Midget Gems down the back of her sweater, which became the signal for Frances to say it was time to go and she would be waiting in the car.

"Seriously Wilson," said Daisy buttoning up her coat, "no more Market Square. And certainly no more Ward 3B and the energy tunnel. It makes me shiver thinking about it."

"Okay, I agree. But it might be we have to stop after tonight."

"Why, what's happening tonight?"

"I can't be certain, but I think there's a good chance I'll be seeing you later, it being your eighteenth birthday and all."

Chapter 49

The fatal attraction

Wednesday 8th November 2017

Wilson was waiting for Daisy in the field filled with poppies. A gentle breeze made the flowers sway like chorus girls with slender green bodies and giant red hats. The outline of The Gateway rippled in the heat as pearl-tinted clouds drifted across the sky. The clouds seemed to pause while passing across the sun, as though basking in a moment of celestial superiority, before fragmenting and dissolving — the price to be paid for impertinence. After a while, Wilson felt a warm, soft hand slip into his. There was no need to look; the birthday girl had arrived. The waves of flowers parted like a biblical special effect and in no time at all Wilson and Daisy stood facing The Gateway.

"Jeeeesssus," said Daisy, craning her neck to take in the momentous scale of the huge building. "Who's palace is this?"

"It's called The Gateway. The place I told you about, remember, where they keep the extinguished spirits."

"You never said it was this big, how do we get inside?"

"Follow me."

They made their way up the wide stone steps hand in hand.

Daisy stopped to look up at the violent battle between the humans and flying figures carved into the portico. Then she caught up with Wilson who was standing in front of two doors, which he explained were completely independent, two separate entrances: one for visitors, the other for residents.

"We're definitely visitors" he said, pushing the door open sufficiently for them both to squeeze through.

Daisy stood transfixed, eyes and mouth agape, taking everything in.

The soft beams of milky light shining through rows of arched windows. The colossal expanse of the interior, like a never-ending cathedral and the mountains of gold bangles.

"Tell me again where we are" asked Daisy, taking a few steps forward while gazing up at rainbow dust sparkling in broad shafts of light.

"He's already told you. It's called The Gateway."

Startled by the voice, Daisy instinctively turned back to Wilson and blinked in surprise at the two comical looking characters, either side of him, dressed in black from head to foot. Wilson had his hands in his pockets and was rocking on his feet, grinning.

"This is The Hall of Extinguished Spirits" said Short Cake, sweeping his arm outwards in an imperious manner.

"Ah, so these are the guys you told me about."

Daisy was coming to terms with the colossal proportions of the hall, the glittering mounds of gold jewellery and now, the men in black.

"Yeah, Big Mac and Short Cake look after the place, but the other way round — cos he's not big and the other one's not short — it can be confusing."

"So what's with all the jewellery then?"

The dumpy figure of Big Mac then waddled towards Daisy — his small, shuffling feet and short legs just about managing to keep his top heavy frame upright. He reminded Daisy of a round-bottomed toy, a Mr Roly Poly or a Wobbly Man.

"Each gold bangle Daisy, is the Shell of a human spirit, the extinguished 'will to live' of a dead person." Big Mac held one of the bangles aloft as he continued to explain. Knowing full well that the forthcoming dialogue was solely for Daisy's benefit, Wilson turned to Short Cake, who swivelled his head ninety degrees, somewhat robotically, in response to Wilson's attention.

"We loved your rescue mission Wilson, we really did. Even The Powers That Be liked it and they usually hate that magnitude of mischief. Yes, you really put the cat amongst the feathered rats with that little stunt. So ingenious, stealing the wedding photo, writing a secret message, the lovely train journey and the chat with Dad. We loved it. We saw you on TV! And The Powers That Be even shed some tears when they saw how concerned you and Daisy were at playing God.

"But Wilson," Short Cake continued, "when I say, The Powers That Be shed tears, I don't mean they were crying. I mean they were splitting their sides laughing." Then he bellowed at the top of his voice "AND NOT IN A GOOD WAY!" Which once again gave Daisy a start.

"I don't get you" said Wilson.

Big Mac had concluded Daisy's introduction to The Gateway and now turned his attention to Wilson.

"Mr Armitage, you are a very clever chap. Over-indulged possibly, and certainly an above-average eleven. But then you were turbo-charged with extra... abilities, shall we say."

"Just for the flippin' hell of it" announced Short Cake, stamping his foot like a spoilt child.

Big Mac ignored him.

"We don't know why they gave you and Daisy the status of eleven-plus Wilson and I believe they're now of the same opinion, especially after your rocket-conjuring trick. That was another first and took us all by surprise."

"Gateway, this is Short Cake. We have a problem."

"Stop, please stop, just for a minute. Can someone tell me what the hell's going on here, in ENGLISH?" Daisy had heard enough of the nonsensical chatter.

"Ah" said Big Mac, his face lighting up, "I'm so happy you asked that Miss Meadowcroft. Happy birthday by the way. Many elevens come here for a meet and greet when they come of age. May I be allowed to answer your question at the macro level?"

Oh, be my guest thought Daisy, wishing he'd quickly get to the bloody point.

"Well, Earth is but part of a universe forever expanding outwards. The space into which the universe expands is where The Powers That Be reside, running their giant train set..."

"It's just the best toy... ever" interrupted Short Cake in the giddy voice of a small boy.

"...and they let uncontrollable variables, like you and Wilson, mess up the schedules on purpose, so they can place bets on all the possible outcomes. You two are very hard to predict and so difficult to wager. The Powers That Be like you Wilson, they really do."

"But stop meddling with stuff that don't concern you!"

Daisy was now certain Short Cake had some sort of mental issue and was so irritated by the conversation she decided to go and explore.

"I'm just going to see if there's a sale on anywhere" she said, nodding at the pathway running between two piles of bangles.

Big Mac returned to the point he was trying to make.

"What we're trying to say Wilson, is that you're only supposed to be in The Market Square to bring a light dusting of snow — not to rescue people and cause blizzards. They gave you too much power Wilson. You make the gambling difficult, harder to calculate the odds — the ripples from some of your actions have the bookies beaten. Not to mention all the damage limitation required and the knock on effects of snow falling on the Amazon. Remember?"

Big Mac raised an eyebrow questioningly.

"Okay, okay, I get the message" said Wilson, "and we're sorry, but we were only trying to help, to do something good. Daisy even reckons it could have been God that made us do it in the first place. That would count in our favour, wouldn't it, with The Powers That Be?"

Wilson knew Daisy would soon return and insist on leaving The Gateway so he jumped to a question that had been on his mind for a while. Also, he was feeling unnerved with the direction the conversation had been taking.

"There's just one thing I don't understand: who decides what The Market Square looks like when we arrive?"

"Ahhh, good question Wilson. Well, to use the terminology of the day, it just happens to be what's trending. The consensus of dream energy mixed with tomfoolery from The Powers That Be — rigged dice, five aces, that sort of thing. But the Blackpool Tower ballroom was all their idea. They thought you might want to celebrate."

"So will they stop me from visiting The Market Square soon?"

Wilson's probing was purposely going off on a tangent.

"They're certainly working on it, but yours is more of a VIP pass and more difficult to nullify. So until the matter is resolved, I suggest, no, I absolutely recommend, you refrain from further disruptive activity."

Big Mac had chosen his words carefully and it seemed to Wilson that he had finally got to the point. He and Daisy were being told in no uncertain terms to stay away from The Market Square, or at the very least, no straddling.

But how is it possible, in practical terms to cease visiting The Market Square? How can Daisy and I choose not to go there?

Wilson put the questions to Big Mac.

Daisy was about twenty metres away, standing at the foot of a towering pile of 2006 bangles. She selected three bangles and slipped them onto her wrist. *Nice and heavy. Definitely real gold* she thought, letting them shake and jangle on her arm as she turned to walk back to Wilson. Big Mac was still droning on. Short Cake was rising and falling on the balls of his feet with a gormless expression on his face.

Whether it was the conversation or the lack of positive ions in his body it's hard to say, but at that moment Wilson began to yawn, he started to fade into a translucent shadow and then his presence dissipated from The Gateway.

Daisy was scratching at what looked like a hallmark or an inscription on one of the 2006 bangles hanging from her wrist, when she also started to yawn and moments later, returned to the 'no longer dreaming' phase of sleep.

At 5.45 a.m. the next morning, Wilson was stirred from slumber by a text from Daisy. The message read:

'Wilson, I'm lying in bed and I've got three effing gold bangles on my effing wrist!'

Wilson thought he was dreaming and so tired, he fell straight back to sleep.

Chapter 50

A spanner in the works

Thursday 9th November 2017

Wilson sent Daisy a text the moment he woke up.

'You've got what??????!!!!!!!!!'

'Three gold bangles on my wrist' she texted back. 'The ones I was trying on in that place last night - still on my wrist when I woke this morning.'

Wilson called as fast as his fingers could move over the phone.

"Daisy, you realise this can only mean one of two things. We're going to become rich beyond our wildest dreams by selling mountains of gold jewellery, or we're in a lot of trouble. But let me tell you for certain: we'll never be allowed to sell gold bangles that represent a person's extinguished spirit. Especially when they've got the name of the owner written on them and that person is DEAD!"

Wilson was shouting as he delivered those last few words.

"But they look really nice. Listen."

He could hear them jangling on her wrist.

"I want to keep them. Nothing bad is going to happen."

"Oh yes it is. Because The Powers That Be are going to say something like 'we're also called The Powers That Are Going To Find Daisy And Wilson And Smash Their Stupid Faces In'."

"Come on Wilson, they won't miss three. They had millions of them."

"Jesus Daisy, of course they will."

"Who will?"

"The people, the spirits, the Residuals who moved on to eternity. The people whose names are on the inside of those bangles! They'll bloody well miss them."

"What names?"

"Daisy, please, the names that are inscribed on the inside of each of those bangles in very small, but very clear writing."

Wilson heard her shake one of the bangles free.

"You mean, err, let me see... God, it's tiny writing. Er, Andrew Latchford. Nineteen fifty-four until two thousand and six."

"Yes, and the others?"

"Er, hold on a minute. Edward Riley, nineteen thirty-two until two thousand and six. And err, Emily Broadstairs. Eighteen forty-five until two thousand and six."

"So Daisy, the name is the name of a person and the numbers are the years they were born and then died. The year they died is the year they entered The Gateway, where we were last night – where I knew we'd end up because it was your eighteenth birthday and for some reason you go there when you're eighteen. The hall is where the will to live, energy that can't be destroyed by death, is turned into three ounces of gold, leaving the final chunk of energy, the soul, to go through the door to eternity and live with The Powers That Be. Didn't Big Mac tell you all this last night?"

Wilson was dismayed, angry and confused.

"Yes, but he didn't say each bangle was personalised. So let me see, Andrew Latchford was fifty-two when he died. And Emily was, err, sixty-one. No, one hundred and sixty-one. Wilson, nobody lives to be a hundred and sixty-one."

"Correct Daisy, they don't. But in her case, she was probably only seventeen when she died, from TB or an accident in a mill – certainly before she wanted to."

Wilson was dismayed with Daisy's inability to grasp the dire situation they were in.

"Listen, if you look on the internet, there's every chance you'll find a ghost called Emily Broadstairs who haunted some old building until about that date on that bangle. I know all this because I did the research. I've got the t-shirt for Eric Murphy!"

Wilson exhaled. He'd just woken up and was already exhausted.

"Maybe they won't notice these three are missing?"

"Yes Daisy, THEY WILL! They already know, I'm sure. The question is; what are they going to do about it? And the other question is; how do we get them back? Sharpish."

"Do you think we're in danger?"

"Yeah I do. I really do. And at this moment, possibly you more than me."

"But I didn't steal them on purpose. I was only trying them on. They're so nice. I wasn't really listening to you talking to Big Cake so I put them on my wrist. And then I became tired and when I woke up, they were here, on my wrist."

"Daisy, I know you didn't steal them on purpose. I tried to borrow a special spanner from Sampson's one night, when I was doing up the Vespa, but it wasn't in my pocket when I woke up the next morning. That's because The Market Square seems to be mostly about two kinds of energy, dreams and time. But The Gateway is different, it's involved with another type of energy altogether, the energy of the human spirit. And somehow you managed to wander back to bed with part of someone's spirit dangling from your wrist. Actually Daisy, those bangles are like spanners, spanners in the works of The Gateway — maybe even spanners in the universe."

"Wow" said Daisy. "Well, if you want to put it that way, yeah, it does sound serious. What're we gonna do?"

"I've not got a clue Daisy, but above all else, don't lose those bloody bangles."

Chapter 51

The red army

Thursday 9th November 2017

A few minutes after he'd finished the call to Daisy, Wilson's mum brought him a cup of tea, a sausage sandwich and two more bottles of Lucozade. She checked his temperature and told him she was nipping out to the shops but would be back in half an hour. He was eating the sandwich when his phone rang again. It was Blamire.

"Hello?"

"Hello Winston?"

"It's Wilson, you idiot."

"Hello Wilton."

"What do you want Blamire?"

"I was just ringing to check on my investment."

"Blamire, overcharging someone for a poxy flat that should be condemned and then ripping them off at some extortionate wide-boy interest rate isn't an investment, it's extortion — an extortion racket by a slum landlord. You've done this before, haven't you? Probably to the people who were in that flea pit before Teaps. You know, I think the police would be interested in your little scam."

"Yeah, I'm sure they would, but going to the boys in blue wouldn't be a smart move would it Winston, cos now I've got another option? You see, I've been talking to a couple of handy lads from Salford, from a well-known firm. I brought them up to speed with my predicament and they made me a business proposition. They expressed an interest on my interest on the interest. Seventy-five pence in the pound. Which means I get six grand today and they become the new debt collectors.

"So I need eight grand by the day after tomorrow, or the reds will

282

come marching in. Those boys really don't give a shit about whether you tell the police or not. They'll definitely be well up for kidnapping Teaps's mum. She's loaded apparently. Two days Winston. You've got my number."

Then the line went dead.

Wilson threw his phone across the bedroom. It bounced off the carpet and hit the skirting board, but didn't break. Which was just as well because just over an hour later it rang again.

"Wilson, it's me."

Daisy sounded stressed and on edge.

"I'm in the nurse's room at college. I think I've got a broken finger. Someone slammed my locker door on my hand. But there was nobody there. I'd forgotten my book and there was just me at the lockers; classes had started. The door really whacked my finger, like a hurricane or a tornado, or something like that had blown it shut. It was so quick and powerful. And I think someone's been following me ever since I left the house this morning."

"Have you seen anyone?"

"No, but I sense someone's watching me. And I think they tried to push me under a bus at the station."

Wilson sat bolt upright.

"What? You're saying you think someone tried to kill you?"

"Yeah. I just felt this shove, and I was about to go under the wheels when this man standing by my side grabbed me and pulled me back. And we couldn't tell who'd pushed me. People thought I was trying to jump. Wilson I'm scared. Really scared. I don't know what to do."

Daisy started crying with deep, heavy sobs.

Wilson knew Daisy's fear was well-founded, the threat was real.

"Daisy, Daisy, listen to me. Where are the bangles?"

"They're in my bedroom at home. I wrapped them in paper and hid them at the back of the drawer in my bedside table."

"Okay, well they're safe there. Daisy, try to pull yourself together. Be strong. Look, I don't know what's going on exactly, but I'm sure what's happening now is all connected to you taking the bangles from The

Gateway. But they're also playing with me, with us, teaching us a lesson because we found Vanessa. They're demonstrating how actions, playing God, can have dire consequences, like Blamire blackmailing Teaps."

"What?"

"Nothing, nothing, another problem. Daisy, stay close to people all the time. Be with someone as you move from class to class; don't be alone. Call me when you get home later. Be careful, okay? I'm going to work out how to sort this."

"I want to call the police."

"You can't do that. What story are you going to give about the bangles? Daisy that's ridiculous. If the forces of the universe are after you, how do you think the police can possibly help. We've got to get those bangles back quickly and hope that's all we need to do."

Wilson then paused for a second as an uncanny sense of awareness of his place in the ongoing drama implanted a thought not based on any rationale or logic.

"Daisy, I don't know why I'm thinking this, but I feel you might be safe with your grandma in Ward 3B."

"With my grandma? She's dying Wilson. She can't move, can't speak, and you think she can protect me from an invisible man pushing me under a bus better than the police? Why would you think that?"

"I don't know, I just do. They want the bangles back above all else, but they know you didn't take them on purpose. They'll have seen your trace. It's just bad timing. They're trying to frighten us and they're doing a good job, but I think we have time. They'll give us time to put it right."

"But what if we can't?"

"We will. I'll think of something. Listen, call me later. Okay?"

"Okay. I will, I promise."

"And don't worry, I'll sort it."

Wilson ended the call with Daisy trying to contain her emotions.

He tried to stay calm and to think logically but the parameters of the problem made any conventional form of solution seeking impossible. What he had to do was think illogically, instinctively. Like the idea that

Daisy would be safe in Ward 3B. There was no logic to that, but it felt right. He was certain The Powers That Be would give them more time to sort things. After all, they were betting on it!

Wilson lay in bed for the rest of the afternoon, charging his batteries and boosting his energy levels with bananas, high-protein bars, three bottles of Lucozade and all kinds of vitamins and mineral supplements.

He would sleep fitfully, then after twenty minutes of tossing and turning, wake up, his mind darting in each and every direction in search of an avenue that would lead to a solution. This routine continued until about seven thirty when his phone rang.

It was Daisy, but now her voice was quiet and strained, it sounded to Wilson like she was in shock.

"Wilson, it's me. I'm home. Dad's with me. He had to come back from work early."

Wilson could hear serious voices in the background.

"Daisy, find somewhere quiet where we can speak."

"I can't now Wilson. I don't know what to say to you."

"Daisy, we have to..."

But she'd closed her phone.

He rang her back constantly for the next two hours and sent umpteen messages. Wilson's mum brought supper to his bedroom and asked if he was feeling okay.

"You look tired son, and all washed out again."

Wilson had been planning to go and see Daisy on the Vespa, but he knew his mum would be devastated if he tried. Besides, he wasn't sure he had the power to steer the scooter.

Daisy called him back around ten thirty.

"Daisy, thank God! I've been calling you all night. What happened?"

"The house was burgled this afternoon, while we were all out."

"Burgled? Is there much damage? Was anything taken?"

"Someone was after the bangles. And they found them, but didn't take them."

"How's that possible?"

"There were no signs of a break-in Wilson. No smashed windows or broken doors. It was like a demonstration of what a burglary looks like. The policeman blamed it on an animal coming down the chimney. With no damage and no fingerprints, that was the best he could come up with. My room was the worst though. Some of my clothes had been ripped to shreds and then placed back into the cupboards – I mean, lacerated with a knife. Sliced into strips. Torn to shreds. It wasn't a squirrel."

Daisy's voice was cold and emotionless, as though she was resigned to accepting a terrible judgement.

"Whoever it was, they found the bangles. The paper I'd wrapped them in was all torn up on the floor, but the bangles had been thrown back in the drawer. It was like a message to say they knew the bangles were there. Wilson, I have to tell my dad."

"Daisy, don't. I'll find a way to stop all this. Just give me a bit longer."

"I don't know Wilson. I'm scared and worried, Mum's crying – what's gonna happen next?"

"Nothing. They're just sending us messages. Playing with us. I'm sure they'll give us more time to give the bangles back."

"How much time though?"

"I don't know. A bit."

"Wilson, I'll probably be at the hospital all day tomorrow. They think Gran will pass away. Mum can't cope. I have to go."

"Alright, sorry for your gran and your mum. I'll call you tomorrow."

"Bye."

"Oh, one thing: take the bangles with you to the hospital tomorrow."

"Okay."

Wilson lay in bed, his mind frantically seeking a way to return the bangles. An illogical solution. Any solution. Over the course of two hours he revisited every dream with Daisy, from that first meeting in Sampson's to their last visit to The Gateway. He was looking for the needle in a haystack that would enable him to stitch something together, but he came up with nothing. Wilson reached the conclusion that he needed to go and search The Market Square, that night, just by himself. Perhaps the answer was waiting there.

Chapter 52

The fragment

Friday 10th November 2017

As Wilson strode into The Market Square he knew a curtain had been pulled across the night's narrative because the stage was empty. Thick, angry clouds, the colour of pewter, were banked in layers across a sky through which flashes of sheet lightning erupted with unpredictable regularity. Deep rumbles of thunder trundled along moments later like a giant's footsteps hurrying to catch up.

A storm. That's a first.

Wilson couldn't help but think the dramatic lighting and sound effects were being orchestrated just for him. A soundtrack and visual to accentuate the drama of the moment, courtesy of The Gateway.

He began his search at L'École but the entrance gates were padlocked and the louvre shutters had been folded and secured over the windows. The tulips in the window boxes were drooping and colourless, a section of loose guttering was hanging at a dangerous angle and paint was peeling from bald patches on the walls.

Wilson walked along the flagged pavement with the Clock Tower to his left. The butcher's shop was closed and just like L'École, the building showed signs of neglect. The broad, bay window, normally filled with fat sausages, was empty. There were no pheasant or grouse hanging to age. Display trays were covered with films of grey dust in which dead flies and wasps were disintegrating.

He was reminded of one of his dad's jokes:

A man walks into a butcher's shop and asks for a pound of dead wasps.

"I'm sorry sir," says the butcher, "we don't sell dead wasps."

"Yes you do," says the man, *"you've got loads in the window."*

The cheese shop and the greengrocer were similarly afflicted — empty, dilapidated and abandoned. The once vivid square was now sepia-tinted and derelict, as though blighted by a wicked spell. No inhabitants, no lights in buildings, just an eerie, flickering glow from street lamps running on economy setting. The rate of lightning flash was increasing and thunderous rumbles were growing louder. The giants were marching with purpose. Wilson crossed over the square and made his way to Sampson's.

There's a possibility he'd know how to return the bangles. After all, he's a resident here.

But Sampson's workshop was also closed. The hanging sign above the door had crashed to the ground and splintered wood littered the pavement. Wilson brushed the dust from one of the windows with the sleeve of his hoodie and peered in. The workshop wasn't just closed, it was completely deserted. The bikes, the scooters, the tools, the wooden workbench — all gone. Wilson turned away.

The Powers That Be are really pulling out the stops with this stunt. An illusion of decay — all for my benefit.

As if to punctuate his thoughts, a slate roof tile crashed to the ground and shattered at his feet, Wilson stepped off the pavement, out of reach of further danger and headed to the Clock Tower to consider his next move. The egg hunt was going nowhere and Wilson's basket was still empty.

The sandstone mouldings around the clock face had started to crumble. Large chunks of stone, with a partly sculpted side or a bevelled edge, lay strewn on the ground. The amber bronze statue of Mr Abingdon — or was it Mr Ludlow? — was tarnished with a dull black patina. His left arm was missing. The slats of the wooden benches were afflicted with wet rot and fungi. An armrest was missing. Wilson sat down.

They're watching me, I know they are. Betting on me finding a solution. Or not finding it. They're gambling on what happens next. That's why I'm here, to up the stakes in their stupid game. Turbocharged Wilson, the loaded dice. It's like I'm in some kind of problem solving computer game or TV show. The Crystal Maze. The Midnight Castle.

Wilson continued to expand on those thoughts, working through each step.

So, if they're betting on me, that means I'm either going to win, or I'm going to lose. So only two things can happen next. I discover how to return the bangles, or I don't. And if a chance exists to win, then the answer must be here, in The Market Square, otherwise there's no bet.

Wilson surveyed his surroundings. From L'École up to the far corner, then past the old coaching house to the corner opposite, then back down past Sampson's to the ominous looking building, directly on his left, The Bank.

What exactly is it I'm looking for? Give me a clue, point me in the right direction.

Seemingly on cue, a huge burst of lightning seared through the heavens above Wilson's head and for a fleeting moment, illuminated a long-forgotten scene in a dream; only a fraction of a second of insight, but it was enough. Wilson closed his eyes and went instantly in pursuit, opening, scanning and closing every dream memory along the way. Tasking the most powerful part of his brain, his side room, to find the clue. As the crack of lightning and deep growls of thunder bounced around The Market Square, Wilson journeyed all the way back to being five years old, to his first arrival in The Market Square, to the night he discovered L'École. There, dimly lit by a single bulb, deep in the darkest recess of his memory, he saw the tell-tale fragment of a dream that could never be extinguished. A trace of polaroid snapshots from a moment long forgotten in time. When the light faded, the gas lamps glowed and the rocket and giraffe exited stage left. When the air turned cold and a doorbell rang as a candle flickered to life. The muffled conversation and two pairs of eyes observing him, then movement from two silhouettes, one round, one tall and thin — looking down from a room above a hanging sign.

I don't want to become the boy that is eaten by the wolf.

Wilson studied the facade and gothic features of the building facing him and the hand-lettered signage that read 'The Bank'. His scrutiny settled on a first floor window.

Wilson sprinted from the bench, across The Market Square and up the four stone steps that led to the entrance. The door was covered with dust and cobwebs, but the round brass handle reluctantly turned and when combined with the push of a shoulder, the door slowly creaked open. It was pitch black inside, Wilson reached for his phone and swiped up the torchlight.

He was standing at the foot of a staircase on a brightly coloured mosaic floor in which a battle scene had been recreated in the pattern of coloured glass tiles. Wilson recognised it as the one from The Gateway. He illuminated the route forward. Each stone step was worn smooth in the centre like a shallow dish. A hardwood bannister spiralled upwards supported by white-painted spindles. As he climbed to the first floor, Wilson tried to keep his bearings in relation to the room above the sign.

This is it, he thought, standing in front of an antique oak door with a lion's-head knocker in polished brass. There was no nameplate or numbering. Wilson twisted the fluted glass door handle and pushed. The door didn't open. He applied his shoulder again, but it still didn't budge. He raised the lion's jaw and let it fall. An authentic roar echoed down and back up the staircase — followed by silence. Wilson almost smiled, he knew the sound effect had been added for his entertainment. He tried the knocker a second time and again, there was no reply.

Wilson smashed his clenched fist against the solid wood.

"Look, I know you two are in there, so open this bloody door."

More silence.

Wilson kicked the door. "Let me in, I need your help, urgently."

More silence.

Then a voice.

"What's the magic password?"

"Err, let me think. Oh yeah, I know it: open this door before I break it down and smash your face in."

"Yes that's it, well done."

The door swung back on its hinges and Wilson entered a spacious room, the corners of which were lost in thick shadow. At the centre, Big Mac and Short Cake sat in their black leather chairs at their black desks with shining lamps poised at the same angle.

"So this is where you jokers hang out, is it?"

"Our office in town" said Short Cake, reclining back in his chair, grinning, with his hands behind his head.

"Listen guys, I'm feeling a bit stressed and tired at the moment; in fact, I could go any minute. But I'm also totally hacked off. You know as well as I do that Daisy didn't steal those bangles on purpose. It was just bad timing."

"Oh, we know about that" said Short Cake.

"So how..." Wilson had stifle a yawn "...how do we get them back? Back in the correct year pile."

"Oh, it's very easy. Someone has to bring them back" said Big Mac, casually spinning his chubby fountain pen on the polished surface of his desk. It seemed the answer was so obvious, he didn't have to think.

"We don't care who. It can be you or Daisy" said Short Cake.

"Any*body* in fact" said Big Mac.

"Good. So where do we bring them?"

"Back to The Gateway of course."

"To The Hall of Extinguished Spirits."

"Through the residents' entrance" said Big Mac.

Wilson's thoughts raced away in search of the methodology, but quickly hit a brick wall. He was stunned.

"Hold on a minute. I thought only dead people could get into the hall through the residents' entrance, the one on the right."

"Spot on" said Short Cake.

"So either Daisy or I have to be dead to bring the bangles back into the hall, is that what you're saying?"

Wilson had to swallow down the lump of something that had risen to the back of his throat.

"Spot on again" said Short Cake, with an inane grin.

"I agree Wilson, it does seem harsh" Big Mac continued, "but the problem is, we don't have a door that's signed 'The Gateway: for the bearers of accidentally stolen human spirit bangles'. Obtaining planning permission for that would take ages. Far longer than *you've* got, I'm afraid."

Wilson paused for a moment and considered the irony of not being in a position to say the next morning, "thank goodness, it was all just a dream." Daylight was not going to bring respite from this nightmare.

"You're having me on, right. You're just joking?"

"Not at all. To bring the bangles back they must come through the residents-only door. With, or more accurately, on, a dead person."

"Choo-choo," said Short Cake, pulling down on the cord of an imaginary steam train whistle.

Wilson had to restrain himself from throwing a punch.

"Listen, I know The Powers That Be are mad with me because I played God and screwed up their train set. And I said I'm sorry. But Daisy and I were only trying to do good."

"Just like The Powers That Be then" said Big Mac.

"That's bollocks, there are people starving in Africa, tsunamis, civil wars, terrorism, diseases and cancers. All The Powers That Be do is play with train sets and cruel gambling games with me — while the rest of the world suffers."

"Wilson, dear Wilson, let me tell you something, let me explain," said Big Mac, rising to his feet. He stood no taller.

"Millions and hundreds of years ago there was a special place created by The Powers That Be for human people. It was what you might call a paradise, with no disease, no crime, no tsunamis. But humanity soon became bored with everything being perfect every day and so animal instincts surfaced to create wars and terrorism and serial killers. So The Powers That Be designed a better paradise. One that wouldn't always lead to Lord of the Flies scenarios. A paradise-lite, if you like. The point is, the accidental car shunt, the odd tsunami is okay. They add the necessary spice to human life."

"And you should be thankful" said Short Cake "for all the civil wars, plagues and terrorist attacks The Powers That Be manage to prevent."

Wilson was taken aback and momentarily lost for words.

"So what you're basically saying is that things would be far worse without The Powers That Be. That they try to minimise the bad things that can happen?"

"Yes. You humans don't like it all controlled and you kill each other if it's not. So they try to maintain the optimal balance of cause and effect, by allowing your mischief, as I've told you on numerous occasions. Gambling on outcomes is their guilty pleasure."

"And there's quite a few bobs on you Wilson, quite a few bobs," said Short Cake, gleefully, "one of The Powers That Be has bet that the ripples from Wilson to the rescue will cause at least twenty-three thousand deaths, a civil war and the suicide of Mr Spinner. They'll be busy trying to keep that down to a manageable level if it all comes to pass."

Wilson stomach churned at the thought.

"And the one behind the burglary at Daisy's, the nasty one, who snapped her finger – well, he really wants to win."

"One more very important thing Wilson, about the bangles" said Big Mac.

Wilson was listening intently. In fact he was hanging on to every word. But he was tired, irresistibly tired and began to panic at thoughts of suddenly vacating the dream.

"No, not now. Wait, give me a minute, just another minute," he pleaded to Big Mac and Short Cake, "don't let me go without knowing, tell me quickly, please."

Short Cake smiled and simply shrugged. His fingertips tapping out a sequence of notes on the hard, black surface of his desk.

"Come on, what is it, what's the one more important thing?"

Wilson lurched forward and grabbed the armrest on Big Mac's chair, trying to anchor himself to that moment, to stay in the dream.

"Big Mac, please, tell me, what's the important thing, how do I save Daisy?" He was desperate for a few more precious seconds of conversation. But it was too late, he'd run out of time, the dream had reached its expiry date. Wilson began to fade and in a moment of extremely bad timing he was gone, never to hear Big Mac's last words.

Big Mac turned to Short Cake.

"Well. How rude was that? You don't just leave without hearing the 'one more thing'."

"Indeed" said Short Cake "particularly when the 'one more thing' relates to the crucial imperative of returning the bangles by tomorrow night if Daisy is to avoid a fatal and inexplicable accident — thereby delivering the bangles by default, *ipso facto*, as they say."

"Correct" said Big Mac with an uncharacteristic, callous chuckle.

Chapter 53

A scratch I can't itch

Friday 10th November 2017

No combination of words could ever convey the magnitude of the emotional maelstrom running through Wilson's head when he woke the next morning. He felt like someone who'd driven to the pub with his mates, free as a bird, only to wake up in a police cell the next morning facing life imprisonment for killing a family of five through drink driving. With no possible way to rewind the clock, he was condemned from that moment to a life of torment.

Gloria called him down for a bowl of soup and he joined her, despondent and forlorn, still in his pyjamas. He considered confessing everything, a plea for help; but his sweet and innocent mum didn't deserve to be involved in his self-inflicted catastrophe.

Teaps was still making news on TV. The latest angle focused on Vanessa's mother and how she'd died of a broken heart barely a year after her daughter had gone missing.

"She'll be watching from heaven with a smile on her face" said Gloria, absorbed in the unfolding story.

Struck by something in his mother's words, Wilson stopped sipping soup, closed his eyes and returned back to last night's dream.

What exactly was it that Big Mac had said?

"Oh, it's very easy. Someone has to bring them back."

"We don't care who. You or Daisy."

"Anybody in fact. To bring the bangles back, they must come through the residents-only door. With, or more accurately on, a dead person."

So anybody can take the bangles back, they don't care who it is — it can be anyone who's just died, or someone who's about to die.

Wilson shot upstairs to get dressed. He called Daisy and started speaking the moment she answered.

"Daisy, Daisy, I've worked it out, I know how to get the bangles back, I know how to do it" he said jubilantly.

For a second there was no reply. Wilson thought the connection had been lost.

"Daisy? Are you there?"

"Yes, I'm here, Wilson."

Daisy's voice sounded eerily distant and devoid of empathy. Like the voice of someone about to narrate the harrowing details of an atrocity.

"Daisy, what's wrong? Don't worry. I have a plan. I know how to get the bangles back — it's all going to be okay."

There was another pause.

"Wilson it's too late. It's gone too far."

"Daisy don't be silly. What do you mean, gone too far?"

"I was attacked in my bedroom last night. I think they're going to kill me."

Wilson's stress level was already in the red, but now the needle was off the gauge.

"What! What do you mean you were attacked in your bedroom? What the...Jesus... Are you okay?"

"Yeah. My back's a bit of a mess. I really can't speak now."

"Why? Where are you?"

"I'm in hospital, but not for me, I'm in Ward 3B. A priest is here. She's going Wilson; she only has a few hours left. Gran's not moved or opened her eyes; she's hardly breathing."

"Have you got the bangles?"

"Yes. But —"

"I'm on my way. Talk to her, anything — just keep her alive."

Wilson dashed downstairs.

His phone beeped with a text from Blamire.

'The red army is moving out in two hours!'

Wilson checked at his watch then quickly texted back.

'Got something loads better than cash. Meet me in the car park at the entrance to Stockport Infirmary in twenty minutes.'

He grabbed his jacket and was on the Vespa, accelerating down the driveway before his mum could object. At the first set of red lights he sent Daisy a text.

'Meet me in the car park, usual place, in ten minutes. Bring the bangles!!!'

The muscles in Wilson's arms and shoulders began to ache as he weaved through traffic, his body working on a thirty per cent charge. He turned onto Bramhall Moor Lane and then pulled into the car park of the hospital. Daisy wasn't waiting but Blamire was and he sprang out of a black Mercedes with tinted windows the moment Wilson parked the scooter. Blamire was accompanied by a stocky, shaven-headed bloke and the phrase 'knuckles trailing on the ground' could never have been more applicable. Wilson removed his helmet and looked anxiously at the hospital building.

Daisy, come on, come out of the doors now, please.

"What you got for me then?"

Blamire thrust his stocky barrel chest out and his pit-bull of a mate did the same.

"It's not money, right, not the eight grand" said Wilson, taking a step backwards.

"Are you wastin' our bleedin' time? Cos if you are, we'll be takin' it out on your face. Broad daylight or not."

"No, wait, give me a second. Look, you have a pawn shop, or a buy-and-sell-gold or whatever it is, on Mersey Square, right?"

"Yeah, what of it?"

"Well I've got some gold, solid gold, the best gold you'll ever see."

"Where is it then?"

"It's coming. My girlfriend's got it. The gold used to be her grandma's. She's in the hospital. I just texted to say I've arrived and she'll be here any second. Check my phone if you don't believe me. It's the best gold, fifty carat. Worth loads more than eight grand."

"I don't friggin' believe this. You call me down here promising the dough and then you tell me it's fifty-carat gold."

Blamire took a step forward.

"Fifty-carat gold don't exist, you numpty."

Blamire then stepped back.

"Give him a slap Andy. Remind him who he's dealing with."

Wilson was focusing on the hospital entrance. What if Daisy hadn't got the message to meet him in the car park? What if her grandma had died and it was all too late?

Blamire's bruiser stepped forward and swung a gym-muscled forearm and a tattooed fist at Wilson's head. But Andy was too slow and too out of condition. His fist slammed into Wilson's crash helmet, which Wilson then smashed back into Andy's jaw, just as he brought his foot down at an angle onto the side of Andy's knee joint, snapping ligaments and tendons. Andy screeched in pain and crumpled to the floor. Wilson stepped back, on his toes, waiting for Blamire to make his move.

"What the...!" Blamire's face was fuming with psychopathic rage. "I'm gonna rip your..."

"Wilson! Wilson!"

It was Daisy. She came waving and running across the car park. Breathlessly, she handed him a paper bag. Her broken finger was fixed straight, in a splint.

"Wilson, she's almost gone. I've got to get back."

As Daisy dashed off between the cars, her sweater lifted and Wilson caught a fleeting glimpse of the thick, red scratches, like claw marks, running across the base of her back.

"So what's your fairy godmother brought ya?"

Wilson handed the package to Blamire, who opened it, lifted out one of the bangles, felt the weight, scratched at the surface with a tooth and whistled.

"Tasty bit of merchandise. Where did you get these then?"

"Like I said, an old family heirloom."

"Nice Winston, very nice."

A second car then pulled alongside and a tinted window came down. Blamire handed the package to the driver with the instructions: "Get these in the safe, in my office, now."

The driver nodded, took the package and drove off.

"You were right Winston, it is the best gold. Vintage twenty-four-carat. Worth about three grand each in the shop. I'll use some of that to get Andy patched up. Don't suppose you know if there's a hospital round here?"

"We finished Blamire?"

"Yeah. For now. Give us a bell if you get any more merchandise like that."

Wilson rang Daisy as he sprinted across the car park towards the hospital entrance.

"Daisy, meet me in the corridor at the corner, just before the turn to 3B. Coming now."

Daisy was waiting, tears running in tracks down her cheeks, as he arrived.

"She's left us Wilson. She's gone."

"No, maybe we have a few seconds more. We've gotta try."

"Try what? What do you want to do?"

"Daisy, hold my arm. I need to get closer to 3B."

"No Wilson, you can't go down there. You almost died the last time."

"Daisy, trust me. We don't have an alternative."

"No, I can't, I can't do it."

"Well then, I'll have to do it myself."

Wilson turned into the corridor and immediately felt a splintering jolt in his forehead. He tried to force a second step, but a dense wall of pain stopped him in his tracks. He tried to push through the agony, but it was impenetrable. Then a soft hand closed around his own, the pain seemed to flow away and his beautiful, reassuring, staff-of-life supported him as they slowly walked in the direction of the swing doors.

Wilson closed his eyes and began to turn his head from side to side, up then down, searching for something in the streaming torrent of time traces and energy flowing down the corridor. They stood in front of the swing doors to 3B as Wilson raised one hand into the air, reaching out to an invisible object, seemingly suspended in mid-air, an arm's length away. Precious moments passed. Daisy could feel Wilson slumping in her arms, his stamina failing, his energy, power, electrolytes being obliterated.

"Wilson, please, we have to go back."

With his eyes still closed, Wilson turned to Daisy. Three gold bangles were resting in the palm of his hand, plucked from thin air, the grand finale to an incredible trick. Daisy stared, astonished, unable to comprehend the reality of the illusion.

"Daisy..." Wilson could hardly speak; he was wheezing and coughing. "put... put them on... your grandma's wrist... now. Run Daisy, we might not be too late... *your life* depends on..."

She let Wilson slump gently to the floor, grabbed the bangles from his hand and ran into the ward, to the side of her grandmother's bed. She slipped the three gold bangles over a still-warm hand and onto a frail, narrow wrist.

Then Daisy turned and sprinted back to Wilson, as though *his life* depended on it. Which it most certainly did. Wilson was lying on his back and he wasn't moving. His lips were turning blue and his face was cadaver grey. Daisy wasn't sure if he was breathing. She dragged his lifeless body back down the corridor, round and out of sight of the swing doors to 3B.

She smashed the glass covering an emergency alarm with her fist and started screaming and screaming for help, from anyone, from everyone, from anywhere.

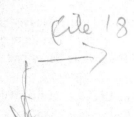

Chapter 54

Who dunnit?

Friday 10th November 2017

Blamire helped Andy hobble to A&E reception where a nurse told them to take a seat and wait to be called. Andy sat in a wheelchair as Blamire inflicted more pain.

"It's not acceptable pal. A skinny kid like that, showing me up. If you work in my team Andy, you've gotta be able to handle yourself. I mean, if word gets out, it's my reputation that takes a batterin', not yours. Everyone'll start taking the mick."

Andy was struggling to reply. Not because Blamire's conversation was too erudite to follow, but because his jaw was fractured.

An urgent message came over the tannoy system.

"Crash team to Ward 3B. Crash team to 3B."

"I think it's better Andy if you find a new career. Something you can handle. Open a flower shop with yer missus. Get a stall on the market and sell cards."

"Doctor Khan to Ward 3B. Doctor Khan, urgent call for Ward 3B."

"Christ, what's goin' on in 3B? Anyway Andy, don't call me right and keep your trap shut. You don't want to be spending time in here again. Over in 3B. Know what I mean?"

Andy grunted in reply. He'd got the message.

Blamire hurried back to his shop on Mersey Square, anxious to check his instructions had been followed to the letter. As he entered, the driver of the second car, now serving behind the counter, nodded to confirm the bangles were secure.

Blamire entered his office, locked the door and opened the safe. It contained a loaded hand gun, eighteen thousand pounds in cash, twelve thousand euros in forged notes and two kilos of cocaine. The gram of dope was purely for personal use. There was also a white paper bag — with nothing in it.

Blamire frantically emptied the safe, leaving the tools of his trade scattered on the office floor. Then he went back out to the shop.

"Are you pullin' my pipe, Dickweed? Okay, very funny. Where's the booty, the bangles?"

The apprentice was serving a customer but immediately raised his head, conditioned to the mention of his name.

"In the safe boss."

The customer scarpered.

The fight didn't last long.

That's assuming you can call Dickweed being thrown through a glass counter, a front door and out into the street, *a fight.*

The police squad car arrived just as Blamire was about to throw Dickweed back into the shop, through the front window, the entrance door no longer being fit for purpose.

The police loved the interior of Blamire's office.

After some considerable effort, three burly officers eventually cuffed an altogether different style of bangle onto Blamire's wrists and dragged the spitting, red-faced maniac back to the sanctity of *their* office.

Chapter 55

Knock, knock – who's there?

Friday 10th November 2017

Blamire had hit the nail on the head. Wilson had indeed been causing trouble outside Ward 3B and was now lying on his back, his eyes wide open, not blinking and fixed on a light hanging from the ceiling directly above.

A team of emergency medical professionals, including Doctor Khan, were desperately trying to jump-start a flat-as-a-pancake heart. Only Wilson's legs from below the knee were visible, protruding from the yellow tent of crash team jackets he was hidden under. The soles of his trainers correctly gave the time of the incident as ten minutes to two. Daisy was collapsed in a heap a metre away – like a marionette with snipped strings. She was crying, her cheek pressed hard against the cold concrete of the corridor wall. A steady stream of tears dripped from her chin, creating a small puddle on the floor. Her bloodied fist was pounding the floor, but the rhythm was slowing, in sync with her sobs and Wilson's heartbeat.

Around the same time, at The Gateway, there was the gentlest of taps on the door of the residents' entrance. Big Mac greeted the new arrival.

"Ah, Gwendolyn, you're finally here, we've been expecting you."

"Do come in" said Big Mac, opening the door fully.

"Looks about a three-ouncer to me" said Short Cake, eyeing up the slight and wrinkled frame of Daisy's grandmother.

Gwendolyn took a step forward and was about to cross the threshold when she stopped, turned her head and looked back over her shoulder.

It was as though she'd heard someone mention her name, from the other side of a room, in a cocktail party conversation.

"Actually" she said "I think I'm a fraction over the three. Better go and spend that last tad of energy on something valuable."

Gwendolyn's Outer Shell then carried her Residual back to Stockport Infirmary where it settled into her recently-pronounced-dead body for just a moment, before returning back to The Gateway.

Big Mac and Short Cake were waiting when she arrived. They knew exactly where she'd been.

"Sorry" she said with a knowing smile "I forgot to bring the bling."

The spirit of Daisy's grandmother then raised a frail and bony wrist and started jangling the bangles.

"Come on in" said Big Mac. "It's time for us to climb that stairway to heaven."

He began singing the words to the song.

"There's a lady who knows all that glitters is gold..."

Short Cake closed the door.

"I wonder who's won all the money then?"

Chapter 56

Daisy's dream

In all the chaos, Daisy never found time to tell Wilson how she got the six claw marks across her back and the bruises all over her body.

Following the burglary, it took Daisy two hours to restore her bedroom to something like its former self and secretly dispose of the shredded clothes. At 11.00 p.m. she took the sedative her mum said would help with sleep and for an hour lay in bed feeling frightened and vulnerable. She cursed The Market Square and her stupidity. She wrestled with ideas on the ways and means to return the bangles to no avail and prayed Wilson was having more success.

Around 3.00 a.m. she woke for no apparent reason, other than the allure of a bead of light shining beneath the bedroom door. After slipping into a dressing gown and the slippers at the foot of her bed — neither of which she'd seen before — Daisy opened the door. The house was silent as she walked across the landing towards the light switch.

A tall figure, half-hidden in darkness was standing at the foot of the stairs. It was covered from head to toe by a black, woollen cassock. A voluminous pointed hood enshrouded the head completely and there was no face, only blackness. As Daisy stood transfixed by the monk-like figure, an invisible force, completely beyond her control, began to draw her down the stairs. Half-falling, half-flying, she landed in a heap at the feet of the figure, who stooped down, enveloped her within the folds of heavy, coarse fabric and began to tickle her.

"Tomorrow is the big day" she heard the figure whisper, before releasing the animal cackle of what could have been a hyena laughing.

When Daisy woke, her body bore the signs of a brutal assault.

Chapter 57

Limboland

Sunday 12th November 2017

After thirty-six hours of intensive care, Wilson's distraught family and friends were finally given the news they'd been dreading; Wilson was in an irreversible coma. Alex, Gloria, Kate, Megan, Daisy, Teaps and Hoover were all in attendance, grief-stricken and inconsolable. Despite my ambivalent indifference, my watchful neglect, I have to admit it was all desperately moving and extremely sad.

But not all bad news. Because Wilson's phone, which was lying on the table beside his bed, let out a sharp ping. Hoover picked up the phone and keyed in Wilson's passcode.

A photo message popped open.

It was a picture of a Japanese boy with a big happy face and an enormously broad smile. He was holding in front of the camera a green sock with a Ralph Lauren logo embroidered onto it.

Hoover turned to face Wilson's dad.

"We've found his missing sock."

The following day, an eminent neurologist met with Alex and Gloria. After a sombre discussion, he told them the Intensive Care Unit had done all it could for Wilson. The brain scans and the consultations between doctors and specialists had all delivered the same conclusion: Wilson was in a persistent vegetative state, or PVS for short and always would be.

Wilson's brain was the equivalent of a dead battery. The component parts were in perfect working order, but the liquid charge being drip-fed into his arm was having no effect. Put simply, Wilson couldn't be jump-started. Eventually, two porters pushed his bed to a small private ward. They passed an arrow pointing out 'The Chapel' on the way.

Wilson's new ward only had space for three beds. One was taken up by Wilson. The second, by a young boy called Tom Rowlands, who'd fallen downstairs and cracked his skull while having a laser-gun fight with his brother. In the third bed was Sally Bennett, the victim of a grisly car crash in Davenport a few weeks earlier. All three were connected to EEG machines and a spot of light was tracing a line across each screen.

On the screen above Sally's bed, the spot was peaking and troughing and occasionally beeping with signs of life.

On the screen above Tom's bed, the spot was active, but subdued.

Above Wilson, the pencil of light was flatlining.

Alex, Gloria and Daisy sat around Wilson's bed. Even the most poignantly crafted sentence could never begin to convey the depths of their torment and suffering. Gloria had brought Wilson's alarm clock and lovingly placed an old toy giraffe with a missing ear on his pillow. Wilson looked to be at peace, like the little boy she remembered, sound asleep under a Batman duvet and dreaming of who knows what — firemen, faces in spoons.

Doctor Khan quietly entered the room and checked Wilson's pulse, then he lifted an eyelid, and shone a torch on the iris. No response. He put the torch back in his pocket and considered Wilson for a long moment that was filled with his disappointment and sympathy.

"I'm sorry, but I can't change my prognosis Mr and Mrs Armitage. In my professional opinion, your son won't be coming back."

Alex had aged ten years in just a few days. Saggy half-moons of skin drooped beneath his eyes and a corrugation of worry lines ran across his forehead. The guilt was almost too much to bear, and the thought of telling Gloria the full story made him feel mentally unstable.

"As you know" Doctor Khan continued, "I've instructed the nurses to implement a regime of 'nil by mouth' in three days' time." He checked the date on his watch.

"Let's say from Friday morning then, shall we?

"Of course, you can appeal against my decision and I can put you in touch with the lawyers here at the hospital. Though speaking as a father, and someone who understands the utter heartache and despair you're facing, and having seen the appeals process and the further pain it brings, I would advise you to put your emotions to one side and do the right thing for Wilson."

Gloria was staring into space, not listening, trying to convince herself that this wasn't happening. She started folding the lace hanky in her lap into increasingly smaller-sized rectangles. She was picturing herself in the kitchen making Wilson his sausage and mash.

"But how can he go, just like that?" Alex's voice was cracking under the strain.

"He was getting better" pleaded Gloria.

"Mr and Mrs Armitage, the brain is a complicated instrument and we still don't fully understand some of its functionality. Take the case of Sally here. Her brain is not... how can I put this? Her brain has always showed some signs of life. Over the last few weeks, her cerebral activity has become stronger as her brain has started to repair and reorganise itself. Patients like Sally will, with time, pull through. In actual fact, she was wide awake yesterday for a few hours. This often happens as the brain continues its running repairs. Some do come out of their coma with a degree of disability it's true, but others make a full recovery.

"But as I said, I can't give you false hope, because that won't be the case with Wilson. There are no impulses, not even the tiniest amount of activity to indicate his brain can come back to life. I'm sorry."

"Doctor Khan" said Daisy, "could Wilson be alive and just... dreaming somewhere? Like resting, recovering in some kind of dream state, just waiting to come back?"

Alex so desperately wanted to clutch at that straw also.

"No Daisy, I'm sorry, that's completely impossible."

Doctor Khan's pager bleeped and after checking the message, he apologised, said goodbye and left the room.

Daisy and Alex sat in silence.

Gloria was silently crying, tears free-falling onto her hanky. Slowly she looked up at Daisy, her eyes crazed with pain, her lips trembling. She was on the verge of hysterics and a primeval plea for truth erupted from the depths of her soul.

"Daisy" she screamed, "what did you do to my son?"

Alex shepherded his distraught wife from the room and told Daisy they were going home for a few hours. He also said that they would need to have a private conversation at some time in the future.

After they'd left, Daisy moved her chair next to Wilson's bed. Her eyes were bloodshot and her cheeks mottled with tear tracks. She held Wilson's hand and smiled at his lovely face, his stupid hair and the small, dark mole on his chin. His skin had a satin, milky sheen and the raised corners of his mouth even suggested a smile. Daisy remembered all the crazy, happy moments. Wilson waltzing with the Medusa in those ridiculous, tight pants. Singing in Fabio's with Chanelle and the Eager Beavers. The first meeting in Starbucks and standing in the rain under the umbrella. And that amazing, wonderful first kiss beneath the fireworks of Ferris the Catherine Wheel.

Daisy leant forward and kissed Wilson's warm lips.

Wilson's eyelids fluttered — as though displaced by rapid eye movement beneath.

Daisy's heart missed a beat.

She kissed him a second time and his eyelids moved slightly, from side to side, then up, then down. Daisy's heart missed a second beat and at that moment, she instinctively knew Wilson was still with her. A message from her heart, from somewhere, from Wilson, was telling her that he was not dead, just dead to the world.

Daisy grabbed her bag and coat, kissed him again and whispered in his ear "Wilson, I know where you are, and I'm coming to get you."

Chapter 58

Calamity Jane

Monday 13th November 2017

Travelling home on the bus, Daisy tried to shackle her euphoria. She didn't want to be overly optimistic but her hope against all hopes was that she would find Wilson and somehow bring him back. She had no idea how, but that wasn't the point. She knew Wilson was still alive, trapped in some kind of limbo between coma-land and being properly alive, breathing and laughing and joking and making her love him. Daisy was fairly certain she needed to start her search in The Market Square, Wilson's eye movements had confirmed that, but her plan had evolved no further. She had to admit it wasn't a great plan, but something inside was saying there would be no need to search elsewhere.

As Daisy opened the front door, her mother was standing in the hallway, expecting the worst. She was holding on to a bannister for support in case her legs gave way. The moment she saw the look on Daisy's face however, she knew something had happened, but it wasn't a tragedy. Daisy wouldn't admit to anything by way of good news though – on the contrary.

"No Mum, he's still the same. They're planning to stop giving him nutrition on Friday and after that, it's just a matter of time."

Frances advanced to give Daisy a hug, fully expecting her to break down in tears, to let it all out, to have a good cry on her shoulder, but she didn't. She simply said "Don't worry, Mum. They have top doctors at the hospital and I'm sure one of them will come up with something. Look, I'm really tired, I haven't slept too much over these last few days. I'm going to lie on my bed for a while. I'm not hungry, so don't bother with any tea for me. Just need to be alone with my thoughts."

She then entered the lounge, grabbed her laptop, said 'hi' to her dad and two steps at a time, raced up to her room.

Daisy's father appeared in the doorway, caught the eye of his wife and shrugged as if to say, 'What in God's name is going on with Daisy?'

Frances scratched her head.

That was odd, she thought, *I could have sworn Daisy was singing a Britney Spears song as she closed her bedroom door.*

It was only half past seven but Daisy changed into a fresh pair of pyjamas, brushed her teeth, combed her hair and climbed into bed. She was a bundle of nervous energy, eager to find Wilson, but first there was prep work to do, just in case. With the laptop resting against her knees, she pulled the duvet under her chin and asked Google to disclose all it knew about PVS, or persistent vegetative states.

Knowledge is a powerful weapon, she thought *and I'm going to need all the help I can get.*

For two hours Daisy read the results of every conceivable search term relating to the word 'coma' including 'coma recovery', 'coma phenomena', 'comas and dreams', 'comas and miracles' and so on. When Daisy finally arrived at the search term 'comas and the human spirit', she knew her work for that part of the evening was done and thankfully, she was tired. It was nine thirty when she switched off the light, closed her eyes and an hour later began the journey to rescue Wilson.

"Hi there little missy."

A cowboy was tipping the brim of a Stetson hat and his grinning face was inches from Daisy's. Most of his stubby, yellow teeth were missing, his hair hadn't been washed in years, he smelt of horse manure and whisky and his clothes were filthy. Two revolvers, nestling in holsters on a belt full of bullets were milliseconds from the grip of his nicotine-stained fingers.

"God," said Daisy, rolling her eyes, "that's all I need, Dodge City."

Slowly she turned on the spot, taking everything in, irritated with the unnecessary antics of The Market Square.

The flagged pavement that normally framed the perimeter of the square was now a raised boardwalk with lines of hitching posts. Saddled horses stood patiently, tethered at the bridle. The cobbles of the square were covered by a thick layer of sun baked, red dirt. The fascias of the once familiar buildings had all been reconstructed from wooden planking, in keeping with the night's theme, and re-branded as a 'Saloon' and a 'Telegram Office', a 'General Store', 'Jail' and an 'Hotel'. Cowboys in leather chaps, waistcoats and thick heeled boots with silver spurs jangling, clomped along the boardwalk. Two American Indians riding bareback trotted past a colourful teepee painted with crude images of a buffalo hunt. Beyond the Clock Tower, (which now resembled a totem pole), at the bottom end of the square, a Mississippi paddle steamer was moored on a wide river alongside a long wooden jetty. The boat was four decks high and the word Casino was emblazoned along the bow.

Daisy walked to a bench, where an old, dappled mare with a long fringe of coarse hair covering one eye was saddled up and reined to the backrest. The horse was chomping on a mouthful of hay.

"Why howdy, ma'am" said the horse.

The protruding yellow teeth and thick lips reminded Daisy of her grandad adjusting his dentures. The image wasn't welcome. She told the horse to 'get lost' and sat down with her arms folded, trying to spot Wilson. In truth, she was surprised that he wasn't already there, waiting for her arrival. Gazing across the square, she understood why. The Wild West backdrop was a dream playground for Wilson.

He'll be out there acting like some bad-ass outlaw or a sheriff laying down the law — so I'll just have to go and round him up.

Daisy was about to start her search in the far corner of the square, where L'École was now masquerading as a saloon called The Golden Nugget, when the horse whinnied for attention and then spoke.

"Can give you a lift, if you like?"

Daisy shook her head at the sheer ludicrousness of the suggestion but then quickly saw sense in the idea.

I'll be able to cover more ground and track him down much quicker.

Daisy had never ridden before but soon got the hang of it, thanks to expert advice, straight from the horse's mouth, so to speak.

"What's your name darlin'?"

"Daisy. What's yours?"

"Trigger" said the horse.

"Come on then Trigger, giddy up, let's go and round up good ol' Sheriff Wilson."

After searching for what could have been hours, Daisy still hadn't found Wilson. He wasn't in the saloon, in jail, or playing poker on the steamboat. He hadn't checked into the hotel and wasn't involved in the gunfight or the brawl in the middle of Main Street. Even the smoke signals from Big Chief Sitting Bull failed to reach him. There was no sign of Wilson anywhere.

Daisy climbed down from Trigger and patted him on the shoulder.

"Sorry we couldn't find him" said Trigger, dejectedly.

"Yeah, I know. Thanks for the help anyway."

Trigger walked away, his nose almost touching the ground and his tail swishing from side to side.

Wilson hadn't arrived back at the benches during Daisy's absence either, and she was stumped.

Cramming all that ridiculous information about comas was a complete waste of time. Reading a book about Billy the Kid would have been more useful.

It was at that moment that Daisy began to feel anxious and deeply uncertain about everything. She had been so sure that Wilson would be waiting for her in The Market Square. Her plan had never allowed for any other possibility. However, what if Wilson really was in a permanent coma and not lost in The Market Square at all? What if she couldn't find and rescue him? What if they did stop feeding him at the hospital? Daisy was finding it difficult to stop disturbing thoughts hijacking her fragile psyche. She began to weep, with real tears, a first for The Market Square. After what could have been an hour or simply a matter of minutes, a strong voice from deep within demanded she pull herself together.

Keep going. Think like Wilson – what would he do? He certainly wouldn't give up on you, ever!

So Daisy thought just like Wilson and three familiar words soon arrived to restore her self-confidence and give fresh impetus to the quest: Sampson's Motorcycle Workshop.

What an idiot! How could I have been so stupid? Wilson knows it's impossible to find him in this Wild West madness, so he's waiting at the obvious meeting place. And all this time I've been prancing around on a bloody horse.

Daisy stood up and laughed through drying tears as she tried to get a fix on the sign outside Sampson's workshop. It wasn't easy to spot because a cloud of thick, red dust was following the one hundred head of cattle slowly being driven across the centre of the square. The Texas Longhorns mooed and bellowed as they succumbed to the shouts and the crack of a whip herding them along. As the stockmen finally steered the last of the stubborn cows past Daisy, she saw the distinctive lettering at the top of The Market Square. She knew that even if Sampson's workshop was masquerading as the Dodge City blacksmith, Wilson would be there and waiting.

She rose from the bench and sprinted in the direction of Sampson's, but strangely, the more she ran, the further away the workshop seemed to be. She was covering the dusty ground, but the ground was slipping back. One step forward became two steps in reverse. Running even harder, meant getting no closer. But she was desperate to reach Wilson. So she ran and ran and ran, faster and harder than any dream could ever follow. Faster than the feeling of panic draining the energy from her legs. Finally, with every muscle burning and her lungs about to explode, she burst through the dream barrier and crashed through the door of Sampson's shop, where she fell to her knees, gasping for air.

As her heart rate dropped and her breathing returned to normal, Daisy looked around the workshop. Nobody was home!

"Wilson" she yelled at the top her voice. "Wilson, it's me, Daisy, I'm here. Wilson, where are you? This isn't funny anymore Wilson. I'm getting scared."

Mark Sampson emerged from his office. He was wiping his hands on a grubby cloth.

"Can I help you?"

"Mark, thank goodness. It's me, Daisy, Daisy Meadowcroft. I'm here for Wilson — you know, Wilson Armitage. Where is he? He should be here waiting for me."

"Can I help you?" Sampson gave the same blank reply for a second time.

"Yes Mark, you can. I just told you, I'm here for Wilson."

"Can I help you?"

"Mark, stop playing silly games. This is serious. Where's Wilson? Wilson Armitage. Where the hell is Wilson?"

"Can I help you?"

Daisy stopped speaking. Something was clearly wrong and terribly confusing.

"Mark, it's me. Don't do this, please, I beg you. We don't have much time, I could go at any moment and still haven't found Wilson."

"Can I help you?"

Standing on the brink of hysteria in a dream, Daisy frantically ran her fingers through her hair. *Please God, please say this madness isn't happening.*

Sampson's facial expression hadn't changed throughout the entire conversation. There was no look of concern, no change of emotion. He was role-playing the robot, dressed in grimy overalls, mechanically cleaning his hands on an oily rag.

"Do you understand me Mark? I'm talking about Wilson — you know, Wilson Armitage, the boy with the Vespa."

At the word 'Vespa', Sampson's entire demeanour changed. He stopped wiping his hands and smiled.

"Ah yes, the 1959 GS 150. A classic. How's he getting on with it?"

Daisy had finally pierced through the false persona. It was all part of an act.

"Hallelujah! Listen Mark, Wilson's had a terrible accident and he's in hospital, in a coma. He fluttered his eyelids this afternoon, telling me to come and find him. I searched all over the wild west, but he wasn't

315

out there, so he has to be here, with you. So where is he?"

"Can I help you?"

Daisy froze, she was still talking to an android.

"Would you recommend a Suzuki?"

"No, cheap and unreliable. Wouldn't touch one with a bargepole. If you want a Japanese bike, get a Yamaha. Can't go wrong with a Yamaha."

Sampson turned to a row of bikes that were lined up for sale.

"You see, take this Yamaha 250. The engine runs..."

Daisy stopped listening because she suddenly understood what was happening. Sampson wasn't real. He couldn't help. He was just a prop, a talking mannequin. Ask him the time and he'd have no answer. Ask about a bike and he'd give a programmed reply, a pre-recorded message activated by the relevant prompt.

"What day is it Mark?"

"Can I help you?"

Daisy left Sampson's shop, agitated and frustrated by a dream not evolving as intended. A new idea was needed, the Plan B that would lead directly to Wilson. The Clock Tower was fading into twilight shadow as Daisy tried in vain to stifle a yawn.

So where do I go now?

Back to bed, came the answer, as she departed to leave Wilson, helpless and alone, somewhere in The Market Square.

Chapter 59

Knockout drops

Tuesday 14th November 2017

'The worries of a sleepless night, are nothing, to the morning light.'

Daisy couldn't recall where she'd heard the quote, but lying in bed, she knew the sentiment wasn't true. Half her mind was still anxiously roaming the The Market Square searching for Wilson; the other half was at his bedside. She dressed quickly and slipped out of the house without saying goodbye to her parents. The note on the bedside table would explain.

An hour later she was in the hospital, one step away from entering Wilson's room, when she paused at the sound of excited chattering and laughter coming from within. Her heartbeat fluttered, Was Wilson back? She cautiously pushed open the door and entered.

But Wilson was still flat out on his bed, in the same position as the previous day. So too was Tom Rowlands. Sally's bed though, was hidden behind a curtain and the thin partition of fabric was struggling to contain the lively conversation on the other side. The car crash victim was awake.

Daisy went for a coffee feeling deflated and guilty for doing so. When she returned half an hour later, the curtain had been pulled back and Sally was propped up on two pillows, sipping juice from a plastic beaker. Her head was bandaged and her arm was in a sling, but apart from that, she appeared well on the way to recovery. All but one of the earlier visitors had gone, so Daisy assumed, quite correctly, that the lady remaining was Sally's mum.

Daisy offered a polite "hello" and sat on a chair beside Wilson.

Sally returned the greeting with a timid wave.

Sally's mum simply said, "Morning love. We've got our fingers crossed for him."

Daisy forced a smile, "thanks, I'm glad you're both okay," and then she turned back to Wilson.

Something was different, he looked older somehow and there was a strange smell coming from his bedclothes. Not body odour; more the sweet, mustiness of decaying fruit. The pallor of Wilson's skin had also changed. It had acquired a sallow, grey yellow tinge and his lips were outlined with a feint blue. Daisy's heart sank. She didn't need to look at the EEG monitor to know that overnight he'd taken a step closer to dying.

"Sorry," she said, pulling the curtain back between the two beds.

Daisy wanted to be completely alone with Wilson.

"It's alright love" said Sally's mum softly, "I was the same."

The conversation between mother and daughter then continued but at muted volume.

Daisy adjusted the bedsheets to fully cover Wilson's shoulders.

On the bus that morning, all the way to the hospital in fact, she couldn't wait to kiss him one more time. To prove that female intuition – no, more than that, her number eleven instincts from the previous day were not just some kind of delusional self-deception.

Wilson's eyelids definitely flickered when I kissed him, without a doubt.

But were they really signalling his dream sleep? Or could the flicker have been a twitch, some kind of involuntary reaction to being kissed? So Daisy kissed Wilson one more time and kept her eyes fixed on his. No response. She repeated the kiss. Still no response. Then she kissed him again, more forcefully, with all the feeling she could impart. But the dream was no longer running in Wilson's head, there was no action for his eyes to follow and the twitch theory was also wrong. When Daisy overheard Sally whisper something to her mum about 'mountains of gold bangles', she had to bite on a clenched fist to stop from shrieking.

Daisy tiptoed round Wilson's bed, stood with her ear to the curtain and checked her feet weren't poking out underneath.

"Yeah, it was such a weird dream Mum. I'll never forget it. This strange white room with people just standing around, all dressed the same. It felt like I was in that white room forever. Then a door opened and I walked into a huge church filled with those golden bangles where two funny men helped me to escape to cowboy-land. Then I woke up and look, all my eczema's nearly gone!"

Daisy held Wilson's hand as she stared blankly into space, her visual senses turned inwards. She was opening, scanning, closing every memory from The Market Square. Looking for a lifeline, a sign that would direct her to the white room in The Gateway. Every dream was mentally dissected into its component parts. Finally, after two hours of searching, at the very end of the road, hidden deep inside the very first night she met Wilson, Daisy found the motif she was seeking — it was on the teacher's desk, in a language class, in L'École.

Ten minutes later, Daisy was in the hospital pharmacy.

"Do you sell sleeping tablets?"

"We do, but I can only sell you certain ones without a prescription. Who are they for?"

"They're for me, I'm going to Australia with my dad tomorrow and I hate flying. I need to knock myself out quickly."

The assistant turned to the various medications on the shelves behind her and asked "How old are you?"

"I was eighteen a few days ago." Daisy flashed her college ID card.

"Well, these will do the job. They're adult strength, so you'll only need to take one, about half an hour before you fly."

"What if I take two?"

"The recommended dose is one in any twenty-four-hour period. So two will certainly send you down under."

She paid for the knockout drops and rushed back to Wilson. Daisy swallowed two pills from the blister pack, drew the curtain to fully enclose Wilson's bed and lay down beside him. She didn't have time to wait for night to arrive — Wilson was dying and she needed to fight for his life there and then. Twenty minutes later Daisy was on her way and knew exactly who to pick a fight with.

Chapter 60

What happened next, but *shouldn't* have

Tuesday 14th November 2017

Daisy hit the ground running when she landed in The Market Square and headed straight for L'École.

She dashed up the flight of steps that led to the main entrance and stopped to get her bearings in the foyer. Through a window to the right she could see a small office in which an elderly lady sat touch-typing at an old fashioned typewriter. The corridor ahead was empty but Daisy could hear the muffled voices of teachers running their crash courses. She couldn't recall the exact room in which she first saw Wilson, but remembered the teacher's name. Following a double tap on the office window, the lady hobbled over and with a warm smile slid the window to one side.

"May I help you?"

"Hi, really sorry to trouble you, as I'm sure you're very busy, but I'm looking for Miss Angeline. She was a French teacher, many years ago. Is she still here, I need to speak with her urgently?"

"Yes child, Miss Angeline still teaches in our language department. I'd be delighted to pass on a message for you."

"No, no you can't. Sorry, it's a personal thing, about a former student; there's been a terrible accident and I have to let her know, face to face. I promised. It'll only take a few minutes."

"Well, up you dash then dearie. She's in Classe 6a, first floor, first on the right."

"Oh thank you, thank you so much."

"Well, I do hope your... our alumni is soon on the road to recovery."

"Yeah, I'll tell him" shouted Daisy as she charged up the stairs.

On reaching the top step, familiarity with the first floor came flooding back. The white mosaic floor tiles, the lilac-painted walls, the smell of fresh violets and on the right, the door to Classe 6a. Daisy knocked and entered.

The classroom was filled with children seated at wooden desks: the boys wore blazers, with a large sun embroidered on the breast pocket, the girls wore stripy pinafore dresses. Daisy felt something glow inside her heart as she noticed the small wooden desk, in the middle of the front row, from which she'd once sent shy smiles to Wilson.

"May I be of some assistance?"

Daisy turned to the voice and instantly recognised Miss Angeline. She was wearing the same, matronly, tweed skirt and jacket, her hair tied in the same tight bun and she hadn't aged a day. Crucially, the large glass vase, filled with flaming-red poppies, was there on her table.

Daisy's hunch was going in the right direction.

"Look, I'm really sorry to trouble you Miss Angeline but I need to know where you got those flowers?"

Miss Angeline faced up to Daisy with a puzzled expression, as though she was being addressed in a language she'd never heard before.

"Please, it's a matter of life and death. I have to know, quickly."

"Why, I cut them myself, just this morning, fresh from the meadow."

"Fresh from which meadow? Where is it and how do I find it?" Daisy's words tumbled out in an anxious rush.

"You'll find it out there of course."

Miss Angeline pointed to a large sash window to the right of the blackboard. It was set in a wall at the back of the room, in an elevation that couldn't be seen from The Market Square.

Daisy dashed to the window, hardly daring to look, too frightened to contemplate the possibility of being wrong. She needn't have worried though, because murmurating like a flock of red starlings in the summer breeze and expanding outwards, for as far as her eye could see, were thousands of vivid crimson flowers. On the horizon, shimmering in a heat haze, were the colossal features of The Gateway itself.

Scarcely able to control her joy, Daisy shot back downstairs and in a flurry of words asked the lady in the office for directions to an exit that would lead out to the poppy meadow. The elderly secretary was happy to oblige.

Daisy stood in the cool shadow of a spacious atrium, facing two familiar doors.

The brass plaque on the left stated: 'The Gateway. Visitors Only'.

The plaque on the right: 'The Gateway. Residents Only'.

Daisy pushed the door on the left, just as Wilson had done, but for some reason, this time it wouldn't budge. She shoved a little harder but it still didn't move. Then she really put her back into it, the door budged an inch and then slammed back shut again.

She heard voices whispering on the other side. Someone had a foot wedged against the door and she didn't need a prize for guessing who.

"Hey, I know you two are there, so let me in. I've come for Wilson. I'm serious. I'll smash this door down if I have to."

She heard further mutterings.

She pushed again with all her might. The door shifted a fraction and again slammed shut. Daisy felt groggy, but not from the exertion, the sleeping tablets were fully kicking in. For a moment she considered the bizarre notion of falling even further asleep in her own dream.

I hope not, please, not right now.

She banged on the door with two sharp raps.

"Look, I'm sorry I stole your bangles. It was a mistake — you know I didn't mean to. But Gran gave them back. And now Wilson is seriously ill as a consequence. I think he's stuck somewhere in a white room and I need to rescue him, urgently."

No answer.

"Please guys, please let me in. Wilson hasn't got much longer. He's going to die if I don't rescue him."

Daisy waited a moment and shoved the door again, to no avail.

Then came the realisation that the miscreants on the other side were aware of this. They knew exactly where Wilson was. They'd kidnapped him and were slowly murdering him as punishment for playing God.

Daisy's blood began to boil and she put her mouth close to the door.

"Listen, if you don't want two new bangles — with *your* bloody names on, open this door!"

Further mutterings, then at last, a reply in a high pitched voice.

"We're closed today."

Daisy took three steps back and charged at the door, but it still held firm. She slumped to the floor rubbing her shoulder. Feelings of despondency began to descend. Wilson was running out of time and every plan was leading to a dead end. Daisy clambered to her feet, walked back along the atrium, down the steps and then turned back to survey the building.

There must be another way to get in. Another door possibly, or perhaps...

A penny dropped.

...an open window. Exactly, I'll climb in through an open window — or break one if I have to.

With renewed optimism, she studied the row upon row of elegant Georgian-style windows along the left and right wings of the building, but they were all shut and more to the point, the lower floor was completely inaccessible, over ten metres above the ground.

So where the hell do I start looking for a ladder.

Daisy thought of the local window cleaner and more specifically, the extension ladder that was always strapped to the roof of his van. She contemplated bringing him to The Market Square, but couldn't be certain he'd bring his ladders as well.

So who else can I reach out to for help?

That train of thought rumbled on and was going nowhere, until a stroke of inspired thinking brought a far more reliable accomplice to mind. Daisy closed her eyes, pictured the sharp image of a familiar face and pulled her personal hero into the drama. When she opened her eyes, Gwen Burton, the six-foot-tall hockey teacher with flaming ginger hair, was standing two feet away, complete with hockey stick.

"Wait" shouted Daisy, "we'll need some reinforcements."

A few moments later, Miss Wetherington, the head of PE and a sixteen stone battleaxe, was also standing beneath the atrium, with *her* hockey stick.

"Morning Miss Burton. Morning Miss Wetherington."

"Morning Daisy, and how are you on this beautiful day?" Gwen Burton was swishing her stick in readiness for a bully-off.

"Well, to be totally honest, I'm not so good. I'm trying to get into this building, through that door on the left, to rescue my boyfriend. But the two guys on the other side, who've kidnapped him, won't let me in."

Miss Wetherington turned to Gwen Burton and her face quickly turned an angry shade of purple, like a beetroot, as her neck and rugby-player shoulders started to bulk up.

"Well, we'll see about that."

As though summoned to quell a disturbance in the sixth-form common room, they both took a combined run at the door and smashed it off its hinges.

All three marched triumphantly into the hall.

Big Mac was lying sprawled out in a daze, on the mound of bangles for 2017.

Short Cake was losing his footing as he tried to scramble down from a pile of 2012s.

"I'm not sure that was completely necessary," said Big Mac, dusting himself off. "You should have said if it was that important."

"Grab 'em both" said Daisy "and follow me."

They marched round the back of the 2015s, where Burton and Wetherington shoved their captives into their matching chairs. The teachers sat, one on each desk, menacingly tapping the business ends of their hockey sticks on the polished wood surface.

"Where's Wilson?" Daisy demanded. "Where are you keeping him? Where's your white room?"

Short Cake was scowling and Big Mac was sulking. Neither of them said a word. Miss Burton raised the tip of her hockey stick as though asking Daisy for permission to use it.

"No, not just yet. Let me think."

Think like Wilson again, act like Wilson.

324

Daisy read the words on the neon signs above the three doors behind the desks. Big Mac had mentioned something about them but neither exit appeared to relate to a white room.

Peering across the cavernous space she was bewildered by the challenge.

The white room could be anywhere in here, and it would take me a year to search it all, maybe forever.

Daisy was still considering how and where to start when she heard a muffled scream, then a prolonged scream, as though someone was being inflicted with pain, or tortured! A third howl was accompanied by a burst of mocking laughter which Daisy was able to trace back to its source; a hole in the wall, roughly thirty metres to the right of the three doors.

Big Mac gasped and then started whimpering as Daisy, with some trepidation, began walking slowly towards the hole. She looked back, Short Cake was shifting uncomfortably in his seat and the skin stretched over his bony face was deathly white. Big Mac gasped for a second time as Daisy peered into the hole. She couldn't see the bottom, it was an inky black void, but there was certainly something bad happening down there; she heard another scream and a desperate plea, "No, please, show mercy for God's sake!" This was followed by an angry booming voice shouting "Oh very funny, we'll show mercy alright, just like you did."

Daisy let out a sigh of relief, neither voice was Wilson's.

Stepping back from the hole she noticed that something had been scratched into the face of a brick that was jutting out like a loose tooth. The impression was faint but clearly spelled out the words, 'A bad un'. Turning to Miss Wetherington, Daisy pointed at Big Mac and motioned for her to bring him over.

"Fetch the fat one and let's push him in, to see if Wilson's trapped down there."

"My pleasure."

The stocky teacher took a firm grip of Big Mac's jacket collar and jerked him to his feet. He made a strange guttural sound, then fainted and slumped to the floor.

"Alright, let's try the other one" said Daisy, nodding at Miss Burton. But Miss Burton didn't have to oblige.

"Go through that white door" said Short Cake, cowering low in his chair and pointing a crabby finger beyond Daisy.

Daisy turned and followed the line of direction for a further twenty metres to a small white box mounted high on the wall. Beneath it, partly hidden by a crest of golden bangles, was the right-angle corner of a door frame.

Daisy rushed round to the far side of the pile of bangles where a narrow strip of exposed marble floor made a pathway to the door.

Wilson had been correct, the white box was indeed an illuminated directional sign. A sign that said: 'The Annexe'.

Daisy referred back to the two teachers.

Miss Burton nodded approval to proceed.

Daisy pushed open the door, stepped inside and was immediately blinded by an intense white light which forced her eyes shut. They needed a moment to acclimatise after the half shadow of the hall.

She slowly opened them and adjusted to the glare of a white room filled with people. Children, men, women, the elderly, lots of the elderly, in regimented row upon row, like soldiers standing on a parade ground. Except there was no ground, just whiteness — and no ceiling or roof or sky, only open space. The people were dressed in the same uniform of white polo-neck sweater, white cotton trousers and white pumps; as though a white army had been called to attention and ordered to stand motionless in a featureless expanse of emptiness.

Daisy stepped up to the front line, face to face with a girl of around her own age. She waved her hand across the girl's face and then touched her shoulder — there was no response, no signs of life. Daisy was reminded of Sally and the words of Doctor Khan.

"Over the last few weeks, her cerebral activity has become stronger as her brain has started to repair and reorganise itself. Patients like Sally will, with time, pull through."

Then it dawned on Daisy, the role of The Annexe, the white room. The girl was in a coma, in a kind of suspended animation, along with thousands of others. She was waiting for her damaged brain to fix itself. But Daisy knew Wilson wasn't brain-damaged; he'd simply run out of charge. She did a quick calculation based on the number of rows and the people in each row, but the sum total would never be accurate, because the rows didn't seem to end. Even with the help of two hockey teachers, Daisy knew it would be hopeless, it would take forever to find Wilson - and only she knew his face. Wilson's face. Wilson's face! She could see Wilson's face. Daisy half laughed in acknowledgement of her stupidity as she became aware of the obvious. She didn't need a search party. There was no need to go looking for Wilson, because all she had to do, was bring Wilson to her. To imagine his presence. She closed her eyes and recalled all the marvellous, wonderful memories of Wilson. Thousands of images rushed to volunteer their services and Daisy slowly pored over them like the pages of a treasured scrapbook. A few minutes later, as she closed the cover and, hardly daring to look, opened her eyes – Wilson was standing there – in the white sweater and trousers she knew he'd be horrified to be wearing. She smiled inwardly at a vision of him complaining about his predicament and tears of happiness and relief ran down her cheeks.

It took the combined strength of the two teachers to carry Wilson back into the Hall of Extinguished Spirits. Daisy closed the door to The Annexe behind her.

Big Mac and Short Cake were standing by their desks. Short Cake was screaming insults and warning Daisy that she had no idea how much trouble she was getting into. Big Mac was chewing the nails off five fingers all at the same time, his eyes virtually popping from their sockets.

"Come on" said Daisy, "let's get out of this place."

They were just about to man-handle Wilson to the Exit to The Market Square when Daisy remembered Tom, the boy in the bed beside Wilson in the hospital.

Perhaps he's also in the White Room somewhere.

Daisy brought to mind her best recollections of his face, framed against a white pillow and ran back into The Annexe.

Don't know if it's going to be enough – but I'll try my best.

Three minutes later, all five of them emerged into the bright sunshine of The Market Square where a triumphant Daisy raised her arms, glared at the heavens and yelled at the top of her voice:

"I found him, I rescued Wilson and I don't care what you Powers That Be do about it. And don't even think about sending your monk-man to cause trouble, cos I'll trap him in a cage and stick him on TV and tell everyone about your stupid gambling games!"

Miss Burton and Miss Wetherington said their goodbyes and left Daisy sitting on a bench by the Clock Tower with Wilson and Tom slumped either side.

Daisy knew she had done the hard part but her work was not completely over. She had pulled people into The Market Square and now she was planning to reverse the process. She wrapped her hand firmly around Wilson's and then clutched Tom's fingers.

When the effects of the knockout drops finally wore off, Daisy's presence in The Market Square dissipated like mist in the morning sun, and she didn't leave empty-handed.

When Daisy awoke, she was lying beside Wilson on his hospital bed and the fingers of her left hand were still clutching at his. Still groggy from the after-effects of the sleeping pills, she propped herself up on one elbow and studied his face. There was still a trace of blue around the line of his lips but the tinge was now barely perceptible. And his skin was losing its parchment like complexion. Daisy heard a soft bleep and was drawn to the EEG monitor above Wilson's bed. The pinhead of white light normally flatlining across the screen had left the trace of a spike. She heard a bleep from a different direction and turned to see a solitary spike in the centre of Tom's screen. A moment later, Wilson's EEG bleeped again, followed quickly by Tom's. Then they both bleeped in unison for a third time and within moments all the bleeps were bleeping every bleeping second.

Wilson slowly opened his eyes. They were shining like sunbeams dancing on a rippling sea. He smiled at Daisy. Then someone tapped Daisy's shoulder. It was Sally, the girl from the other bed.

"Your boyfriend saved my life" she said "is he a number eleven?"

Chapter 61

What *should've* happened next, but *didn't*

So that, dear reader, completes the story of Wilson Armitage. A cautionary tale with the inevitable twist. Actually, it was more a comedy of errors, because Wilson wasn't supposed to die. It was all bad timing really, what with Daisy accidentally taking the bangles from The Gateway and Wilson taking too long to break into Blamire's safe to retrieve them.

You see, we originally planned for Blamire to put the bangles in his jacket pocket while they were both together in the car park – making it easy for Wilson to then pick his pocket from outside 3B. But we realised Blamire would smell a rat, as though Wilson had performed a trick and had never really given him the gold in the first place. So we projected the traces into the future and it all looked very messy. Vanessa is kidnapped by the gang of thugs. Wilson visits The Market Square to discover her whereabouts and confronts the thugs.

The thugs give Wilson a serious beating and then the ambulance taking him to A&E, hits a VW, gravely injuring the driver. The driver is a heart surgeon racing to operate on the ruler of a politically stable republic in Africa – who as a consequence of his surgeon being injured, has a fatal coronary.

The politically stable ruler, as a consequence of being dead, is then replaced by a politically unstable nutter, who starts a civil war – which, without major intervention on my part, looked as though it could lead to Russia and America having a right old barney.

So, as I said, the prognosis for the 'bangles in the pocket scenario' didn't look good. So that's why we decided to send along the second car and make Blamire give the bangles to the driver, rather than put them in his pocket. And to be honest, when we ran the future projections for that scenario, they all came up trumps. No major knock-on effects.

Wilson does his stuff: Granny brings the bangles back. The Gateway are happy and call off the monk-man scaring Daisy and Blamire gets sent down for GBH.

So my fellow Powers That Be thought the second car scenario was just the job. But yours truly didn't, I never thought it'd work. I told them Wilson's electrolyte levels were too low to take the chance and I was right. It took Wilson far longer than anticipated to open Blamire's safe. A few seconds less spent searching, would have saved him precious energy — and his life! Energy, eh? It's a bugger.

However, on the positive side, running with the second car scenario meant that there was an awful lot of bobs riding on Wilson. Virtually all of my colleagues thought he'd pull it off. So I'm in line for quite a windfall after backing Wilson to fall at the last fence. The good news is, the bookies have agreed to pay out early, so tonight it's my shout. We're going to have a big party here in eternity. Elvis and John Lennon are providing the entertainment, with some new songs. Can't wait. There's even a chance Wilson will join us, given the state the poor lad's in. Big Mac says he can doctor the scales to make sure he's a three-ouncer and I think that's for the best. Because, knowing Wilson, even if he's only a gram over, he'll go straight back, messing up his dad's research, mixing up the clothes in his mum's charity shop and getting up to all kinds of Cathy and Heathcliff nonsense with Daisy.

Let me just check the time. I've only got a few minutes and I need to prepare for the party, but before I toddle off, I thought I'd look at some of our predictive traces for the future and see what life holds in store for the rest of the cast. Not that I can be totally certain of course. There's always the possibility of another Wilson coming along and flapping his flipping cabbage whites.

So, let's have a quick look. What's this first projection?

Oh good it's Daisy's. That's nice, really nice.

It looks as though Daisy will go on to marry Teaps. And have a baby.

Wait a minute, the images are coming thick and fast.

Here we are. And it's a baby girl.

There's the christening.

And it seems, Teaps and Daisy are going to call their daughter... Wilson. Oh, wouldn't you just know it.

So who's next? Kate and Megan?

Here they are, let's see.

Well, no surprises by the looks of it. Kate and Megan are going to have a fashion label together. Looks very successful. World famous in fact. Designs based on Bratz dolls. Big platform boots, giant press studs the size of satellite dishes. It all looks good for the peas in a pod.

Now here's Hoover's projection.

He goes on to uni, gets married, good job. Ditches the website. Wonder why? Ah. They only found the one sock. And I think I was responsible for that.

Now Spinner. Hey, here's a turn-up for the books. Spinner turns out to be a number eleven but they don't give him a pass for The Market Square. Thank goodness. Oh, but look, he turns over a new leaf because he goes on to work for Teaps, at the recruitment company in London.

As for Wilson's mum and dad — let's have a look.

Strange, there's nothing showing on the horizon for those two. Well, actually there is, but it's a bit fuzzy. Possibly being updated as I speak, so I can't really see what happens to them.

I think someone's straddling in their neck of the woods.

Blowing the smoke around. Come back to them in a minute.

So what about Michael? What does the future hold for him?

Blimey, he looks like a new man. Happy, confident. Big gardening business. Doing well; will only drink wine in the future.

And finally, finally, here she is: Vanessa.

The star of the show, and the cause of all the trouble. So let... me... see... what's in store for her.

Well, it doesn't look like she is going to get her memory back.

Tut. And she seems to be happier living in residential care.

That's a shame.

Hey, but looks like she's in a very posh nursing home, very smart, like a five-star hotel, and her son and husband go and visit her every...

every...

Uh, that's odd. There's a new scenario coming along. What's this all about? That's not supposed to happen. Let's have a look.

Ah, that's better. Here's the very latest projection. Updated just a few seconds ago. In fact I was wrong. Vanessa is going to get her memory back after all, and... she goes on to be the boss of her old firm again — excellent news!

Wonder how she got her memory back?

Let me look at... Here we are.

She gets her memory back because... because Daisy... and... Wilson... are in The Market Square... and... bloody hell!

"Big Mac, Short Cake! Come here! You two can't be trusted to get anything right. I thought I told you both to make sure Wilson takes the Exit to Eternity. Well, look at the projections. He didn't! Daisy rescued him and now he's up to mischief again!

With thanks to everyone involved in the production of this book, to family and friends for putting up with me and to Carol, Jacki, Dave K and Natalie for their contributions.